THE DANGEROUS
BOOK FOR BOYS

Other books by Conn Iggulden:

Emperor: The Gates of Rome
Emperor: The Death of Kings
Emperor: The Field of Swords
Emperor: The Gods of War

Blackwater

Conn Iggulden

The DANGEROUS Book for Boys

Hal Iggulden

HarperCollins*Publishers*

To all of those people who said 'You *have* to include...'
until we had to avoid telling anyone else about the
book for fear of the extra chapters. Particular thanks
to Bernard Cornwell, whose advice helped us through
a difficult time and Paul D'Urso, a good father
and a good friend.

HarperCollins*Publishers*
77–85 Fulham Palace Road,
Hammersmith, London W6 8JB

www.harpercollins.co.uk

Published by HarperCollins*Publishers* 2006
3

A catalogue record for this book
is available from the British Library

ISBN-13: 978 0 00 723274 1
ISBN-10: 0 00 723274 8

Set in Centennial

Printed and bound in the UK by
Butler and Tanner Ltd, Frome

This book contains a number of activities which may be
dangerous if you do not follow the advice given. For those
who are under 18, these activities should be carried out under the
supervision of an adult. The authors and the publishers exclude all
liability associated with this book to the extent permitted by law.

'Don't worry about genius and don't worry about not being clever. Trust rather to hard work, perseverance, and determination. The best motto for a long march is "Don't grumble. Plug on."

'You hold your future in your own hands. Never waver in this belief. Don't swagger. The boy who swaggers – like the man who swaggers – has little else that he can do. He is a cheap-Jack crying his own paltry wares. It is the empty tin that rattles most. Be honest. Be loyal. Be kind. Remember that the hardest thing to acquire is the faculty of being unselfish. As a quality it is one of the finest attributes of manliness.

'Love the sea, the ringing beach and the open downs.

'Keep clean, body and mind.' –

– Sir Frederick Treves, Bart, KCVO, CB, Sergeant in Ordinary to HM the King, Surgeon in Ordinary to HRH Prince of Wales, written at 6 Wimpole Street, Cavendish Sqare, London, on 2 September 1903, on the occasion of the twenty-fifth anniversary of the *Boy's Own Paper*

CONTENTS

—— ✳ ——

I DIDN'T HAVE THIS BOOK
WHEN I WAS A BOY

———✦———

IN THIS AGE OF video games and mobile phones, there must still be a place for knots, tree-houses and stories of incredible courage. The one thing that we always say about childhood is that we seemed to have more time back then. This book will help you recapture those Sunday afternoons and long summers – because they're still long if you know how to look at them.

Boyhood is all about curiosity and men and boys can enjoy stories of Scott of the Antarctic and Joe Simpson in *Touching the Void* as much as they can raid a shed for the bits to make an electromagnet, or grow a crystal, build a go-cart and learn how to find north in the dark. You'll find famous battles in these pages, insects and dinosaurs – as well as essential Shakespeare quotes, how to cut flint heads for a bow and arrow and instructions on making the best paper aeroplane in the world.

How do latitude and longitude work? How do you make secret ink, or send the cipher that Julius Caesar used with his generals? You'll find the answers inside. It was written by two men who would have given away the cat to get this book when they were young. It wasn't a particularly nice cat. Why did we write it now? Because these things are important still and we wished we knew them better. There are few things as satisfying as tying a decent bowline knot when someone needs a loop, or simply knowing what happened at Waterloo and the Somme. The tales must be told and retold, or the memories slowly die.

The stories of courage can be read as simple adventures – or perhaps as inspiration, examples of extraordinary acts by ordinary people. Since writing them, it's been a great deal harder to hop about and curse when one of us stubs a toe. If you read Douglas Bader's chapter, you'll see why. They're not just cracking stories, they're part of a culture, a part we really don't want to see vanish.

Is it old fashioned? Well that depends. Men and boys today are the same as they always were, and interested in the same things. They may conquer different worlds when they grow up, but they'll still want these stories for themselves and for their sons. We hope in years to come, that this will be a book to dig out of the attic and give to a couple of kids staring at a pile of wood and wondering what to do with it.

When you're a man, you realise that everything changes, but when you're a boy, you know different. The camp you make today will be there forever. You want to learn coin-tricks and how to play poker because you never know when the skills will come in handy. You want to be self-sufficient and find your way by the stars. Perhaps for those who come after us, you want to reach them. Well, why not? Why *not*?

Conn Iggulden and Hal Iggulden

ESSENTIAL KIT

---❋---

IT ISN'T THAT EASY these days to get hold of an old tobacco tin – but they are just the right size for this sort of collection. One of the authors once took a white mouse into school, though considering what happened when he sat on it, that is not to be recommended. We think pockets are for cramming full of useful things.

1. Swiss army knife.

Still the best small penknife. It can be carried in luggage on planes, though not in hand luggage. It is worth saving up for a high-end model, with as many blades and attachments as you can get. That said, there are good ones to be had for £20. They are useful for jobs requiring a screwdriver, removing splinters and opening bottles of beer and wine, though this may not be a prime consideration at this time.

Leather holders can also be purchased and the best ones come with a few extras, like compass, matches, pencil, paper and plasters.

2. Compass.

These are satisfying to own. Small ones can be bought from any camping or outdoor shop and they last for ever. You really should know where north is, wherever you are.

3. Handkerchief.

There are many uses for a piece of cloth, from preventing smoke inhalation or helping with a nosebleed, to offering one to a girl when she cries. Big ones can even be made into slings. They're worth having.

4. Box of matches.

It goes without saying that you must be responsible. Matches kept in a dry tin or inside a plastic bag can be very useful on a cold night when you are forced to sleep in a field. Dipping the tips in wax makes them waterproof. Scrape the wax off with a fingernail when you want to light them.

5. A taw.

Your favourite big marble.

6. Needle and thread.

Again, there are a number of useful things you can do with these, from sewing up a wound on an unconscious dog to repairing a torn shirt. Make sure the thread is strong and then it can be used for fishing.

7. Pencil and paper.

If you see a crime and want to write down a car number or a description, you are going to need one. Alternatively, it works for shopping lists or practically anything.

8. Small torch.

There are ones available for keyrings that are small and light. If you are ever in darkness and trying to read a map, a torch of any kind will be useful.

9. Magnifying glass.

For general interest. Can also be used to start a fire.

10. Plasters.

Just one or two, or better still, a piece from a cloth plaster roll that can be cut with penknife scissors. They probably won't be used, but you never know.

11. Fish-hooks.

If you have strong thread and a tiny hook, you only need a stick and a worm to have some chance of catching something. Put the hook tip into a piece of cork, or you'll snag yourself on it.

THE GREATEST PAPER PLANE
IN THE WORLD

IN THE 1950s, a secondary school headmaster found a boy throwing paper planes from a high window. The head was considering punishments when he noticed the plane was still in the air, flying across the playground below. The boy escaped a detention, but he did have to pass on the design to the schoolmaster – who passed it on to his own children. You will find more complicated designs. You may be sold the idea that the best planes require scissors and lessons in origami. This is nonsense.

  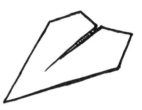

The plane on the right – the Harrier – is simple, fast and can be made from a sheet of A4. It is the best long-distance glider you'll ever see – and with a tweak or two, the best stunt plane. It has even won competitions. One was to clear the entire road from a hotel balcony next to Windsor Castle on New Year's Eve. Four other planes hit the tarmac – this one sailed clear across. The one on the left – the Bulldog Dart – is a simple dart, a warm-up plane, if you like. It's a competent glider.

THE BULLDOG DART

1. Fold a sheet of A4 lengthways to get a centre line.
2. Fold two corners into the centre line, as in the picture.
3. Turn the paper over and fold those corners in half, as shown.
4. Fold the pointy nose back on itself to form the snub nose. You might try folding the nose underneath, but both ways work well.
5. Fold the whole plane lengthways, as shown.
6. Finally, fold the wings in half to complete the Bulldog Dart.

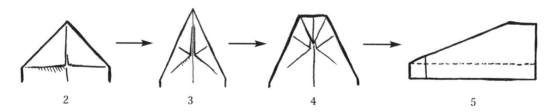

Good – now you know a design that really works. You may have noticed the insect-like plane in the middle of the first picture. It does have complicated 'floats' and inverse folds. However, it just doesn't fly very well and neither do most of the overcomplicated designs. We think that matters. Yes, it looks like a locust, but if it nose-dives, what exactly is the point?

Here, then, is the gold standard. It flies.

THE HARRIER

1. Begin in the same way as the Bulldog Dart. Fold in half lengthways to find your centre line and then fold two corners into that line, as shown.
2. Fold that top triangle down, as you see in the picture. It should look like an envelope.
3. Fold in the second set of corners. You should be able to leave a triangular point sticking out.
4. Fold the triangle over the corners to hold them down.
5. Fold in half along the spine, leaving the triangle on the outside, as shown.
6. Finally, fold the wings back on themselves, finding your halfway line carefully. The more care you take to be accurate with these folds, the better the plane will fly.

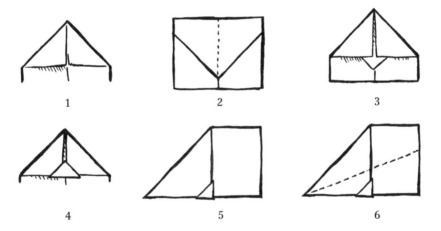

This plane does well at slower launch speeds. It can stall at high speed, but if you lift one of the flaps slightly at the back, it will swoop and return to your hand or fly in a great spiral. Fiddle with your plane until you are happy with it. Each one will be slightly different and have a character of its own.

THE SEVEN WONDERS
OF THE ANCIENT WORLD

THE FAMOUS SEVEN WONDERS of the ancient world were: the Great Pyramid of Cheops at Giza, the Hanging Gardens of Babylon, the Temple of Artemis at Ephesus, the Mausoleum at Halicarnassus, the Colossus of Rhodes, the Statue of Zeus at Olympia and the Pharos Lighthouse at Alexandria. Only the pyramid at Giza survives to the modern day.

1. **The Great Pyramid** is the largest tomb ever built, created for the 4th Dynasty Egyptian pharaoh Khufu (2898–2875 BC), though he is better known by the Greek form of his name, Cheops.

THE GREAT PYRAMID OF CHEOPS.

It is one of the three great pyramids at Giza near Cairo, the other two being constructed for the pharaohs Menkaure and Khafre. The largest, for Cheops, was the tallest structure on earth for more than four thousand years, until the nineteenth century AD. Though the capstone was removed at some point, it would have stood at 481 ft (146.5 m) high.

The base is perfectly square – a feat of astonishing accuracy considering the sheer size of it. Each side of the base is 755 ft 8 in (231 m) long and each side slopes at 51 degrees, 51 minutes. It is composed of two million blocks of stone, *each one* weighing more than two tons. They fit together so well that not even a knife blade can be slid between them.

2. **The Hanging Gardens of Babylon** were built in what is now modern-day Iraq, on the banks of the river Euphrates. They were created by King Nebuchadnezzar for his queen between the seventh and sixth centuries BC.

Famously, they employed complex hydraulic systems to raise thousands of gallons from the river and keep the gardens blooming. We can only guess at the exact method, but an Archimedean screw, as shown here, may have been employed.

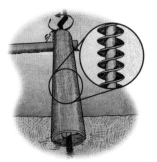

3. **The Temple of Artemis (Diana) at Ephesus** in what is modern-day Turkey is said to have awed Alexander the Great with its extraordinary beauty, though the citizens refused his offer to bear the cost of a restoration. Originally built in the sixth century BC, the temple was destroyed and rebuilt on more than one occasion, though the most famous was the night of Alexander's birth, when a man named Herostratus burned it so that his name would be remembered – one of the greatest acts of vandalism of all time. It finally fell into ruin around the third century AD.

THE HANGING GARDENS OF BABYLON.

TEMPLE OF DIANA AT EPHESUS.

4. **The Mausoleum at Halicarnassus** was created for King Mausolus of Persia, who ruled from 377 to 353 BC. Halicarnassus is now the city of Bodrum in Turkey. On top of the rectangular tomb chamber, thirty-six columns supported a stepped pyramid crowned by statues of Mausolus and his wife (and sister) Artemisia in a chariot, reaching a height of approximately 140 ft or 42.5 m. It was destroyed in 1522 when crusading Knights of St John used the stone to build a castle that still stands today. The polished marble blocks of the tomb are visible in the walls. From Mausolus, we have the word 'mausoleum', meaning an ornate tomb.

5. **The Statue of Zeus at Olympia** is also lost to the modern world. Only images on coins and descriptions survive to tell us why the statue was considered so astonishing in the fifth century BC.

MAUSOLEUM AT HALICARNASSUS

STATUE OF ZEUS AT OLYMPIA.

THE SEVEN WONDERS OF THE ANCIENT WORLD

Olympia was the site of the ancient Olympic games – giving us the word. The site was sacred to Zeus, and Phidias of Athens was commissioned to carve the statue. The statue was of wood layered in gold for the cloth and ivory sheets for the flesh. In his right hand stood the winged figure of the goddess Victory (Nike), made of ivory and gold. In his left, he held a sceptre made of gold, with an eagle perched on the end.

The Roman emperor Caligula tried to transfer the statue to Rome in the first century AD, but the scaffolding collapsed under the weight and the attempt was abandoned. Later on, the statue was moved to Constantinople and remained there until it was destroyed by fire in the fifth century.

6. **The Colossus of Rhodes** in Greece is perhaps the most famous of the seven ancient wonders. It was a statue of Helios, over a hundred feet (30 m) high.

   It did not actually stand across the harbour, but instead rested on a promontory, looking out over the Aegean Sea. The base was white marble and the statue was built slowly upwards, strengthened with iron and stone as the bronze pieces were added. It took twelve years and was finished around 280 BC, quickly becoming famous. An earthquake proved disastrous for the statue fifty years later. It broke at the knee and crashed to the earth to lie there for eight hundred years before invading Arabs sold it.

THE COLOSSUS OF RHODES.

7. **The Pharos Lighthouse at Alexandria** was built by the architect Sostratus of Cnidus for the Greco-Egyptian king Ptolemy Philadelphus (285–247 BC).

   Ptolemy's ancestor had been one of Alexander the Great's generals. His most famous descendant is Cleopatra who was the first of her Greek line actually to speak Egyptian.

THE PHAROS OF ALEXANDRIA.

When Julius Caesar arrived in Alexandria, he would have passed by the great lighthouse on Pharos island. Its light was said to be visible for 35 miles (55 km) out to sea. Its exact height is unknown, but to have shed visible light to that distance, it must have been between 400 and 600 feet high(121–182 m).

It was so famous that, even today, the word for lighthouse in Spanish and Italian is 'faro'. French also uses the same root, with 'phare'.

As you can see, even the greatest wonders can be lost or broken by the passage of millennia. Perhaps the true wonder is the fact that we build them, reaching always for something greater than ourselves.

THE FIVE KNOTS EVERY
BOY SHOULD KNOW

---✦---

BEING ABLE TO TIE KNOTS in rope is extremely useful. It is amazing how many people only know a reef and a granny knot. Rather than naming hundreds, we've narrowed it down to five extremely useful examples.

However, they take endless practice. I learned a bowline on a sailing ship in the Pacific. For three weeks, I used an old bit of rope on every watch, night and day. On my return to England, I attempted to demonstrate the knot – and found it had vanished from memory. To be fair, it didn't take long to recall, but knots should be practised every now and then, so they will be there when you need them. There are hundreds of good books available, including expert levels of splicing and decorative knots. These are the standard basics – useful to all.

1. THE REEF KNOT

This knot is used to reef sails – that is, to reduce the amount of sail area when the wind is getting stronger. If you look at a dinghy sail, you'll notice cords hanging from the material. As the sail is folded on the boom, the cords are tied together using reef knots. It is symmetrical and pleasing to the eye.

The rule to remember is: left over right, right over left.

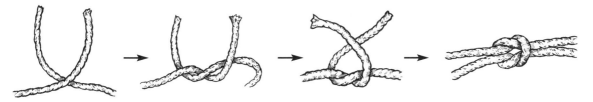

2. THE FIGURE OF EIGHT

This is a 'stopper' – it goes at the end of a rope and prevents the rope passing through a hole. A double figure of eight is sometimes used to give the rope end weight for throwing. It's called a figure of eight because it looks like the number eight.

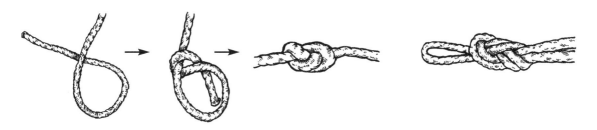

3. The Bowline (pronounced bow-lin)

This is a fantastically useful, solid knot. It is used whenever a loop on the end of a rope is needed – for a post, a ring, or anything else really.

i.   Make a loop towards yourself, leaving enough free at the end to go around your post, tree or similar object
ii. Now – imagine the loop is a rabbit hole and the tip is the rabbit. The other end of the rope is the tree. Feed the tip up through the hole – the rabbit coming up.
iii Pass the rabbit round the back of the tree.
iv   Pass the rabbit back down the hole – back into the original loop.
v.   Pull tight carefully.

NOTE: You can make a simple lasso by making a bowline and passing the other end of the rope through the loop.

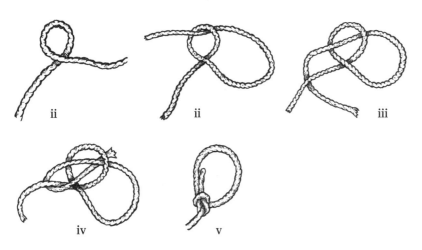

4. Sheet Bend

This is a useful knot for joining two ropes together. Reef knots fail completely when joining ropes of different diameters – but a sheet bend works very well.

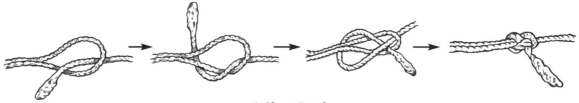

A Sheet Bend

5. A Clove Hitch – for hitching two things together very quickly

This is a short-term knot – the sort of thing you see used by cowboys in westerns to hitch their horses. Its main benefit is that it's very fast to make. Basically, it's wrapping a rope around a post and tucking an end into a loop. Practise this one over and over until you can do it quickly.

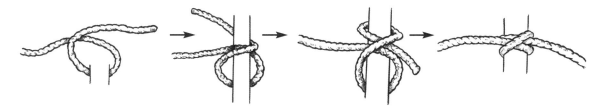

These five knots will be useful in a huge variety of situations, from building a treehouse to camping, to sailing, to tying up your horse outside a saloon. They will not come easily. They take practice and patience. Knowing this will not impress girls, but it could save your life – or your horse.

QUESTIONS ABOUT THE WORLD – PART ONE

1. Why is a summer day longer than a winter day?
2. Why is it hotter at the Equator?
3. What is a vacuum?
4. What is latitude and longitude?
5. How do you tell the age of a tree?

1. Why is a summer day longer than a winter day?

In Australia, the shortest day is 21 June, and the longest falls on 21 December. In the northern hemisphere, 21 June is midsummer and midwinter falls on 21 December. Christmas in Australia is a time for barbecues on the beach.

Although the North Pole points approximately at the star Polaris, the Earth's axis is tilted twenty-three and a half degrees in respect to the path it takes around our sun.

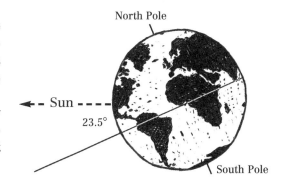

While the northern hemisphere leans towards the sun, more direct sunlight reaches us. We call this period summer. 21 June is the day when the North Pole points directly towards the sun, and the tilt is at maximum. The days are longest then as most of the northern hemisphere is exposed. Down in the south, the days are shortest as the Earth itself blocks light from reaching the shivering inhabitants.

As the Earth moves around the sun, the tilt remains the same. The autumnal equinox (22 or 23 Sept) is the day when day and night are of equal length – twelve hours each, just as they are on the vernal equinox in spring on 20 March. 'Equinox' comes from the Latin for 'equal' and 'night'.

When the northern hemisphere leans away from the sun, less light reaches the surface. This is autumn for us, and eventually winter. Longer days come to the southern hemisphere as shorter days come to the north. The summer solstice of 21 June is also the moment when the sun is highest in the sky.

The Earth is actually closer to the sun in January rather than June. It's not the distance – it's the tilt.

The best way to demonstrate this is by holding one hand up as a fist and the other as a flat palm representing the Earth's tilt. As your palm moves around the fist, you should see how the tilt creates the seasons and why they are reversed in the southern hemisphere. Be thankful that we have them. One long summer or one long winter would not support life.

At the midsummer and midwinter solstices, the conditions can become very peculiar indeed. The summer sun will not set for six months at the North and South Poles, but when it does set, it does not rise for another six. Northern countries such as Finland also experience the 'midnight sun' effect.

2. Why is it hotter at the Equator?

There are two reasons why the Equator is hotter than the rest of the planet. Strangely enough, the fact that it is physically closer to the sun than, say, the North Pole is not relevant. The main reason is that the Earth curves less in the equatorial region. The same amount of sunlight is spread over a smaller area. This can be clearly seen in the diagram below.

Also, the sun's rays have to pass through less atmosphere to reach the equatorial band – and so retain more of their heat.

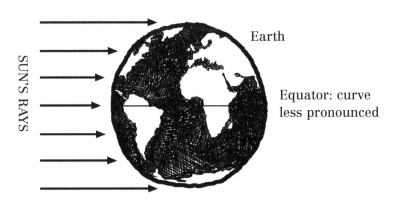

SUN'S RAYS

Earth

Equator: curve
less pronounced

3. What is a vacuum?

A perfect vacuum is a space with absolutely nothing in it – no air, no matter of any kind. Like the temperature of absolute zero (–273.15 °C/0 Kelvin), it exists only in theory. The light bulbs in your home have a 'partial vacuum', with most of the air taken out as part of the manufacturing process. Without that partial vacuum, the filament would burn far faster, as air contains oxygen.

The classic science experiment to show one quality of a vacuum is to put a ticking clock inside a bell jar and expel the air with a pump. Quite quickly, the sound becomes inaudible: without air molecules to carry sound vibrations, there can be no sound. That is why in space, no one can hear you scream!

4. What is latitude and longitude?

The Earth is a globe. The system of latitude and longitude is a man-made system for identifying a location anywhere on the surface.

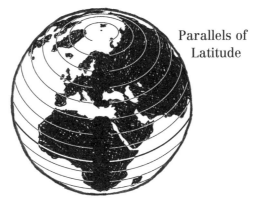

Parallels of Latitude

Latitude takes the Equator as a line of zero. If you cut the world in half at that point, you would have a horizontal plate. The centre point of that plate is at ninety degrees to the Poles above and below it.

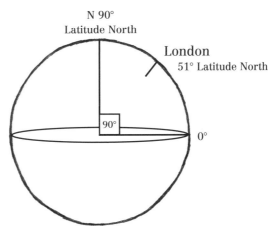

N 90°
Latitude North

London
51° Latitude North

90°

0°

Latitude is not measured in miles but in the degrees between ninety and zero in both hemispheres. London, for example is at 51° latitude north. The curve representing the ninety-degree change is split into imaginary lines called 'parallels' – because they are all parallel to each other and the Equator.

With something as large as the Earth, even a single degree can be unwieldy. For both longitude and latitude, each degree is split into sixty 'minutes of arc'. Each minute of arc is split into a further sixty 'seconds of arc'. The symbols for these are:

Degrees: °   Minutes: ′   Seconds: ″

With something as large as a city, the first two numbers would suffice. London would be 51° 32′ N, for example. The location of a particular house would need that third number, as well as a longitude coordinate.

There is an element of luck in the fact that a latitude degree turned out to be almost exactly sixty nautical miles – making a minute of latitude conveniently close to one nautical mile, which is 6,000 feet (1852 metres).

The *longitude* of London is zero, which brings us neatly into longitude.

Longitude is a series of 360 imaginary lines stretching from Pole to Pole. London is zero and 180 degrees stretch to the west or east.

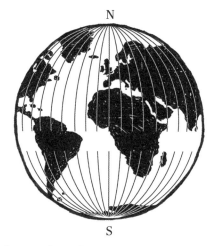

If the world turns a full circle in a day, that is 360 degrees. 360 divided by 24 = 15 degrees turn every hour. We call the fifteen-degree lines 'meridians'. ('Meridian' means 'noon', so there are twenty-four noon points around the planet.)

Now, this is how it worked. On board your ship in the middle of nowhere, you took a noon sighting – that is, took note of the time as the sun passed its highest point in the sky. You could use a sextant and a knowledge of trigonometry to check the angle. If you were at noon and your ship's clock told you Greenwich was at nine in the morning, you would have travelled three meridian lines east or west – which one depending on your compass and watching the sun rise and set. You would be at longitude +/– 45°, in fact.

Having a clock that could keep the accurate time of Greenwich even while being tossed and turned on a ship was obviously crucial for this calculation. John Harrison, a clock maker from Yorkshire, created a timepiece called H4 in 1759 that was finally reliable enough to be used.

All that was left was to choose the Prime Meridian, or zero-degree point of longitude. For some time it looked as if Paris might be a possibility, but trade ships in London took their time from the Greenwich clock at Flamstead House, where a time ball would drop to mark 1 p.m. each day. Ship chronometers were set by it and Greenwich time became the standard. In 1884 a Washington conference of twenty-five nations formalised the arrangement. If you go to Greenwich today, you can stand on a brass line that separates the west from the east.

On the opposite side of the world, the two hemispheres meet at the International Date Line in the Pacific Ocean. It's called the International Date Line because we've all agreed to change the date when we cross it. Otherwise, you could travel west from Greenwich, back to 11 a.m., 10 a.m., 9 a.m., all the way round the planet until you arrived the day before. Obviously this is not possible, and so crossing the line going west would add a day to the date. Complex? Well, yes, a little, but this is the world and the systems we made to control it.

Like latitude, longitude is broken down into a three-figure location of degrees, minutes and seconds. Common practice puts the latitude figures first, but it's always given away by the North or South letter, so they can't really be confused. A full six-figure location will look something like these:

38° 53′ 23″ N, 77° 00′ 27″ W	Washington DC
39° 17′ 00″ N, 22° 23′ 00″ E	Pharsalus, Greece, where Julius Caesar beat Pompey and ended the civil war.
39° 57′ 00″ N, 26° 15′ 00″ E	Troy

6. HOW DO YOU TELL THE AGE OF A TREE?

You cut it down and count the rings. For each year of growth, a dark and a light ring of new wood is created. The two bands together are known as the 'annual ring'. The lighter part is formed in spring and early summer when the wood cells are bigger and have thinner walls which look lighter. In autumn and winter, trees produce smaller cells with thicker walls which look darker. They vary in width depending on growing conditions, so a tree stump can be a climate record for the life of the tree – sometimes even centuries. The age of a tree, therefore, can be told by counting the annual rings.

MAKING A BATTERY

A BATTERY AT ITS SIMPLEST is a cathode (the positive end), an anode (the negative end) and electrolyte (the bit in the middle). There are quite a few different combinations out there. Electricity is the movement of electrons, tiny negatively charged particles. The anode tends to be made of a substance that gives up electrons easily – like zinc, which gives up two electrons per zinc atom. The cathode tends to be made of substances that accept electrons easily, like copper.

The electrolyte inside can be a liquid, a gel or a paste. All that matters is that it contains positive and negatively charged ions that flow when the anode and cathode are activated. When the Italian physicist Alessandro Volta made the first battery, he used copper for the cathode, zinc for the anode and an electrolyte of blotting paper and sea water. His name gives us the word 'volt', as in a 12-volt car battery. If you think of electricity as a water pipe, a volt will be the speed of the water, but it also needs a big hole to flow through – or 'amps'. You can have enough voltage to make your hair stand on end, but without amps, it won't do more than cause a tiny spark. A house supply, however, has 240 volts and enough amps to kill you as dead as a doornail.

You will need

- Ten two-pence pieces.
- Metal kitchen foil.
- Blotting paper.
- Two pieces of copper wire (taken from any electrical wire or flex).
- Malt vinegar.
- Salt.
- Bowl.
- LED – a light emitting diode (available from model and hardware shops).
- Masking tape.

The copper coin will be the cathode, the foil the anode.

Cut the foil and blotting paper into circles so they can be stacked on top of each other. The blotting paper will be soaked in the vinegar, but it is also there to prevent the metals touching – so cut those paper circles a little larger than the foil or coins.

1. Mix vinegar and a little salt together in the bowl. Vinegar is acetic acid and all acids can be used as an electrolyte. Sulphuric acid is found in car batteries, but don't fool around with something that powerful. It eats clothing and can burn skin – unlike vinegar, which goes on your chips.

   Common salt is sodium chloride, a combination of a positive and negative ion (Na+ and Cl–). These will separate in the electrolyte, increasing its strength.

2. Soak your circles of blotting paper in the ion-rich electrolyte.

3. With the masking tape, attach the end of one wire to the underneath of a foil disc. This is the negative terminal. Now stack in this sequence – foil, paper, coin, foil, paper, coin. Each combination is its own tiny battery – but to light even an LED (light-emitting diode) you'll need quite a few. A car battery tends to have six of these, but with a much larger surface area for each 'cell'. As a general rule, the bigger a battery is, the more power it has. (Power measured in Watts = amps × volts.)

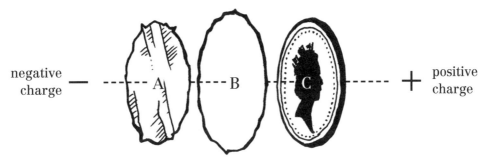

All the positive ions will go to one terminal, all the negative ions to the other. In effect, you are charging your battery.

4. When you have a stack, you can attach a wire to the last coin with tape. This will be the positive terminal. They can now light an LED, as in the picture below, or with enough coin batteries, even a small bulb.

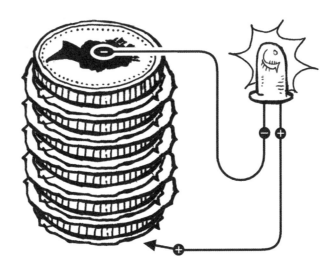

There may come a time when batteries go on to a new generation, but if you can understand the battery you have just made, you can understand every type of battery currently available, from nickel-cadmium, to lithium-ion, from rechargeable phone batteries, to the ones that drive toy rabbits. You won't hear acid sloshing in alkaline batteries, where a paste or gel is used, but the principles are identical.

CONKERS

THE FIRST THING TO DO is spend an autumn afternoon throwing sticks into the branches of horse chestnut trees. For conkers, the bigger the better is a good rule and any that still have white spots should be given to friends – they are useless. Collect more than you need.

This is only your practice year. Next year, you'll take out all the ones you prepared and win constantly, but this is the year you learn your skills.

The trickiest part is making a neat, small hole. You will be tempted to use a nail, a spike or anything else with a point. This does work, but there's always a chance of spoiling a good conker in the process. Better to get your dad to use a drill on them. Don't try that one yourself. The conkers spin round at high speed, or crack when you put them in the vice. Much better to ask an adult to do it, but give them your worst conkers to start with until they have learned the knack.

Once you have your holes, you need a strong trainer lace. Don't waste time with the ones from school shoes – they just cut into the conker.

Getting the lace through is always tricky and takes patience. Start by licking the end and twisting it into the hole, pushing and twisting to feed it in. Once you have it started, you'll need a bit of stiff wire to poke it through. Don't be tempted to use a fork, they never worked for us. Prod and twist until you can see the other end and then tweak it through with the wire. It's a good moment when you can finally pull the whole length through.

You need a big knot to stop it slipping back into the conker. The classic is the simple overhand knot, but you'll need three or four of them to be sure of avoiding catastrophic match slippage. (Loop it over itself and then put the end back through the hole. Everyone knows this one and it's too basic to put in the chapter on knots.)

Now you should have a conker that looks a little like this:

Yours will be round and shiny where this one is like a bit of wood, but that's because this is a year old and has been hardened using the techniques at the end of this chapter.

If you can find a lot of old laces, you might think of taking ten or twenty conkers to school and selling them for 10 or 20p each. The aim is not to make money, but to create an instant conker club one lunchtime. You are going to need people to beat, after all.

NOTE: Sell them ALL before you start playing. People won't enjoy losing to you and then having to buy another conker from the same person.

The Rules
1. Choose who goes first by tossing a coin. Wrap the conker securely around your hand. If it goes flying away on the string when someone hits it, the rule of 'Stompies' comes into play. Anyone, including teachers, can stamp it flat and laugh in a menacing fashion.

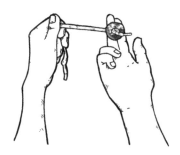

2. When it is your turn on strike, keep the string tight with two fingers under the conker. Wallop your opponent's conker as hard as you can.

3. When you're being hit, let it dangle a little less than the length of your forearm. Any shorter will be too easy to send into a windmill. (See Rule 4.)

4. Windmills. If your conker is sent in a complete circle, your opponent gets another go. Whether this rule is applied or not is agreed before starting play.

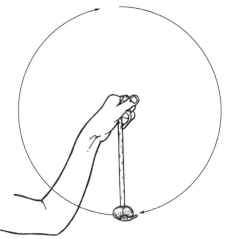

5. Strings. If the strings become entangled by a bad shot, the person on strike loses their go.

6. Take shots in turns until one conker is destroyed.

Scoring

There is an element of trust here, but if you win one contest, you now have a 'one-er'. If you win another, you have a 'two-er' and so on.

If a 'three-er' beats a 'two-er', you add the numbers together to make a 'five-er'. That conker is now responsible for the deaths of five conkers in battle. Do not lie about this. Honour is at stake.

How to Prepare Your Conker

The best conkers are the ones you left in an airing cupboard the year before. If you do this, remember to make the holes first as it's practically impossible when they're rock hard. By all means, play the first year – but at the same time, prepare for the next by securing a supply.

Apart from the passage of time, the classic methods of conker hardening are:

1. Soak in vinegar for an hour, then bake in an oven at 250 °C for five to ten minutes. All you're trying to do is speed up the effect of drying out for a year, so don't leave them to roast and go black. It's best to let your parents do the oven bit, as well. They will probably pat you on the head and talk about their own conker triumphs many years ago. Try not to go glassy-eyed in case they have a secret technique we've never heard of. If they have, send it to the publishers. We want to know and we like to win.

2. This one probably steps over the line of clever competition preparation into outright cheating, but a single coat of matt varnish is difficult to detect and helps to hold the conker together. Do not try more than one coat as a conker that looks like a cricket ball will be noticeable.

Avoid trying to fill the conker with something hard, like glue or fibreglass resin. At some point, the conker will break open and reveal what you have been up to.
Bear in mind that suspicious opponents may want to check your conker. It's best to play 'clean' and be sporting.

Now go out and find a big stick.

CATAPULTS

CATAPULTS HAVE INTRIGUED boys for as long as they have had access to strips of rubber. Before then, slingshots of leather were used right back to Biblical times, as when David slew Goliath by hitting him in the forehead with a stone. They do have a serious use in hunting, of course, or for launching bait into a river whilst fishing. However, the classic images are more to do with Dennis the Menace and Bart Simpson. They can be astonishingly powerful and accurate, though this is not something to demonstrate by telling a younger brother 'Run,' and laughing in an unpleasant fashion. **Never** aim or fire a catapult at someone else.

You will need

- A forked stick.
- A piece of rubber – 2 ft (60 cm) long.
- Twine to tie the ends.
- A piece of leather, such as the tongue from an old shoe.

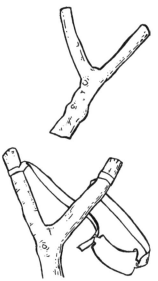

1   Find and cut a forked stick. We found our example in a large holly bush, but the 'Y' shape can come from almost anywhere

A Swiss army knife has a saw attachment that makes short work of small branches. You don't want the diameter of the wood to be any thicker than your thumb. If you are not confident in your 'eye', cut a little more than you think you will need. A good top to bottom height is six or seven inches (15–17 cm).

2. Cut rings from the bark at the top of the 'Y' to anchor the rubber – a Swiss army knife is perfect for this, too.

3. Finding the rubber is the hardest part. After a fruitless search in hardware and toy shops, we found that a strip cut from a bicycle inner tube works very well. Cut a two-foot length of tube and then make two cuts lengthways to remove a long strip. Some experimentation will be necessary to get the right pull tension and power.

[Note that we have used two pieces of rubber. It was tempting to use one long piece, with the central pouch threaded through. In practice, we found that the pouch piece moved after one or two shots and suddenly we had a catapult that could fire almost anywhere without warning. It is far better to tie two pieces securely.

4. The central pouch piece is easy enough if you have an old shoe. Either the tongue of the shoe or some part of the body can be cut to produce a rectangle of material around 4 × 2 inches (10 × 5 cm). Leather is best for this as it can be holed without splitting. Make two holes with a sharp point and attach the ends of the rubber. You now have a catapult.

FOSSILS

HALF A BILLION YEARS ago there was no life on land and only worms, snails, sponges and primitive crabs in the seas. When these creatures died, their bodies sank into silt and mud and were slowly covered. Over millions of years, the sea bottom hardened into rock and the minerals of the bones were replaced, molecule by molecule, with rock-forming minerals such as iron and silica.

Eventually, this process turns the bones into rock – and they become known as fossils, a slowly created cast of an animal that died hundreds of millions of years ago. Other fossils are formed when dying animals fall into peat bogs or are covered in sand. As each new sedimentary layer takes millions of years to form, we can judge the age of the fossils from their depth. You can travel in time, in fact, if you have a spade. You can reach Roman times in just six or seven feet down in some places. To reach levels millions of years ago, you'll need to find a cliff where the layers are already revealed – like Lyme Regis and Charmouth in Dorset or the Lake District in Cumbria.

Those sea animals can move a long way in the time since they were swimming in dark oceans! Geological action can raise great plates of the earth so that what were undersea fossils can be found at the peak of a mountain or in a desert that was once a valley on the sea floor.

In parts of New Zealand, you can see the fossilised remains of ancient prehistoric forests in visible black bands on the seashore. This particular compressed material is coal and it burns extremely well as fuel. Oil too is a fossil. It is formed in pockets, under great pressure, from animals and plants that lived three hundred million years ago. It is without a doubt the most useful substance we have ever found – everything plastic comes from oil, as well as petrol for our planes and cars.

By studying fossilised plants and animals, we can take a glimpse at a world that has otherwise vanished. It is a narrow view and the information is nowhere near as complete as we would like, but our understanding improves with every new find.

Even the commonest fossils can be fascinating. Hold a piece of flint up to the light and see creatures that last crawled before man came out of the caves – before Nelson, before William the Conqueror, before Moses. It fires the imagination.

Here are some of the classic forms of fossils.

Ammonite. A shelled sea creature that died out at the KT boundary 65 million years ago (see Dinosaurs). Sizes vary enormously, but they can be attractively coloured.

Trilobite. These are also a fairly common find, though the rock must usually be split to see them. Fossil hunters carry small hammers to tap away at samples of rock.

Sea urchin. Fossilised sea urchins and simple organisms like starfish are all very well, but remnants of woolly mammoths have been found in the south of England, as well as remnants of Jurassic period great carnivores and herbivores. However, you are likely to find a few ammonites on the Dorset coast in a single afternoon, while a Jurassic skeleton would be the find of a lifetime. That said, if you don't look, you won't find.

BUILDING A TREEHOUSE

LET'S BE BLUNT. Building a decent treehouse is really hard. It takes something like sixty man-hours start to finish and costs more than a hundred pounds in wood and materials. In other words, it's a job for dads. You could spend the same amount on a games console and a few games, but the treehouse won't go out of date – and is healthier, frankly. We are well aware of the satisfaction gained from nailing bits of wood to a tree, but for something that looks right, is strong and safe and will *last* more than just a few months, you need a bit more than that.

Along with a canoe or a small sailing dinghy, a treehouse is still one of the best things you could possibly have. It's worth the effort, the sweat, the cost, even the blood if whoever builds it is careless with power tools. It is a thing of beauty. It really should have a skull and crossbones on it somewhere, as well.

You will need

- Thirty 6-inch (15 cm) coach screws with heavy square washers.
- Eight 8-inch (20 cm) coach screws with washers.
- Thirty-two 4-inch (10 cm) coach screws with washers.
- 4 × 3 inch beams – at least 16 ft, but better to get 20 ft (6 m).
- 2 × 6 inch (5 × 15 cm) pine planking – 64 ft (19.5 m).
- 2 × 4 timber for roof joists and walls – 32 ft + 152 ft (10 m + 46 m): 184 ft (56 m).
- Pine decking to cover the area of the platform – 49 sq ft (4.5 sq m).
- Pine decking for the ladder – 27 sq ft (2.5 sq m).
- Jigsaw power tool, electric drill, rip saw. (Preferably an electric table saw.)
- Spirit level.
- Large drill bits of 14, 16 and 18 mm.
- Stepladder and a long ladder.
- Safety rope
- Bag of clout nails and a hammer.
- 'Shiplap' planking – enough to cover four half walls with a total area of 84 sq ft (7.8 sq m) Add in approximately 49 sq ft (4.5 sq m) for the roof.
- Ratchet spanner with a set of heads to tighten the coach screws.
- Chisel to cut trenches for the trapdoor hinges. Two hinges.
- Four eyebolts that can be screwed into the trunk.
- Cloth bag for trap-door counterweight.

To build the platform, you need some 2 × 6 inch (5 × 15 cm) pine planking, available from any large wood supplier. Our base was 7 ft by 7 ft (2.1 m × 2.1 m) and that worked out as eight 7 ft (2.1 m) lengths, with one more for bracers. Altogether: 64 ft (19.5 m) of 2 × 6.

Most dads will be concerned with making this as safe as possible. You really don't want something this heavy to fall down with children in it. Wherever possible, we went for huge overkill with materials, working on the principle that 'in the event of nuclear war, this treehouse would remain standing'.

Choose your tree and check if the treehouse will overlook a neighbour's garden. If it does and they object, the local council could ask you to take it down again. Choose the height of the base from the ground. This will depend in part on the age of the children, but we put ours eight feet up. Higher ones are more impressive, of course, but are harder to make. If the ground is soft, use a board to stop the feet of the ladders from sinking in.

THE PLATFORM

The coach screws need to have holes pre-drilled, so make sure you have a suitable drill bit and a long enough extension lead to reach the tree. We ended up using three leads attached to each other and a double socket on the end. For a previous job, we had attached a table saw to an old table and it proved extremely useful to be able to cut wood as required.

Build the platform as shown in the diagrams below. Use the safety rope to support the planks until they are secure, putting the rope over a higher branch and tying it off when they are in position. Do not try and walk on the platform before it is supported at each corner. For it to drop, it would have to sheer off a number of steel coach screws, but the turning force of someone standing on a corner is immense and could be disastrous. Supporting the platform is technically the hardest part of the job.

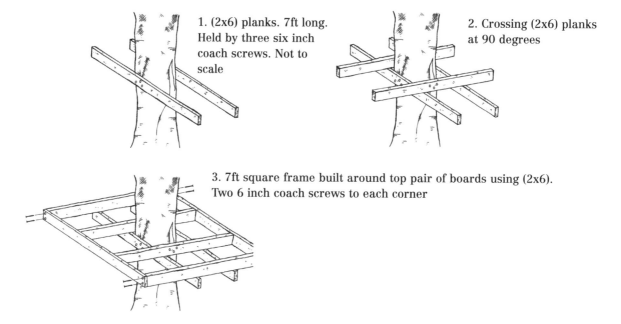

1. (2x6) planks. 7ft long. Held by three six inch coach screws. Not to scale

2. Crossing (2x6) planks at 90 degrees

3. 7ft square frame built around top pair of boards using (2x6). Two 6 inch coach screws to each corner

Beams measuring 4 × 3 inches (10 × 7.5 cm) are immensely strong – probably far too strong for the job. Given that the trunk is likely to be uneven, they will almost certainly have to be different lengths. First cut them roughly to size, being generous. The hard part is cutting the join where the top of the beam meets the platform.

The strength comes from the fact that the platform sits on a flat surface at all four corners. The joint for this looks a little like a bird's open mouth. Cut it by hand, marking it out carefully. The first task is cutting a ninety-degree triangle with two saw lines.

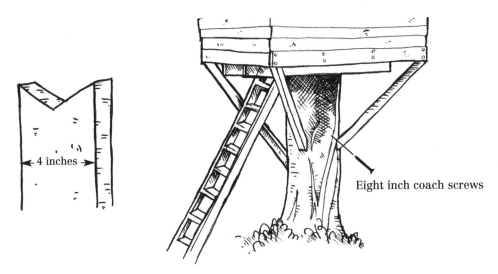

4 inches

Eight inch coach screws

Mark a point 4 inches (10 cm) from the end on both sides, then draw a line to it from the opposite edge. Repeat to give you two diagonal lines. Where they meet is a neat centre point. Measure it all twice. Cut from the edge inwards.

The second and spatially trickier cut is straight down on one of the cut edges. Again, measure carefully and cut. It might be worth practising on a bit of scrap wood first. You should end up with four ends that fit neatly inside the corner of the main platform and support it as well.

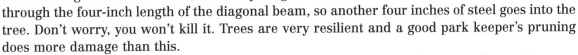

Eight-inch (20 cm) coach screws might seem excessive to attach the four diagonals to the trunk, but everything rests on them. Drill through the four-inch length of the diagonal beam, so another four inches of steel goes into the tree. Don't worry, you won't kill it. Trees are very resilient and a good park keeper's pruning does more damage than this.

When the four diagonals are in place, the platform cannot tip without actually crushing one of them. This is practically impossible. We tested the strength by putting six adults up in the finished treehouse, with a combined total of more than sixty stone (380 kg).

We used offcuts of 2 × 6 to add bracers to any spare gap in the platform. Rather than our usual overkill, this was to support the decking. Make sure you leave a gap for the trap door. We used standard pine decking available from any DIY store. It has the advantage of being treated against damp – as were all the timbers here. Getting them treated is a little more expensive but makes the difference between a treehouse lasting ten years and twenty. We screwed the decking straight into the bracers and main beams of the platform, using a jigsaw to shape it around the actual trunk. Leave a little gap to allow for tree movement and somewhere to sweep dust and dead leaves.

THE WALLS

It is easiest to assemble these rectangles on the ground, then hoist them into place. That said, they are extremely heavy, so use ropes and two people at least. Do not attempt to lift the section without it being held by a strong rope.

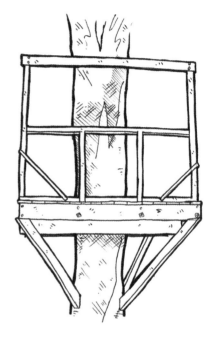

For each wall, 4 × 2 inch (10 × 5 cm) beams were used, with four-inch coach screws holding them together. We planned to cover the lower half of each wall with overlapping shed planking, except for one left open with just wire to stop the children falling through. It was absolutely crucial to have a drill powerful enough to send screws straight into the wood without pre-drilling. If we'd had to drill every hole first, we'd probably still be there now.

The shape was a simple rectangle with a ledge and a couple of support uprights. When you are deciding how tall it should be, remember that it is a treehouse for children. We went with five foot six inches, which was probably generous.

Each wall just sat on top of the decking and was screwed into it from above. Please note that it is going to feel wobbly at this stage. The four walls all support each other and when the last one is put in place, it becomes extremely solid. The roof will also add stability.

Also note that two of the walls will be shorter than the other two, so plan and measure these *carefully* or you'll have an awful time. You may also have trouble with the heads of the coach screws getting in the way. Although it's time-consuming, you may have to countersink these with a ¾ inch (16/18 mm) wood drill bit. As well as the four-inch coach screws, we used four six-inch bolts and nuts to bring the sides together.

THE ROOF

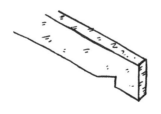

Once the four walls are in place and solid, you can think about the roof. We used eight joists of 2 × 4. The length will depend on the angles involved, but allow at least four feet for each one.

Cut them roughly to size, then take out a triangle near the end so that they will fit neatly over the top corner of the walls. In theory, this is the exact opposite of the lower diagonals, but we didn't think it was worth cutting more 'bird-mouth' joints.

Measure and cut very carefully here as one end will be in contact with an uneven trunk. Use six-inch coach screws (8) to anchor them to the tree. The roof supports only its own weight.

After placing the four diagonal joists for the corners, add four more between them, one to a side. Use a spirit level to be certain they are all at the same height, or your roof will be uneven.

There are various ways of finishing a roof, of course. We used a plastic roof membrane tacked to the eight joists with clout nails. Over that, we nailed strips of overlapping shed planking, known as 'shiplap'. It looked very natural, but each piece had to be cut to size and then taken up the tree. We also nailed very thin battens on the diagonals for cosmetic effect.

The roof was probably the most time-consuming part of the whole process – and a good safety rope at that height was absolutely crucial. In fact, to reach the highest point of the roof, we had to stand on the window ledges, make a loop out of the rope and sit on the loop as we leaned out. To say the very least, this is extremely dangerous and for adults only.

Finally, we used the same overlapping planking to cover the lower half of the walls, then made a ladder out of decking planking. We attached the top of the ladder with loose bolts on the basis that it could be pulled up at some point in the future. It probably never will be though – far too heavy.

We made the trap door from offcuts of decking and some pine planking, screwing it all together. To pull the trap door closed behind you, a piece of rope hanging from an eyebolt is perfect.

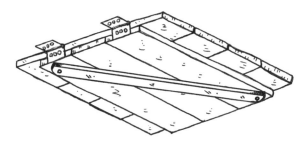

To prevent the trap door dropping on small fingers, it's worthwhile counterweighting it. To do this, get yourself a cloth bag of the sort you sometimes get shoes in. Run a rope through the trapdoor, with the knot on the underside. The other end should go through an eyebolt higher up the trunk and a third one out on the wall. Tie the bag of stones to the end and leave it dangling where the children can reach it. To open the trap door from below, they can pull on the bag. To close it, they pull on the knotted rope hanging down from the trap door. You'll have to adjust the weight of the bag to suit the child, of course, and it means the trap door has to be pressed shut with a foot when you're up there, but it's much safer.

The important thing when it's all done is to wait for a nice summer evening, take some cushions, blankets and a torch and spend the night up there under the stars. Take snacks – all that fresh air will give you an appetite.

THE LAWS OF FOOTBALL

NEATLY ENOUGH, there are only seventeen main laws for the most popular game on earth. These are based on rules put together in England as far back as 1863 and formally ratified by the International Football Association Board in 1886.

1. **The pitch.** Length: 100–130 yds (90 m–120 m). Width: 50–100 yds (45 m–90 m). The two long lines are called touchlines, the two short lines are called goal lines. The pitch is divided by a halfway line, with a centre point where the 'kick-off' occurs to begin the match. At each goal, there is a 6-yard box (5.5 m) known as the goal area. Outside that, there is an 18-yard box (16.5 m) known as the penalty area. A penalty spot is drawn 12 yards (11 m) in front of the goalposts. The goalposts are 8 yards (7.32 m) apart and 8ft (2.44 m) high.

2. **The ball.** Circumference: between 27 and 28 inches (68–70 cm). Weight: between 14 and 16 oz (410–450 g).

3. **The teams.** No more than eleven players can be fielded by each team, including the goalkeeper. Depending on the competition, between three and seven substitutes can be used. In addition, any player can change places with the goalkeeper provided that the referee is told and the change occurs while play has stopped.

4. **Clothing.** Players wear football shirts, shorts, shinguards under long socks and football boots. Goalkeepers wear different-coloured kits.

5. **The referee.** All decisions by the referee are final. Powers include the ability to give a verbal warning, a more serious yellow card warning, or a red card, which results in immediate sending off. A second yellow card is equivalent to a red. The referee also acts as timekeeper for the match and controls any restarts after stopped play.

6. **Assistant referees** (linesmen). These indicate with a raised flag when a ball has crossed the lines and gone out of play, and let the referee know which side is to take the corner, goal kick, or throw-in. They also raise their flags to indicate when a player may be penalised for being in an offside position.

7. **Duration.** Two halves of forty-five minutes, with a half-time interval of no more than fifteen minutes.

8. **Starting.** Whichever team wins a coin-toss kicks off and begins play. The ball returns to the centre spot after a goal and at the start of the second half. All opposing players must be in their own half at kick-off – at least ten yards (9.15 m) from the ball.

9. **In and out.** The ball is out of play when it crosses any of the touchlines or goal lines, or if play has been stopped by the referee. It is in play at all other times.

10. **Scoring.** The whole ball has to pass over the goal line. If a member of the defending team knocks it in by accident, it is an 'own goal' and still valid. Whoever scores the most goals wins.

11. **Offside.** The offside rule is designed to stop players hanging around the goal of their opponents, waiting for a long ball to come to them. A player is given offside if the ball is passed to him while he is nearer to the goal than the ball and the second-last defender. Note that players are allowed to sit on the goal line if they want, but the ball cannot come to them without offside being called by the referee. An 'offside trap' is when defenders deliberately move up the field to leave a forward player in a position where he cannot take the ball without being called offside. It is not an offside offence if the ball comes to a player from a throw-in, a goal kick or a corner kick.

12. **Fouls.** Direct and indirect free kicks can be given to the opposing team if the referee judges a foul has been committed. The kick is taken from where the foul occurred, so if it is close to the opponent's goal, the game can easily hinge on the outcome. Fouls can range from touching the ball with the hands to kicking an opponent. In addition, the player can be cautioned or sent off depending on the offence.

13. **Free kicks.** Direct free kicks can be a shot at goal if the spot is close enough, so are given for more serious fouls. The ball is stationary when kicked. Opposing players are not allowed closer than ten yards (9.15 m), which has come to mean in practice that the opposing team put a wall of players ten yards from the spot to obscure the kicker's vision.
    Indirect free kicks cannot be directly at goal, but must first be passed to another player.

14. **Penalties.** These are awarded for the same offences as direct free kicks – if the offence happens inside the penalty area of the opposing team. This is to prevent what are known as 'professional fouls', where an attacker is brought down deliberately to stop him scoring.
    The goalkeeper must remain on his goal line between the posts until the ball has been kicked. Other players must be outside the penalty area and at least ten yards from the penalty spot – that's why there's an arc on the penalty area.
    The penalty must be a single strike at the goal. As long as it goes in, it can hit the posts and/or goalkeeper as well. In the normal run of play, a penalty kick that rebounds off the keeper is back in play and can be struck again. In a penalty shootout, this does not apply and there is only one chance to score.

15. **Throw-ins.** A player must face inwards to the field and have both feet on the ground, on or behind the touchline. Both hands must be used and the ball must be delivered from behind the head. The thrower must pass the ball to another player before he can touch it again.

16. **Goal kicks.** These are given when the opposing team kick the ball over the opposing goal line, after a missed shot at goal, for example. The goal kick is taken from anywhere within the goal area and the ball must pass out of the penalty area before another player can touch it.

17. **Corner kicks.** These are given when a member of the defending team knocks the ball over his own goal line. The goalkeeper may do this in the process of saving a goal, for example, or a defender may do it quite deliberately to prevent a shot reaching goal. Many goals are scored from corner kicks, so the tension is always high when one is given.

Defending players must remain at least ten yards (9.15 m) from the ball until it is kicked. In practice, they group themselves around the goalmouth. Defenders work hard to prevent attackers finding a free space. Attackers work to drop their marking defender, get the ball as it comes in and either head or kick it into the goal. A goal-keeper is hard-pressed during corners. Visibility is reduced due to the number of people involved and the ball can come from almost anywhere with very little time to react.

OTHER POINTS OF INTEREST

The goalkeeper is the only player able to use his hands. However, apart from the lower arms and hands, any other part of the body can be used to help control the ball.

If the game must be played to a conclusion (in a World Cup, for example), extra time can be given. There are various forms of this, but it usually involves two halves of fifteen minutes each. If the scores are still tied at the end of extra time, a penalty shootout is used to decide the winner. Five pre-arranged players take it in turns to shoot at the goal. If the scores are *still* tied, it goes to sudden-death penalties, one after the other until a winner is found.

One advantage that football has over rugby and cricket is the fact that if you have a wall, you can practise football forever. The other games really need someone else. There are many ball skills that must be experienced to be learned. It's all very well reading that you can bend the ball from right to left in the air by striking the bottom half of the right side of the ball with the inside of your foot, or left to right by using the outside of your foot on the bottom half of the left side of the ball. Realistically though, to make it work, you'll have to spend many, many hours practising. This is true of any sport – and for that matter any skill of any kind. If you want to be good at something, do it regularly. It's an old, old phrase, but 'use makes master' is as true today as it was hundreds of years ago. Natural-born skill is all very well, but it will only take you so far against someone who has practised every day at something he loves.

DINOSAURS

THE TERM 'dinosaur' means 'terrible lizard', coined by a British scientist, Richard Owen, in 1842. These reptiles roamed the earth for over a hundred and fifty million years, then mysteriously died out. They varied from fierce killers to gentle plant eaters.

The largest dinosaurs were also the largest land animals ever to have existed. In 1907, the immense bones of a Brachiosaurus were discovered in east Africa. When alive, the animal would have been 75 ft (23 m) long and weighed between fifty and ninety tons. Its shoulder height would have been 21 ft (6.4 m) off the ground. These giants rivalled the largest whales in our present present-day oceans. In comparison, the largest living land animals today, elephants, weigh only five tons!

Brachiosaurus – the 'Arm lizard'.

The Age of the Dinosaurs

The age of the dinosaurs is known as the Mesozoic era. This stretched from 248 to 65 million years ago. It divides into three separate time spans: the Triassic, the Jurassic and the Cretaceous. At the start of the Mesozoic era all the continents of today's earth were joined

Eras		Periods
Cenozoic		Quaternary
		Tertiary
Mesozoic		Cretaceous
		Jurassic
		Triassic
Paleozoic		Permian
		Pennsylvanian
		Mississipian
		Devonian
		Silurian
		Ordovician
		Cambrian

Millions of years ago

0
50
100
150
200
250
300
350
400
450
500

together in one super continent – Pangaea. This was surrounded by a massive ocean called Panthalassa. These names sound quite impressive until you realise they mean 'the whole earth' and 'the whole sea'. The German geophysicist, Alfred Wegener first came up with the theory of moving tectonic plates, or 'continental drift', in 1912. He examined similarities in rocks found as far apart as Brazil and southern Africa and realised they came from a single landmass.

The Triassic world saw the first small dinosaurs, walking on their hind legs. This period lasted from 248 to 206 million years ago. Over millions of years Pangaea split into continents and drifted apart. After separation, different groups of dinosaurs evolved on each continent during the Jurassic period from 206 to 144 million years ago. This was the era of the giants. Huge herbivorous dinosaurs roamed in forests and grassland that covered entire continents.

The continental 'plates' are still moving today. In fact, wherever an area is prone to earthquakes or volcanoes, the cause is almost always one plate pushing against another, sometimes deep under the sea. The vast mountain ranges of the Andes and the Rockies were formed in this way.

The Cretaceous period lasted from 144 to 65 million years ago. This age included armoured plant eaters like Triceratops, browsers like Hadrosaur and huge meat eaters like the Tyrannosaurus Rex.

The seas too were filled with predators and prey that were very different from the inhabitants of today – except for sharks, oddly enough, who seem to have reached a perfect state of evolution and then stuck there for millions of years. Crocodiles are another example of a dinosaur that survived to the modern world. Modern crocodiles and alligators are smaller than their prehistoric cousins, but essentially the same animals. A crocodile from the Cretaceous period would have stretched to 49 ft (15 m)!

Tyrannosaurus – 49 ft (15 m) of ferocious predator. Note that we have no idea of the actual skin colour.

The World of the Dinosaurs

The dinosaurs' world was hot and tropical and dinosaurs of many shapes and sizes roamed pre-historic earth. One of the most interesting things about studying dinosaurs is seeing how evolution took a different path before the slate was wiped clean in 65 million years BC. Carnivores developed into efficient killing machines, while their prey either grew faster, or more heavily armoured as the eras progressed – the original arms race, in fact. Huge herbivores could nibble leaves from tree tops as tall as a five-storey building. The largest were so immense that nothing dared attack a healthy adult, especially if they moved in herds. The herbivores must have eaten huge amounts of greenery each day to fill their massive bodies – with stones, perhaps, to grind up the food in their stomachs.

As well as the giants, the age of dinosaurs overshadowed a smaller world of predators and prey. Compsognathus was only about the size of a modern house cat. We know it ate even smaller lizards as one has been found preserved in a Compsognathus stomach cavity.

The fastest group of dinosaurs were probably the two-legged ornithomimids – the 'ostrich mimics'. It is always difficult to guess at speed from a fossil record alone, but with longer legs than Compsognathus, they may have been able to run as quickly as a modern galloping horse. They have been found as far apart as North America and Mongolia.

Compsognathus – meaning 'pretty jaw'.

Ornithomimids.

Carnivores and Vegetarians

During the Cretaceous period, gigantic meat-eaters such as Tyrannosaurus, Daspletosaurus and Tarbosaurus ruled the land. The Tyrannosaurus Rex had up to sixty teeth that were as long as knives and just as sharp. Although the T-Rex was a fierce hunter, its huge size may have prevented it from moving quickly. It is possible that it charged at and head-butted its prey to stun them, then used its short arms to grip its victims while it ate them alive – though behaviour is difficult to judge from a fossil record alone. Much of the study of dinosaurs is based on supposition and guess-work – and until time travel becomes a reality, it always will be!

The Velociraptor was made famous by the film 'Jurassic Park' as a smaller version of Tyrannosaurus, hunting in packs. It may have used team work to single out and attack victims. Velociraptors were certainly well equipped to kill, with sharp claws, razor-sharp teeth and agile bodies.

Our experience of evolution and the modern world suggests that carnivore hunters are more intelligent than herbivores. In the modern world, for example, cows need very little intelligence to survive, while wolves and leopards are capable of far more complex behaviour. We apply the patterns we know to fill the gaps in the fossil record, but intelligence is one of those factors that are practically impossible to guess. If it were simply a matter of brain size, elephants would rule the land and whales would rule the sea.

Velociraptor claw and toe bones.

Armour

One aspect of the age of dinosaurs that has practically vanished from ours is the use of armour for defence. It survives in tortoises, turtles and beetles, but otherwise, it has vanished as a suitable response to predators. By the end of the Mesozoic era, the arms race between predator and prey had produced some extraordinary examples of armoured herbivores. The Stegosaurus, meaning 'covered' or 'roof lizard', is one of the best-known examples and evolved in the mid to late Jurassic period, some 170 million years ago.

Stegosaurus was a huge plant eater about the length of a modern 16 sixteen-wheel truck. The plates along its back would have made it

Stegosaurus

much harder for a predator to damage a Stegosaurus spine. In addition, it had a viciously spiked tail to lash out at its enemies. Some dinosaurs, like the Ankylosaurus, even had their eyelids armour-plated.

Triceratops means 'three-horned face' and was named by Othniel C. Marsh, an American fossil hunter. It looked armoured for both attack and defence. It weighed up to ten tons and its neck protector was a sheet of solid bone – clearly designed to prevent a biting attack on that vulnerable area. It was very common 65 to 70 million years ago in the late Cretaceous period.

The camouflage dinosaurs used is unknown. Skin just doesn't survive the way bones do and, for all we know, some dinosaurs could have been feathered or even furred. Today's animals leave some clues, however. Living relatives of dinosaurs such as birds and crocodiles show how some dinosaurs may have been coloured. Large plant eaters like Iguanodon probably had green scaly skin and predators would have found them hard to spot among the forest ferns, very similar to today's lizards. Some carnivores may have also had green or brown colouring, to help them sneak up on prey. Successful hunters like the Velociraptor may have evolved light sandy skin if they hunted in desert regions or brown savannah, just as leopards have done today.

Like modern crocodiles, dinosaurs laid eggs. Some dinosaurs would look after these until they hatched, like the Maiasaur, which means 'mother lizard'. The evidence for this comes from the first one found in Montana, in a preserved nest containing regurgitated vegetable matter – suggesting that the parents returned to feed their babies as modern birds do. In addition, the leg bones of the fossilised babies do not seem strong enough to support the infants after birth, suggesting a vulnerable period spent in the nest. In comparison, modern-day crocodiles leave the egg as a fully functioning smaller version of the parent, able to swim and hunt.

In the skies of the Mesozoic, the reptile ancestors of birds ruled. There were many varieties, though most come under the species genus name of *Pterodactylus* – meaning 'winged fingers'. Of all species on earth, the link to birds from the Mesozoic era is most obviously visible, with scaled legs, hollow bones, wings and beaks. Many of them resembled modern bats, with the finger bones clearly visible in the wing. As might be expected, however, the Jurassic produced some enormous varieties. The biggest flying animal that ever lived may have weighed as much as a large human being. It was called Quetzalcoatlus – named after the feathered serpent god of Mexican legend. To support its weight it had a wing span of 39 ft (12 m) – like that of a light aircraft. It was almost certainly a glider, as muscles to flap wings of that size for any length of time would have been too heavy to get airborne.

There were no icebergs in Mesozoic seas. In

the strict sense of the word, there were no dinosaurs either, as dinosaurs were land animals. However, pre-historic oceans brimmed with a variety of strange and wonderful reptiles, like the giant sea serpent Elasmosaurus. The neck alone grew up to 23 ft (7 m) long and today people believe that 'Nessie', the Loch Ness monster, is a surviving descendant of an Elasmosaurus or some other plesiosaur, a similar breed.

Elasmosaurus

Extinction

Hundreds of different dinosaurs roamed the earth seventy-five million years ago, yet ten million years later they had all but died out. Only the birds, their descendants, survived and what happened is still uncertain. An enormous crater in the Gulf of Mexico was almost certainly caused by a giant asteroid hitting earth. The impact occurred sixty-five million years ago, at the same time that the dinosaurs disappeared. Soil samples from the boundary between the Cretaceous and Tertiary periods – the moment of geological time known as the KT boundary – are found to be rich in iridium, an element commonly found in meteors and asteroids.

The asteroid would have hit earth at an incredible speed and dramatically changed the planet's atmosphere. Huge clouds of rock and dust would have covered the sun, blocking out light and, crucially, warmth. Some animals lived through the changes; scorpions, turtles, birds and insects were just some of those resilient enough to survive. There is no definite explanation for why the dinosaurs vanished, although the asteroid strike is widely supported in the scientific community – at least for the moment.

MAKING A BOW AND ARROW

A**T SOME POINT**, you may consider making a bow and arrow. Perhaps because of the British history of using longbows at Agincourt and Crécy, firing an arrow can be immensely satisfying – not to hit anything, even, but just to see it fly and then pace out the yards. The bow in this chapter sent a heavy-tipped arrow 45 yards (41 m), landing point first and sticking in.

Despite the fact that English archers at the battle of Crécy fired arrows *three hundred yards* (275 m), it was a glorious moment. The current world record is held by Harry Drake, an American, who fired an arrow in 1971, while lying on his back, to a distance of 2,028 yards (1854 m) – more than a mile (more than a km).

Don't spoil such moments by doing something stupid with yours. The bow and arrow here could be used for hunting or target practice in a garden. Remember at all times that it is a weapon. Weapons are **never** pointed at other children.

Arrows and Arrowheads

You will need

- Flint or bone for arrowheads.
- Baked bean tin.
- Strong scissors and penknife.
- Straight 4 ft (1.2 m) lengths of springy wood – elm, ash or yew.
- Straight 1 yd (0.9 m) lengths for arrows.
- Thread, glue.
- Crosshead screwdriver.
- String.
- Feathers, usually found, or bought from a butcher.
- Strip of leather to protect fingers.

There are a number of ways to make an arrowhead. Stone-Age man used flint and it is still intriguing to make a simple arrowhead with this material. Flint is the fossilised remnant of small organisms. It is extremely common in Britain and can be found both in the north and south, in Edinburgh, Yorkshire and Dorset. Our selection came from a ploughed field that was absolutely littered with pieces bigger than a fist. It is usually found with chalk – on what was once the bed of an ocean millions of years ago.

Find yourself a good big piece like the one on the right of the picture. One of the very few benefits of wearing glasses is that your eyes are better protected from shards. If you don't wear glasses, look away as you bring it down sharply on another flint lump or wear goggles.

You'll find that with enough of an impact, flint breaks like glass, forming razor-sharp edges that almost instantly suggest axeheads and arrows to you. We found that with a bit of luck, five or ten of these impacts would give you a handful of suitable pieces – shards that look as if they could be shaped into an arrowhead.

You may have seen pictures of Stone-Age flints with a series of scalloped semi-circles around the edge. These circles are formed by 'knapping' (sometimes spelled 'napping'), which is a difficult skill. Many people still do it as a hobby, producing ornate as well as functional arrowheads.

Using a pointed implement such as a small crosshead screwdriver, it is possible to nibble away at the sharp edge of a flint until the right shape is achieved. Place the flint on a piece of soft wood, with the edge touching the wood, then press the screwdriver head downwards against the very edge.

It's a slow and tiring process, but it does work and if it was the only way to kill a deer to feed your family, the time would be well spent. A grindstone, patience and spit can also produce quite decent arrowheads, though without that classic look. A combination of the techniques would also work well.

Remember to leave enough of a 'handle' to bind into the arrow shaft – and expect to have

a few break in half and be ruined before you have one you like.

The next one we produced with only a grindstone. It is very small at ¾ in (17 mm) long – but much larger and the arrow range will be reduced.

Bone also works well – and can be shaped on a sanding block very easily. We found that if you give a lamb bone to a big dog, the splinters he leaves behind can be turned into arrowheads without too much trouble.

The easiest arrowheads to make come from tin cans – baked beans, spaghetti hoops, anything. The base and lid will be a flat metal surface. Use a good pair of scissors, and you might find it is very easy to cut yourself and spend the rest of the day at your local hospital. Ask an adult to help with this bit. Leave a long 'handle', as in the picture. It will help keep the head securely in place.

Note that these are not that useful for target practice – they bend. They are probably better for hunting rabbits, though we found the movement of drawing an arrow scared living creatures away for half a mile in every direction. For target practice, the best thing is simply to sharpen the wooden arrow tip with a penknife and use a soft target – an old jumper stuffed with newspaper or straw.

The arrows themselves are traditionally made out of very thin, straight branches, whittled, trimmed and sanded until they are perfectly smooth. Dowel rods, however, are already perfectly straight and smooth and can be bought from any large hardware shop. The arrow we made is from an English elm, but any wood that doesn't splinter easily will do.

There are three important parts to making an arrow – getting it straight, attaching the point and attaching the feathers. The old word for 'arrow maker' was 'fletcher', and it is a skill all to itself.

If you have a metal tip, simply saw a slit in the end of your arrow, push the head into place and then tie strong thread securely around the arrow shaft to keep it steady. Attaching a flint head like this is only possible if it is a flat piece.

Now to fletch the arrow, you are going to need feathers. We used pheasant ones after seeing a dead pheasant on the side of the road. If this isn't possible, you'll have to go to any farm, ask at a butcher's or look for pigeon feathers in local parks. Goose feathers are the traditional favourite, but are not easy to find. Make sure you have a good stock of them to hand. Feathers are much lighter than plastic and are still used by professional archers today.

With a penknife, or just scissors, cut this shape from the feather, keeping a little of the central quill to hold it together. You can still trim it when it's finished, so it doesn't have to be fantastically neat at this stage.

You should leave an inch of bare wood at the end of the arrow to give you something to grip with your fingers as you draw. We forgot this until actually testing the bow.

Also note that the three feathers are placed 120° apart from each other ($3 \times 120 = 360$). The 'cock feather' is the one at 90° to the string slot, as in the picture below. Use your eye to place them on the shaft for gluing. During a shot, the arrow rests on the outside of the hand gripping the bow and the cock feather points towards the face of the archer. The other two feathers can then pass the bow at speed without hitting it.

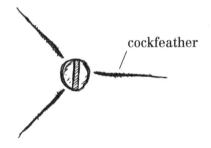

cockfeather

A touch of glue holds the feathers in place, but for tradition and for the look of the thing, you should tie a thread securely at one end, then wind it carefully through each of the three feathers until you reach the other end. This is a fiddly job, but strong thread will create an arrow that is a joy to behold. Tie both ends off carefully, trimming the ends of the thread.

It's a good idea to prepare five or six of these arrows. There is an excellent chance you are going to break a couple, or lose them. Use a little common sense here and don't fire them where they can disappear into someone else's garden.

The Bow

Ideally, the wood for your bow should be straight and springy. It should be cut green and then left somewhere to dry for a year. However, our childhood experience of bow-making was that they were always made on the same day they were cut, so we did that again here. Elm works well, as does hazel and ash. The most powerful bows come from a combination of yew sapwood and heartwood, the dense hedge tree found in every churchyard in Britain. In earlier times, Druids considered yew trees sacred and built temples close to them, beginning an association with places of worship that continues to this day. The red yew berries are extremely poisonous. Do not cut yew trees. They are ancient.

Freshly cut bows do lose their power after a day or two. They should not be strung unless you are ready to shoot and you should also experiment with different types of local woods for the best springiness.

The thing to remember is that the bow actually has to bend. It is tempting to choose a thick sapling for immediate power, but anything thicker than three-quarters of an inch is probably too thick.

If you have access to carpentry tools, fix the bow gently into a vice and use a plane to taper the ends. Most ones you find in woods will have some degree of tapering, which can be redressed at this stage.

We cut all the notches and slots for this bow and arrow with a standard Swiss army knife saw blade. However, a serrated-edge bread knife would do almost as well.

Cut notches in the head and foot of the bow, two inches from the end. Use a little common sense here. You want to cut them just deep enough to hold the bowstring without slipping.

You'll need very strong, thin string – we found nylon to be the best. Fishing line snapped too easily. Traditional bowstrings were made from waxed linen or woven horse hair, forming miniature cables of immense strength. The Romans even used horsehair to form great springs for their war catapults!

The knot you'll need is a good all-rounder, from tying up a canal boat to stringing a bow. Its advantage is that the actual knot isn't tightened under pressure, so it can always be loosened when you need to move on. It is called 'the round turn and two half-hitches'.

First wind your rope fully around the bow end, as shown. This is the 'round turn'. Then pass the end under the bowstring and back through the loop – a half hitch. Pull tight. Finally, do another hitch in the same way: under the string, back through the loop and away. You should end up with a knot that doesn't touch the bow wood but is very solid.

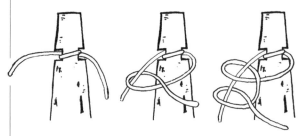

As a final note, it is a very good idea to wear a glove on the hand that holds the bow as you draw back the string. The arrow passes over it at speed and can take skin off. Also, we found it much easier to pull the string back if we had strips of leather wound around the second and third fingers. You can probably get a piece of leather from a furniture shop as a sample, or an upholsterer's offcut bin. Alternatively, you could just wear another glove. It may interest you to know that the rude gesture of sticking two fingers up at someone came from the English archers at Agincourt. The French had said that they would cut off the arrow-pulling fingers of those men when they beat them. Instead, the French were defeated and the archers mocked them by showing off their fingers – still attached.

Archery can be a fascinating and highly skilful sport and this isn't a bad way to start.

UNDERSTANDING GRAMMAR – PART ONE

IT'S STRANGE HOW SATISFYING it can be to know right from wrong. Grammar is all about rules and structure. It is *always* 'between you and me', for example. If you hear someone say 'between you and I', it isn't a matter of opinion, they're just wrong.

The grammar of English is more complex than can be contained here, but a skeleton of basics is well within our reach. You wouldn't use a chisel without knowing how to hold it. In the same way, you really should know the sharp end from the blunt one in everything else you use – including your language. The English language is spoken by more people on earth than any other, after all.

The first thing to know is that there are only nine kinds of words. Nine.

1. **Nouns** are the names of things. There are three kinds. Proper nouns have capital letters e.g. 'Newcastle'. Abstract nouns are the things that exist but you can't touch: 'courage', 'loyalty', 'cruelty', 'kindness'. Common nouns are the words for everything else: 'chair', 'eyes', 'dog', 'car' and so on.

2. **Verbs** are words for action or change: 'to become', 'to wash', 'to dissect', 'to eat' and so on. There are six parts to each verb, known as first person singular, second person singular, third person singular, first person plural, second person plural and third person plural.
   Most verbs follow this simple pattern.

To deliver	
First person singular:	*I deliver*
Second person singular:	*You deliver*
Third person singular:	*He/She/It delivers* – note the 's'
First person plural:	*We deliver*
Second person plural:	*You deliver*
Third person plural:	*They deliver*

Irregular verbs like 'to be' and 'to have' are not as... well, not as regular. They must be learned.

To be	To have
I am	*I have*
You are	*You have*
He/She/It is	*He/She/It has*
We are	*We have*
You are	*You have*
They are	*They have*

Note that the second person 'you' is the same in the singular and plural. In older forms of English, you would have used 'thou' as second person singular. In modern English it makes no difference whether you are addressing one man or a thousand, you could still begin as follows: 'You are responsible for your behaviour.'

ADVERB

3. **Adverbs** are the words that modify verbs, adjectives and other adverbs. They are important as there is a huge difference between 'smiling nastily' and 'smiling cheerfully'. Clearly the verb is not enough on its own.

Most adverbs end in '-ly', as with the examples above.

If you say, 'I'll go to the shops tomorrow,' however, 'tomorrow' is an adverb, because it adds detail to that verb 'go'. Words like 'soon' and 'often' also fall into this category. As a group, these are sometimes known as 'adverbs of time'.

As mentioned above, an adverb can also add detail to an adjective. 'It is really big' uses 'really' as an adverb. 'It is very small' uses 'very' as an adverb. He walked 'extremely quietly' uses 'extremely' as an adverb for an adverb! This is not rocket science. Take it slowly and learn it all bit by bit.

ADJECTIVE

4 **Adjectives** are words that modify nouns. In 'the enormous snake', 'enormous' is the adjective. More than one can be used together, thus: 'the small, green snake'. Note the comma between the two adjectives. Putting a comma between adjectives is correct.

As a general rule, adjectives come before the noun. However, as always with English, rules have many exceptions: 'That snail is *slimy*!', for example.

PRONOUN

5. **Pronouns** are words that replace nouns in a sentence. It would sound clumsy to say 'John looked in John's pockets.' Instead, we say 'John looked in *his* pockets'. 'His' is a pronoun.

   Here are some examples: *I, you, he, she, we, they – me, you, him, her, us, them – my, your, his, her, our, their*

   'One' is also used in place of 'people in general', as in the following sentence: 'One should always invest in reliable stocks.' The informal form of this is 'you', but it does sometimes lead to confusion, which keeps this unusual use of 'one' alive. The Queen also uses the 'we' form in place of 'I' during formal announcements.

CONJUNCTION

6. A **conjunction** is a word that joins parts of a sentence together. 'I tied the knot *and* hoped for the best.' Tying the knot is a separate action to hoping for the best, joined by the word 'and'. Conjunctions can also join adjectives, 'short and snappy', or adverbs 'slowly but surely'.

   Examples: *and, so, but, or, if, although, though, because, since, when, as, whilst, nor.*

   The general rule is: 'A sentence does not begin with a conjunction.' Yes, you will find examples where sentences do begin with a conjunction. Professional writers do break this rule, but you should know it to break it – and even then do it carefully.

   The examples above are fairly straightforward. It does get a little trickier when a conjunction is used to introduce a subordinate clause. (Clauses are covered in Grammar Part Two.)

   'Although he was my only friend, I hated him.' (Although)

   'As I'm here, I'll have a drink.' (As).

   In these two examples, the sentences have been rearranged to change the emphasis. It would have been clearer, perhaps, to write, 'I'll have a drink as I'm here', or 'I hated him although he was my only friend.' It's easier to see 'although' and 'as' are being used as joining words in that way, but many sentences begin with a subordinate clause.

ARTICLES

7. **Articles** are perhaps the easiest to remember: 'a', 'an' and 'the'. That's it.

'A/an' is the **indefinite article**. Used when an object is unknown. 'A dog is in my garden.' 'An elephant is sitting on my father.'

'The' is the **definite article**. 'The dog is in the garden' can refer to a particular dog. 'The elephant is sitting on my father' can mean only one elephant – one we already know: a family pet, perhaps.

'An' is still sometimes used for words that begin with a clearly sounded 'h': 'an historical battle', 'an horrendous evil' and so on. It is seen as old-fashioned, though, and using 'a' is becoming more acceptable.

PREPOSITION

8. **Prepositions** are words that mark the position or relationship of one thing with respect to another. Examples: *in, under, over, between, before, behind, through, above, for, with, at and from.*

'He fell from grace' demonstrates 'from' as a preposition. Another example is 'He lived *before* Caesar', or 'I stood *with* Caesar.'

The general rule for prepositions is: 'Don't end a sentence with a preposition.'

It is not correct to say 'This is my son, who I am most pleased with.' It should be 'This is my son, with whom I am most pleased.'

INTERJECTION

9. This is another of the easier types. **Interjections** are simple sounds used to express an inward feeling such as sorrow, surprise, pain or anger. This can be a wide group, as almost anything can be said in this way. Obvious examples are: *Oh! What? Hell! Eh? Goodness gracious!*

Note the last one – interjections don't have to be a single word. It could be a whole phrase like 'By the Lord Harry!' or a complex oath. They tend to stand on their own and often have exclamation marks following them.

That is all nine.

Bearing in mind that English has more words than any other language on earth, it is quite impressive that there are only nine kinds. The first part of grammar is to learn those nine well and be able to identify them in a sentence. If you have, you should be able to name each of the eight kinds of words used in the following sentence. If it helps, we didn't use a conjunction.

'No! I saw the old wolf biting viciously at his leg.'

(Answer: 'No!' – interjection, 'I' – pronoun, 'saw' – verb, 'the' – definite article, 'old' – adjective, 'wolf' – common noun, 'biting' – verb, 'viciously' – adverb, 'at' – preposition, 'his' – pronoun, 'leg' – common noun. Eight different types.)

TABLE FOOTBALL

THIS IS A SIMPLE GAME, but it does require some skill and practice. It used to keep us occupied during French lessons.

You will need

- A flat, smooth surface – a school table, for example.
- Three two-pence pieces are best.

1. Place the coins on the close edge of the table, as in the diagram. The first blow must be struck with the heel of the hand against the coin half over the edge. The three coins will separate. From then on, only the coin closest to the player can be touched.

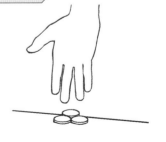

2. The aim of the game is to pass the coins up the table by firing the closest through the two further up. If you don't get the coin through, that's the end of your go and your opponent begins again from his side of the table. Just one finger is usually used to flick the coins. They should always be in contact with the table, so a great deal of the skill is in judging the force as well as planning ahead.

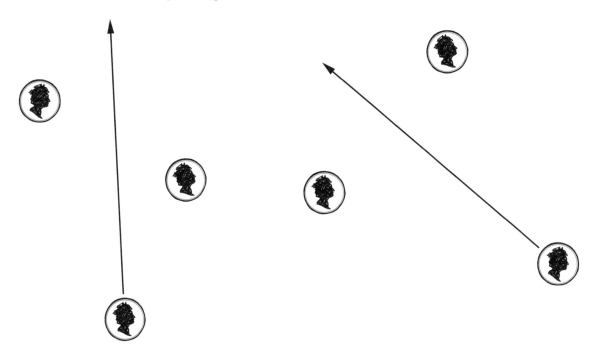

3. After a few of these 'passes', the opposing goal comes into range. This is provided by the other player, as shown.

4. If the goal shot misses, the game is lost. If the shooting coin strikes one of the other two, the game is also lost.

In the rugby version of the game, tries are scored rather than goals, and they are worth five points. The scorer then has an opportunity to gain two more points by converting the try. This is difficult, to say the very least.

1. The opposing player rearranges his goal into a rugby-post formation, as in the picture.

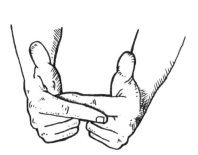

2. The goal or shooter coin must first be spun in place. *As it spins*, the coin must be gripped as shown in the picture and flipped over the posts in one smooth motion. No hesitation is allowed for aiming. This is not at all easy to do, which is as it should be.

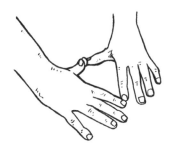

3. Play to an agreed number, or perhaps to win the coins.

FISHING

FISHERMEN ARE *NOT* PATIENT. Anticipation and concentration can make fishing an exhausting sport. It is a mainly solitary occupation. You hardly ever see people fishing in groups, laughing and chatting with each other, or drinking alcohol and singing. Fishermen can spend the day in silence. Even if you never catch anything, lazy afternoons spent fishing in the summer can be relaxing, rewarding – and addictive.

A simple starter kit – a rod, bait, a float, a lead weight and a hook – can be put together for about £30. As a legal requirement, you'll also need to purchase a rod licence, available at any post office. You have the choice of a day, week or annual licence costing up to around £25 – though a salmon and sea trout licence is more than double that. Note that you *do not need a licence* if you are under twelve. Twelve to sixteen-year-olds can buy a 'junior' version which is cheaper than adult ones.

The local fishing shop will have the equipment and also be able to tell you if there are free fishing grounds nearby. Most towns have a stretch where no extra fees are required. The largest is in London between London Bridge and Staines. Richard I gave it to the citizens of London and it has remained free ever since.

Otherwise, any canal or good-sized freshwater river will do. You may be asked to pay a small extra fee for a day's permit. If expensive fish like trout or salmon are involved, you will almost certainly be asked to show your rod licence and be required to get the owner's permission. Technically, fishing cannot be poaching as fish are *ferae naturae* – wild animals. However, if you don't obtain permission, you can be prosecuted for trespass and fishing without a licence. A water bailiff also has the right to confiscate your equipment but, again, not the fish you have caught.

The classic fishing method is with a float. Maggots from bluebottle or greenbottle flies are spiked on a hook suspended from a float that bobs on the surface. Push the hook through the blunt end of the maggot, taking care not to burst it, as it dies faster.

It tends to be necessary to place a couple of ball lead weights on the line to keep the float upright. Ask in the fishing shop if you're not sure how.

Cast carefully as a hook catching in your eyebrow is a deeply unpleasant experience. Watch out for overhead cables or tree branches. Your spool will have two settings – one for casting and one for retrieving the hook. Allow it to run loose and cast the hook and float upstream and allow the hook to come downstream towards you in the current. The first moment when that float dips is an experience to be treasured. Otherwise, wind back in slowly and try it again, replacing your maggots when they no longer move. If it's a nice day, find a place to sit and enjoy the peace that lasts until someone comes along and says, 'Any luck?'

The second classic method is known as 'ledgering'. It involves a heavier lead weight that keeps the hook on the bottom. Fish taking the bait feel no resistance. This works well with carp.

It should be clear that the method depends on the fish. Pike and perch tend to attack injured or dying fish. As a result, they can be caught using a 'spinner', a device that resembles a wounded fish as it moves through the water. Many anglers use complex lures that mimic insects on the surface. For a beginner, though, you'd hope to catch one of the following:

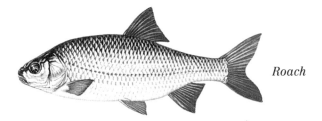

Roach

Roach (*Rutilus rutilus*). The ideal beginner's fish. Roach feed in all conditions, at all levels, in summer and winter. Found in lakes, ponds, rivers and canals in England, Scotland, parts of Wales and Ireland. They are not large – a pound roach would be a reasonable catch.

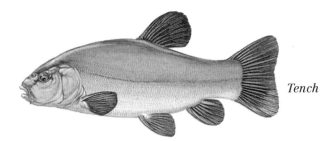

Tench

Tench (*Tinca tinca*). A member of the carp family. Golden brown to olive green in colour, more likely to take the bait in warm weather. Usually found in deeper water – ponds, weirs and lakes. They can range in weight from a couple of pounds up to six or seven, though it would have to be deep water such as a gravel-pit lake for them to grow as large as that.

Chub (*Leuciscus cephalus*). Found in rivers fast and slow, under overhanging banks, rafts of waterweed and any other shelter. Omnivorous, chub will take almost any bait. They are common at around 5 lb in weight.

There is also a good chance of you picking up 'small fry' – fish no larger than a thumb that are used either as live bait for pike and perch, or thrown back. In the UK, these are:

Gudgeon. A small bottom feeder, found everywhere.

Stickleback. An even smaller fish with harmless spines. Often caught in nets by very small children.

Minnows. The tiny fish whose name has actually come to mean 'small and insignificant'.

There are too many other types to include here – the rivers and lakes teem with them.

'Game fishing' is a specific reference to the salmon family: salmon, trout, char and grayling. 'Coarse' fish have five fins – ventral, anal, dorsal, pectoral and caudal. Members of the salmon family all have one extra fin close to the tail – known as the adipose fin. Salmon are born from eggs laid in rivers and swim to the sea, where they live for one to three years. After that, they return by instinct to the river where they were born to breed, in what is known as the 'spawning season'. They are caught as they travel upstream, with a lure containing a hook.

Catching a fish can be exciting – the real skill is not in hooking one but in bringing it in without breaking the line or losing the fish. As a final note, try reading the classic fishing tale by Ernest Hemingway – *The Old Man and the Sea*. Happy fishing.

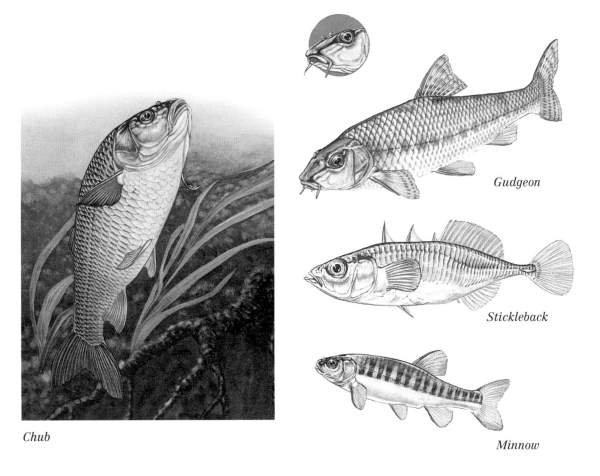

Gudgeon

Stickleback

Chub

Minnow

TIMERS AND TRIPWIRES

> You will need
>
> - An old alarm clock.
> - Bulb.
> - Two pieces of insulated electrical wire with bare copper ends.
> - Adhesive tape.
> - A battery – C or D size.

These are very simple to make – and deeply satisfying. For the timer, any wind-up alarm clock will do – preferably one with plastic hands. The idea is to use the clock to complete a circuit and turn on a light. You want the bulb to turn on in twenty minutes – to win a bet perhaps, or to frighten your little sister with the thought that a mad axe murderer is upstairs.

First, remove the plastic front of the clock. Tape wire to each hand, so that when one passes under the other, the bare ends will touch. It should be clear that a circuit can now be made with a time delay of however long it takes the minute hand to travel around and touch the hour hand.

Attach one of the wires to a positive battery terminal. Tape a torch bulb to the negative terminal and the end of the other wire to the end of the bulb. Test it a few times by touching the hands of the clock together. The bulb should light as the wires on the hands touch and complete the circuit.

Bear in mind that the hour hand will have moved by the time the minute hand comes round, so it's worth timing how long it takes for the bulb to light after setting the minute hand to, say, fifteen minutes before the hour. You can then terrify your young sister with the tale of Hamish McGee, the butcher of Margate.

TRIPWIRE

This is almost the same thing, in that it uses a battery circuit with a bulb linked to a switch – in this case a tripwire. With a long enough wire, the bulb can be lit some way from the actual trip switch for longer warning times.

Wrap foil around the ends of the wooden or plastic clothes peg. Attach your wires with tape to those foil ends, running both to exactly the same battery and bulb set-up as the alarm-clock switch above.

The important thing is to have a non-conducting item between the jaws of the clothes peg. We found a wine cork worked quite well. The wire itself must also be strong enough to pull the cork out – if it snaps, the bulb won't light. Fishing wire is perfect for this as it's strong and not that easy to see. It is also important to secure the clothes peg under a weight of some kind. Only the cork should move when the wire is pulled.

When the cork is pulled out, the jaws of the peg snap shut, touching the foil ends together, completing the circuit and lighting the bulb to alert you.

This works especially well in long grass, but its main disadvantage is that whoever trips the switch tends to know it has happened. Enemy soldiers would be put on the alert, knowing they were in trouble. Of course, in a real conflict, the wire would have pulled out the pin to a grenade.

PRESSURE PLATE

One way of setting up a trip warning without the person realising is with a pressure plate. Again, this relies on a simple bulb circuit, but this time the wires go to two pieces of cardboard held apart by a piece of squashable foam such as you might find in children's toy letters. A bit of sponge would also be perfect.

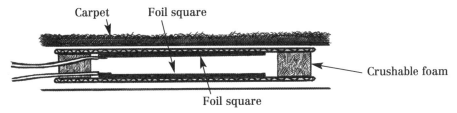

Carpet   Foil square

Crushable foam

Foil square

This time, tape foil squares over the bare ends of the wires on the inner surfaces of the cardboard and set up a simple bulb and battery circuit as before. With only light pressure from above, the two bits of cardboard come together, bringing the foil squares into contact. The circuit is made and the warning bulb comes on. Enjoy.

KINGS AND QUEENS OF
ENGLAND AND SCOTLAND

SCOTLAND

House of Alpin (Scotland)

843–859	Kenneth Macalpin.
860–863	Donald I
864–877	Constantine I
877–878	Aed
878–889	Eochaid
889–900	Donald II
900–942	Constantine II

House of Dunkeld

942–954	Malcolm I
954–962	Indulf
962–967	Dubh
967–971	Cuilean
971–995	Kenneth II
995–997	Constantine III
997–1005	Kenneth III
1005–1034	Malcolm II
1034–1040	Duncan
1040–1057	Macbeth
1057–1058	Lulach 'The Fool'

The House of Canmore

1058–1093	Malcolm III
1093–1094	Donald Ban
May to November 1094	Duncan II
1094–1097	Donald Ban and Edmund
1097–1107	Edgar 'The Peaceable'
1107–1124	Alexander the Fierce

1124–1153	David I
1153–1165	Malcolm IV 'The Maiden'
1165–1214	William the Lion.
1214–1249	Alexander II
1249–1286	Alexander III
1286–1290	Margaret (Maid of Norway)

Disputed succession.

The House of Balliol

1292–1296	John Balliol. Resigned his Kingdom to Edward I of England. Died In Normandy.

The House of Bruce

1306–1329	Robert I (The Bruce)
1329–1371	David II

The House of Stewart

1371–1390	Robert II
1390–1406	Robert III
1406–1437	James I
1437–1460	James II
1460–1488	James III
1488–1513	James IV
1513–1542	James V
1542–1567	Mary Queen of Scots
1567–1603	James VI – who later became king of England in 1603 when Elizabeth I died without heirs.

House of Wessex (England)

802–839	Egbert
839–858	Ethelwulf
858–860	Ethelbald
860–866	Ethelbert – first Christian king
866–871	Ethelred I
871–900	Alfred the Great
900–924	Edward I 'the Elder'
924–939	Athelstan – first king of all England
939–946	Edmund I
946–955	Edred
955–959	Edwig
957–975	Edgar
975–978	Edward II 'the Martyr'
978–1016	Ethelred II 'the Unready'
1016	Edmund II Ironside
1016–1035	King Canute (Danish king by conquest)
1035–1040	Harold I 'Harefoot'
1040–1043	Hardicanute
1042–1066	Edward III 'the Confessor'
1066	Harold II – killed at Hastings

House of Normandy

1066–1087	William I
1087–1100	William II
1100–1135	Henry I
1135–1154	Stephen

House of Plantagenet

1154–1189	Henry II
1189–1199	Richard I (also King of Jerusalem)
1199–1216	John
1216–1272	Henry III
1272–1307	Edward I
1307–1327	Edward II
1327–1377	Edward III
1377–1399	Richard II

The House of Lancaster

1399–1413	Henry IV
1413–1422	Henry V
1422–1461	Henry VI

House of York

1461–1483	Edward IV
1483	Edward V
1483–1485	Richard

House of Tudor

1485–1509	Henry VII
1509–1547	Henry VIII
1547–1553	Edward VI
1553–1558	Mary I
1558–1603	Elizabeth I

House of Stuart

1603–1625	James I (King of England and Scotland)
1625–1649	Charles I (King of England and Scotland)

Commonwealth and Protectorate

1649–1653	Government by a council of state
1653–1658	Protectorate of Oliver Cromwell
1658–1659	Protectorate of Richard Cromwell

House of Stuart (Restored)

1660–1685	Charles II (King of England and Scotland)
1685–1688	James II (King of England and Scotland)

House of Orange

1689–1694	William III and Mary II (jointly)
1694–1702	William III (sole ruler)
1702–1714	Anne (First Queen of Great Britain after Act of Union 1707.)

House of Hanover

1714–1727	George I (First King of Great Britain)
1727–1760	George II
1760–1820	George III
1820–1830	George IV
1830–1837	William IV
1837–1901	Victoria (First Empress of India)

House of Saxe-Coburg-Gotha

1901–1910	Edward VII (First Emperor of India)

House of Windsor

1910–1936	George V (Saxe-Coburg-Gotha until 1917)
1936	Edward VIII (abdicated)
1936–1952	George VI
1952–	Elizabeth II

You may find it easier to remember this rhyme. Memorise it and you'll use it and take satisfaction from the knowledge for the rest of your life.

> Willie, Willie, Harry, Steve,
> Harry, Dick, John, Harry Three,
> Edward One, Two, Three, Dick Two,
> Henry Four, Five, Six, then who?
> Edward Four, Five, Dick the Bad,
> Harrys twain and Ned the lad,
> Mary, Bessie, James you ken,
> Charlie, Charlie, James again.
> William and Mary, Anne of Gloria,
> Georges (4), Will Four, Victoria.
> Edward Seven, Georgie Five,
> Edward, George and Liz (alive).

Another excellent mnemonic is for Henry VIII's wives. In order, he married: Catherine of Aragon, Anne Boleyn, Jane Seymour, Anne of Cleves, Catherine Howard, and Catherine Parr. Their respective fates were: 'Divorced, beheaded, died, divorced, beheaded, survived.'

King Canute
and Queen Aelgifu

Henry VIII

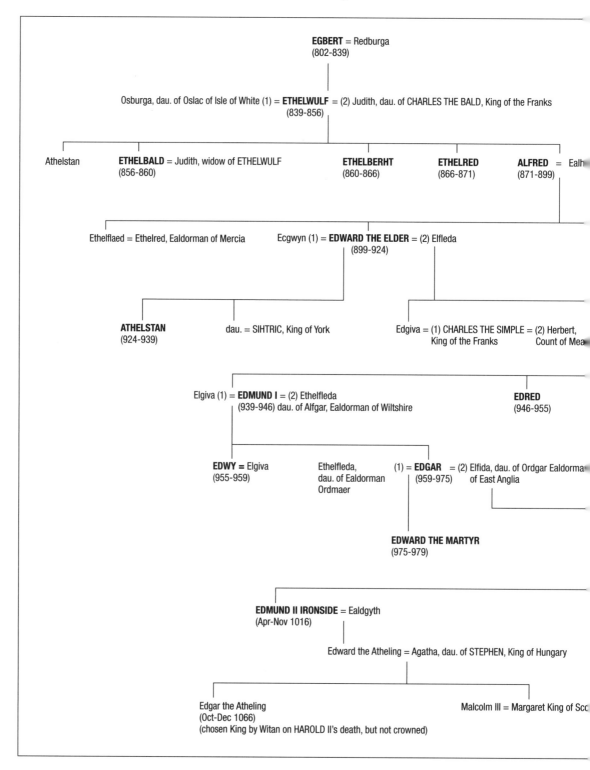

EGBERT = Redburga
(802-839)

Osburga, dau. of Oslac of Isle of White (1) = ETHELWULF = (2) Judith, dau. of CHARLES THE BALD, King of the Franks
(839-856)

Athelstan

ETHELBALD = Judith, widow of ETHELWULF
(856-860)

ETHELBERHT
(860-866)

ETHELRED
(866-871)

ALFRED = Ealh
(871-899)

Ethelflaed = Ethelred, Ealdorman of Mercia

Ecgwyn (1) = EDWARD THE ELDER = (2) Elfleda
(899-924)

ATHELSTAN
(924-939)

dau. = SIHTRIC, King of York

Edgiva = (1) CHARLES THE SIMPLE = (2) Herbert,
King of the Franks   Count of Mea

Elgiva (1) = EDMUND I = (2) Ethelfleda
(939-946) dau. of Alfgar, Ealdorman of Wiltshire

EDRED
(946-955)

EDWY = Elgiva
(955-959)

Ethelfleda,
dau. of Ealdorman
Ordmaer

(1) = EDGAR = (2) Elfida, dau. of Ordgar Ealdorma
(959-975)   of East Anglia

EDWARD THE MARTYR
(975-979)

EDMUND II IRONSIDE = Ealdgyth
(Apr-Nov 1016)

Edward the Atheling = Agatha, dau. of STEPHEN, King of Hungary

Edgar the Atheling
(Oct-Dec 1066)
(chosen King by Witan on HAROLD II's death, but not crowned)

Malcolm III = Margaret King of Sco

KINGS OF WESSEX AND ENGLAND 802-1066

(Note: Ealdorman was a Shire Officer who took part in the Witan, an early Saxon form of Parliament. The title later evolved into Earl.)

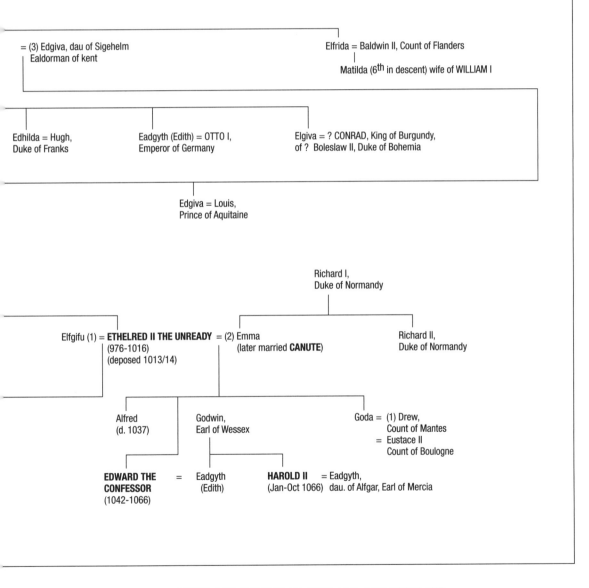

= (3) Edgiva, dau of Sigehelm
Ealdorman of kent

Elfrida = Baldwin II, Count of Flanders

Matilda (6th in descent) wife of WILLIAM I

Edhilda = Hugh,
Duke of Franks

Eadgyth (Edith) = OTTO I,
Emperor of Germany

Elgiva = ? CONRAD, King of Burgundy,
of ? Boleslaw II, Duke of Bohemia

Edgiva = Louis,
Prince of Aquitaine

Richard I,
Duke of Normandy

Elfgifu (1) = **ETHELRED II THE UNREADY** = (2) Emma
(976-1016)   (later married **CANUTE**)
(deposed 1013/14)

Richard II,
Duke of Normandy

Alfred
(d. 1037)

Godwin,
Earl of Wessex

Goda = (1) Drew,
Count of Mantes
= Eustace II
Count of Boulogne

EDWARD THE   = Eadgyth   **HAROLD II**   = Eadgyth,
CONFESSOR   (Edith)   (Jan-Oct 1066)   dau. of Alfgar, Earl of Mercia
(1042-1066)

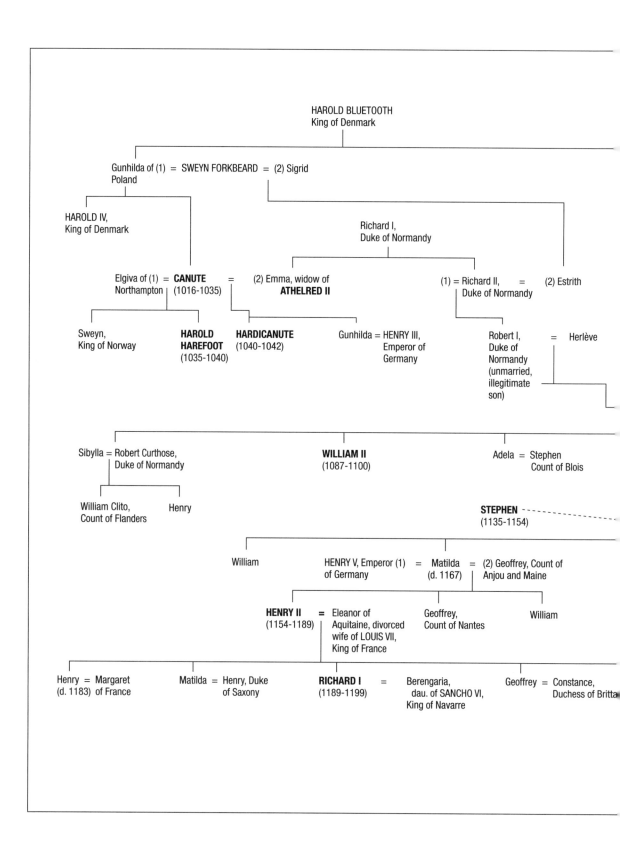

HAROLD BLUETOOTH
King of Denmark

Gunhilda of (1) = SWEYN FORKBEARD = (2) Sigrid
Poland

HAROLD IV,
King of Denmark

Richard I,
Duke of Normandy

Elgiva of (1) = **CANUTE** = (2) Emma, widow of   (1) = Richard II, = (2) Estrith
Northampton (1016-1035)   **ATHELRED II**   Duke of Normandy

Sweyn,   **HAROLD**   **HARDICANUTE**   Gunhilda = HENRY III,   Robert I, = Herlève
King of Norway **HAREFOOT** (1040-1042)   Emperor of   Duke of
                (1035-1040)   Germany   Normandy
                                                                      (unmarried,
                                                                      illegitimate
                                                                      son)

Sibylla = Robert Curthose,   **WILLIAM II**   Adela = Stephen
          Duke of Normandy   (1087-1100)   Count of Blois

William Clito,   Henry   **STEPHEN** - - - - - - - - -
Count of Flanders   (1135-1154)

William   HENRY V, Emperor (1) = Matilda = (2) Geoffrey, Count of
                 of Germany   (d. 1167)   Anjou and Maine

                 HENRY II = Eleanor of   Geoffrey,   William
                 (1154-1189)   Aquitaine, divorced Count of Nantes
                               wife of LOUIS VII,
                               King of France

Henry = Margaret   Matilda = Henry, Duke   **RICHARD I** = Berengaria,   Geoffrey = Constance,
(d. 1183) of France   of Saxony   (1189-1199)   dau. of SANCHO VI,   Duchess of Britta
                                                               King of Navarre

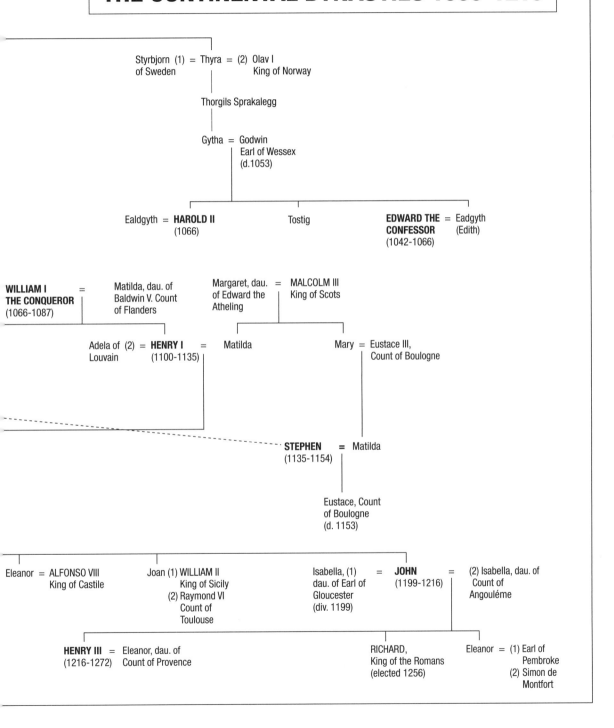

THE CONTINENTAL DYNASTIES 1066-1216

Styrbjorn (1) = Thyra = (2) Olav I
of Sweden   King of Norway

Thorgils Sprakalegg

Gytha = Godwin
Earl of Wessex
(d.1053)

Ealdgyth = **HAROLD II**   Tostig   **EDWARD THE** = Eadgyth
(1066)   **CONFESSOR** (Edith)
                                        (1042-1066)

WILLIAM I   =   Matilda, dau. of   Margaret, dau. = MALCOLM III
THE CONQUEROR   Baldwin V. Count   of Edward the   King of Scots
(1066-1087)   of Flanders   Atheling

Adela of (2) = **HENRY I**   =   Matilda   Mary = Eustace III,
Louvain   (1100-1135)   Count of Boulogne

STEPHEN   =   Matilda
(1135-1154)

Eustace, Count
of Boulogne
(d. 1153)

Eleanor = ALFONSO VIII   Joan (1) WILLIAM II   Isabella, (1)   =   **JOHN**   =   (2) Isabella, dau. of
       King of Castile   King of Sicily   dau. of Earl of   (1199-1216)   Count of
                        (2) Raymond VI   Gloucester   Angouléme
                        Count of   (div. 1199)
                        Toulouse

HENRY III   =   Eleanor, dau. of   RICHARD,   Eleanor = (1) Earl of
(1216-1272)   Count of Provence   King of the Romans   Pembroke
                                (elected 1256)   (2) Simon de
                                                       Montfort

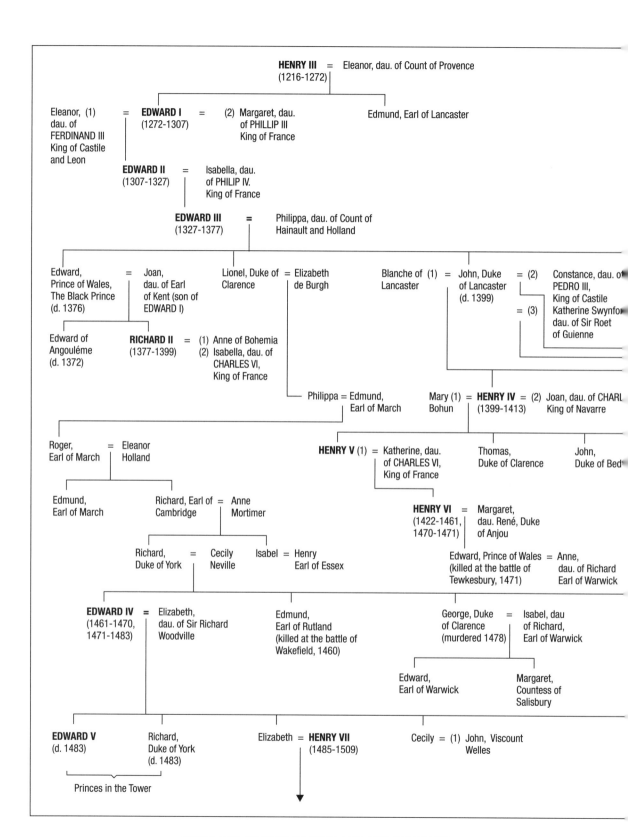

THE PLANTAGENET DYNASTIES 1216-1485

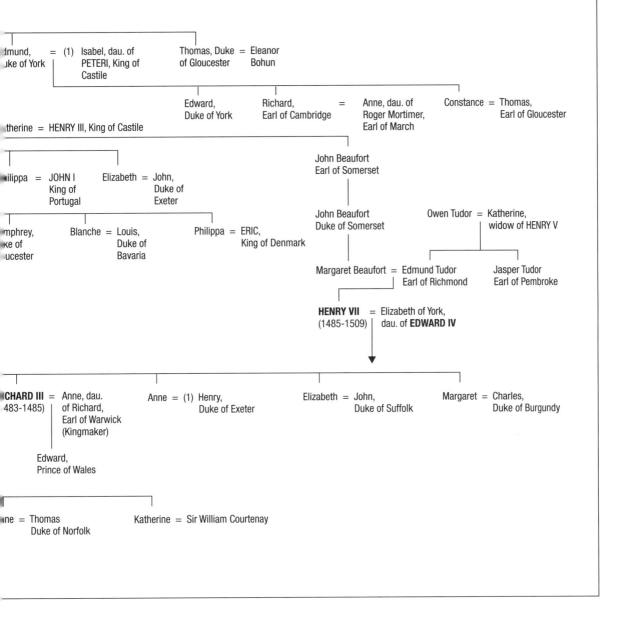

dmund, = (1) Isabel, dau. of   Thomas, Duke = Eleanor
uke of York   PETER I, King of   of Gloucester   Bohun
                   Castile

                        Edward,   Richard,   =   Anne, dau. of   Constance = Thomas,
                        Duke of York   Earl of Cambridge   Roger Mortimer,   Earl of Gloucester
                                                               Earl of March
atherine = HENRY III, King of Castile

                                                          John Beaufort
                                                          Earl of Somerset

ilippa = JOHN I   Elizabeth = John,
           King of   Duke of
           Portugal   Exeter

                                                          John Beaufort   Owen Tudor = Katherine,
mphrey,   Blanche = Louis,   Philippa = ERIC,   Duke of Somerset   widow of HENRY V
ke of   Duke of   King of Denmark
ucester   Bavaria
                                                                                  Margaret Beaufort = Edmund Tudor   Jasper Tudor
                                                                                                      Earl of Richmond   Earl of Pembroke

                                                          HENRY VII = Elizabeth of York,
                                                          (1485-1509)   dau. of **EDWARD IV**

CHARD III = Anne, dau.   Anne = (1) Henry,   Elizabeth = John,   Margaret = Charles,
483-1485)   of Richard,   Duke of Exeter   Duke of Suffolk   Duke of Burgundy
             Earl of Warwick
             (Kingmaker)

     Edward,
     Prince of Wales

ne = Thomas   Katherine = Sir William Courtenay
       Duke of Norfolk

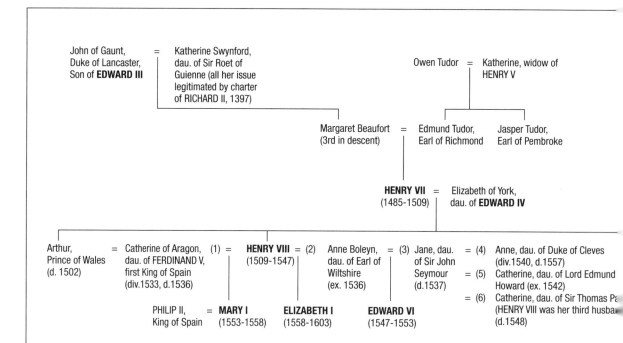

John of Gaunt, = Katherine Swynford,
Duke of Lancaster, dau. of Sir Roet of
Son of **EDWARD III** Guienne (all her issue
legitimated by charter
of RICHARD II, 1397)

Owen Tudor = Katherine, widow of
HENRY V

Margaret Beaufort = Edmund Tudor, Jasper Tudor,
(3rd in descent) Earl of Richmond Earl of Pembroke

HENRY VII = Elizabeth of York,
(1485-1509) dau. of **EDWARD IV**

Arthur, = Catherine of Aragon, (1) = **HENRY VIII** = (2) Anne Boleyn, = (3) Jane, dau. = (4) Anne, dau. of Duke of Cleves
Prince of Wales dau. of FERDINAND V, (1509-1547) dau. of Earl of of Sir John (div.1540, d.1557)
(d. 1502) first King of Spain Wiltshire Seymour = (5) Catherine, dau. of Lord Edmund
(div.1533, d.1536) (ex. 1536) (d.1537) Howard (ex. 1542)
= (6) Catherine, dau. of Sir Thomas Pa
(HENRY VIII was her third husba
(d.1548)

PHILIP II, = **MARY I** **ELIZABETH I** **EDWARD VI**
King of Spain (1553-1558) (1558-1603) (1547-1553)

THE STUARTS 1603-1714

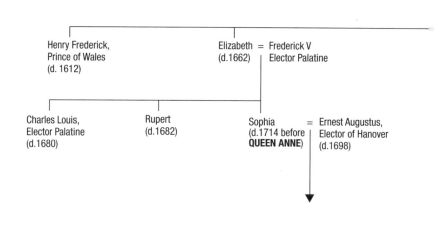

Henry Frederick, Elizabeth = Frederick V
Prince of Wales (d.1662) Elector Palatine
(d. 1612)

Charles Louis, Rupert Sophia = Ernest Augustus,
Elector Palatine (d.1682) (d.1714 before Elector of Hanover
(d.1680) **QUEEN ANNE**) (d.1698)

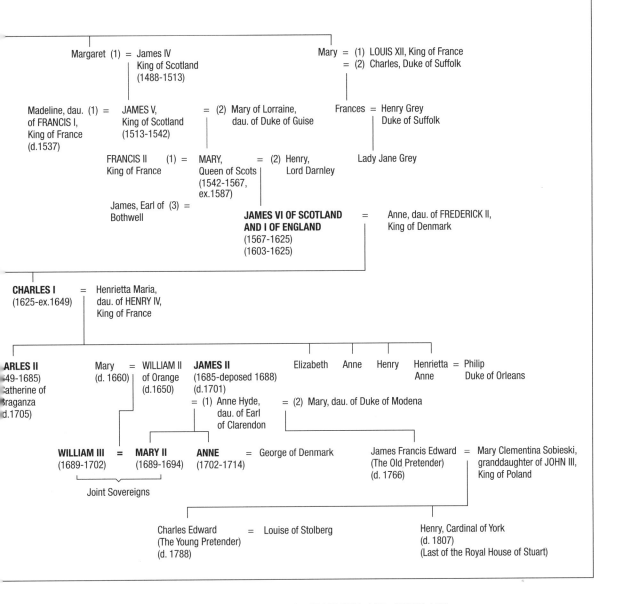

THE TUDORS 1485-1603

Margaret (1) = James IV
King of Scotland
(1488-1513)

Mary = (1) LOUIS XII, King of France
= (2) Charles, Duke of Suffolk

Madeline, dau. (1) = JAMES V,
of FRANCIS I, King of Scotland
King of France (1513-1542)
(d.1537)

= (2) Mary of Lorraine,
dau. of Duke of Guise

Frances = Henry Grey
Duke of Suffolk

FRANCIS II (1) = MARY, = (2) Henry,
King of France Queen of Scots Lord Darnley
(1542-1567,
ex.1587)

Lady Jane Grey

James, Earl of (3) =
Bothwell

JAMES VI OF SCOTLAND = Anne, dau. of FREDERICK II,
AND I OF ENGLAND King of Denmark
(1567-1625)
(1603-1625)

CHARLES I = Henrietta Maria,
(1625-ex.1649) dau. of HENRY IV,
King of France

ARLES II
49-1685)
Catherine of
Braganza
d.1705)

Mary = WILLIAM II
(d. 1660) of Orange
(d.1650)

JAMES II
(1685-deposed 1688)
(d.1701)
= (1) Anne Hyde,
dau. of Earl
of Clarendon

Elizabeth   Anne   Henry   Henrietta = Philip
Anne   Duke of Orleans

= (2) Mary, dau. of Duke of Modena

WILLIAM III = MARY II
(1689-1702)   (1689-1694)

ANNE = George of Denmark
(1702-1714)

James Francis Edward = Mary Clementina Sobieski,
(The Old Pretender)   granddaughter of JOHN III,
(d. 1766)   King of Poland

Joint Sovereigns

Charles Edward = Louise of Stolberg
(The Young Pretender)
(d. 1788)

Henry, Cardinal of York
(d. 1807)
(Last of the Royal House of Stuart)

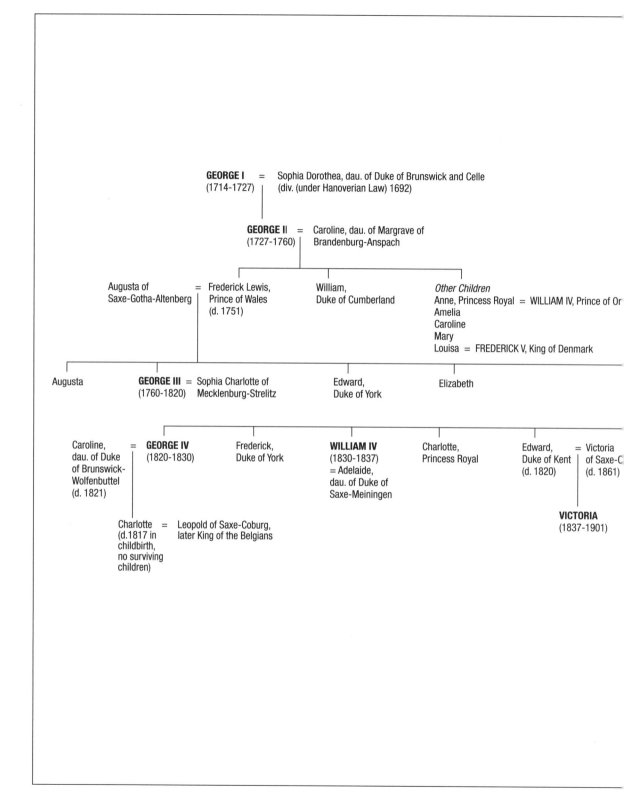

GEORGE I = Sophia Dorothea, dau. of Duke of Brunswick and Celle
(1714-1727) | (div. (under Hanoverian Law) 1692)

GEORGE II = Caroline, dau. of Margrave of
(1727-1760) | Brandenburg-Anspach

Augusta of = Frederick Lewis,
Saxe-Gotha-Altenberg | Prince of Wales
(d. 1751)

William,
Duke of Cumberland

Other Children
Anne, Princess Royal = WILLIAM IV, Prince of Or
Amelia
Caroline
Mary
Louisa = FREDERICK V, King of Denmark

Augusta

GEORGE III = Sophia Charlotte of
(1760-1820) Mecklenburg-Strelitz

Edward,
Duke of York

Elizabeth

Caroline, = **GEORGE IV**
dau. of Duke (1820-1830)
of Brunswick-
Wolfenbuttel
(d. 1821)

Frederick,
Duke of York

WILLIAM IV
(1830-1837)
= Adelaide,
dau. of Duke of
Saxe-Meiningen

Charlotte,
Princess Royal

Edward, = Victoria
Duke of Kent | of Saxe-C
(d. 1820) | (d. 1861)

Charlotte = Leopold of Saxe-Coburg,
(d.1817 in | later King of the Belgians
childbirth,
no surviving
children)

VICTORIA
(1837-1901)

THE HANOVERIANS 1714-1837

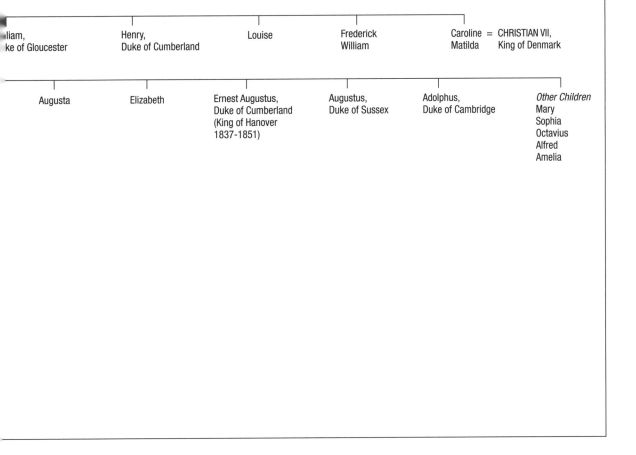

| liam, ke of Gloucester | Henry, Duke of Cumberland | Louise | Frederick William | Caroline Matilda | = | CHRISTIAN VII, King of Denmark |

Augusta   Elizabeth   Ernest Augustus, Duke of Cumberland (King of Hanover 1837-1851)   Augustus, Duke of Sussex   Adolphus, Duke of Cambridge   *Other Children* Mary Sophia Octavius Alfred Amelia

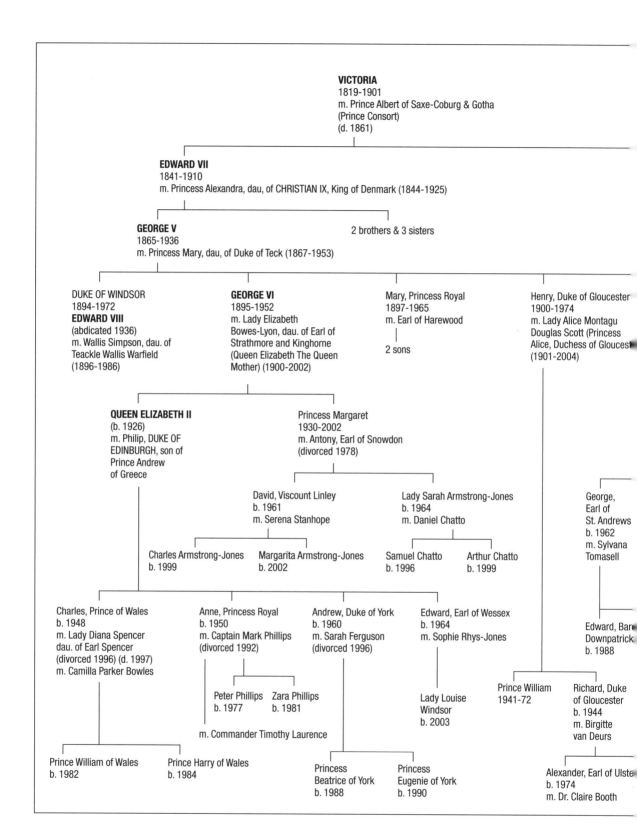

VICTORIA
1819-1901
m. Prince Albert of Saxe-Coburg & Gotha
(Prince Consort)
(d. 1861)

EDWARD VII
1841-1910
m. Princess Alexandra, dau. of CHRISTIAN IX, King of Denmark (1844-1925)

GEORGE V
1865-1936
m. Princess Mary, dau. of Duke of Teck (1867-1953)

2 brothers & 3 sisters

DUKE OF WINDSOR
1894-1972
EDWARD VIII
(abdicated 1936)
m. Wallis Simpson, dau. of
Teackle Wallis Warfield
(1896-1986)

GEORGE VI
1895-1952
m. Lady Elizabeth
Bowes-Lyon, dau. of Earl of
Strathmore and Kinghorne
(Queen Elizabeth The Queen
Mother) (1900-2002)

Mary, Princess Royal
1897-1965
m. Earl of Harewood

2 sons

Henry, Duke of Gloucester
1900-1974
m. Lady Alice Montagu
Douglas Scott (Princess
Alice, Duchess of Gloucest▪
(1901-2004)

QUEEN ELIZABETH II
(b. 1926)
m. Philip, DUKE OF
EDINBURGH, son of
Prince Andrew
of Greece

Princess Margaret
1930-2002
m. Antony, Earl of Snowdon
(divorced 1978)

David, Viscount Linley
b. 1961
m. Serena Stanhope

Lady Sarah Armstrong-Jones
b. 1964
m. Daniel Chatto

George,
Earl of
St. Andrews
b. 1962
m. Sylvana
Tomasell▪

Charles Armstrong-Jones
b. 1999

Margarita Armstrong-Jones
b. 2002

Samuel Chatto
b. 1996

Arthur Chatto
b. 1999

Charles, Prince of Wales
b. 1948
m. Lady Diana Spencer
dau. of Earl Spencer
(divorced 1996) (d. 1997)
m. Camilla Parker Bowles

Anne, Princess Royal
b. 1950
m. Captain Mark Phillips
(divorced 1992)

Andrew, Duke of York
b. 1960
m. Sarah Ferguson
(divorced 1996)

Edward, Earl of Wessex
b. 1964
m. Sophie Rhys-Jones

Edward, Bar▪
Downpatrick
b. 1988

Peter Phillips
b. 1977

Zara Phillips
b. 1981

m. Commander Timothy Laurence

Lady Louise
Windsor
b. 2003

Prince William
1941-72

Richard, Duke
of Gloucester
b. 1944
m. Birgitte
van Deurs

Prince William of Wales
b. 1982

Prince Harry of Wales
b. 1984

Princess
Beatrice of York
b. 1988

Princess
Eugenie of York
b. 1990

Alexander, Earl of Ulste▪
b. 1974
m. Dr. Claire Booth

KINGS AND QUEENS OF ENGLAND AND SCOTLAND

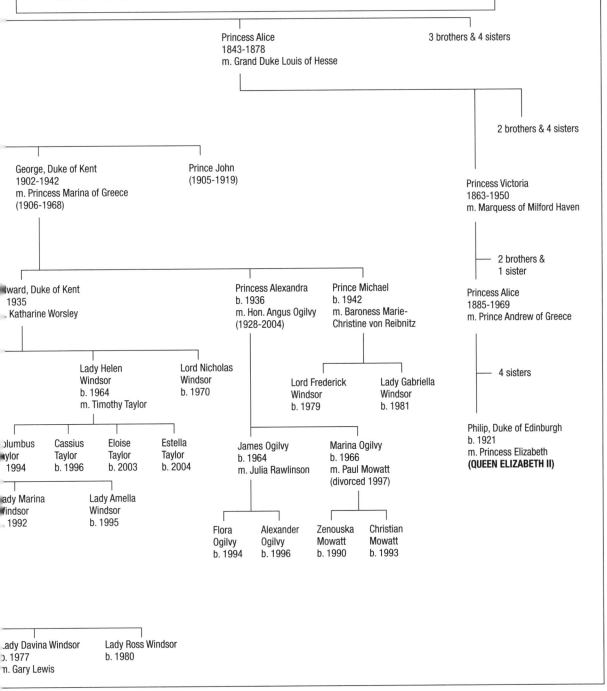

SAXE-COBURG & GOTHA 1837-1917 and THE WINDSORS 1917 – PRESENT DAY

Princess Alice
1843-1878
m. Grand Duke Louis of Hesse

3 brothers & 4 sisters

2 brothers & 4 sisters

George, Duke of Kent
1902-1942
m. Princess Marina of Greece
(1906-1968)

Prince John
(1905-1919)

Princess Victoria
1863-1950
m. Marquess of Milford Haven

...ward, Duke of Kent
1935
. Katharine Worsley

Princess Alexandra
b. 1936
m. Hon. Angus Ogilvy
(1928-2004)

Prince Michael
b. 1942
m. Baroness Marie-
Christine von Reibnitz

2 brothers &
1 sister

Princess Alice
1885-1969
m. Prince Andrew of Greece

Lady Helen
Windsor
b. 1964
m. Timothy Taylor

Lord Nicholas
Windsor
b. 1970

Lord Frederick
Windsor
b. 1979

Lady Gabriella
Windsor
b. 1981

4 sisters

...olumbus
...aylor
...1994

Cassius
Taylor
b. 1996

Eloise
Taylor
b. 2003

Estella
Taylor
b. 2004

James Ogilvy
b. 1964
m. Julia Rawlinson

Marina Ogilvy
b. 1966
m. Paul Mowatt
(divorced 1997)

Philip, Duke of Edinburgh
b. 1921
m. Princess Elizabeth
(QUEEN ELIZABETH II)

...ady Marina
...indsor
. 1992

Lady Amella
Windsor
b. 1995

Flora
Ogilvy
b. 1994

Alexander
Ogilvy
b. 1996

Zenouska
Mowatt
b. 1990

Christian
Mowatt
b. 1993

...ady Davina Windsor
). 1977
m. Gary Lewis

Lady Ross Windsor
b. 1980

FAMOUS BATTLES – PART ONE

IN THE MAIN, history springs from both noble and petty sources – from jealousy and murder as much as the dreams of great men and women. As well as being formed in new laws and sweeping cultural movements, history is made on the battlefield, with entire futures hanging on the outcome. You will find further study of these examples both enlightening and rewarding. Each is an extraordinary story in itself. Each had repercussions that helped to change the world.

1. Thermopylae – 480 BC

Darius the Great ruled the Persian lands known today as Iran and Iraq, pursuing an aggressive policy of expansion. He sent his heralds to Greek cities to demand submission. Many accepted, though Athens executed their herald and Sparta threw theirs down a well. War followed and Darius' ambitions came to an abrupt end when he was beaten at the Battle of Marathon in Greece. Although he planned another great invasion, his death prevented his return. It would fall to his son, Xerxes, to invade northern Greece with a vast army of more than two million in the spring of 480 BC.

The Persian fleet had already won control of the sea and the Greeks could not hold the north against such a vast host. Instead, they chose to defend the pass at Thermopylae in the south. Here, the way through the mountains was a tiny path only fourteen feet wide at its narrowest point. Thermopylae means 'Hot Gates', named after thermal springs in the area.

The Spartan king, Leonidas, took his personal guard of three hundred Spartans and about 7,000 other foot soldiers and archers to the pass. Of all the Greek leaders, he alone seemed to understand the desperate importance of resisting the enemy horde. When he

reached the pass, his men rebuilt an ancient wall and 6,000 of them waited at the middle gate, the other thousand guarding a mountain trail above. They did not expect to survive, but Spartans were trained to scorn fear and hardship from a young age. They prided themselves on being elite warriors. The Royal Guard were all fathers, allowed to attend the king only after they had contributed to the gene pool of Sparta. They revered courage above all else.

The Persian king sent scouts to investigate the pass. He was surprised to hear that the Spartans were limbering up and braiding their hair for battle. Unable to believe that such a small group would honestly wish to fight, he sent a warning to withdraw or be destroyed. They made him wait for four days without a reply. On the fifth, the Persian army attacked.

From the beginning, the fighting was brutal in such a confined space. The Spartans and the other Greeks fought for three solid days, throwing the Persians back again and again. Xerxes was forced to send in his 'Immortals' – his best warriors. The Spartans proved they were poorly named by killing large numbers of them. Two of Xerxes' brothers were also killed in the fighting.

In the end, Leonidas was betrayed by a Greek traitor. The man went to Xerxes and told him about a mountain track leading around the pass at Thermopylae. Leonidas had guarded one track, but for those who knew the area, there were others. Xerxes sent more of his Immortals to the secret path and they attacked at dawn. The other Greek soldiers were quickly routed, but Leonidas and the Spartans fought on.

When Leonidas finally fell, he had been cut off from the rest of the Spartans. A small group of the guard fought their way into the heaving mass, recovered his body and carried him to where the others were surrounded, fighting all

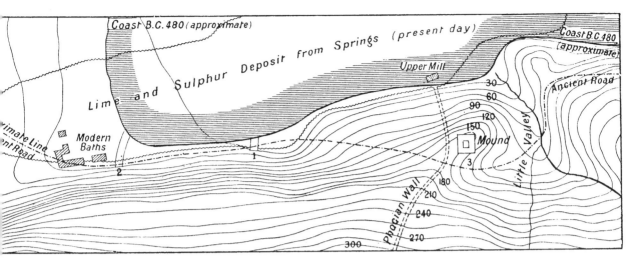

COAST AT MIDDLE GATE OF THERMOPYLÆ IN 480.
Scale, 8″ to 1 mile.
1, 2, 3, mark the three positions of the defenders of the Pass.

the way. The Persians simply could not break their defence and finally Xerxes ordered them to be cut down with flight after flight of heavy arrows. He was so furious at the losses his army had suffered that he had Leonidas beheaded and his body nailed to a cross.

The Spartans went on to play a crucial part in the war against the Persians. Leonidas and his small guard had established an extraordinary reputation, and larger forces of Spartans struck terror into the Persians at later battles. They had seen what only 300 could do and no one wanted to face 10,000 or 20,000. The Greeks won classic sea battles at Salamis and Eurymedon, destroying the Persian fleet. Over the next eight years, they beat the Persian host on land with battles at Plataea and Mycale. They lost Athens twice to the enemy and saw it completely destroyed. Much of the war has been forgotten, but the battle at Thermopylae still inspires writers and readers today. When peace returned, the Spartans placed a stone lion at the Hot Gates to mark where Leonidas created a legend. The epitaph reads: 'Go tell the Spartans, Stranger passing by, that here, obedient to their laws, we lie'.

2. Cannae – 216 BC

When the Latini tribe consolidated their hold on southern Italy, they joined two settlements into a city named Rome on seven hills. In the centuries that followed, they continued to explore their lands and boundaries, north and south, eventually crossing into Sicily. There, they came face to face with an outpost of the ancient and sophisticated Carthaginian empire. It was a clash of force and culture that launched generations of bitter conflict in what have come to be known as the Punic Wars and the first real test of Rome.

The Battle of Cannae is famous in part because the Roman legions were utterly annihilated. This is a surprisingly uncommon event. History has many more examples of battles where the defeated enemy were allowed to leave the field, sometimes almost intact. Cannae was a complete destruction of an army in just one day. It was very nearly the death knell for Rome herself.

The Romans had actually won the First Punic War, which lasted for seventeen years (264–241 BC), but it had not been a crushing defeat for the Carthaginians. They had had a gifted general in Hamilcar Barca, who had brought southern Spain under the rule of Carthage. Yet it was his son Hannibal who would invade Italy from Spain, cross the Alps with elephants and threaten the very gates of Rome. He commanded Carthaginian forces for the Second Punic War (218–201 BC).

Cannae is in southern Italy, near the heel of the 'boot'. Hannibal had come south the previous year, after destroying Roman armies of 40,000 and 25,000. Rome was in real danger.

The senate appointed a Dictator, Fabius, who tried to wear Hannibal's forces down by cutting lines of supply. It was a successful policy, but unpopular in a vengeful city that wanted to see the enemy destroyed rather than starved to death. New consuls were elected: Gaius Terentius Varro and Lucius Aemilius Paullus. The senate mustered an army of 80,000 infantry and 6,000 cavalry over which the consuls assumed joint leadership.

Hannibal's army had very few actual Carthaginians. When he entered what is today northern Italy, his forces consisted of 20,000 infantry (from Africa and Spain) and 6,000 cavalry. He recruited more from Gallic tribes in the north, but he was always outnumbered. In fact, the Romans had every possible advantage.

The two armies met on 2 August 216 BC. Hannibal and his army approached along the bank of a river, so he could not easily be flanked. He left 8,000 men to protect his camp. His cavalry was placed on both flanks and his infantry took position in the centre.

Varro was in command on the Roman side that day. He was not an imaginative leader and marched the Roman hammer straight at Hannibal's forces, attempting to smash them. Varro thought he had protected his wings from flanking manoeuvres with his own cavalry. In fact, Hannibal's horsemen were far superior. They crushed one Roman flank almost immediately, *circling behind* them to destroy the

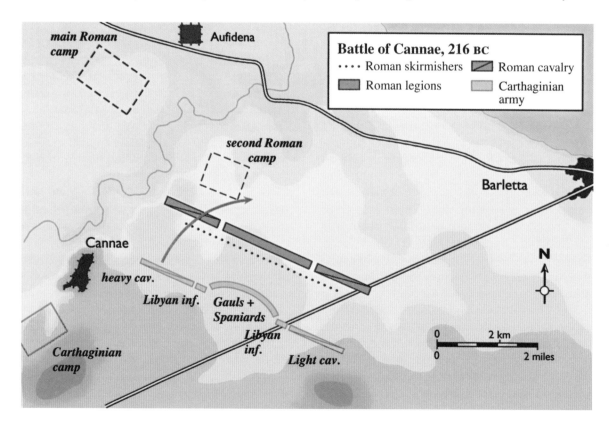

Battle of Cannae, 216 BC
- •••• Roman skirmishers
- ▨ Roman cavalry
- ▬ Roman legions
- ▢ Carthaginian army

main Roman camp

Aufidena

second Roman camp

Barletta

Cannae

heavy cav.

Libyan inf.

Gauls + Spaniards

Libyan inf.

Light cav.

Carthaginian camp

N

0   2 km
0   2 miles

other wing as well. They then wreaked havoc on Roman lines from behind.

Varro pressed on, however, his front line pushing the forces of Carthage further and further back, like a bow bending. Hannibal's front line had become completely concave and Varro had no idea that it was part of the plan. The Roman force marched further and further into the cup Hannibal had created for them. They believed they were winning.

Hannibal signalled for the wings to move and the cup began to close. Hannibal's cavalry completed the boxing-in of the Roman legions behind. They were so compressed they could hardly move and their numerical advantage had been completely cancelled out. More than 60,000 died over the next few hours as they were butchered, unable to escape. Hannibal lost 6,000 men.

One result of this battle was that the Romans learned from it. Three years later they had more than 200,000 men under arms and had renewed the struggle. There were successes and disasters on both sides, and Rome teetered on the brink of destruction until they appointed Publius Cornelius Scipio – known as Scipio Africanus. He had the vision and tactical skill to counter Hannibal. Though Rome was near bankruptcy and Italy was starving, the fortunes of Rome began to turn.

3. Julius Caesar's Invasions of Britain – 55 and 54 BC

Though neither invasion really came to anything, this has traditionally been the official starting point of recorded British history. In fact, Julius Caesar's own commentary is the *only* written source for some of the information that has survived today, such as the names of tribes around the south coast.

The Romans' first landing was on the beaches near Deal in Kent, having sailed from Gaul (France). The Britons (meaning 'painted ones', as they painted themselves blue) fought in the sea to prevent the landing, accompanied by huge dogs. Caesar's reference to the dogs

makes the English mastiff the oldest recorded breed. The Roman force fought their way onto dry land and made a truce with the local inhabitants. It is important to remember that Britain was practically off the edge of maps at this time. The existence of 'foggy islands' or 'tin islands' somewhere past Gaul was considered a myth in some places. Caesar was overstretched and spent only three weeks in Britain before heading back across the Channel to Gaul.

The second landing in 54 BC was much better organised. Caesar returned with a fleet of 800 ships, five legions and 2,000 cavalry. As the Spanish Armada would discover fifteen hundred years later, the coast can be violent and a storm smashed a large number of his ships, scattering many more.

Caesar marched north, destroying the tribes who had gathered under their war chief, Cassivellaunus of the Catuvellauni. Cassivellanus was forced to sue for peace near modern St Albans. Caesar accepted and returned to Gaul. Events such as the great Gaul rebellion under Vercingetorix, a civil war in Rome, falling in love with the Egyptian queen Cleopatra and, finally, assassination would prevent him ever returning. The Romans did not come back to Britain until AD 43, under Emperor Claudius.

4. Hastings – 14 October 1066

This is one of the most famous dates in English history – the last successful invasion up to modern times. At first, after the Romans left, Britain was almost constantly invaded. First the Saxons proved bothersome, then just as everyone was settling down to being Anglo-Saxon, the Vikings arrived. The Danish king, Canute (sometimes written Cnut), created a small, stable empire early in the eleventh century, ruling England, Norway, Sweden and Denmark. He had taken the English throne from Ethelred the Unready and after Canute's death, his feckless sons lost it back to Ethelred's son Edward, known as the Confessor for his piety. He named Harold Godwinson as his heir, crowned King Harold in January 1066 – the last Anglo-Saxon king before the Normans arrived and spoiled it for everyone.

In fact, William of Normandy had probably been named heir by Edward the Confessor – as far back as 1051. William had also extracted a promise from Harold Godwinson to support that claim when Harold was shipwrecked off Normandy in 1064. In that sense, the 1066 landing was to protect his rightful throne, though that isn't the usual view. We don't know the exact size of his army and estimates vary enormously. It was probably around 12,000 cavalry and 20,000 infantry.

In September, Harold was busy repulsing Norwegian invasions. They had promised Harold's brother Tostig an earldom for his aid. Harold marched north from London to relieve York from a Norse army. He met them at Stamford Bridge on 25 September, fighting for many hours. Of the 300 ships the Norwegians had brought over, only twenty-four were needed for the survivors. Tostig was killed. Stamford Bridge resulted in heavy casualties amongst Harold's best soldiers, which was to prove of vital importance to the later battle at Hastings.

On 28 September, William of Normandy landed on the Sussex coast. Harold heard of the landing by 2 October and immediately marched 200 miles south – which his army covered in less than five days. That is forty miles a day with weapons and armour.

Harold rested his men in London from 6 to 11 October, then marched to Hastings, covering fifty-six miles in forty-eight hours. Again we have only estimates of the size of his army, but it is believed to have been around 9,000 men. He was badly outnumbered and only a third of his men were first-rate troops. Still, it is difficult to see what else he could have done.

Harold took position on Senlac Ridge, about eight miles north-west of Hastings. On 14 October, the Norman army advanced in three lines: archers, pikemen and cavalry. William's archers fired first at too long a range, then fell back through their own lines to allow the pikemen to reach the enemy. The second line stormed forward, but were battered back from the ridge by rocks, spears and furious hand-to-hand fighting.

William then led a charge up the ridge, but it too failed to penetrate. The Normans' left wing fell back and Harold's soldiers rushed forward to take advantage of their weakness. Harold's army was set to crush the invaders as a rumour went around that William had fallen.

William threw off his helmet and rode up and down his lines to let his men see he was alive. As well as being a splendid moment, his action does show the importance of charismatic leadership at this time, a tradition going back to Thermopylae and beyond. When they saw William, the Normans rallied and crushed their pursuers. Seeing how this strategy had worked to his advantage, William used the technique again. He staged a false cavalry panic and succeeded in drawing more of Harold's men from their position, his cavalry returning to cut them down. Yet most of Harold's men remained on the ridge and the battle was far from over.

Many assaults by infantry, archers and cavalry followed. Harold's forces were exhausted by mid-afternoon, but their courage had not faltered and they had sent back every attack against them. At that point, a chance arrow struck Harold in the eye, wounding him mortally. Morale plummeted and the English lines began to fail.

In terms of historical effect, this battle was the seed that would flower into the largest empire the world has ever known. Countries like Germany, Belgium and Italy have only existed as nation states in the last couple of centuries, but England has maintained her identity through a thousand years.

On Christmas Day 1066, in Westminster Abbey, William I was crowned King of England.

5. Crécy – 26 August 1346

This battle was part of the Hundred Years War. Fighting was not absolutely constant between 1337 and 1453, but there were eight major wars over the period between France and England. In addition, the French supported the Scots in their almost constant wars with England. It was a busy time and the period is fascinating and well worth a more detailed look than can be attempted here.

Edward III of England had declared himself King of France in 1338, a statement that did not go down well with the French King, Philip VI. In support of his claim, Edward invaded with a professional, experienced army of 3,000

heavy cavalry knights, 10,000 archers and 4,000 Welsh light infantry. An additional 3,000 squires, artisans and camp followers went with them. It is worth pointing out that the English longbow took more than a decade to learn to use well. It could not simply be picked up and shot, even after weeks of training. The strength required to fire an arrow through iron armour was only developed after years of building strength in the shoulders. It was necessary to start an archer at a young age to

achieve the skill and power of those at Crécy.

Edward had failed to bring Philip to battle on two previous occasions. In 1346, he landed near Cherbourg and began a deliberate policy of the utter destruction of every French village and town he came to. In this way, Philip had to make an active response and his army marched against the English at the height of summer.

(The story of the early manoeuvres make excellent reading, especially Edward's crossing of the Somme river, made possible only by his

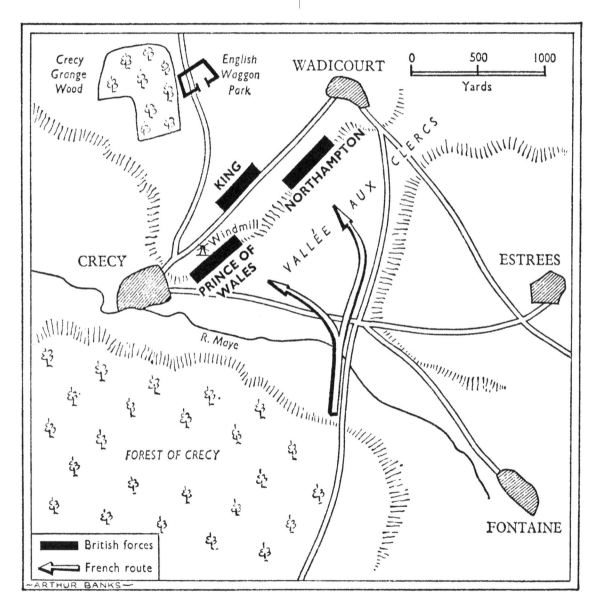

archers and neat timing. The Osprey Military book *Crécy 1346: Triumph of the Black Prince* by David Nicolle is well worth buying.)

To counter the English longbows, Philip did have Italian crossbowmen, but they needed a protective wicker shield while they reloaded and these were still with the baggage train for this battle, leaving them vulnerable. Nevertheless, the French force outnumbered the English three to one, with 12,000 knights and men at arms, 6,000 crossbowmen, 17,000 light cavalry and as many as 25,000 foot conscripts. They were not well prepared when they came up against the English lines, however.

Philip's first action was to send his crossbowmen out to lay down fire. They moved forward and shot at 150 yards. Most of the bolts fell short and they advanced to fire again. This brought them inside the killing range of the English longbows and a storm of arrows struck them.

The French knights saw the Italian crossbowmen falter and assumed they had lost their nerve. The knights were so keen to attack that they rode down their own allies to get through to the front, killing many. Then they too were in range of the English longbowmen and the thundering cavalry charge was torn apart. Those who did make it to the English lines were met by unsmiling veterans carrying axes and swords.

Charge after wild charge followed and was destroyed by the archers and the grim men behind them. Edward's son, the Prince of Wales, played a part, though at one point his position was almost overrun by the maddened French. His father refused to send him aid, saying that he must win his spurs.

We know the exact number of French aristocracy killed, as careful records were kept: 1,542 knights died that day. The number of common dead is less certain – somewhere between ten and twenty thousand is the best estimate. In comparison, the English forces lost two hundred men, including two knights, forty men-at-arms and the rest from the Welsh infantry.

Crécy was a humiliation for the French king. It meant that Edward was able to go on to capture Calais on the north coast of France, which remained an English possession for almost two centuries.

Philip died in 1350, succeeded by his son, John, who was captured at the Battle of Poiters in 1356 by the Prince of Wales, then kept in London and held for a ransom of three million gold crowns. He never regained his father's throne.

This was not the last battle where cavalry played a part, far from it. After all, Winston Churchill took part in a cavalry charge in his youth some five hundred years later. Yet Crécy does mark the end of the *dominance* of cavalry. It showed the future was with infantry and projectile weapons, at least until the tank was invented.

THE LAWS OF RUGBY UNION
AND RUGBY LEAGUE

A PUPIL OF RUGBY SCHOOL, William Webb Ellis, is credited as the first player to pick up a football and run with it – inventing the game of 'Rugby Football' in 1823. The trophy competed for at the Rugby Union World Cup is named in his honour, as is Ellis Stadium in Johannesburg.

The modern game still has two distinct codes – Rugby Union and Rugby League. The most obvious difference at first glance is that Rugby Union has fifteen players and Rugby League has only thirteen. Rugby Union was played first, with Rugby League splitting off after disagreements over payments in the late nineteenth century. Union matches were originally for amateurs only and a player who had played professional Rugby League was, until recently, banned from ever playing Rugby Union.

In 1995, the International Rugby Board removed all restrictions on Union games, allowing players to be paid as they are in other sports at the top level. However, the games themselves are still different in a number of ways. The Six Nations Championship (between Italy, France, Scotland, Wales, England and Ireland) and the Rugby World Cup are both played to Union rules, though there is also a Rugby League World Cup

RUGBY UNION

RUGBY UNION SHIRT NUMBERS		
	No.	**Position**
F O R W A R D S	1.	Loosehead prop
	2.	Hooker
	3.	Tighthead prop
	4.	Second row (lock)
	5.	Second row (lock)
	6.	Blindside flanker
	7.	Openside flanker
	8.	Number 8
B A C K S	9.	Scrum-half
	10.	Fly-half (outside half)
	11.	Left wing
	12.	Inside centre
	13.	Outside centre
	14.	Right wing
	15.	Full-back

Two teams of fifteen players compete for two halves of forty minutes on a grass pitch to gain points through tries, conversions, drop goals or penalties. A referee is in charge of the game and is supported by two flag-carrying 'touch judges' on the touchlines. The maximum distance between the H-shaped posts at each end is 110 yards (100 m), though behind each post there is an 'in-goal area', ending in a 'dead-ball line' that is between 11–24 yards (10–22mm) long.

Kick-off. Which team kicks off is decided by the referee tossing a coin. The successful team drop-kicks the ball from the centre of the halfway line. (A drop kick is when the ball is kicked after bouncing on the ground – usually at the moment of impact with the ground.) It must travel at least ten metres or the opposing team can restart with a scrum on the halfway line or ask for the kick to be taken again. In the same way, after every try and every successful penalty kick or drop goal, the team that didn't score restarts play with a drop kick from the halfway line.

Rucks. If a player is holding the ball, he can be tackled, ideally around the lower legs. Tackles around the neck are considered dangerous play and not permitted. Once he is down, he has to release the ball immediately. His own team want to keep possession, while the opposing team want to gain it. Both teams are allowed to pile in from behind the ball, but not from the side without earning a penalty, and players must bind onto a team-mate. If the ball comes free, it can be picked up and play can continue. A ruck always involves the ball being on the ground. It cannot be handled and must be 'rucked' backwards with the feet.

Mauls. A maul resembles a fast-moving, fast-forming scrum, with the ball still being held (and so not touching the ground). They form when a tackle holds up the ball rather than slamming the opposing player into the ground. As with rucks, players can only come charging in from behind the ball. A maul can collapse as it moves forward, in which case a scrum or penalty will usually be given, depending on circumstances.

Scrums. A scrum is a way of restarting play after a number of different infringements. For example, players are only allowed to pass backwards. Even if the ball is accidentally knocked forward, the referee will stop play and award a scrum to the other team. It is a huge advantage to be the team putting the ball into the scrum. Scrums are also given when the ball doesn't come out quickly from a ruck or a maul.

Unlike a ruck or maul, only the eight forwards take part in a scrum – usually the heaviest, toughest men in the team, though not always. The hooker, two props, two second rows, two flankers and the number 8 all link arms in a 3-4-1 formation, ready to lock heads with the opposing forwards. The hooker in the middle of the front row is the most important player in the scrum – it's their job to hook the ball out backwards for the scrum-half.

Offside takes many forms in rugby, but in open play it occurs when a player is in front of a team-mate with the ball. It's all to do with the fact that they must not obstruct opposing players – whereas in American Football, 'running interference' is actually a crucial part of the game.

Finally, the **line-out** is a way of restarting the game when the ball passes out of play on the touch lines. Whichever team didn't send it out of play throws the ball to a line of between two and eight players from each team. Whichever team throws the ball also chooses the number in the line-out and tends to have the advantage. The ball is thrown straight down the middle, and the throwing team usually wins the line-out because, by using secret calls, they know the likely length of the throw.

A **try** brings five points and is awarded when the ball is grounded in the opponents' in-goal area. The try must then be 'converted' for another two points. A **conversion** is a kick taken from a point in line with where the try was touched down. The ball must pass above the cross-bar and through the top uprights of the H. The easiest conversions are directly in front of the posts, which is why you will sometimes see players reach the opponents' try line and then run along to touch the ball down under the goalposts.

If a **penalty** is awarded when the team is in range of the posts, a penalty kick will usually be attempted – for three points. As with conversions, this is normally a stationary place kick. A **drop goal** is a ball in normal play that is drop-kicked from the hands between the uprights for three points. Penalty kicks and drop goals have come to be an important part of the modern game.

RUGBY LEAGUE DIFFERENCES

RUGBY LEAGUE SHIRT NUMBERS		
	No.	**Position**
Backs	1.	Full-back
	2.	Wing
	3.	Centre
	4.	Centre
	5.	Wing
	6.	Stand-off
	7.	Scrum-half
Forwards	8.	Prop forward
	9.	Hooker
	10.	Prop forward
	11.	Second row
	12.	Second row
	13.	Loose forward

In Rugby League, a try is worth four points, though the conversion is still worth two. A penalty goal is also worth two and a field or drop goal just one point. Apart from scoring, the two most important differences are 'play-the-ball' and the 'six-tackle rule'.

Play-the-ball is one of the things that makes Rugby League a fast-moving, exciting game to watch, with fewer stoppages than Rugby Union games. When a player is tackled, all opposing players but two must retreat ten metres from the tackled player. The two markers remain in front as he places the ball on the ground and rolls it backwards with his foot to the player behind them. It is also acceptable for the player to roll the ball back, step over it and pick it up himself.

The **six-tackle rule** further differentiates the two kinds of rugby. In League, there can only be five of these tackles where the ball is passed back into play. If a sixth tackle occurs, the ball is handed over to the opponents, so it's usually kicked high as it comes back into play after the fifth tackle, gaining ground in the process. Ideally, of course, the set of six would gain enough ground to go for a try or a drop goal.

Both kinds of rugby can be exciting to watch and the sport has not suffered from some of the crowd troubles that have affected football in recent years. A single chapter cannot cover every aspect of a complex game, unfortunately. For those who wish to go further, there are local clubs all over the country. A definitive collection of Union rules is published by the International Rugby Board: *The Laws of the Game of Rugby Union* (ISBN 0954093909). Alternatively, the Rugby Football League publish a 52-page booklet: *Rugby Football League: Laws of the Game and Notes on the Laws* (ISBN 0902039032).

SPIES – CODES AND CIPHERS

THE PRACTICE OF SENDING secret messages is known as 'steganography', Greek for 'concealed writing'. The problem with hiding a message in the lining of a coat or tattooed on the scalp is that anyone can read it. It makes a lot of sense to practise 'cryptography', as well, Greek for 'hidden writing'. Cryptography is the art of writing or breaking codes and ciphers.

The words 'code' and 'cipher' are sometimes used as if they mean the same thing. They do not. A code is a substitution, such as the following sentence: 'The Big Cheese lands at Happy tomorrow.' We do not know who the 'Big Cheese' is, or where 'Happy' is. Codes were commonly used between spies in World War II, when groups of numbers could only be translated with the correct codebook. Codes are impossible to break without a key or detailed knowledge of the people involved. If you spied on a group for some months, however, noticing the President of France landed at Heathrow airport the day after such a message, a pattern might begin to emerge.

'Ciphers', on the other hand, are scrambled messages, not a secret language. In a cipher, a plain-text message is concealed by replacing the letters according to a pattern. Even Morse Code is, in fact, a cipher. They are fascinating and even dangerous. More than one person has gone to his grave without giving up the secret of a particular cipher. Treasures have been lost, along with lives spent searching for them. In time of war, thousands of lives can depend on ciphers being kept – or '*deciphered*'.

Edgar Allan Poe left behind a cipher that was only broken in the year 2000. The composer Elgar left a message for a young lady that has not yet been fully understood. Treasure codes exist that point the way to huge sums in gold – if only the sequence of symbols can be broken.

At the time of writing, the state-of-the-art cipher is a computer sequence with 2048 figures, each of which can be a number, letter or symbol. The combinations are in trillions of trillions and it is estimated that even the fastest computers in the world couldn't break it in less than thirty billion years. Oddly enough, it was created by a seventeen-year-old boy in Kent, named Peter Parkinson. He is quite pleased with it. To put it in perspective, it is illegal in America to export an encryption program with more than *forty* digits without providing a key. It takes three days to break a 56-bit encryption.

Combinations to computer locks are one thing. This chapter contains some classic ciphers – starting with the one used by Julius Caesar to send messages to his generals.

1. **The Caesar Shift Cipher**. This is a simple alphabet cipher – but tricky to break without the key. Each letter is moved along by a number – say four. A becomes E, J becomes N, Z becomes D and so on. The number is the key to the cipher here. Caesar could agree the number with his generals in private and then send encrypted messages knowing they could not be read without that crucial extra piece of information.

   'The dog is sick' becomes 'WKH GRJ LV VLFN', with the number three as the key.

   As a first cipher it works well, but the problem is that there are only twenty-five possible number choices (twenty-six would take you back to the letter you started with). As a result, someone who really wanted to break the code could simply plod their way through all twenty-five combinations. Admittedly, they would first have to recognise the code as a Caesar cipher, but this one only gets one star for difficulty – it is more than two thousand years old, after all.

2. **Numbers**. A = 1, B = 2, C = 3 etc, all the way to Z = 26. Messages can be written using those numbers. This cipher is probably too simple to use on its own; however, if you combine it with a Caesar code number, it can suddenly become very tricky indeed.

   In the basic method, 'The dog is better' would be '20 8 5 – 4 15 7 – 9 19 – 2 5 20 20 5 18', which looks difficult but isn't. Add a Caesar cipher of 3, however, and the message becomes '3 23 11 8 – 7 18 10 – 12 22 – 5 8 23 23 8 21', which should overheat the brain of younger brothers or sisters trying to break the encryption. Note that we have included the key number at the beginning. It could be agreed beforehand in private to make this even harder to break. (With the Caesar combination, a difficulty of two stars.)

3. **Alphabet ciphers**. There are any number of these. Most of them depend on the way the alphabet is written out – agreed beforehand between the spies.

   A B C D E F G H I J K L M

   N O P Q R S T U V W X Y Z

With this sequence, 'How are you?' would become 'UBJ NER LBH?'

A	B	C	D	E	F	G	H	I	J	K	L	M	N	O	P	Q	R	S	T	U	V	W	X	Y	Z
Z	Y	X	W	V	U	T	S	R	Q	P	O	N	M	L	K	J	I	H	G	F	E	D	C	B	A

In this one, 'How are you?' would become 'SLD ZIV BLF?' It's worth remembering that even simple ciphers are not obvious at first glance. Basic alphabet ciphers may be enough to protect a diary and they have the benefit of being easy to use and remember.

4. Most famous of the alphabet variations is a code stick – another one used by the Romans. Begin with a strip of paper and wind it around a stick. It is important that the sender and the receiver both have the same type. Two bits from the same broom handle would be perfect, but most people end up trying this on a pencil. (See picture.)

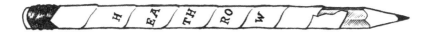

Here the word 'Heathrow' is written down the length of the pencil, with a couple of letters per turn of the strip. (You'll need to hold the paper steady with tape, or better still, Blu-Tack.) When the tape is unwound, the same pen is used to fill in the spaces between the letters. It should now look like gibberish. The idea is that when it is wound back on to a similar stick, the message will be clear. It is a cipher that requires a bit of forethought, but can be quite satisfying. For a matter of life and death, however, you may need the next method.

5. **Codeword alphabet substitution.** You might have noticed a pattern developing here. To make a decent cipher, it is a good idea to agree the key beforehand. It could be a number, a date, the title of a book, a word or even a kind of stick. It's the sort of added complexity that can make even a simple encryption quite fiendish.

Back to one of our earlier examples:

A	B	C	D	E	F	G	H	I	J	K	L	M	N	O	P	Q	R	S	T	U	V	W	X	Y	Z
Z	Y	X	W	V	U	T	S	R	Q	P	O	N	M	L	K	J	I	H	G	F	E	D	C	B	A

If we added the word 'WINDOW', we would get the sequence below. Note that no letters are repeated, so there are still twenty-six in the bottom sequence and the second 'W' of 'WINDOW' is not used.

A	B	C	D	E	F	G	H	I	J	K	L	M	N	O	P	Q	R	S	T	U	V	W	X	Y	Z
W	**I**	**N**	**D**	**O**	A	B	C	E	F	G	H	J	K	L	M	P	Q	R	S	T	U	V	X	Y	Z

This is a whole new cipher – and without knowing the codeword, a difficulty of three stars to crack.

6. **Cipher-wheels.** Using a pair of compasses, cut four circles out of card, two large and two small – 5 inch (12 cm) and 4 inch (10 cm) diameters work well. For both pairs, put one on top of the other and punch a hole through with a butterfly stud. They should rotate easily

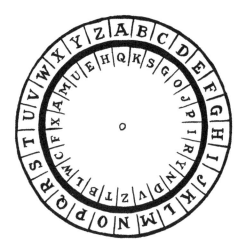

A circle = 360 degrees. There are twenty-six letters in the alphabet, so the spacing for the segments should be approximately 14 degrees. Mark off the segments as accurately as you can for all four circles. When they are ready, write the normal alphabet around the outside of the large circles in the usual way – A to Z. For the inner circles, mark the letters in random order. As long as the matching code wheel is done in the same way, it doesn't matter where the letters go. The code sequence will begin with the two-letter combination that shows the positions of the wheels – AM or AF, for example.

You should end up with a cipher-wheel encrypter that can *only* be read by someone with the other wheel. Now *that* is a difficulty of four stars.

7. **Morse Code** is the most famous substitution cipher ever invented. It was thought up by an American inventor, Samuel F.B. Morse, who patented a telegraph system and saw it explode in popularity. He realised that a pulse of electricity could act on an electromagnet to move a simple lever – transmitting a long or short signal. He arranged a moving strip of paper to pass underneath the metal point and a new method of communication was born. Using his cipher, he sent the first inter-city message in 1844 from Washington to Baltimore. The marvellous thing about it is that the code can be sent using light if you have a torch, or sound, if you can reach a car horn, or even semaphore, though that is fairly tricky.

The first message Morse sent was 'What hath God wrought?', which gives an idea of just how impressive it was to pick up messages as they were written on the other side of America. In Morse's lifetime, he saw telegraph lines laid across the Atlantic.

The example *everyone* knows is SOS – the international distress call. ('May-day' is also well known. That one comes from the French for 'Help me' – 'M'aidez'.)

The SOS sequence in Morse is dit dit dit – dah dah dah – dit dit dit.

MORSE CODE

A	• —	N	— •	1	• — — — —
B	— • • •	O	— — —	2	• • — — —
C	— • — •	P	• — — •	3	• • • — —
D	— • •	Q	— — • —	4	• • • • —
E	•	R	• — •	5	• • • • •
F	• • — •	S	• • •	6	— • • • •
G	— — •	T	—	7	— — • • •
H	• • • •	U	• • —	8	— — — • •
I	• •	V	• • • —	9	— — — — •
J	• — — —	W	• — —	0	— — — — —
K	— • —	X	— • • —		
L	• — • •	Y	— • — —		
M	— —	Z	— — • •		

This really is one worth learning. Rescuers have heard messages tapped out underneath fallen buildings, heard whistles or seen the flashes from a capsized dinghy. This cipher has saved a large number of lives over the years since its invention. It has also sent quite a few train timetables.

If you *do* have a flag handy, it's left for a dash, right for a dot. This is not so well known.

8. This last one is actually designed to make meaning clearer rather than to hide it. The **Nato Phonetic alphabet** is just useful to know, so...

NATO PHONETIC ALPHABET

A	Alpha		**N**	November
B	Bravo		**O**	Oscar
C	Charlie		**P**	Papa
D	Delta		**Q**	Quebec
E	Echo		**R**	Romeo
F	Foxtrot		**S**	Sierra
G	Golf		**T**	Tango
H	Hotel		**U**	Uniform
I	India		**V**	Victor
J	Juliet		**W**	Whiskey
K	Kilo		**X**	X-ray
L	Lima		**Y**	Yankee
M	Mike		**Z**	Zulu

A previous RAF version (c.1924-1942) was Ace, Beer, Charlie, Don, Edward, Freddie, George, Harry, Ink, Johnnie, King, London, Monkey, Nuts, Orange, Pip, Queen, Robert, Sugar, Toc, Uncle, Vic, William, X-ray, Yorker, Zebra. This was more suited to British English accents, apparently. The Nato version was created in 1956 and has become the accepted standard phonetic alphabet. It is used to minimise confusion when reading letters aloud on the radio or telephone. 'P' and 'B' sound very similar – but 'Papa' and 'Bravo' do not.

MAKING CRYSTALS

HAVING A CRYSTAL growing on your windowsill can be good fun. With food colouring, you can make them any colour you wish.

The problem is finding a suitable chemical. You may have seen copper sulphate and potassium permanganate in school. Both can be quite toxic and are therefore not easily available in local chemists. Your science teacher may allow you to have a sample, if you ask very politely.

For this chapter, we decided to use Potassium Aluminium Sulphate, better known as Alum powder. It is a non-toxic substance that used to be used to whiten bread. As with any household substance, you shouldn't get it in your eyes. It is available from the following website: www.panspantry.co.uk. 100 grams will cost you two pounds at the time of writing, not including postage and packing. That is enough for crystal making, but Alum can be used for fire-proofing and tanning skin – as discussed in other chapters. It also works as an astringent on small cuts, or the crystals can be used as an underarm deodorant. You might want to get more. Alternatively, you can grow crystals with common salt or sugar.

> You will need
>
> - 10 grams of potassium aluminium sulphate (alum).
> - A glass tumbler.
> - A lolly stick (clean).
> - Warm water.
> - Thread.
> - Small stones, preferably with sharp edges.

METHOD

1. Make sure the stones are clean – wash them thoroughly in running water.

2. Put enough warm water in the tumbler to cover the stones. (About a third of the cup.) Do not put the stones in yet.

3. Add the alum and stir furiously with the lolly stick until it stops dissolving easily. You may be left with a few grains at the bottom. Ignore them. You can either put the stones straight in or, for the classic look, tie a thread around a small stone and the other end around the lolly stick, as in the pictures. We did both.

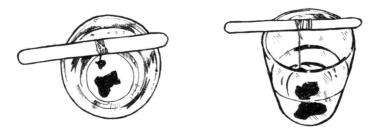

4. If you are intending to add food colouring, do it now. Show proudly to parents, who will pat your head for being a 'little genius'.

Evaporation is the key for these small crystals, so make sure it is in a warm place. It will take a few days for the first ones to appear, and the full effect can take a few weeks. Larger crystals can be made by repeating the process – after tying a small crystal to the thread.

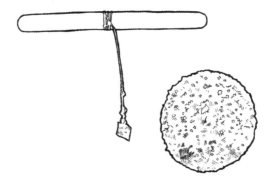

The crystal you see here is a picture of the one we grew – the one on the left, not the enormous thing. The huge circle came from the bottom of the glass and in many ways is more impressive than the actual crystal. It took about six weeks in total, and we refilled the alum once.

EXTRAORDINARY STORIES – PART ONE

STORIES OF COURAGE and determination are sometimes underrated for their ability to inspire. It is true that once-famous names can slip from the memory of generations, names like Charles George Gordon, Richard Francis Burton, Florence Nightingale, Robert Scott, Herbert Kitchener, Henry Morton Stanley, Rudyard Kipling, Isambard Kingdom Brunel and a host of others. Their lives, their stories, were once known to every schoolboy; held up as examples of fortitude and honour. These values have not ceased to be important in the modern world, nor have the stories become less moving. We have chosen five of our favourites. They range from Nelson's death at Trafalgar to the astonishing modern story of Joe Simpson's struggle in the mountains of Peru. These are all tales worth knowing.

Robert Scott and the Antarctic

Robert Falcon Scott was born on 6 June 1868. All his life, he was known as 'Con', a short form of his middle name. He came from a seafaring family, with uncles, grand-uncles and grandparents all serving in the Royal Navy. His father owned a small brewery in Plymouth that had been bought with prize money from the Napoleonic wars.

'Con' Scott joined HMS *Boadicea* at the age of thirteen as a midshipman. It was a hard world, requiring instant obedience and personal discipline. By twenty-two, he was a lieutenant with first-class certificates in pilotage (steering/navigation), torpedoes and gunnery, with the highest marks in his year for seamanship.

He had met Sir Clements Markham, the President of the Royal Geographical Society, more than once in the course of his naval duties, impressing the older man with his intelligence and demeanour. When, at the turn of the century, the Royal Society wanted someone to head an expedition to the South Pole, Sir Clements Markham fought to have Scott lead the group.

Scott had no experience of the extremes he would be facing at that point in his career. He solved this problem by consulting those who had, travelling to Oslo to consult Fridtjof Nansen, a Norwegian explorer of Arctic regions who would later become the Norwegian ambassador to London. They became firm friends and Scott accepted Nansen's advice to get dogs to pull sleds, buying twenty dogs and three bitches in Russia for his first attempt on the South Pole.

Robert Scott

By 1900, the first members of the team were appointed. Scott had insisted on personal approval of all appointments and was able to make quick decisions. With an idea of the hardship ahead, most were young and fit, though when Scott met Edward Wilson, a young doctor and artist, the man was suffering from an abscess in his armpit, blood poisoning and lungs weakened by tuberculosis. Nonetheless, Scott appointed him. He also chose one Ernest Shackleton, whose own courageous story would become famous later on.

With the money Sir Clements Markham had raised, the ship *Discovery* was built, costing £49,277, and launched on 21 March 1901. Scott also purchased a balloon for the voyage, costing £1300. The young King and Queen, Edward VII and Alexandra, came on board to see the ship at Cowes. Sir Clements Markham said of the crew, 'No finer set of men ever left these shores, nor were men ever led by a finer captain.'

The trip south was slow and difficult. *Discovery* leaked and could not make more than seven knots under full steam. However, they reached New Zealand and had the leak fixed as well as taking on supplies. They sailed on into the ice packs and the high southern latitudes. Scott and Shackleton were the first people ever to take a balloon trip in the Antarctic, though that too developed a leak and was used only once.

Their lack of experience showed in a number of ways, from misjudging distances and the difficulties of driving dogs, to protecting the skin and cooking in low temperatures. They had to learn vital skills very quickly in an environment where sweat froze and a blizzard could strike without warning. However, they did learn, spending a year in an icy landscape, out of which their ship seemed to grow.

In November 1902, they made a push to the Pole, but the dogs sickened. They were the first to cross the 80th parallel, after which all maps were blank. They began to kill the dogs, feeding them to the others. Shackleton developed the first symptoms of scurvy due to a lack of vitamins in his diet and the pain of snow blindness became so great for Wilson that he had to use a blindfold and follow Scott's voice. After an attempt lasting ninety-three days, they were four hundred and eighty miles from the Pole when Scott gave the order to turn back on 31 December. More dogs died on the way back to the ship, but the men all survived to try again.

A support ship, the *Morning*, resupplied the expedition and took some members home, including Shackleton. Research trips continued, despite recording temperatures as low as −67°F. The *Discovery* had become solidly wedged and it took a combination of relief ships and dynamite to free her after two years on the ice. They returned to Portsmouth in September 1904. Still on special leave from the Royal Navy, Scott was appointed Captain on the strength of his achievements. There were exhibitions of drawings and scientific samples, lectures and tours. Scott became something of a celebrity, publishing a two-volume account of the expedition, complete with Wilson's dramatic pictures. Despite his relative success, the government ignored Scott's plea to save the *Discovery* and she was sold.

In 1907, Scott went back to sea as Captain on various ships, and met and married Kathleen Bruce in 1908. Shackleton tried a trip of his own, but his team turned back when they were only ninety-seven miles from the Pole. The lure of the Antarctic had struck deep in both Scott and Shackleton, but it was Scott's second expedition of 1910 that was to become famous around the world.

Scott wrote that 'the main object of the expedition is to reach the South Pole and secure for the British Empire the honour of that achievement.' Science would play a lesser part in the second strike for the Pole.

Scott had learned from his previous experiences and consulted once again with Nansen while the money was raised and the team came together. Funds came slowly and more than one member of the expedition collected money to earn their place. Captain L.E.G. Oates was in charge of ponies. Wilfred Bruce, Scott's brother-in-law, was sent to Russia to buy the vital sled-dogs and Siberian ponies. They also experimented with motor sledges.

The Norwegian explorer Roald Amundsen was also heading south. Originally, his intentions had been to explore the Arctic, but an American, Robert Peary, claimed to have reached the North Pole in 1909 and Amundsen now had his sights set on the unconquered southern pole. He had a hundred dogs with him and supplies for two years. He knew the conditions and he had planned the route. Scott was still struggling to collect funds in New Zealand and Australia. The final stores were loaded and the ship *Terra Nova* sailed on 29 November 1910. Two months before, Scott had received a telegram from Amundsen, sent after he had sailed. It had read only, 'Beg leave inform you proceeding Antarctic. Amundsen.'

Terra Nova entered the pack ice on 9 December, smashing its way through and finally anchoring to solid ice in January 1911. The sledges, base equipment and supplies were unloaded – and the heaviest motor sledge broke through the ice, disappearing into the sea. The slow process of a pole attempt began, with camps established further and further south. The ponies did not do at all well and frostbite appeared very early on amongst the men.

Conditions were awful, with constant blizzards pinning them in their tents. The ponies were all dead by the time they reached the last camp, after dragging the sledges up a 10,000-foot glacier. Scott picked Wilson, Evans, Oates and Bowers for the final slog to the Pole, with each man hauling 200 pounds on sledges.

The smaller team of five battled through blizzards to reach the 89th parallel, the last before the Pole itself. It was shortly afterwards that they crossed the tracks of Amundsen and his dog teams. Scott and the others were touched by despair, but went on regardless, determined to reach the Pole.

They finally stood at the southernmost point on earth on 17 January 1912. There they found a tent, with a piece of paper that bore the names of five men: Roald Amundsen, Olav Olavson Bjaaland, Sverre Hassel, Oscar Wisting and Hilmer Hanssen. The note was dated 14 December 1911. The disappointment weighed heavily on all of them – there have been few closer races in history with so much at stake.

Captain L.E.G. Oates

The return journey began well enough, but Evans had lost fingernails to the cold, Wilson had strained a tendon in his leg, Scott himself had a bruised shoulder and Oates had the beginnings of gangrene in his toes. In such extreme conditions of exhaustion, even small wounds refused to heal. They had all paid a terrible price to be second.

Food began to run short and every supply dump they reached was a race against starvation and the cold. Oil too ran low and freezing to death was a real possibility. Evans collapsed on 16 February and never fully recovered. He struggled on the following day, but he could barely stand and died shortly afterwards.

Wilson too was growing weak, so Scott and Bowers made camp by themselves in temperatures of –43 °F.

On 16 or 17 March, Oates said he could not go on and wanted to be left in his sleeping bag. He knew he was slowing them down, and that their only slim chance may have been vanishing. The next morning, there was a blizzard blowing. Oates stood up in the tent and said, 'I am just going outside and may be some time.'

Scott wrote in his diary, 'We knew that poor Oates was walking to his death, but though we tried to dissuade him, we knew it was the act of a brave man and an English gentleman.' Oates was not seen again and his body has never been found.

By 20 March, Scott knew he would lose his right foot to frostbite. They were only eleven miles from a camp, but a blizzard prevented them from moving on and staying still was a slow death for the three men remaining. They had run out of oil and had only two days of starvation rations left. They had run out of time and strength. Scott made the decision to try for the depot, but it was beyond them and they did not leave that last position. Scott's final diary entry was, 'It seems a pity, but I do not think that I can write more. R. Scott. For God's sake look after our people.'

With the diary ended, Scott wrote letters to the families of those who had died, including a letter to his own wife, where he mentioned their only son.

I had looked forward to helping you to bring him up, but it is a satisfaction to know that he will be safe with you... Make the boy interested in natural history if you can. It is better than games. They encourage it in some schools. I know you will keep him in the open air. Try to make him believe in a God, it is comforting... and guard him against indolence. Make him a strenuous man. I had to force myself into being strenuous, as you know – had always an inclination to be idle.

He also wrote a letter to the public, knowing that his body would be found.

We took risks, we knew we took them; things have come out against us, and therefore we have no cause for complaint, but bow to the will of providence, determined still to do our best to the last... Had we lived, I should have had a tale to tell of the hardihood, endurance and courage of my companions which would have stirred the heart of every Englishman. These rough notes and our dead bodies must tell the tale, but surely, surely, a great rich country like ours will see that those who are dependent on us are properly provided for.

Scott knew that the expedition funds were crippled by debt and his last thoughts were the fear that their loved ones would be made destitute by what was still owed. In fact, enough donations came in when the story was known to pay all debts and create grants for the children and wives of those who had perished.

The men were found frozen in their tent by the team surgeon, Atkinson, in November of that year. The diaries and letters were recovered, but a snow cairn was built over their last resting place ready for the day when the moving pack ice would ease them into the frozen sea. The search party looked for Oates without success, finally erecting a cross to him with the following inscription.

HEREABOUTS DIED A VERY GALLANT GENTLEMAN, CAPTAIN L.E.G. OATES OF THE INNISKILLING DRAGOONS. IN MARCH 1912, RETURNING FROM THE POLE, HE WALKED WILLINGLY TO HIS DEATH IN A BLIZZARD TO TRY TO SAVE HIS COMRADES, BESET BY HARDSHIP.

'. . . for my own sake I do not regret this journey, which has shown that Englishmen can endure hardships, help one another, and meet death with as great a fortitude as ever in the past.'
— Robert Falcon Scott

MAKING A GO-CART

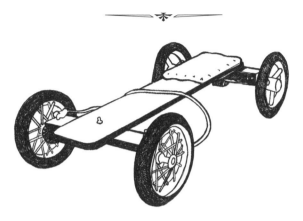

THE HARDEST PART of making a go-cart is finding the wheels. The sad truth is that most modern prams have tiny wheels, so the classic idea of finding a pram and removing the axles intact isn't really possible any more. Those prams that do survive are antiques and too valuable for our purposes.

THE DESIGN

You will need

- Two fixed axles with wheels attached.
- Plank to sit on – we used ¾ in (18 mm) pine.
- Axle wood. Length will depend on your axles, but we used a plank of 3½ × 1½ inches (88 mm × 37 mm).
- Rope for the handle.
- Two eye-screws to attach the rope.
- Four electrician's metal 'saddles' (see explanation below).
- Wood paint (colour of your choice).
- 1½ inch screws (40 mm).
- Vinyl and foam if you intend to add a seat.
- A steering bolt (see explanation).
- Upholstery tacks for the seat.

First, cut the wood. We cut two lengths of 17 in (43 cm) for the axles but this will be different for each project. We also cut quite a long central plank at 3 ft 9 in (114 cm). Again, that depends on the length of your legs. Allow some growing room at least. It really is a good idea to let an adult cut the wood for you, especially if power tools are involved. If you ignore this advice and cut off a finger, please do not send it to us in the post as proof.

However, the good news is that there are other things you can use. We found our two axles after many visits to three local refuse centres – dumps. It is against council regulations to buy or sell at dumps, but if you hold a five-pound note visibly in your hand, you might be lucky. It took many weeks to find ours, so the best planning you can do is to go out now and make your face known to the employees in every dump for ten miles. Our rear axle came from a golf trolley and our front from a modern three-wheel pram – used ones are just starting to appear in these dumps, so you might find one faster than we did. The other possibility was to find a tricycle and use the rear wheels from that. As long as it has a fixed axle that doesn't turn with the wheels, you needn't worry. If at all possible, use metal wheels rather than plastic ones. Plastic is an awful material and has a tendency to shatter under stress – while going down a hill, for example.

It is also a good idea to paint the wood – or varnish it – at this stage. We completely forgot to do this and painting it at a late stage was very fiddly. Better to do it now. We used a wood primer and black matt paint. As we had an old can of varnish in the shed, we then varnished it as well. You can, of course, buy paint, but digging out old cans with just a dab still wet at the bottom is somehow more satisfying.

When the painted wood is dry, attach the axles. Twenty years ago, we used U-shaped nails, and these were perfectly reliable. This time we found our axles were much wider and had to find an alternative. This is the sort of problem you might have to solve.

Above is an electrical 'saddle', available for a few pence from any electrical shop. They are also quite useful for attaching axles and come in a variety of sizes.

We used three of them on the front axle. The original plan was two, but one of the screw holes seemed weak and we wanted it to be reliable. Make sure you place the saddles carefully so that the axle is straight on the plank. Given identical saddles, we measured the distance from the top of each one to the edge of the wood. You can place this by eye, but it's better to measure and be certain.

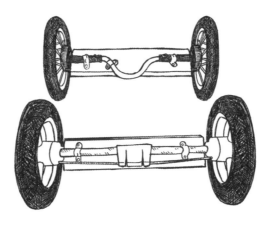

1½ in (40 mm) screws will secure the rear of the main plank, as shown below. It looks easy, but some careful measuring is necessary to make the angle between the main plank and the axle plank exactly ninety degrees. You must also make sure that the overhang on each side is the same. We clamped the pieces together quite loosely and then used a rubber mallet to tap it into place, measuring again and again until we were satisfied.

The steering is the only tricky thing left to do. We were extraordinarily lucky in finding that the single wheel bolt on a three-wheel pram is perfect for this, but you can't depend on that kind of luck. You must find a bolt with a thread only part-way along.

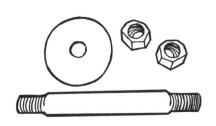 

Bolt from a three-wheel pram   *More likely to use this one.*

The benefit of this is that a nut can be tightened on the bolt and yet the bolt can still turn freely in the hole. They are available from any hardware shop. Find one a little over the length you need and add a washer at both ends – or more if it's too long.

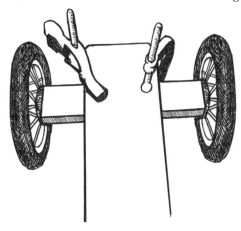

Getting the front position right wasn't as hard as the rear. It was crucial to have the same distance of axle poking out on either side as before, but it didn't have to be at ninety degrees as the axle was going to pivot – otherwise there could be no steering. The nice thing about this design is that you sit with your feet on the steering bar, also holding onto ropes. As a result, it is extremely manoeuvrable.

We decided to put a seat on ours. We asked in a carpet shop and were given a bit of carpet and a vinyl sample for free. We folded the vinyl around a piece of pine, using the carpet as padding between. We then tacked it down with upholstery nails from a hardware shop and screwed the whole thing to the main plank from underneath. The rope was attached using a bowline knot on each end.

Cost

Getting a pram and a golf trolley from two different dumps cost us two five-pound notes. We think it might have been possible to get them for less, but after weeks of asking, we were so pleased to find them that we offered too much. Begin by offering two or three pounds. The wood came to £13, the screws, nuts and washers cost around another £5. The paint came from old tins in the shed. We had the rope already. Altogether, it came to around £30. However, to buy a go-cart of this sort of quality, you would have to pay at least £50 and possibly even £80 or more. This one has the benefit of lasting longer than pedal versions (room to grow), being much faster down hills and, well, being something *you* made rather than a company in China.

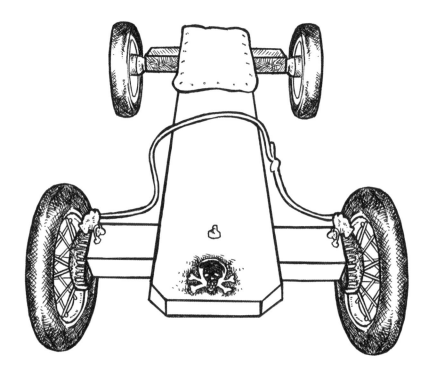

INSECTS AND SPIDERS

A Meadow Grasshopper

'INSECT' AS A WORD is from the Latin, meaning 'cut into' or 'segmented'. An insect is any creature with a head, a thorax, an abdomen and six legs. They usually have an exoskeleton – protective plating on the outside. They are by far the largest class in the animal kingdom. There are hundreds or even thousands of different species to be found in any field or stretch of open water in the country. They are part of fantastically complex ecosystems and in a single village pond a hundred thousand lives can come into existence, fly and perish, sometimes even in a single day. Their variety is astounding and their lives can be endlessly fascinating. Here are some of the ones you might find near where you live.

GRASSHOPPERS (ORTHOPTERA)

Although, with tiny differences, there are more than two dozen varieties of **grasshopper**, they can be put into two main groups: long-horns (Locustidae) and short-horns (Acrididae). Both make the familiar rhythmic creaking noise on sunny days, though short-horned varieties are much more common. The long-horned grasshopper can be as much as five times larger than their cousins and are capable of flight, though usually only in very short bursts. When they are stationary, they are practically invisible. To find them, walk very slowly through long grass, the longer the better. In the summer, you will see small darting specks of small meadow grasshoppers leaping away from you. They are usually bright green, but can also be found in brown or grey. If you are lucky, you will see a larger long-horned one. By all means try to catch the small grasshoppers, but the long-horns are always damaged when they are caught by hand.

Crickets are far less common in this country, though there are three varieties: the field cricket, the house cricket and the mole cricket, which spends most of its time underground. The British field cricket is an endangered species and came close to dying out in the 1980s. They have been bred and reintroduced to the wild since then, but sightings are still relatively rare. They are more common in France, Italy and many warmer countries, however.

Cricket

Earwigs (Dermaptera)

These are so common that it might seem odd to put them here – the reason is merely to say that **earwigs** are completely harmless. They are nocturnal insects, with one flying variety. The fierce-looking clippers are for holding, not killing. The female cares for and feeds her young, after laying eggs in a tiny nest dug with the male.

Earwig

Mayflies (Ephemeroptera)

The most fascinating thing about **mayflies** is their life cycle. They live for only a few hours, emerging from a chrysalis without even a mouth to feed. The final brief flight of its life comes after a much longer period as a nymph grub underwater. More than one poet or writer has seen within the story of the mayfly a metaphor for our own short time in the sun. A lifetime is just a matter of scale.

Mayfly

The mayfly lives only to mate and despite the apparent fragility of such a system, they have been found preserved in fossil form in Paleozoic era rocks, three hundred and fifty million years ago – before even the dinosaurs!

Dragonflies and Damselflies (Odonata)

Another harmless and beautiful group of insects. Both **dragonflies** and **damselflies** belong to the order Odonata, meaning 'toothed jaw'. Their lower jaws are serrated, which may explain the name. Even large ones are incapable of breaking human skin, however. Having four wings makes them wonderfully alien, though it is their bright colours that catch the eye in summer. In addition, they consume gnats and mosquitoes, so are a very welcome presence in a garden.

Damselfly

As with the mayfly, the grub stage hatches underwater, then crawls up a reed or aquatic plant until it reaches air. The skin hardens and splits and a dragonfly struggles out of its old carcase, born anew. Damselflies are a suborder (Zygoptera), with four wings of roughly equal size. In comparison, dragonflies (Anisoptera) have hind wings that are shorter and broader than the forewings. Overall, there are more than forty different types, though by far the most common are the blue-tailed and common blue 'needle' damselflies, found in eastern and southern England in particular.

Dragonfly

All dragonflies have excellent eyesight and flying skills – they need them to survive fast attacks from birds and slower ones from frogs if they come down to water to lay eggs or to drink.

They are strictly summer insects and do not survive cold weather. Wet weather too can starve them as neither dragonflies nor their prey fly in the rain.

WATER SURFACE INSECTS

Pond Skater

The **pond skater** (*Gerris lacustris*) uses the surface tension of water to scull itself along without getting wet. Its already tiny weight is spread on long legs, as can be seen in the image here. The front legs row it along at an astonishing speed for its size.

The **water boatman** (*Notonecta glauca*) rows along on its back, again at a fair clip for such a tiny insect. Unlike the pond-skater it is carnivorous. Neither of these poses any danger to us, they are simply strange and fascinating members of the insect world.

Water Boatman

BUTTERFLIES AND MOTHS (LEPIDOPTERA)

Gatekeeper

Red Admiral

There are many hundreds of species to be seen in the British countryside. Moths fly by day and night, though butterflies restrict themselves to daylight hours only. Another difference is that butterflies generally raise their wings erect when at rest and have little buds or clubs at the end of their antennae. Although most moths are brown or black in colour, some can be as bright as butterflies.

Here are a few of the ones you are most likely to see in fields and gardens.
Gatekeeper or **Hedge Brown** (*Pyronia tithonus*).

The **Red Admiral** (*Vanessa atalanta*) is one of the best known, though it is often confused with the similar Painted Lady. The Red Admiral is an attractive flutterer found wherever there are wild nettles, fruit or hops. The Latin name is from Atalanta, a Greek girl who refused to marry unless a man could beat her in a foot race. As suitors chased her, so children still chase the Red Admiral today.

The **Peacock Butterfly** (*Inachis io*) is named for the eyes on its wings. Like the Red Admiral, they eat and lay their eggs on stinging nettles. They can be seen in spring and summer.

The **Cabbage White** (*Pieris rapae*) is a bit of a pest to gardeners, as the name suggests. Nonetheless, it is one of the most common British butterflies.

Peacock

Large White

The **Small Blue** (*Cupido minimus*) is the smallest British butterfly and is no larger than the tip of a finger. It is found on moors and grasslands in summer and produces a similarly small brown caterpillar from its eggs that has fine brown bristles and a glossy black head.

Small Blue

MOTHS

Moths are a common sight whenever a window is left open at night. Their variety is immense. In fact, of around 130,000 species of Lepidoptera in the world, moths account for 110,000 of them. Famously, their senses are confused by bright light and they can spend many unhappy hours bumping against bulbs. In previous generations, the light would have come from a flame and the moth would be drawn to it and then burned. The metaphor is obvious when considering anything else lured to its own destruction.

Like butterflies, they spend time as caterpillars, emerging as adults from a chrysalis. Some are brightly coloured and fly by day; only the lack of clubbed antennae can show that you are looking at a moth rather than a butterfly.

The **Six-spot Burnet** or **Ten O'clock Riser** (*Zygaena filipendulae*). Can be found in Scotland in July and August.

Finally, one of the most useful moths in the world is *Bombyx mori*. The moth is practically unknown, but its caterpillar larvae are silkworms and still produce all the world's natural silk, unwound from their cocoons. They have been bred in China for five *thousand* years.

Six-spot Burnet

BEETLES (COLEOPTERA)

Beetles are insects with a hard carapace protecting wings. Many are scavengers and play a vital role in consuming dead animals and birds. There are around 3,600 different species in this country.

The **Dor Beetle** or 'Dumble-Dor' (*Geotrupes stercorarius*) shown here, buries cow dung as a food source. It is benign and relatively common. Other species are positively destructive, however, such as the brown **Deathwatch Beetle** (*Xestobium rufovillosum*) that bores holes in wood and can destroy old beams and buildings.

Dor Beetle

INSECTS AND SPIDERS

Glow-worms (*Lampyris noctiluca*) are not worms at all. They too are beetles. Sightings are quite rare. The males fly, but their light is very dim. The females are flightless, but give off a much brighter yellow-green light that can be seen in country hedges at dusk in May. One grisly fact about the glow-worm is that its larvae seek out inhabited snail shells when they hatch, feeding on the defenceless snails within.

Glow-worms

Ladybirds (Coccinelidae) are a very familiar beetle and can be found in any grassy meadow. They eat greenfly and are welcome in any garden. If annoyed, they eject an unpleasant-tasting fluid as a defence, just as a grass snake does. (If you ever pick up a grass snake, be prepared for a cupful of the worst-smelling filth you have ever experienced. One of the authors was caught unawares trying this and the smell lingered for days despite endless hand-washing in powerful detergent.)

Ladybirds

The **Stag Beetle** (*Lucanus cervus*) is not particularly uncommon, though the authors have only ever seen one. We kept him in a matchbox until he somehow escaped. As with earwigs, the horns of Britain's largest beetle are completely harmless. Males cannot be kept with other males as they will fight and damage or even kill each other. Also, pairs must be kept apart after mating, or they will bite each other's legs off. The life of a Stag Beetle is not an easy one! They can be bred in captivity, but the pupae are very easy to damage and should not be touched by bare skin.

Stag Beetle

BEES AND WASPS

Bees are fascinating insects – and extremely unlikely to sting unless you make them afraid. If you sit on one, it will sting you, but in the circumstances, who could blame it? Otherwise, they are harmless and, of course, they produce delicious honey. The **Bumble Bee** (*Bombus terrestris*, sometimes called the Humble Bee) can be seen bumbling around looking for nectar in the summer, though it is less common than the common **Honey Bee** or **Hive Bee** (*Apis mellifera*). Very few Honey Bees are wild in Britain any more. Their lives could fill a chapter on their own, but the main types are workers, drones and queens. The drones live only for a single season, while the queen lives three or four years.

Bumble Bee

Wasps are almost universally disliked. The **Common Wasp** (*Vespula Vulgaris*) comes in varieties of non-reproductive workers, males and queens, the queens being larger than the rest. They can be aggressive if attacked and will sting with very little

Common Wasp

provocation. If they are trapped under clothing, they can sting more than once.

The **Hornet** wasp (*Vespa crabro*) is much larger than the common variety and has brown bands rather than black. Thankfully, they are not common.

The pain-causing chemical injected by a bee or wasp sting is called 'melittin'. A bee sting usually rips out the whole sting apparatus from the bee in the process, wounding it fatally. Sadly, the wasp has no such handicap and can fly away happily after stinging.

Hornet

There are around fifty different species of ants in Britain, though most are harmless. Black or yellow ants of any size, whether winged or not, cannot harm humans. Black **Wood Ants** (*Formica rufa*) can eject an unpleasant spray of formic acid, however, which smells like bitter vinegar. Anyone who has ever sat down on a red ant nest will know how painful their bites can be. **Red Ants** (*Myrmica ruginodis*) are aggressive and unfortunately seem to enjoy the garden habitat as much as their black cousins (*Lasius niger*).

Ants

FLIES AND MOSQUITOES

Bluebottle

Hoverfly

Horsefly

Bluebottles (*Calliphora vomitoria*) and **Greenbottles** (*Lucilia caesar*) lay eggs which hatch into maggots. Apart from being useful for fishing, they spread dirt and disease and should be kept away from food if at all possible. They are attracted to rotting meat, household rubbish and excrement in any form. There really isn't anything pleasant to say about them.

Hoverflies (Syrphidae) look a little like small wasps, but can be recognised by their hovering, darting motion and are harmless. **Horseflies** (Tabanidae), on the other hand, are an absolute menace, as one of the authors found out on a Scottish hillside once. Their bite leaves a tiny bleeding hole. Both authors have been subject to the attention of **Midges** (Ceratopogonidae) in Scotland. They leave itchy red marks on the skin and swarm around water in extraordinary numbers.

The **Common Gnat** (*Culex pipiens*) is very similar-looking to the more dangerous **Malarial Mosquito** (*Anopheles maculipennis*). Both are members of the same family and females from both species feed off humans if they get the chance, making a characteristic whining sound just

as you are trying to get to sleep. In countries like Italy and France, they are a serious pest and whole areas have to be sprayed regularly. Malaria carried by the Anopheles Mosquito is still a terrible killer in parts of Africa. They are not common in Britain.

Midge

Gnat

WOODLICE

The **Pill Woodlouse** (*Armadillidium vulgare*) is capable of rolling itself into a tight ball, hence the name. They are harmlessly amusing creatures and less common than the blue-grey **Common Woodlouse** (*Porcellio scaber*), which can be found wherever there is rotting wood or dampness.

SPIDERS (ARACHNAE)

Spiders are not insects. They have eight legs rather than six, have only two sections to their bodies and have eight single eyes instead of two compound ones. Britain is extremely lucky in the six hundred varieties of spiders found naturally within her borders. None are dangerous. In comparison with many other countries, a small child can be allowed to wander barefoot in, say, Wales, without worrying that they will be bitten or even killed.

The common **House Spider** (*Tegenaria atrica*) is completely harmless, though it can be quite large in country settings and moves worryingly quickly across the floor when it senses danger.

Another common sight in wooden sheds everywhere is the **Garden Spider** (*Arachneus diadematus*). Again, these can grow quite large with a good supply of flies and smaller spiders. It makes funnel-style webs and can be tempted out by touching a leaf or pencil to the edge of one.

There are many other species of spider and many thousands more insects with different and interesting lives and habits. The more you learn about insects, the more you understand what an incredibly complex world this actually is.

▲▲
House Spider
▲
Garden Spider

INSECTS AND SPIDERS

JUGGLING

THIS IS THE SKILL of tossing objects in the air and catching them. First of all you will need three round balls, about the size of cricket balls. You can make excellent ones by putting a couple of handfuls of rice or flour into a balloon. If you use fruit, it will be very messy, so be prepared to eat them bruised. Alternatively, juggling balls can be bought from any toy shop. It looks difficult, but on average it takes about an hour to learn, two at most.

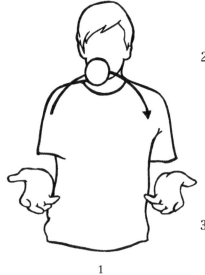

1

1. Hold one ball in your right hand and gently lob it into your left. Now lob it back in the direction it came. Go back and forth with this until you are comfortable.

2. Now let's add another ball! Hold one ball in your right hand and one in your left. As you lob the ball from your right hand to your left, release the ball in your left hand and catch the incoming ball. The hard part is releasing the left-hand ball so that you lob it back to your right hand and catch it. This will take some practice, or you might pick it up immediately. Make sure both balls are flowing in a nice arc from hand to hand. This will give you more time to release and catch.

3. Ball three! Hold two balls in your right hand. Hold the third ball in your left hand. Lob the first ball from right to left and as you catch it in your left hand, release the second ball lobbing it back to your right. (This is just step 2, holding a third ball.)

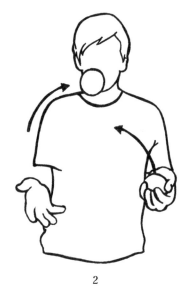

2

3

The hard bit is releasing that third ball as you catch the second ball in your right hand, and lobbing the third ball back to your left hand. You must keep this lob-release-catch going from hand to hand. Practise, practise, practise!

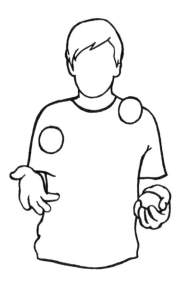

Now for a fancy trick. Start in the beginning position (two balls in the right hand, one in the left), put your right hand behind your back and throw the two balls forward over your shoulder. As they sail over to the front, lob the left hand ball up as normal and catch the two coming over in your left and right hand. Yes, this is as hard as it sounds. Quickly lob the right-hand one to your left and catch the one in the air coming down. You are into the routine. This is an impressive start to juggling three balls, but it *is* very hard, so the best of luck.

QUESTIONS ABOUT THE WORLD – PART TWO

1. **How do we measure the earth's circumference?**
2. **Why does a day have twenty-four hours?**
3. **How far away are the stars?**
4. **Why is the sky blue?**
5. **Why can't we see the other side of the moon?**
6. **What causes the tides?**

1. HOW DO WE MEASURE THE EARTH'S CIRCUMFERENCE?

The simple answer is that we use Polaris, the Pole Star. Imagine someone standing at the Equator. From their point of view the Pole Star would be on the horizon – as in the diagram. If the same person stood at the North Pole, Polaris would be almost directly overhead. It should be clear, then, that in moving north, Polaris appears to rise in the sky. A sextant can confirm the changing angle.

The angle through which the Pole Star rises is equal to the change in the observer's latitude. If Polaris rises by ten degrees, you have travelled ten degrees of latitude.

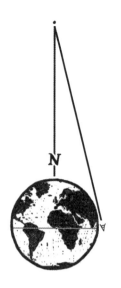

All the observer has to do is measure how far he has travelled when Polaris has risen by one degree. Multiply that distance by 360 and you have your circumference of the earth. Easy.

The actual circumference is 24,901 miles (40,074 km) around the Equator and 24,859 miles (40,0006 km) around the poles – or in rough terms 25,000 miles around, with a slightly fatter Equator. As you can see, this is not a perfect globe. The correct term is 'geoid', which just means 'shaped like the earth'. When you're a planet, you get your own word.

2. WHY DOES A DAY HAVE TWENTY-FOUR HOURS?

Well, because we say it does. The modern world uses the Roman system of measuring time from midnight to midnight – as opposed to the Greek system of measuring from sunset to sunset. The Romans also divided daylight into twelve hours. This caused difficulties as summer hours would be longer than winter hours. When the system was made more accurate, it was sensible enough to double the twelve for the night hours. Most of the way we measure time is based on the number twelve, fractions and multiples of it, in fact – which is why we have sixty minutes and sixty seconds. The architects of the French Revolution were keen not only on introducing a decimal number system and metres to the world, but also a ten-day week, a hundred-minute hour and a hundred-second minute. Needless to say, no one else was quite as keen.

3. HOW FAR AWAY ARE THE STARS?

Light travels at 186,000 miles (300,000 km) a second. In a year it would travel almost 6 million, million miles. (The American billion, or one thousand million, is now all-conquering in terms of usage. The British billion is traditionally one million million. Realistically, this is such a large number that it doesn't come up that often. There are no billionaires by the British standard, for example. A US 'trillion' is a thousand US billion. You may have noticed it's the same as the old British billion, but let's not overcomplicate this.)

Using the US definition, a light year is 6 trillion miles. That is a long way by anyone's standards.

The closest star to us is Proxima Centauri – about four and a third light years away. That is even further. To put it another way, the light from Proxima Centauri has taken four and a third years to get here. The actual star could have blown up yesterday, but we wouldn't know for almost five years.

The furthest stars we can see are more than a thousand light years away.

4. Why is the sky blue?

To understand this, it's important to understand that colour doesn't exist as some separate thing in the world. What we call blue paint just means paint that reflects light in certain wavelengths we have learned to call 'blue'. Colour-blind people have eyes that work perfectly well but are different from most other eyes in just this area – how they register light wavelengths. Take a moment and think about this. Colour does not exist – only reflected light exists. In a red light, blue paint will look black as there is no blue light to reflect. In a blue light, red paint will look black.

Now, the sky is blue because blue light comes in on a short wavelength and wallops into oxygen atoms of roughly the same size. When we look up and see a blue sky, we are seeing that interaction.

At sunset, we see more red because the sunlight is passing through many more miles of atmosphere at that low angle near the horizon. The blue light interacts with the oxygen and is scattered as before – but cannot reach the eye through the extra miles this time. Instead, we see the other end of the spectrum, the red light.

5. Why can't we see the other side of the moon?

Until the late twentieth century, mankind had no idea what lurked on the dark side of the moon. This is because the same face was presented to observers on earth all the way through the lunar cycle.

The moon takes twenty-nine and a half days to go around the earth. It does actually rotate on its own axis, completing a full turn in … twenty-nine and a half days. As these two are the same, it always shows the same face.

The best way to demonstrate this is with a tennis ball and a football. Mark the side of the tennis ball and place the football somewhere where it can't roll away – or have someone hold it. Now move the tennis ball around your earth, keeping the same side always inwards. By the time you have gone all the way around, the tennis ball will also have turned on its own axis.

6. What causes the tides?

Following neatly on from the last question, the answer is gravity – from the moon and the sun. The moon's massive presence overhead actually pulls oceans out of place. These two diagrams are deliberately exaggerated to show the effect. They are *not* to scale!

Spring Tide – New Moon

Moon
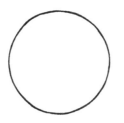

Spring Tide – Full Moon

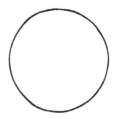

The seas move more easily than land, though the whole planet is actually affected. What happens in practice is that the earth's own spin produces two high and two low tides each day. It takes twelve hours to expose the other side of the earth to the moon's gravity, a little like squeezing a balloon twice around the middle in twenty-four hours. Both ends bulge to create high tides and then withdraw to create low tides.

The diagram above is actually of a 'spring' tide, which occurs twice a month at the new and full moon. The name has nothing to do with the season. When the moon is in line with the sun and the earth, the tide is particularly strong. The weakest tides are known as 'neap' tides, and occur at the quarter moon, as in this diagram. The moon's effect is lessened by being out of line with the sun.

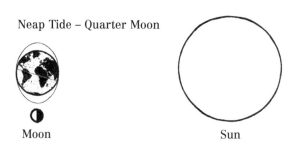

Neap Tide – Quarter Moon

Moon

Sun

ASTRONOMY – THE STUDY
OF THE HEAVENS

ASTRONOMY IS NOT ASTROLOGY. Astrology is nonsense. The idea that our lives can be affected by the flight of planets is not even slightly plausible. Venus may have been named after a goddess of love, but its movement can have no bearing on our own chances for romance. The planet could equally have been called by another name, after all. The first (and last) point about star watching is that it is science and not superstition – but the stories of ancient heroes like Orion can be fascinating. Knowing Orion chases Taurus works as a mnemonic – an aid to memory.

There are eighty-eight constellations that can be seen in the night sky at different times of the year and all the visible stars have names, or at least numbers. As the earth rotates, so their positions change and you can follow them through the seasons (see Star-Maps).

This chapter is an introduction to sky watching. Most of us live and work in noisy, artificial environments. Light pollution from cities hides the glories of the night sky, but those who are curious always find ways to explore beyond them. Naked-eye astronomy is easy and fun and can be done alone or with friends. This chapter will make you more familiar with the wonders of the universe.

Look at the stars! look, look up at the skies!
O look at all the fire-folk sitting in the air!
The bright boroughs, the circle-citadels there!

Gerald Manley Hopkins

Since the dawn of time, mankind has grouped stars into constellations, filling the heavens with heroes, gods and fantastic creatures. The myths and histories of lost civilisations can be found above us and help us understand the legends and stories that chart our own time.

One of the most easily recognisable constellations, and a great way to start finding your way around the skies, is **Ursa Major**, the **Great Bear**.

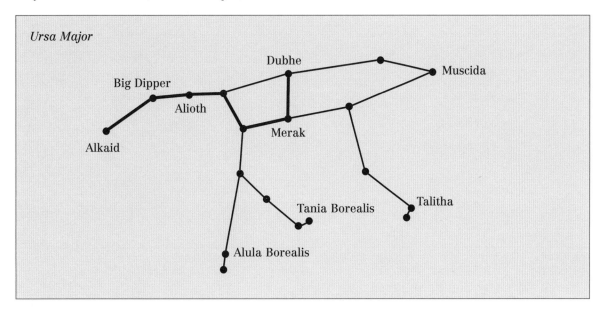

This constellation gets its name from the Greek legend of Callisto, a nymph transformed by Zeus into a she-bear. Many Native American tribes have also seen this constellation as a bear. Maybe the ancient Greeks sailed further than we realise! Particularly famous is the group of seven stars often called the **Big Dipper** or the **Plough**. In Cherokee legend, the handle of the Big Dipper is seen as a team of hunters chasing the bear who is visible high in the sky in spring until he sets on autumn evenings. Each day they chase the bear further west. Boys, you will need your compass.

This distinctive star system has been noted by Shakespeare and Tennyson. In Hindu mythology, the Big Dipper is seen as the home of the seven great sages. The Chinese saw them as the masters of heavenly reality; the Egyptians, as the thigh of a bull. The Europeans saw a wagon and the Anglo-Saxons associated it with the legends surrounding King Arthur.

In ancient times, north could be plotted using the star **Alkaid**, in the Big Dipper. Today north can be found in **Ursa Minor**, a constellation that lies almost alongside Ursa Major. In Greek legend this constellation was named after Arcas, the son of Callisto. He too was changed into a bear and left to follow his mother eternally around the north celestial pole.

Finding north, and with it all other points on the compass, is as important as knowing your address. It is one of the first steps to understanding where you are. The key star is called **Polaris** (see below), the Pole Star for the northern hemisphere.

From the Big Dipper, mentally draw a line through the stars Dubhe and Merak, extend upwards five times its length and you hit Polaris. Face Polaris and you are facing north. If there is light pollution, it may be the only star visible in Ursa Minor.

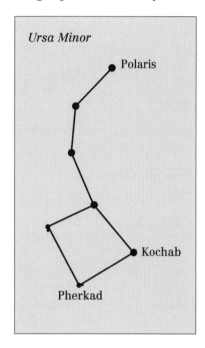

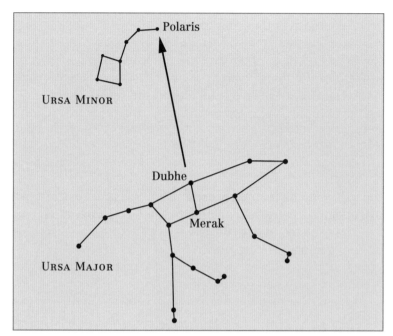

If you are in the southern hemisphere then finding south is just as important, and almost as easy. First identify the **Southern Cross** (see right) and mentally extend a line down from the long arm. To the left are two stars, Rigil Kentaurus and Hadar, known as the pointers. Extend a line down from between them until it crosses the first line. This point is directly above south.

On a clear night in winter in the northern hemisphere if you face south, away from the Pole Star, the constellation of **Orion** is the chief attraction. It is characterised by its three belt stars with the red star Betelgeuse above and Rigel below.

In Greek mythology, Orion was a great hunter. Artemis, the goddess of the moon and the hunt, fell in love with him and neglected her duties of lighting the night sky. As punishment, her brother, Apollo, tricked her into slaying him from afar with an arrow. When she realised what she had done, she put his body in

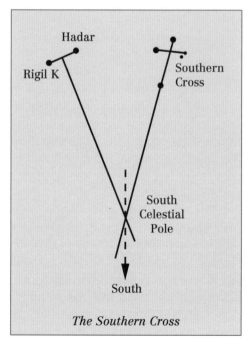

The Southern Cross

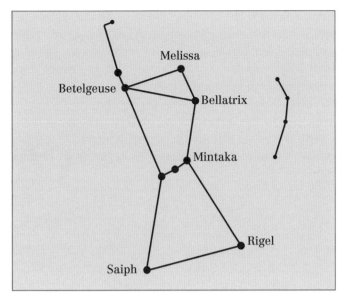

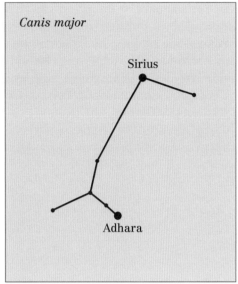
Canis major

the sky with his two war dogs, Canis Major and Canis Minor. According to ancient Greek astronomers, her grief explains the sad, cold look of the moon.

The brightest star in the sky is in Canis Major – **Sirius**, the **Dog Star**. Sirius rises in the east in late summer, at the heels of Orion, hunting with him through the winter.

Above and to the right of Orion and his dogs is their prey, **Taurus**, the bull. Its red eye looks back nervously – the star Aldebaran. Since the time of the ancient Babylonians, some 5000 years ago, this constellation has been seen as a bull. Bulls have been worshipped since ancient times as symbols of strength and fertility. The Greeks saw the constellation as Zeus disguised as a bull. In this form he seduced the princess Europa and swam to Crete with her on his back. Only the forequarters are visible in the constellation, as it emerges from the waves.

In the shoulder of Taurus is the most famous open star cluster in the sky, the **Pleiades**, also known as the **Seven Sisters**.

The legend tells that the sisters were being chased by Orion and called out to Zeus to protect them. Zeus turned them into doves and placed them in the sky. In a Native American tale,

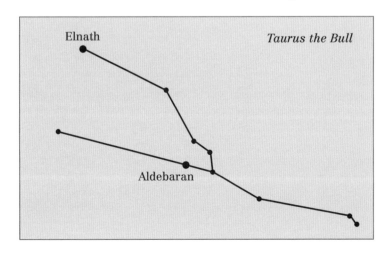
Taurus the Bull

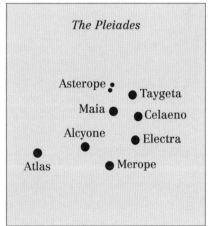
The Pleiades

the Pleiades are seven girls who are walking through the sky and get lost, never making it home. They remain in the sky, huddled together for warmth. The seventh sister is hard to see because she really wants to go home and her tears dim her lustre. On a reasonably clear night you should be able to pick out six of the sisters. The whole star cluster actually has more than 500 stars, but it is possible to see as many as nine with the naked eye.

On the other side of Polaris from the Big Dipper is the striking W-shaped figure of **Cassiopeia**. (Careful not to mix this up with the Little Dipper.) This is the most prominent constellation in the winter sky, visible all year round in the northern hemisphere. If the Big Dipper is low in the sky then the W of Cassiopeia will be high. It is not as accurate in finding north but it does point in the general direction of the Pole Star.

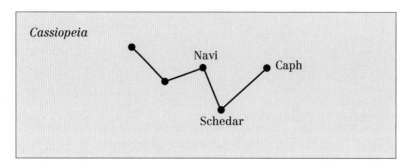

In Greek mythology, Cassiopeia was the Queen of Ethiopia. The Romans saw her as being chained to her throne and placed in the heavens to hang upside down, for boasting that her daughter, Andromeda, was more beautiful than Aphrodite. Arab cultures pictured the constellation as a kneeling camel.

Finding your way around the night sky can be quite a challenge for the beginner. In this chapter we have described a few of the brighter stars and constellations from which you will be able to explore further. There are many good periodicals about astronomy which will open up the sky to you. The stories that surround our heavens are wonderful and colourful and as easy as reading a road map, with a little work!

Remember that all stars twinkle – the light shifts and flickers as you concentrate on it. Planets do not. If you narrow your eyes, you can see the disc of Jupiter even without binoculars.

MAKING A PAPER HAT,
BOAT AND WATER BOMB

THERE IS SOMETHING ridiculously simple about these, but how to make them is something every boy should know. After all, with a little luck, you may one day have children of your own and seeing a paper boat bobbing along on water is a pleasure.

THE HAT

First – the hat. The boat is just a few extra folds on the hat.

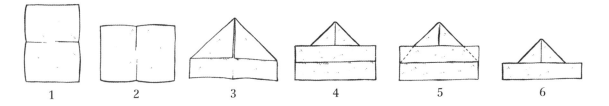

1. Fold a sheet of A4 in half, as shown.
2. Fold a central line in the half-page and open out again.
3. urn down the corners to that central line.
4. Fold one long strip up.
5. Fold over the corners on the dotted lines.
6. Fold up the other edge and you now have a paper hat – open it. This also works well with newspaper, but printer paper A4 can be painted or coloured. In theory, you don't need to fold the corners over if you're stopping at a hat – but we're going on to turn it into a boat.

THE BOAT

Turning this into a paper boat is only a fraction more complicated.

1. Holding the hat upside down, join the two ends together.
2. It will fold into a neat diamond that looks like the picture on the next page.
3. Next fold each side of the diamond onto itself along the dotted line shown.
4. You will now have a triangle.
5. Open it as before and fold in the opposite corners.
6. Now this final bit doesn't look like it will work, but it does. Take hold of the two loose corners and gently pull them apart.
7. The boat will form. It might take a bit of tweaking to get exactly the right shape, but when the bottom is opened a little, it does float.

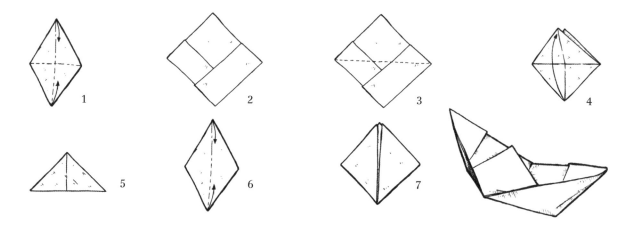

THE WATER BOMB

Finally, as we're folding paper, we might as well do the last one every boy should know – the water bomb.

Turn an A4 sheet into a square piece by folding down a corner to the edge and tearing off a strip. When you have a perfect square of paper, fold it in half across both diagonals and horizontally as well. Concentrate – this is tricky to get right.

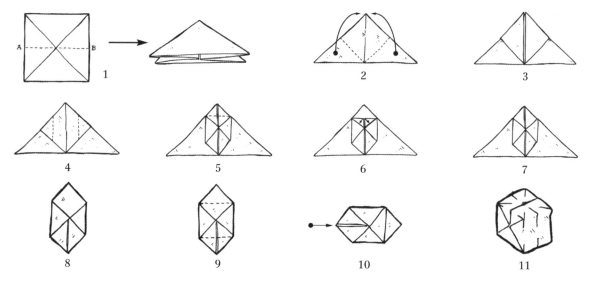

1. Put points A and B together, flattening the whole thing down so that it looks like the next diagram
2. Fold upwards on the line on the right and on the left.
3. Then it must look like this.
4. Fold on the lines.
5. Then it must look like this.
6. Fold the two little triangles on the lines downward. Put the triangles in the two pockets on the right and on the left. This is a little bit fiddly.

7. Then it must look like this.

Turn the whole triangle over and repeat the steps 2, 3, 4, 5, 6 and 7.

8. Then it must look like this.
9. Fold and unfold on the dotted lines to help with the last stage.
10. Take the folded cube in your hand and blow into the hole at the top to unfold the cube. It's pretty satisfying when it works.
11. The cube is ready.

Fill it with water – find a high place and drop it.

INTERESTING FACT: No piece of paper can be folded in half more than seven times. Try it.

THE LAWS OF CRICKET

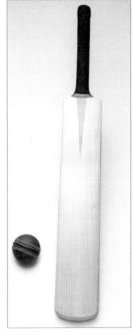

Bowling a man out or hitting a six is right up there with learning to drive, catching a fish, sailing a boat through a storm, shooting a rabbit, finishing a race, winning a fight and climbing a mountain. There are moments to be treasured in every life. Some of them can be found on the sports field. It is a myth that Wellington ever said that the Battle of Waterloo was 'won on the playing fields of Eton' – but the concept is revealing. Sport teaches discipline and aids fitness. There are few better ways of spending a summer than learning to play cricket. The game dates back as far as 1700, making it one of the oldest organised team sports in the world.

THE GAME

Cricket is a game for two teams of eleven. It is played on a pitch with wickets twenty-two yards apart – one 'chain' in imperial measurements. The wickets are made of three upright stumps with two horizontal wooden 'bails' resting on top. Each team scores runs by hitting the ball and running between the wickets, scoring one 'run' for each complete trip. Batsmen stay in to bat until they are 'out', which can happen in a variety of ways. When the tenth batsman is out, the team can no longer continue and the innings is over.

The cricket field or 'ground' itself is an oval shape and may range in size from 450 ft by 500 ft (137 × 150 m) to 525 ft by 550 ft (160 × 168 m). The wicket is in the middle of the oval and the boundary is usually marked with a rope.

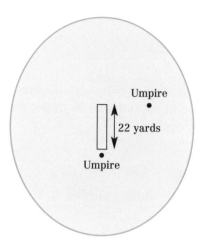

Note the position of the umpires. There are two in a professional game. One stands behind the bowling end wicket, facing the batsman at the other end. The other stands square on to the batsman, watching the wicket from the side angle. (In international cricket, there is also a 'third umpire' off the field, who can be requested by the on-field umpires to use video evidence to help with difficult decisions.)

In each team of eleven, there will be a captain, who is often a good batsman. There will also be a wicketkeeper who takes position directly behind the wicket when fielding. All players

have to bat and field, but some specialise in bowling, some in batting and some are skilled in both – 'all-rounders'. A toss of a coin decides who bats first, then one team take up fielding positions and the other send out their first pair of batsmen – one at each wicket.

The captain and the bowler confer to decide the placing of the fielders. The bowler may find that a particular batsman has a tendency to reach for dangerous shots on one side. The captain would then put more men in that area to catch a ball off the bat.

A lot of cricket terms, including fielding positions, refer to the 'leg' and 'off' sides. From the bowler's point of view, if the batsman is right-handed, the **leg side** is to the right and the **off side** is to the left. So the stump of the batsman's wicket on the right is called the leg stump. The other stump is called the off stump, and the middle stump? Well that's just called the middle stump. It's important to note that if the batsman is left-handed, then this is reversed. This is a good thing to get straight in your head early on.

Even at schoolboy level, you will still be expected to wear pads, gloves and possibly a helmet when you bat, though probably not forearm and chest protectors. A groin cup, or 'box', is also a good idea. Cricket balls are solid cork wrapped in twine and leather. They are very hard and a good fast bowler can produce both fear and awe in batsmen.

The game goes forward in 'overs' – groups of six balls. The umpires usually keep six coins in their coats, moving one from one pocket to the other for each ball bowled. They change position at the end of the over. The bowler and fielders also move around and only the batsmen remain in the same places. In this way, both batsmen face the bowler. In theory, if single runs are scored, a batsman could find himself at the other end every time an over is called, but this evens out over long play. At anything greater than three schoolboys in a park, there is a bowler at each end bowling alternate overs.

The bowler bowls a ball of between 5½ and 5¾ ounces (155–163 g). Its circumference must be between $8^{13}/_{16}$ and 9 inches (22.4–22.9 cm). Smaller versions are available for women's and junior cricket.

A bowler can bowl from either side of the wicket, as long as he mentions it to the umpire, who will then inform the batsman. The terms used are 'over' and 'around' the wicket. **Over the wicket** – the most common method – is when the bowler bowls from the side where his bowling arm is closest to the wicket. For a right-handed bowler, this would be the left side. **Around the wicket** is when the bowler bowls from the side where his bowling arm is furthest away from the wicket.

By the wicket there are several lines or 'creases'. The line 4 ft (1.2 m) down the pitch is called the 'popping' or 'batting' crease. When bowling, the bowler's front foot can touch the popping crease, but must not step past it or a **no ball** is called by the umpire. There is another pair of creases at right angles to the popping crease – the 'return' creases. The bowler's trailing foot must end up between these two creases, or again a no ball can be called. The batsman can hit a no ball and can even be caught without being out – though he can be run out off a no ball. Even if he swings and misses, one run is added to the team's score – though not to his personal total. 'No balls' are also called if the bowler chucks the ball rather than bowls it – that is, he throws it with a bent elbow.

A **wide** can be called if the ball is too high or far from the wicket for the batsman to reach using a normal cricket stroke. If the batsman, by moving, manages to hit a wide ball anyway, or gets close enough to hit it, the wide is not given after all. A wide is well worth leaving as it adds a run to the score – and another ball to the over. In theory, an over can go on for ever with wides and no balls.

Byes are runs scored when the ball whips straight past the batsman and wicketkeeper, touching nothing. Fast schoolboy bowlers are particularly prone to this. The runs are added to the team score and not the batsman's. One reason to have a fielder at deep fine leg behind the wicketkeeper is to stop byes.

Leg byes are balls that whip through after striking some part of the batsman apart from his hands – an elbow, for example. This must not be deliberate on the part of the bats-man. Leg byes are given only when the batsman tries for a shot. The runs are added to the team score, unless it's a glove deflection when they are added to the batsman's.

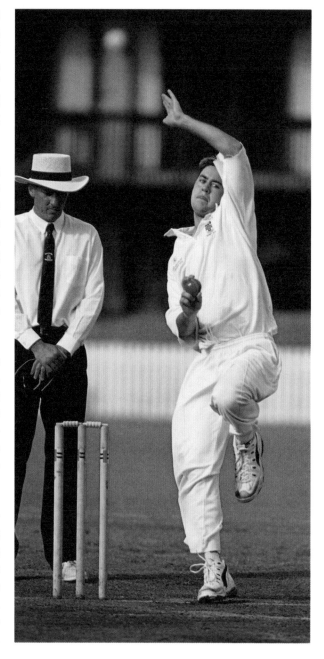

The bowler is allowed to rub the ball on his trousers to give it a shine, but not to use any external product. Running a hand through brilliantined hair and then rubbing the ball is strictly forbidden, as is picking at the seam to help the ball jump further on striking the ground. As with most sports, there are a thousand ways to cheat at cricket. It should not need to be said, but it is a matter of honour to play within the laws and within the spirit of the game.

The main different kinds of bowlers are fast bowlers, who rely primarily on speed, seamers, who aim to have the ball bounce on the seam, and spinners, who use either their wrists or their fingers to impart spin to the ball. Leg spinners normally bowl balls that turn from right to left – that is, from leg to off for a right-handed batsman. Off spinners bowl balls that turn from left to right – that is, from off to leg for a right-handed batsman. Bowlers will usually specialise in one of these areas, though a fast bowler will be quite capable of bowling with a bit of leg spin if the situation requires it.

The aim of bowling is obviously to take the wicket and send the batsman back to the pavilion. However, there are a number of ways to do this. It is extraordinarily satisfying to send a wicket tumbling through the air with a well-placed ball, but more wickets come from catches. For example, the bowler might place the ball with just a little spin so that the batsman tries a mighty blow and misjudges it, snicking a shot straight into the hands of the fielder. Not every bowl is aimed straight at the wicket. Bowlers are tactical thinkers. They tempt a batsman with an easy shot, perhaps, then lay another one in exactly the same place, but spinning the opposite way. The wicket falls. The only way to gain skill as a bowler is to practise in nets, learning how to be accurate.

LBW – leg before wicket. The batsman is not allowed to use his body or his pads to block the wicket. If a ball would have struck the stumps but was blocked, the bowler shouts 'How's that?' and the umpire raises a finger, indicating the man is out. Note that the point of impact has to be in a straight line between the wickets. If the batsman plays a shot, a ball outside that line cannot take an LBW, no matter how it swings in. You can see this rule applied occasionally when a batsman deliberately uses his pad to knock a leg-side ball away. The contact is outside the line and within the rules. LBW decisions are often a matter of controversy, but the umpire's decision is final.

A batsman can be bowled out, caught out, run out and given LBW. If he is caught out, the hand is allowed to touch the ground, but the ball must not. He can also be out if he breaks his own wicket, by accident or otherwise. A careless step back while batting has been the end of many a good innings. He is **run out** when the wicket is broken by the ball while he is between creases. At the highest level, this can come from a ball thrown by a fielder with extraordinary accuracy. At schoolboy level, it is usually thrown from a fielder to a wicketkeeper, who 'stumps' him, by knocking off the bails with the ball. Note that this can happen any time the ball is in play and a batsman steps outside his crease. If the batsman steps too far down the pitch to hit the ball and misses, there is a real danger that the wicketkeeper will take his wicket by catching the ball and stumping him.

An umpire also has the power to send a player off the field for misconduct, effectively out. This can be for something as simple as deliberately obstructing an opposing player, disputing an umpire's decision, hitting the ball twice or even losing their temper and throwing the bat, which we once witnessed at a schoolboy match. It should be an indication of how despicable such behaviour is that the incident is still talked about a decade later. Team conduct is the responsibility of the team captains and in the first instance of poor behaviour, the umpire will have a word with the captain in question.

The only thing a batsman can do when he is called out is to walk. The best batsman do not even wait for the umpire to call it. They know when they are out and they leave the pitch without argument – though they may be internally furious with themselves.

UMPIRE SIGNALS

Out – raising one finger above the head.

4 scored – waving one arm from side to side at chest level.

6 scored – raising both arms above the head.

Wide – extending both arms to the sides.

No ball – extending one arm straight out to the side.

Bye – raising an open hand above the head.

Leg bye – touching a raised knee with a hand.

New ball – holding the ball above the head.

5 penalty runs to batting side score – repeated tapping of one shoulder with the opposite hand.

5 penalty runs to fielding side score – one hand placed on opposite shoulder.

The umpire will wait for the scorer to acknowledge the signal before play continues.

BATTING

The best bats are famously made of willow. A bat should be no more than 3 ft 2 in (96.5 cm) in length and no more than 4¼ inches (10.8 cm) at its widest point. The handle is normally wrapped in rubber. It is crucial to have a firm grip and individual bats will depend on your height and build. Expert advice is needed when choosing a good bat. If you are left-handed, you will need to say so, as left-handed bats are fractionally different from right-handed ones.

Bats where the wood is covered are generally cheaper, as a poorer grade of willow is used. That said, they can still be good starter bats. Linseed oil should be used on the wood, with a small amount rubbed in and left for twenty-four hours. Be careful not to use more than a very small amount of oil. All bats need 'knocking in', a process of tapping the surface and edges with a mallet to compress the willow wood and make it better able to stand the impact of a hard ball.

You will also need a pair of pads, gloves, a box and a good stance. Stand with your legs slightly apart, with your weight on the balls of your feet, equally distributed. Point your front shoulder down the pitch at the other wicket. The knees should be slightly bent, the head still. The bat should rest on the ground near your back foot. The crucial thing is to be well balanced – able to move forward or backward easily. As the bowler runs in, you may find it helps balance to lift the bat towards third slip or gully – but bring it down *straight*.

A batsman's sole aim is to score runs. To do this, he must not lose his wicket. Cricket is not a slogger's game. A batsman who attempts to score four or six from every shot may manage it a few times in a row, but he will inevitably snick a ball and give someone an easy catch. A good batsman uses his judgement with every ball of every over. He watches the bowler carefully, observing how his hand moves to get an idea of the spin on the ball. He does not take his eyes off the ball as it leaves the bowler's hand.

There are seven main shots in batting: front-foot defence, back-foot defence, a drive, a square cut, a pull, a sweep and a loft shot. Which one used will depend on how the ball moves and where it hits the ground. Note that reading about them is not a substitute for practising them! The first thing to remember is that you are less likely to get out if the ball is hit along the ground.

1. **Front-foot defence**. A good forward defensive stroke will smother a ball completely, stopping it almost dead. Step to where the ball pitches, angling the bat forward to knock the ball down. Played to balls pitched on a good length.

Front-foot defence

2. **Back-foot defence**. (Putting someone on the 'back foot' comes from this.) Used in response to fast balls pitching on a short length. When you see it is short, rock backwards, get the elbow high and knock the ball down with the angle of the bat. Keep the lower hand soft.

3. **Drives** – off-drive, square drive, cover drive, straight drive. The names come from the area of the pitch where you make the driving shot. Similar body position to the defensive shots, but the stroke is followed through rather than simply playing the ball into the ground. Front-foot and back-foot drives begin as the defensive shots do, but the bat comes down fast and straight, swinging through. The front-foot drives are easier and less risky for inexperienced batsmen. The bat tends to end up above shoulder level.

Back-foot defence

4. A **square cut** is a shot to an off-stump short ball that pitches a little wide – usually a real wallop with a horizontal bat. The batsman's weight should come onto the back foot as soon as you see it pitching short. Keep your head forward and roll your wrists to keep it down.

▲ *Drive*
◄ *Square cut*

5. A **pull shot** is another response to a short ball. Weight on the back foot as it moves quickly towards off stump.The front foot moves out to the leg side, opening up the body. The bat comes across horizontally, with the face angled down into the ground to prevent an easy catch. Note that any shot where the bat is brought round horizontally is potentially dangerous and requires a good eye to hit it cleanly.

6. The **sweep shot**. This is played to a ball of good length, usually to a spin bowler. The front foot goes forward and the back foot goes down to kneel. This is another horizontal shot and must not be employed against short-pitched balls, as they're likely to take your wicket – or your head off, one or the other.

7. The **loft**. Similar to a lob in tennis, in theory. It is crucial to keep your head down and still, with hands firm on the bat. Do not try this with an overpitched delivery – only to short balls.

Pull shot

If a ball is pitched short and bounces high, a pull (or hook) shot or a loft could be used. Alternatively, you can just duck if you see it coming and react fast enough. No matter what you choose to do, however, never ever take your eye off the ball.

Part of the pleasure of batting is the partnership between the two players at either end. When scoring, partnerships are recorded as faithfully as individual scores, such is its importance to the game. Both partners call for runs, depending on who can see the ball. It is a responsibility that either builds or destroys trust in a very short time. A simple 'Yes!' or 'No!' or 'Wait!' are the usual calls from whichever batsman can see the ball. When you run, you must ground your bat at the far crease. At some point, we have all been run out after a bad call and had to leave the field through no real fault of our own. Calling is a matter of lightning judgement and remaining calm under pressure. Tempers and friendships rest on it.

Sweep shot

If a batsman is injured, the umpires can allow a substitute to run and field for him. The substitute cannot bat, bowl or keep wicket, however.

Finally, a brief word on the ashes. On 29 August 1882, Australia beat England for the first time on English soil. A journalist, Reginald Shirley Brooks, wrote a mock obituary for English cricket that appeared in the *Sporting Times*.

Loft

THE LAWS OF CRICKET

In affectionate remembrance of English cricket which died at the Oval on 29th August, 1882, deeply lamented by a large circle of sorrowing friends and acquaintances. RIP. NB – The body will be cremated and the ashes taken to Australia.

Arrangements had already been made for a return match and Ivo Bligh, later Lord Darnley, set out out three weeks later to 'recover the ashes'. A tiny urn containing the ashes of a bail was in fact presented to him in Australia after his team won two of the three test matches. After Darnley died in 1927, the urn was given to the MCC by his widow and can be viewed in the cricket museum at Lord's today.

A single chapter can never hope to cover every aspect of cricket. For the definitive answer to any question, buy *The Laws of Cricket* issued by Marylebone Cricket Club (ISBN: 1845790278).

UNDERSTANDING GRAMMAR – PART TWO

GRAMMAR DOES BECOME more complicated when you look at sentences, as you might expect. However, there are in fact, only four *kinds* of simple sentences.

The Four Kinds of Sentence

1. **Imperative** (Command) – 'Get out of my office!'
2. **Interrogative** (Question) – 'Did you take my keys?'
3. **Exclamative** (Exclamation) – 'Fantastic!'
4. **Declarative** (Statement) – 'You are not my friend.'

As you see, a simple sentence can be very simple indeed. It needs a subject and a verb to be a sentence – so you need to know what a subject is.

Subject and Object – Nominative and Accusative

The **subject** of a sentence is the person or thing acting on the verb. 'The man kicked the dog' has 'the man' as the subject. It does get a little harder to spot with the irregular verbs – 'John is sick' still has 'John' as the subject. The **nominative** form of words all have to do with the subject. This is crucial when it comes to pronouns, as the pronoun you use will depend on whether it is the subject or object in a sentence.

The **object** of the sentence is the person or thing on which the verb acts. 'The man kicked the dog' has 'the dog' as an object. The **accusative** forms of words all have to do with the object.

Before we go on to explaining nominative and accusative in more detail, you should know that Imperative or Exclamative sentences often have an invisible or implied subject. 'Get out!' does have a subject – the person doing the getting out, though the word isn't included. 'Fantastic!' as an exclamation implies 'That is . . .' The verb is there in a sense, but not seen. All other sentences have a subject and a verb. Easy.

Nominative/ Accusative Pronouns

When a pronoun is in the subject part of a sentence, we use nominative case pronouns. These are : *I*, *you*, *he*, *she*, *it*, *we*, *they*, *who* and *which*.

He went home.	*not*	'Him went home.'
He and I were good friends.	*not*	'Him and me were good friends.'
She and Susan were going home.	*not*	'Her and Susan were going home.'
We went to the park.	*not*	'Us went to the park.'
Who struck Tim?	*not*	'Whom struck Tim?'

In the above examples, the pronouns are all acting on the verbs, making it correct to use the nominative or subject form.

The accusative is the object part of a sentence. In the case of a pronoun, if it has the verb acting on it, we use *me*, *you*, *him*, *her*, *it*, *us*, *them*, *whom* and *which*.

Susan went with him.	*not*	'Susan went with he.'
John loved her.	*not*	'John loved she.'
David enjoyed playing chess with them.	*not*	'…chess with they.'
Why not come with us?	*not*	'Why not come with we?'
We did not know whom to thank.	*not*	'…who to thank.'

Some of these examples are blindingly obvious. No one with the most casual knowledge of language would say 'John loved she'. However, 'who' and 'whom' cause problems still. It is worth giving those two words a small section of their own.

Who and Whom

Learn this: If the word in question is acting on a verb (subject/nominative), use 'who'. If it is being acted upon (object/accusative), use 'whom'. Be careful – this is tricky.

Examples:

1. *The man who walked home was hit by a bus.* Correct or incorrect? Well, the 'who' in question is doing the walking, so it is in the subject form = accusative = correct. (You would not say 'Him was hit by a bus', but 'He was hit by a bus.')

2. *The man whom we saved was hit by a bus.* Correct or incorrect? This time, the man has been saved. The verb is acting on him. He is not doing the saving, so it is in the object form = accusative = correct to use 'whom' here. (You would not say 'We saved he', but 'We saved him'.)

3. *He was walking with his mother, whom he adored.* Correct or incorrect? She is not doing the adoring. The 'who' or 'whom' in question is being acted upon by the verb and therefore should be in the object form = accusative = correct.

Finally, for the 'who' and 'whom' section, prepositions must be mentioned. Most examples of 'whom' are used when it is the object of a preposition. Note that it is still the accusative form. There is nothing new here, but this one gives a great deal of trouble. The form often comes as sentences are rearranged so as not to leave a preposition at the end. It has the added bonus of putting a key word at the end of the sentence, which works very well for emphasis.

1. *He was a man for whom I could not find respect.* If this had been written, 'He was a man I could not find respect for', it would have been wrong. 'For' is a preposition and you just don't end a sentence with them. Note that it could have been written 'He was a man I could not respect' – to avoid the problem. This is laziness, however. Learn it and use it.

2. *To Whom it may concern* – a formal opening in letters. Note that such a letter should be ended, *Yours faithfully*. If the letter begins with a name, *Dear David*, for example, it should end with *Yours sincerely*.

A final mention of pronouns in the accusative must be made. It should now be clear enough why it's 'between you and me' – the 'me' is in the accusative, acted on by the preposition 'between'. You would not say, 'He gave the car to I', which has 'to' as a preposition, or 'Come with I'. Similarly, you don't say, 'Between you and I'.

For the record, **Genitive** has to do with possessive words: *mine, my, his, hers, ours* etc. Easy.

Dative is the term used to describe an indirect object. In the sentence 'Give me the ball', 'the ball' is the object, or accusative. However, 'me' is also in the accusative, as if the sentence had been written 'Give the ball to me.' The word 'me' is 'in the dative' – an indirect object.

Note that dative is of very little importance in English. In Latin, sentence word order is less important. 'The man bites the dog' can be written as 'The dog bites the man' – and only the endings will change. As a result, the word endings become crucial for understanding. English has evolved a more rigid word order and so the dative, for example, has become less important. It's still satisfying to know it though and most modern English teachers can be made to glaze over with a question on this subject. That said, if you try it on a Latin teacher, you'll be there all day . . .

The **Ablative** case is another one more relevant to the study of Latin than English. It involves words that indicate the agent or cause of an event, its manner and the instrument with which the action is done. The ablative case is likely to be used in sentences with the words 'from', 'in', 'by' and 'with' – prepositions. 'They proceeded *in silence*,' for example, shows the manner in which they proceeded. 'He was beaten *with sticks*,' shows how he was beaten. Those phrases are 'in the ablative'.

Clauses and Phrases

Simple sentences are not the whole story, of course. A complex sentence is one that has 'two or more clauses', but what is a clause?

The simplest working definition of a **clause** is that it has a subject and a verb and is part of a larger sentence. Sometimes the subject is understood, or implied, but the verb should always be there. The following example is a sentence with two clauses, joined by the conjunction 'so': 'I could not stand the heat, so I leaped out of the window.'

In a sense, clauses are mini-sentences, separated either by conjunctions or punctuation.

This sentence has four clauses: 'Despite expecting the voice, I jumped a foot in the air, smashed a vase and rendered my daughter speechless.'

'Despite expecting the voice' is a subordinate clause, separated by a comma from the rest. (Subordinate means lesser – a clause that could be dropped without destroying the sentence.) 'I jumped a foot in the air' is the second clause, 'smashed a vase' is the third, and 'rendered my daughter speechless' is the last. The final two are joined with the conjunction 'and'.

Note that 'smashed a vase' has the subject implied from the 'I' earlier on.

Subordinate clauses cannot stand on their own. Main clauses like 'I jumped a foot in the air' are complete sentences, but 'Despite expecting the voice,' is not. On its own, it would beg the question 'Despite expecting the voice...what?'

Phrases are groups of words that do not necessarily contain a verb and subject. Expressed simply, they are every other kind of word grouping that is not a clause or main sentence. A phrase can even be a single word.

The main kinds of phrase: Adjectival (works like an adjective); Adverbial (works like an adverb),; Noun (works like a noun);. Prepositional (works like a preposition); and Verb (works like...um, a verb). If you want to impress an English teacher, ask them if part of a sentence is using an adjectival or prepositional phrase.

Examples:

1. 'I lived *in France*.' 'in France' is a prepositional phrase, as it is a group of words indicating position.

2. 'I thought you wanted to leave *early tonight*' is an adverbial phrase, as 'early tonight' modifies the verb 'leave'.

3. 'It was an elephant *of extraordinary size*.' 'Of extraordinary size' is an adjectival phrase as it adds information to the noun 'elephant.'

4. '*The bearded men in the room* stood up and left.' This is a noun phrase – it's just a more complicated name for the men, using more than just one word.

5. A verb phrase is a group of words often containing the verb itself – an exception to the general rule that phrases won't have verbs. 'You *will be going* to the play!' has 'will be going' as a phrase of three words combining as the verb.

In contrast to complex sentences, 'compound' sentences have either multiple subjects: 'You and I are going to have a little chat', or multiple verbs: 'He choked and died.'

GIRLS

———— ✳ ————

Y̲O̲U̲ ̲M̲A̲Y̲ ̲A̲L̲R̲E̲A̲D̲Y̲ have noticed that girls are quite different from you. By this, we do not mean the physical differences, more the fact that they remain unimpressed by your mastery of a game involving wizards, or your understanding of Morse Code. Some will be impressed, of course, but as a general rule, girls do not get quite as excited by the use of urine as a secret ink as boys do.

We thought long and hard about what advice could possibly be suitable. It is an inescapable fact that boys spend a great deal of their lives thinking and dreaming about girls, so the subject should be mentioned here – as delicately as possible.

ADVICE ABOUT GIRLS

1. It is important to listen. Human beings are often very self-centred and like to talk about themselves. In addition, it's an easy subject if someone is nervous. It is good advice to listen closely – unless she has also been given this advice, in which case an uneasy silence could develop, like two owls sitting together.

2. Be careful with humour. It is very common for boys to try to impress girls with a string of jokes, each one more desperate than the last. *One* joke, perhaps, and then a long silence while she talks about herself . . .

3. When you are older, flowers really do work – women love them. When you are young, however, there is a ghastly sense of being awkward rather than romantic – and she will guess your mother bought them.

4. Valentine's Day cards. Do *not* put your name on them. The whole point is the excitement a girl feels, wondering who finds her attractive. If it says 'From Brian' on it, the magic isn't really there. This is actually quite a nice thing to do to someone you don't think will get a card. If you do this, it is even more important that you never say, 'I sent you one because I thought you wouldn't get any.' Keep the cards simple. You do not want one with padding of any kind.

5. Avoid being vulgar. Excitable bouts of wind-breaking will not endear you to a girl, just to pick one example.

6. Play sport of some kind. It doesn't matter what it is, as long as it replaces the corpse-like pallor of the computer programmer with a ruddy glow. Honestly, this is more important than you know.

7. If you see a girl in need of help – unable to lift something, for example – do not taunt her. Approach the object and greet her with a cheerful smile, whilst surreptitiously testing the weight of the object. If you find you can lift it, go ahead. If you can't, try sitting on it and engaging her in conversation.

8. Finally, make sure you are well-scrubbed, your nails are clean and your hair is washed. Remember that girls are as nervous around you as you are around them, if you can imagine such a thing. They think and act rather differently to you, but without them, life would be one long rugby locker room. Treat them with respect.

MARBLING PAPER

IF YOU'VE EVER WONDERED how the marbled paper inside the covers of old books is created, here it is. It is a surprisingly simple process, but the results can be very impressive. Once you have the inks, there are all sorts of possibilities, like birthday wrapping paper or your own greeting cards.

You will need

- Marbling ink – available from any craft or hobby shop and some large stationers.
- A flat-bottomed tray – a baking tray for example.
- A4 paper for printing and newspaper ready to lay out the wet sheets.
- Small paintbrush, a toothpick, comb or feather to swirl ink.

At about £3.50 a pot, marbling ink is expensive, but you only need a tiny amount for each sheet, so they last for years. We began with red, blue and gold.

We used A4 printer paper as it was handy, but almost any blank paper will do. You could do this in the bath, but remember to clean it later or you will have a blue father or mother the following morning. The paper must not have a shiny surface, or the inks won't penetrate.

1. Fill the tray with water to the depth of about an inch (25 mm). It is not necessary to be exact.
2. Using the small brush, or a dropper, touch the first colour to the water surface. It will spread immediately in widening circles.
3. Speckle the water with circles of your colours, then when you are satisfied, swirl the colours with a toothpick, a comb or a feather. Anything with a point will do for the first attempt.
4. When the pattern is ready, place the sheet of paper face down onto it and wait for sixty seconds. That is long enough for printer paper, though times may vary with different types.

5. Take hold of one end of the paper and draw it upwards out of the liquid. There really isn't any way to do this incorrectly, as far as we could tell – it really is easy. Wash your paper under the tap to get rid of excess ink. Place the wet sheet on newspaper and leave to dry.

If you have access to a colour photocopier or printer, you could make a copy with certain sections blanked off. The spaces could then be used for invitation details, or the title of a diary or story – perhaps an old-fashioned Victorian ghost story, with an old-fashioned marble-paper cover. Dark green, gold and black is a great combination.

CLOUD FORMATIONS

IT REALLY IS AMAZING just how many times you can look up at the sky in a lifetime and say 'I can never remember, is that Cumulocirrus, or Strato-whatsit?' Everyone is taught them at school and, frankly, we all forget. You'll read them now and when you *really* want to know, you'll have forgotten. The solution is to get spare copies of the book, so that you always have one with you.

THERE ARE ONLY THREE BASIC TYPES OF CLOUDS

This image is of **Cirrus** – light, wispy clouds, which can be as high as fifteen thousand feet and are made of ice crystals. The formation is sometimes referred to as 'mare's tails'.

After that comes the most common – **Cumulus.** These are the fluffy cotton-wool clouds you can see on most days.

The last member of our big three is **Stratus** – a dark, solid blanket of cloud at low level.

All cloud formations are combinations of these three basic forms. The only other word that crops up is Nimbus – meaning a dark grey rain cloud. You could for example, see Cumulonimbus, which would be large and fluffy, but dark and just about to rain. The leading edge of a storm is usually Cumulonimbus. Nimbostratus would be a heavy dark layer covering the sky and again just about to pour down.

Cirrus

THE MAIN CLOUD FORMATIONS

HIGH ALTITUDE
(above 18,000 ft/5500 m)

Cirrus – high and wispy

Cirrostratus – high thick layer

Cirrocumulus – high cotton wool

Cumulonimbus – cotton-wool storm clouds

MEDIUM ALTITUDE
(6,500–18,000 ft/2000–5500 m)

Altostratus – medium-height heavy band

Altocumulus – medium-height cotton wool

LOW ALTITUDE
(up to 6,500 ft/2000 m)

Stratus – heavy flat layer

Stratocumulus – fluffy and flat combined

Cumulus – cotton wool

Nimbostratus – raining flat layer

▲▲ *Cumulus*   ▲ *Stratus*

You know a storm is coming when you see Stratus and Stratocumulus cloud formations getting lower. If the clouds descend quickly into Nimbostratus, it is time to find shelter as the rain will be coming at any moment. If you happen to have a barometer, check the mercury level. A sudden drop in pressure indicates a storm is on the way.

These ten can be further subdivided, with names such as Cumulonimbus Incus, an anvil-shaped storm cloud often called a 'thunderhead'. For most of us, however, just remembering and identifying all ten major types would be enough.

FAMOUS BATTLES – PART TWO

1. Waterloo – 18 June 1815

NAPOLEON HAD OVERREACHED himself by 1814. He had lost more than 350,000 men in his march on Russia, one of the most ill-advised military actions in history. Wellington had beaten his armies and their Spanish allies in Spain. In addition, the armies of Austria and Prussia stood ready to humble him at last. Yet Napoleon was not a man to go quietly into obscurity. When he abdicated as Emperor, he was exiled to rule the tiny island of Elba off the west coast of Italy. Perhaps cruelly, he was allowed to keep the title he claimed for himself. Many lives would have been saved if he and his honour guard had stayed there. Instead, eleven months after his arrival, a frigate picked him up and he returned to France.

The French king, Louis XVIII, sent troops with orders to fire on him. Famously, Napoleon walked fearlessly out to them, threw open his coat and said, 'Let him that has the heart, kill his Emperor!' The soldiers cheered him and Napoleon turned them round and marched on Paris. By 20 March, 1815, the French king had fled and Napoleon was back. The period of March to June is still known as the 'Hundred Days' war.

With extraordinary efficiency, Napoleon put together an army of 188,000 regulars, 300,000 levies (conscripts) and another 100,000 support

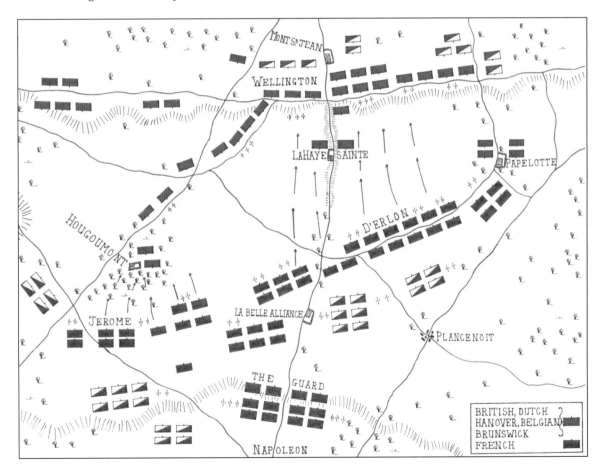

personnel. In addition, he had his veteran Army of the North around Paris – 124,000 men.

Wellington's Anglo-Dutch army of 95,000 was in Flanders (Belgium) at this point, with the Prussian army of 124,000 under Marshall Blücher. The Austrians had 210,000 men along the Rhine and another army of 75,000 in Italy. The Russian army of 167,000 under Barclay were coming through Germany to attack France. In many ways, Napoleon had overreached himself in 1815, as well.

Napoleon moved quickly against the armies in Belgium, attempting to crush his enemies one or two at a time. Unfortunately for his hopes, Wellington's forces stopped one of his marshals at Quatre-Bras, south of Brussels, counter-attacking and preventing the support Napoleon needed to destroy the Prussians. Blücher's men did take terrible casualties when they met Napoleon at Ligny, but were still able to retreat in good order. Napoleon did not follow up his advantage and Wellington was able to move from Quatre-Bras to a better position, ready for battle. He chose a ridge named Mont St-Jean, to the south of the village of Waterloo. It was the evening of the 17 June and that night it rained in torrents.

Blücher had given his word to Wellington that he would reinforce the British position. His deputy Gneisenau was convinced Wellington would fail to hold the ridge and would be gone by the time the Prussians arrived. He wanted to abandon their allies and return to Prussia. Despite exhaustion and being wounded himself, the seventy-two-year-old Blücher overrode him and gave orders for his men to support Wellington. It is an interesting detail that Gneisenau arranged the Prussian marching order so that the units furthest away from Wellington would go first. It seems he knew this would delay their arrival. The furthest unit, however, was General von Bülow's IV Corps, one of the best units the Prussians had. The eventual arrival of the Prussians would force Napoleon to respond, just as he should have been attacking the British centre. This was a vital part of the victory.

The ground was a quagmire after the downpour of the night before, and Napoleon delayed the attack until it began to dry. On noon of the 18 June, he attacked at last with 72,000 against Wellington's 67,000. Napoleon's troops moved forward in a feint attack, while his 'belles filles' (beautiful daughters) guns hammered at Wellington''s army for an hour. At 1 p.m., 20,000 veterans moved in line formation towards the British-held ridge. They too had to march through artillery fire and the carnage was horrific. Yet two of the veteran divisions made it to the crest through fierce hand-to-hand fighting. This was a crucial point in the battle, but it was saved by the Household Brigade and Union Brigade cavalry under the Earl of Uxbridge, who smashed the French attackers with a charge over the ridge.

The two brigades continued on across the valley, attacking the French guns. They took about twenty and most of them were exhausted as they were broken in turn by the French cavalry reserves. The damage was done, however. The only truly formidable French infantry left on the field were his Imperial Guard, his elite.

There were some confused orders in the French lines at this point. Wellington ordered his men to pull back 100 ft out of range of the French guns. Marshal Ney thought they were retreating and ordered a brigade of French cavalry to attack. His order was queried and in an angry response, Ney led them himself, taking around 4,000 cavalrymen forward without support. If Napoleon had sent in his Imperial Guard at this point, Wellington could well have lost the battle. Napoleon had become aware of the approach of the Prussians and refused to commit them. Unsupported, the cavalry failed to damage the British square formations in any significant way. Volley fire repulsed them and the survivors eventually retreated. The heavy French cannons opened up again and more on the ridge began to die.

By four in the afternoon, the Prussians were there in force, led by the IV Corps. They took a strategic position on Napoleon's right flank and had to be dislodged by vital troops from the Imperial Young and Old Guard regiments. By the time that was done it was getting on for seven in the evening. So close to midsummer, the days were long and it was still light when Napoleon sent in his Imperial Guard at last to break the British centre. They wore dark blue jackets and wore high bearskin hats. In all their history, they had never retreated.

The Imperial Guard marched up the hill towards a brigade of British Foot Guards under Colonel Maitland and a Dutch brigade under Colonel Detmer. Volley fire and a bayonet charge made the Imperial Guard retreat. Wellington sent in more men after them as they tried to re-form and they were finished. The British Guard regiments were well aware of the reputation of the Napoleonic elite and took their hats as souvenirs. The high bearskin headgear is still worn today by the Grenadier, Welsh, Irish, Scots and Coldstream Guard regiments.

Blücher attacked the French right as Wellington counterattacked in force. The French army collapsed. Afterwards, Blücher wanted to call the battle 'La Belle Alliance', but Wellington insisted on his old habit of naming battles after the place where he'd spent the night before. As a result, it became known as the Battle of Waterloo.

Napoleon returned to Paris and abdicated for the second time on 22 June, before surrendering to the British. HMS *Bellerophon* took him on board, one of the ships that had fought at the Nile and Trafalgar with Nelson. Ironically, *Bellerophon* (known as 'Billy Ruffian') was one of those that had fired on Napoleon's flagship *L'Orient* before she exploded at the Battle of the Nile.

Napoleon was taken to the island of St Helena and would not leave it until his death. Waterloo was Wellington's last battle, though he did become Prime Minister in 1828.

Blücher died in his bed at home in 1819.

France was forced to pay damages to Britain, Austria, Prussia and Russia. Those countries met in Vienna to settle the future of Europe. A neutral country, or buffer zone, was created from those talks, its peace guaranteed by the others. It was later known as Belgium when it became completely independent in 1830. Interestingly, it is true that the 'Wellington boot' takes its name from a leather boot style popularised by Wellington. Originally, it was made of leather and only later produced in the rubber form we know so well today.

2. Balaclava – 25 October 1854

In 1853, Tsar Nicholas I saw a chance to topple an ageing Ottoman Empire, control Turkey and extend Russian influence right into the Mediterranean. Both France and England were intent on resisting Russian encroachment on that part of the world. In a highly unusual alliance, both countries sent fleets to support Turkey.

The allied force was jointly commanded by Lord Raglan and the French Marshal Saint Arnaud. With their arrival, Turkey declared war on Russia and had some initial success before the Russians sank the Turkish fleet and invaded Bulgaria. Various skirmishes followed. Dysentery and cholera were already causing problems for the allied expeditionary force at Varna when orders arrived to take the Russian seaport of Sevastopol. The fleet of 150 warships and transports landed 51,000 French, British and Turkish soldiers thirty miles north of the port. As the cold months arrived, some of them wore woollen headgear that left only a part of the face exposed. These quickly became known as 'Balaclavas'.

On 20 September, Prince Alexander Menshikov fought them at the River Alma. His army was defeated but left almost intact as it withdrew. The allied force moved on to Sevastopol and laid siege to it while the fleet under Sir Edmund Lyons blockaded the port at sea. Menshikov decided to divert their attention from Sevastopol by attacking the main British supply base at Balaclava. He had 65,000 men and expected another 25,000 in reinforcements. In comparison, the allied forces had been reinforced to 75,000.

Balaclava is a great plain in the Crimean

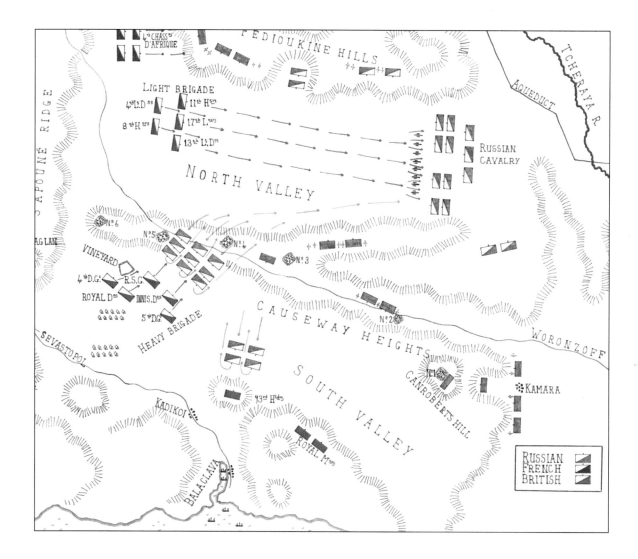

Peninsula with high ground in the form of the Sapoune Ridge at one end and a central spine known as the Causeway Heights. To reach the British camp at Balaclava, Menshikov had to cross the River Tchernaya and the Fedioukine Hills, coming into the North Valley. His task then was to take the British redoubts on Causeway Heights, manned by Turkish militia. Beyond them lay the British 93rd Highlanders, a thousand Royal Marines and another thousand Turkish troops, all under General Sir Colin Campbell.

The British cavalry were camped at the northern foot of the Causeway Heights to protect the flank. They were under the command of Lords Lucan and Cardigan, two men who disliked each other intensely and rarely spoke.

The battle of 25 October began when Menshikov used artillery and bayonet charges to storm three of the redoubts in two hours, routing the Turkish militia within.

The Russian cavalry burst through the allied defences and charged through the battlefield towards the suddenly defenceless British camp further south.

The only thing in their path was the 93rd Highland Regiment with Campbell. They formed a double rank as the cavalry thundered towards them and Campbell said, 'There is no retreat from here, men. You must die where you stand.' John Scott on the right, replied, 'Ay, Sir Colin. An needs be, we'll do that,' and the rest of them echoed the reponse.

They began volley fire at the oncoming wall of charging Russian horse and stood their ground until the charge collapsed against their rifle fire. It is said that one of the Highlanders was able to reach out and touch the face of a fallen mount as it lay within arm's length of him. Ever after, the stand was known as 'The Thin Red Line'.

The second main action of the day occurred when the main body of Russian horse entered the southern valley. General Sir James Scarlett had brought up the Heavy Brigade at this time. The name is no exaggeration, as both men and horses were large and stronger than usual, a hammer rather than a rapier on the battle-field. General Scarlett ordered 300 of these from the 2nd and 6th Dragoons *uphill* against the Russian force of 2,000. It seemed foolhardy but the Heavy Brigade cavalry smashed through their lighter Russian counterparts, driving them from the field with almost 300 dead. The Heavy Brigade lost only ten that day, not all of them at that charge with Scarlett.

The third and final action of the day is by far the most famous. By this time, Menshikov was entrenched in the North Valley and had cannons lining the position. It was never the intention of Lord Raglan to send the Light Brigade down into the 'Valley of Death'. He saw that the guns in the captured redoubts on Causeway Heights were being removed by the Russians and sent a message to Lord Lucan that could have been better phrased. He also made the mistake of sending it with a galloper named Captain Lewis Edward Nolan, who added his own twist to the disaster.

The message to Lucan read as follows: 'Lord Raglan wishes the cavalry to advance rapidly to the front – follow the enemy and try to prevent the enemy carrying away the guns. Troop Horse Artillery may accompany. French cavalry is on your left. Immediate.'

Raglan also gave the verbal instruction: 'Tell Lord Lucan the cavalry is to attack immediately.'

Captain Nolan reached Lord Lucan with the message and passed it on. Lucan could not see the guns to which the note referred and queried which ones were meant. In exaspera-tion, Captain Nolan replied, 'There, my lord, is your enemy, there are your guns!' and he ges-tured angrily in the direction of the redoubts, which was also the direction of the main Russian position. The arrogant Lucan was infuriated by the man's tone – and perhaps the implication that he was deliberately delaying going into action.

Lord Lucan ordered the Light Brigade and Lord Cardigan into the North Valley – against the wrong guns. Cardigan pointed out that three sides of the valley were covered in entrenched cannon positions, but Lucan told him haughtily that Raglan had ordered it and 'We have no choice but to obey.'

The Light Brigade were also thirsty for glory. The Heavy Brigade had seen action, but the Lights had hardly been used. Without the slightest hesitation, all 660 of them advanced into the North Valley, led by Cardigan. As the Russian guns opened up, Captain Nolan galloped alongside Cardigan, but was killed before he could point out the error.

On the north and south sides of the valley were almost fifty cannon and nineteen infantry battalions. At the end were eight more cannon pointing directly at the Light Brigade and four full Russian regiments – the entire remaining army under Menshikov.

The Light Brigade cantered at first under heavy fire, slowly building to a full gallop towards the Russian guns. Men were torn from their saddles by rifle bullets and shell frag-ments. The Russians could not believe what they were seeing and reacted too slowly to protect the guns once it became clear the Lights were going to make it to the end of the valley. The Cossacks around the guns panicked and ran. The Light Brigade killed any remain-ing gunners and then charged the Russian cav-alry, driving them back. They had taken the guns, but without support could not dream of holding them. The horses were exhausted and many of the surviving men were wounded. They turned then and began to make their way back to their starting place – and the cannon fire began once more as they rode.

It took only twenty minutes, start to finish. 195 survived out of 661. Six of the then new Victoria Crosses were awarded for bravery.

The charge should be put in context. The Crimean War had its fair share of horrors, from the silent terror of cholera, to the stench of men dying of dysentery and infected wounds. It was here that Florence Nightingale introduced the idea of nursing and the concept of sanitation to a British battlefield. There were few things to lift the spirits of the British public as they read the reports. The Battle of Balaclava provided one of the most extraordinary examples of courage in warfare – equal to the Spartans at Thermopylae. You must remember that the Russians had broken before the Thin Red Line – and again against a small number of heavy cavalry. The Light Brigade faced almost fifty cannon and literally thousands of rifles and yet did not falter. As one French officer said, '*C'est magnifique, mais ce n'est pas la guerre.*' – 'It is magnificent but it is not war.' Tennyson's poem 'The Charge of the Light Brigade' is still one of the most famous pieces in the English language.

3. Rorke's Drift – 22 and 23 January 1879

The Boer Wars between Dutch and British forces were over control of lands in southern Africa, rich with diamonds, gold and timber. The Zulu armies of Shaka, then Cetewayo fought against the encroachment of their lands by both sides. Britain attempted to arrange a 'protectorate' with Cetewayo, but when he refused, they invaded Zulu lands, led by Lord Chelmsford. He entered Cetewayo's territory with only 5,000 British troops and 8,000 natives. His objective was to occupy Cetewayo's royal kraal (cattle enclosure or village), advancing on it from three directions. Accordingly, he split his force into three columns.

Chelmsford entered Zulu lands at Rorke's Drift, a farm named after its deceased owner,

James Rorke. They made the farm buildings into a supply depot and moved on.

The battle of Isandlwana involved Chelmsford's No. 3 central column, a mixed force of cavalry, infantry and Royal Engineers. They had made steady progress into Zulu land, attacking a minor cattle kraal and crossing a river. Mounted troops scouted ahead to Isipezi Hill and found no sign of a Zulu force in the area, so Chelmsford decided to make a camp at Isandlwana. Perhaps because of the stony ground, he did not give orders to fortify the camp in any way.

On the morning of 22 January, Chelmsford went with about half his full force (2,500) in scouting parties, searching for signs of Zulu forces. There were many sightings as the area began to fill with Cetewayo's warriors. A message came through from the camp at Isandlwana: 'For God's sake come with all your men; the camp is surrounded and will be taken unless helped.'

By the time Chelmsford made it back to Isandlwana, the camp had been overrun and 1,300 men killed. The defenders had fought bravely, but a Zulu force of 10,000 had attacked with ferocious energy, using their assegai spears to cut their way in, despite rifle fire and bayonets. They lost about 3,000 warriors in the attack.

Chelmsford did not believe this could have happened at first. Not everyone under his command had been killed – about 55 British and 300 natives survived, while the Zulus paraded in the red uniforms and raided the stores before moving off. The whole area was filled with hostile impis (attack groups), right back to Rorke's Drift. Chelmsford chose to retreat back to the border. His small column formed a hostile camp for the night and as darkness fell, they saw the flames of Rorke's Drift in the distance. It too had been attacked by the warriors of Cetewayo that day.

The main house at Rorke's Drift had been converted into a hospital as well as a supply store. It had eleven rooms, stone exterior walls and a thatched roof. There was also a stone

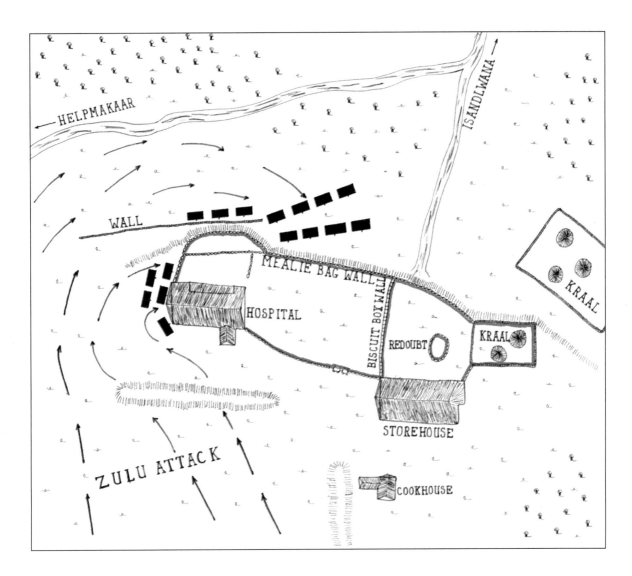

walled chapel being used as a store, and a few other outbuildings in the compound. When firing was heard on the morning of 22 January, an evacuation was considered, but the extraordinary speed of the Zulu impis across open ground meant that any attempt to move the sick and injured would be overtaken. Although they only had a hundred men fit to fight, the decision was taken to fortify the compound and wait it out.

A Zulu impi of 4,500, under Prince Dabulamanzi kaMpande, attacked the compound late in the afternoon. Their assegais could not reach through the piled grain bags and biscuit boxes at first and they were thrown back by point-blank rifle fire. The initial attacks were unsuccessful before they managed to set fire to the hospital building, get in and start killing the helpless patients. Private Alfred Henry Hook used his bayonet to hold them back while Private John Williams cut through an internal wall and pulled the sick and injured through to relative safety.

The battle raged on all day and long into the night before the Zulus finally moved on at dawn on the 23 January. They left four to five hundred of their dead around the barricaded compound. The British had lost 17 dead and

10 seriously wounded. For the individual acts of bravery during the siege, eleven Victoria Crosses were awarded to the following: Lieutenants Chard and Bromhead, Privates Alfred Hook, Frederick Hitch, Robert Jones, William Jones, James Dalton, John Williams and Corporal Allen. Surgeon James Reynolds was awarded his VC for tending to the wounded under fire. Christian Schiess received the first VC awarded to a soldier serving in the Natal Native force. He was a Swiss volunteer and had killed three men in hand-to-hand fighting, preventing a break into the main house.

You could do a lot worse than seeing the film *Zulu*, with Michael Caine playing Lieutenant Bromhead. It gives an idea of the sort of extra-ordinary bravery witnessed on both sides of this conflict.

4. The Somme

One of the many and complex reasons that World War I began was that Germany invaded Belgium. Britain was bound by treaty to defend the country. Similar alliances across Europe drew in all the great powers one by one. It may have begun with the assassination of Archduke Franz Ferdinand in Serbia, but that was merely the spark that set the world on fire.

The Somme was the river in France that Edward III crossed just before the battle of

Crécy. The area has had a great deal of British blood soaking into its earth over the centuries, but never more so than on the first day of the Battle of the Somme, 1 July 1916.

Before the British army marched into the machine-gun tracks criss-crossing the battlefield, General Sir Douglas Haig had ordered eight days of artillery bombardment. This had not proved a successful tactic over the previous two years and it did not on that day. One flaw was that the barrage had to stop to allow the allies to advance, so as soon as it stopped, the Germans knew the attack was coming and made their preparations. They had solid, deep bunkers of concrete and wood that resisted the barrage very well indeed. Their barbed-wire emplacements were also still intact after the shells stopped.

At 7.28 in the morning, the British forces detonated two huge mines, then three smaller ones near German lines. The idea was probably to intimidate the enemy, but instead, they acted as a final confirmation of the attack.

The slaughter began at 7.30, when the British soldiers rose up out of their trenches and tried to cross 800 yards in the face of machine-gun fire. A few actually made it to the German front line in that first surge before they were cut down. There were 60,000 British casualties and 19,000 dead. An entire generation fell on a single morning, making it the worst disaster of British military history. Who can say what their lives would have meant and achieved had they survived?

There is a touching poem called 'For the Fallen' written by Laurence Binyon in 1914 that is quoted at every Remembrance Day service. This is an extract from it, remembering those who gave their lives for their country. The second verse is particularly poignant.

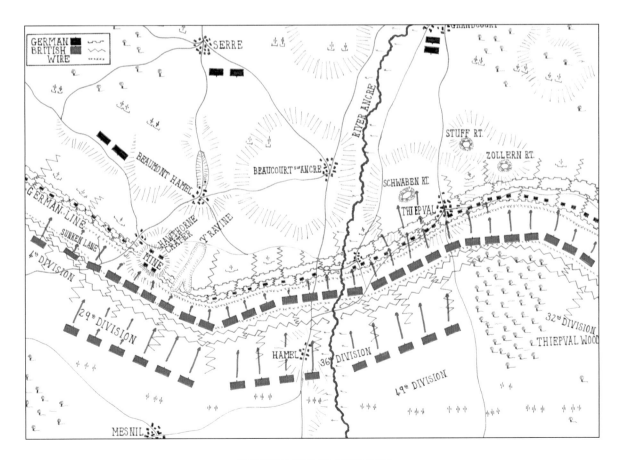

They went with songs to the battle, they were young,
Straight of limb, true of eye, steady and aglow.
They were staunch to the end against odds uncountered:
They fell with their faces to the foe.

They shall grow not old, as we that are left grow old:
Age shall not weary them, nor the years contemn.
At the going down of the sun and in the morning
We will remember them.

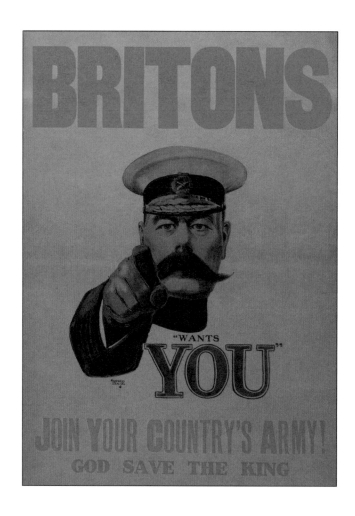

MAKING CLOTH FIREPROOF

—✦—

PERHAPS THE MOST impressive use for alum (potassium aluminium sulphate) is in fireproof-ing material. This could be very useful for tablecloths where there is a fire hazard, as in a laboratory or on a stage. It works with any porous cloth, but should not be considered fool-proof. To demonstrate it, we used household dusters.

First prepare a solution of alum and water. Hot water works best in dissolving the powder. 1 lb 1 oz (500 g) of alum dissolves easily in a pint of water. Dip the material you wish to fire-proof in the solution and make sure it is completely covered. Remove immediately and leave to dry. Be careful not to let it drip onto valuable carpets. If you leave it outside and it happens to rain, it will probably still work.

Once dry, the cloth should be a little stiffer than usual, but otherwise unchanged. An untreated duster burned almost completely in twenty seconds. The treated duster could *not be lit*, though there was some light charring after thirty seconds of applied flame.

FIRST AID

—✦—

ACCIDENTS ARE GOING TO HAPPEN. You can't spend your life worrying about them or you'd never get anything done. However, using common sense and taking a few simple precau-tions is well worth a little of your time. Really, everyone should have a basic knowledge of first aid. If you were injured, you'd want someone close to you who doesn't panic and knows what to do. It's not being dramatic to say a little knowledge can be the difference between life and death.

When dealing with more than one casualty, a decision has to be made about which person to treat first. This process is called 'triage'. One rule of thumb is that if someone is screaming, they are clearly alive, conscious and almost certainly in less danger than someone silent and still.

These are your priorities:

1. Breathing and heartbeat
2. Stop bleeding
3. Bandage wounds
4. Splint fractures
5. Treat shock

When dealing with blood and wounds, there is a risk of AIDS infection. Wear gloves if you have them, or put plastic bags over your hands. Avoid touching your mouth or face with bloody hands. Wash thoroughly as soon as possible. This advice is almost always ignored in high-stress situations, but it could save your life.

When you approach an injured person, make sure whatever hurt them isn't likely to hurt you – falling debris on a building site, for example. If there is an imminent threat, move the patient before treatment. Weigh the risk of spinal injury against the immediate danger. If they have been electrocuted and the current is still running, stand on something dry and non-conductive and use a stick to heave them away from the source.

If you do have to move them, avoid twisting motions that could make spinal injuries worse. Pull by the ankles until they are clear.

ARE THEY BREATHING?

If they are breathing, turn them on their side and bend one leg up in support. This is the 'recovery position'. It helps to prevent choking caused by vomit or bleeding.

If breathing is poor, use a finger to remove any obstructions from the mouth and throat. Check they have not swallowed their tongue and if they have, pull it back into the mouth. If breathing is blocked, put them onto their back, sit astride them, place your hands just above their navel and thrust upwards into the ribcage. If this does not work, grasp them around the chest under the armpits from behind, joining your hands in front if you can. Then grip hard, compressing their chest. This is the 'Heimlich manoeuvre'.

Once the blockage is clear, if they are still not breathing, start artificial resuscitation.

Note that babies require special delicacy. If a baby stops breathing, support them face down on your forearm. The pressure alone is enough in some cases, but if not, press three or four times between the shoulder blades with the heel of your hand. If there is still no response, support the head and turn the baby face up, then use just two fingers to press down on the chest four times. Repeat this action. Finally, cover the baby's mouth and nose with your mouth and breathe into their lungs.

IS THE HEART BEATING?

To take the pulse at the wrist, press your fingers on the front of the wrist, just below the thumb at the lower end of the forearm. To take the pulse at the neck, turn the face to one side and press your fingers under the jaw next to the windpipe.

The normal pulse rate for the relaxed adult is 60–80 beats per minute. For a child it is 90–140 beats per minute. In high-stress situations, it can spike as high as 240, though a heart attack is very close at that point.

Use your watch to count the beats in thirty seconds and then double it. If you cannot feel a pulse and the pupils of the eyes are much larger than normal, start cardiac compression. (See below.)

Artificial Respiration

The first five minutes are the most crucial, but keep going for up to an hour while you wait for emergency services. This can be exhausting, so take turns if there are more of you.

'The Kiss of Life'

1. Lay the patient on their back.
2. Tilt the head back.
3. Hold jaw open and nostrils closed.
4. Check airway is clear with a finger.
5. Place mouth over patient's mouth and blow firmly. It takes more effort than you might expect to inflate someone else's chest.

Watch for the chest to rise, and take your mouth away. Repeat this five or six times in succession. After that, get a rhythm going of one breath every five seconds. After ten or twelve, begin cardiac compression.

With a baby, put your mouth over the nose and mouth and use short gentle breaths twenty times a minute. A baby's lungs can be damaged by too forceful treatment.

With an animal, such as a dog, hold the mouth closed with both hands and blow into the nose to inflate the chest. Whether you do this will of course depend on how much you love the dog. Use a strong mouthwash afterwards.

Cardiac Compression

1. First thump hard onto the centre of the chest and check to see if the heart has restarted.
2. Place heel of hands on the breastbone.
3. With arms straight, push down about 1½ inches (4 cm).
4. Do this four or five times between breaths, counting aloud.

Never try compression when the heart is beating, even if it is very faint. This could stop the heart.

Check for a pulse after one minute and then at three-minute intervals. Do not give up.

As soon as a pulse is detected, stop compressions but continue mouth-to-mouth until the patient is breathing normally, then put them into the recovery position.

Bleeding and injury

If anything is embedded in the wound, you will need a 'doughnut' bandage. Roll a piece of cloth into a tube, then join the ends to make a doughnut shape. Put this around the wound before bandaging, so the bandage won't press glass or other fragments in deeper.

An adult has up to eleven pints of blood. Losing three of them will cause unconsciousness.

Even one pint can cause someone to faint, which is why blood donors are asked to sit down and have a biscuit and orange squash after donating.

Immediate steps must be taken to stop the flow of blood. Pressure is the key. It slows down the blood flow enough to allow the body's own repair mechanisms to start vital clotting. Apply pressure for five to fifteen minutes and don't keep checking it. Talk to the patient as you do, keeping an eye on their state of mind and alertness. If you have no dressing, make a pad of a shirt or any other cloth.

Raise the injured part above the heart to aid clotting. Squeeze the edges of a gaping wound together before applying the pad.

Apply a tourniquet only if the patient is likely to bleed to death. Tie a belt or cord above the wound, tightening it until the blood flow slows. You cannot keep this on for more than a few minutes without causing permanent damage, so loosen it at intervals.

If you don't have anything to tie it, apply pressure on the main artery above the wound. To do this, find a pulse in the side of the jaw or wrist, underside of upper arm, crook of the elbow, top of the shoulder (clavicle), the temples on the side of the head, top of the thighs by the groin, back of the knees and the front of the ankles. Find the closest one and press it hard into the bone. It is a good idea to try and find these on yourself, before you try to do it in real life with someone screaming in your ear.

Soap is an antiseptic and can be used to wash a wound to avoid infection. Hot water or boiled wine will also sterilise the site, though the application will be extremely painful. In an emergency, fresh urine will also work, as it is sterile.

Serious internal bleeding may be shown by cold clammy skin, a rapid pulse, restlessness and rapid bruising under the skin. Try to minimise shock by elevating their legs, keeping them warm and getting help fast.

BREAKS

If someone fractures a bone in an accident it may be necessary to splint the damaged limb before trying to move them. This is done by placing two pieces of wood around the damaged area and securing them with rope or a belt.

A wrist or a dog's leg can be secured in a rolled-up magazine and held with shoelaces. Damaged arms will need to be put in a sling and secured against the body.

A sling can be formed by a large triangular bandage which folds over the arm and is secured at the neck. If it's a broken forearm, you could tie the wrist, then take the cloth around the neck and back down. A simple loop would work, but the arm will not be secure.

BURNS

Burns destroy the skin and carry a risk of infection. Run cold water over a burn for at least ten minutes. Try not to break any blisters that form. Give the injured person lots to drink. Remove any jewellery and clothing from the burnt area. Do not apply ointments to the skin. Cover with a loose bandage if you have one, or if not, a plastic bag. Put dressings between burnt fingers and toes to stop them sticking together.

SHOCK

This can occur after any serious accident and can be fatal. The symptoms are loss of colour from the lips, dizziness, vomiting, cold and clammy skin, and a rapid pulse.

Reassure the patient and talk to them. If they can talk, ask them their name and then use it often. Keep them warm and check their breathing and pulse. Lay them down and elevate their legs. Be ready to give mouth-to-mouth and cardiac compression if they fall unconscious. Hot sweet tea is useful if they are conscious and alert. Never leave a shock victim on their own, however.

Staying calm is most important for your own safety and other people who may be relying on you. It helps to prepare. When the injury occurs, the first thing you should do is take a deep breath and reach for the first-aid kit you have prepared long before. Remember the ABC of 'Airway, Breathing, Compression' and check one at a time.

Make sure you have considered methods of contact in the event of an emergency. A mobile phone is a good idea, but is it in a waterproof bag? Is it charged? Remember that the best captains look after their men.

NAUSEA

Nausea from some external cause, like car sickness, sea sickness or morning sickness, can sometimes be eased with an acupressure point in the wrists. To find it, lay the other hand at right angles to the wrist, as shown in the diagram.

The point lying underneath the index finger between the first and the second joints can relieve nausea after about five minutes of pressing. It is possible to have each hand press on the other's nausea point. It does not work for everyone, but it can be very useful to know.

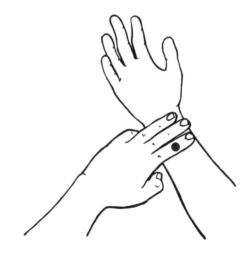

MEDICAL KITS

Whether this is intended for a house or emergencies will alter the contents. There isn't much point putting athlete's foot powder in an emergency kit. However, the basics are:

1. Plasters and scissors. Cloth plasters are the best and can be cut to any shape.
2. Antiseptic cream and TCP antiseptic liquid.
3. Needle and thread. Stitching cuts is possible if the patient is unconscious. (Dogs will occasionally let you do this, though most of them struggle like maniacs.)

FIRST AID

4. Painkillers. Ibuprofen also works as an anti-inflammatory drug, but can be dangerous to asthmatics. Aspirin is useful in cases of heart attack or a stroke as it thins the blood. Paracetamol is good for pain and to bring down a high temperature. Oil of cloves can be dabbed on for tooth pain.
5. Golden Eye ointment. Available in chemists, it is fantastically good stuff for any eye soreness or infection. Works brilliantly on dogs as well.
6. Bandages. Including one large square that can be folded diagonally into a sling.
7. Gauze pads to go under the bandage and soak up blood.
8. Lip balm.
9. High-factor sun block.
10. Tweezers and safety pins.
11. A couple of pairs of latex gloves.
12. Antihistamine pills for insect stings or allergic reactions.

If there is a chance of you needing antibiotics away from civilisation, such as on a mountaineering trip, your local GP will supply a private prescription, which is more expensive. It will probably be for a general-purpose antibiotic, like amoxicillin.

THE COMMONWEALTH

FACTS AND FIGURES

The Commonwealth is an organisation of fifty-three nations. With the exception of Mozambique, which joined at the end of the twentieth century, the other fifty-two were all part of the British Empire. In fact, the Commonwealth was created as the peaceful twilight organisation of that empire. It has been largely successful, remaining a surprisingly influential group today. More than 1.8 billion people live in Commonwealth countries and Queen Elizabeth II broadcasts an address to them on Commonwealth Day (the second Monday in March) each year. All fifty-three take part in the Commonwealth Games.

1. Antigua and Barbuda*	19. Jamaica	37. St Vincent and the Grenadines*
2. Australia*	20. Kenya	38. Samoa
3. The Bahamas*	21. Kiribati	39. Seychelles
4. Bangladesh	22. Lesotho	40. Sierra Leone
5. Barbados*	23. Malawi	41. Singapore
6. Belize*	24. Malaysia	42. Solomon Islands*
7. Botswana	25. Maldives	43. South Africa
8. Brunei Darussalam	26. Malta	44. Sri Lanka
9. Cameroon	27. Mauritius	45. Swaziland
10. Canada*	28. Mozambique	46. Tanzania
11. Cyprus	29. Namibia	47. Tonga
12. Dominica	30. Nauru	48. Trinidad and Tobago
13. Fiji Islands.	31. New Zealand*	49. Tuvalu*
14. The Gambia	32. Nigeria	50. Uganda
15. Ghana	33. Pakistan	51. United Kingdom*
16. Grenada*	34. Papua New Guinea*	52. Vanuatu
17. Guyana	35. St Kitts and Nevis*	53. Zambia
18. India	36. St Lucia*	

The * symbol indicates the constitutional monarchies where Queen Elizabeth II is head of state. Up to 1947, there were no republics in the British Commonwealth. To allow India to remain a member whilst becoming an independent republic, the word 'British' was dropped from the description. Today, thirty-two members are republics and five (Brunei, Lesotho, Malaysia, Swaziland and Tonga) have national monarchs of their own. All, however, accept the British monarch as 'Head of the Commonwealth'. In addition, Crown Dependencies like Guernsey, Jersey and the Isle of Man can take part in the Commonwealth Games.

This is an extract from a speech on the Commonwealth by the Right Honourable Owen Arthur, Prime Minister of Barbados:

It is the oldest living political association of states, yet in many ways the most adaptable to modern realities and thus the most responsive to the changing needs of its membership. It is rich in its diversity, yet remarkable in its cohesiveness, forged in no small measure by the sense of common identity we derive from our shared historical experience and the administrative, legal and institutional structures.

The Commonwealth promotes democracy, equality and good governance not only amongst its own members, but also throughout the world. It gives aid and disaster relief to its members and provides funds for development and the eradication of poverty.

MAPS OF CHANGING BRITAIN –
ROMAN BRITAIN TO THE NORMAN CONQUEST

BRITAIN WAS SEMI-MYTHICAL to the Greeks and Phoenicians, who knew it as 'Cassiterides', the 'tin island' on the edge of the world. The Greek writer Herodotus wrote that he had heard of a sea on the other side of Europe from Greece, but personally doubted its existence. However, a Greek explorer, Pytheas, successfully circumnavigated Britain in the fourth century BC.

Map 1
Julius Caesar landed in 55 and 54 BC, but did not remain. In 45 AD, Rome invaded in force.

Map 2
When the Romans left in AD 440, Vortigern, the British king of Kent, invited mercenary Saxons to Britain to fight the Scots and Picts invading over Hadrian's Wall. The historian Gildas describes a dispute over payment and rations which led to a Saxon revolt. They ravaged the whole island as far as the western sea, achieved strongholds in East Anglia and Kent and so began the English conquest of Britain.

Map 3
5th to 8th century England went from a barbarous pagan land to a settled Christian one of eight Saxon kingdoms. This period is known as the Dark Ages, but the spread of Christianity also brought civilisation and the written word.

Map 4
Alfred became king in AD 871. This was a time when the 'great heathen army' of the Danes was fighting for control in England. Alfred defeated the Danes at Edington in Wiltshire. They signed the Treaty of Wedmore, which divided England, with Alfred controlling Wessex and the south and the Danes controlling northern England. It also stipulated that the Danes become Christian. Alfred created a powerful navy, built schools and ruled wisely. He is the only English king to be given the title 'Great'.

Map 5
Athelstan (reigned AD 924–939) was the first king of all England. He continued the re-conquest of what was left of the Danelaw area as laid down in the Treaty of Wedmore. In January 1066, Harold Godwinson was made king after the death of Edward the Confessor. He beat an invading Norwegian army at Stamford Bridge and marched south to face William of Normandy at Hastings in Sussex. William was victorious and was crowned king in Westminster Abbey on Christmas Day, 1066.

Map 1

ROMAN
BRITANNIA

Scale 1 : 6,000,000
English Miles

0   100

MAEATAE

(Abercorn)   (Edinburgh)

Bodotia Aest.

ANTONINE WALL

Trimontium

Clota Aest.

Blatum Bulgium
(Birrens)

Magnae

Hunnum
(Halton Chesters)

Segedunum
(Walls End)

Corstopitum
(Corbridge)

HADRIAN'S WALL

Luguvallium
(Carlisle)

(Chester-le-Street)

Ituna Aest.

Uxellodunum
(Maryport)

Brocavum
(Brougham)

Bravoniacun
(Kirkby Thore)

Vinovia

Veterae
(Brough)

Lavatrae

(Ravenglass)

Caractonium
(Catterick Bridge)

BRIGANTES

PARISII

OCEANUS
GERMANICUS

Monapia

(Lancaster)

Isurium

Eburacum
(York)

Olicana
(Ilkley)

Calcaria
(Tadcaster)

OCEANUS
HIBERNICUS

Bremetennaeum
(Ribchester)

Mancunium
(Manchester)

Abus Fl.

Wigan
(Warrington)

Seteia
Aest.

Danum
(Doncaster)

MELANDRA
CASTLE

Mona

Canovium

(Buxton)

Sherwood
Forest

Lindum
(Lincoln)

Seaontium
(Carnarvon)

Deva (Chester)

CORNAVII

CORITAVI

Metaris Aest.
(The Wash)

Branodunum
(Brancester)

ORDOVICES

Causennae
(Ancaster)

Venta Icenorum

Vernentetum

Viroconium
(Wroxeter)

Letocetum

WATLING STREET

RYKNIELD WAY

FOSSE WAY

Ratae
(Leicester)

CENTI

Forest
of Arden

Venonae

Rockingham
Forest

Durobrivae

ERMINE STREET

TRINOBANTES

ICKNIELD WAY

Magnae

DEMETAE

SILURES

Gobannium
(Abergavenny)

Glevum
(Gloucester)

Venta
Silurum

DOBUNI

Camulodunum
(Colchester)

Octapitarum Pr.

Mariduniun
(Carmarthen)

ATREBATES

Corinium
(Cirencester)

AKEMAN STREET

CATIVELLAUNI

Verulamium
(St. Albans)

Londinium

Isca
(Caerleon)

FOSSE WAY

WATLING STREET

ICKNIELD WAY

Durobrivae
(Rochester)

Tamesa

Regulbium
(Reculver)

Sabrina Aest (Severn)

Aquae Sulis
(Bath)

BELGAE

Cunetio

Calleva Atrebatum
(Silchester)

CANTII

Durovernum
(Canterbury)

Rutupiae
(Richborough)

Herculis Pr.

Ilchester

Sorbiodunum
(Salisbury)

Venta Belgarum
(Winchester)

ANDERIDA SILVA

Dubrae
(Dover)

DUROTRIGES

Isca Dumnoniorum
(Exeter)

Durnovaria
(Dorchester)

Portus Magnus
Clausentum

REGNI

Regnum
(Chichester)

Dortus

Lemanae
(Lymne)

Anderida
(Pevensey)

DAMNONII

Vectis

LITTUS SAXONICUM

Bolerium Pr.   Ocrinum Pr.

OCEANUS BRITANNICUS

MAPS OF CHANGING BRITAIN – ROMAN BRITAIN TO THE NORMAN CONQUEST

Map 2

THE
ENGLISH
CONQUEST
OF
BRITAIN

Scale 1 : 6,000,000

English Miles

0   100

APPROXIMATE	...in 550	
EXTENT OF	...in 600	
ENGLISH	...in 650	
CONQUEST...	...in 800	

Edinburgh

Tweed

Clyde

STRATHCLYDE

BERNICIA

Holy I.

GALLOWAY

CUMBRIA

Heavenfield

Eden

Wearmouth

Tees

Whitby

CLEVE-
LAND

DEIRA

Man

Ribble

Mersey

ELMET

York

Ouse

Aire

GAINAS

LINDISWARA

IRISH SEA

NORTH
SEA

Anglesey

Chester

Faddiley

PECSAETAN

Derby

Nottingham

Lincoln

Elmham

NORTH
WALES

Maserfield

MERCIANS

Trent

Leicester

MIDDLE
ANGLES

Nen

Crowland

NORTH
GYRWAS

NORTH
FOLK

Dunwich

MAGESAETAN

Severn

Ouse

SOUTH
GYRWAS

EAST ANGLES

SOUTH
FOLK

Gloucester

Usk

HWICCAS

Cirencester

Burford

Bampton

SOUTH
ANGLES

Dorchester

Bensington

Bedford

Colchester

EAST
SAXONS

Wanborough

MIDDLE
SAXONS

London

Deorham

Avon

Barbury Hill

Wimbledon

SURREY

Crayford

Aylesford

Canterbury

Ebbsfleet

SUMORSAETAN

Parret

WELSAETAN

Gharford

WEST SAXONS
(GEWISSAE)

Winchester

MEONWARA

CANTWEARA

SOUTH SAXONS

WEST WALES

Exe

DORSAETAN

Wight

Pevensey
(Anderida)

ENGLISH CHANNEL

MAPS OF CHANGING BRITAIN – ROMAN BRITAIN TO THE NORMAN CONQUEST

Map 3

ENGLAND
IN THE
EIGHTH
CENTURY

Scale 1 : 6,000,000

English Miles

0   100

PICTS

Edinburgh   LOTHIAN

Clyde   Tweed   BERNICIA   Lindisfarne
                                                Bamburgh

STRATHCLYDE   NORTHUMBRIA

GALLOWAY   Tyne   Jarrow

Carlisle   Hexham

Whithorn   Eden   DEIRA   Whitby

CUMBRIA

Tees

Man   Ouse   York

                    Ribble   Aire

IRISH SEA   Humber   NORTH
                                                        SEA

                    Mersey

Anglesey   Dore   LINDSEY
                                    Lincoln   The Wash
        Chester   Elmham
            Dee   Derby   Nottingham   EAST
                                                        ANGLIA
        Maserfield   MERCIA   Trent

NORTH WALES   Lichfield   Leicester   Stamford   Dunwich

OFFA'S DYKE   Tamworth   Bury St. Edmunds
        Bridgnorth   Severn   Nen   Ouse   Witham
                                                                ESSEX
        Wye   MAGE-   Cirencester   Burford   Chelmsford
                SAETAS   Oxford   MIDDLE   London
            Gloucester   HWICCAS   Bensington   -SEX
    Usk   Canterbury   Sandwich
Deorliam   Merton   KENT   Dover
Chippenham   Ashdown   Englefield   Reading   Ockley
                Avon   Ethandun   Basing   SUSSEX
    Wedmore   Winchester
WESSEX   Wilton   Chichester   Pevensey
Glastonbury   Parret
Athetney
        Exe   Avon
Tintagel   Exeter   Dorchester   Wight

Tamar

WEST WALES   Hengest's
                Dun   ENGLISH CHANNEL

MAPS OF CHANGING BRITAIN – ROMAN BRITAIN TO THE NORMAN CONQUEST

Map 4

ENGLAND
AT THE
TREATY OF WEDMORE
OR CHIPPENHAM

Scale 1 : 6,000,000

English Miles

0   100

STRATHCLYDE

Edinburgh

Clyde

Tweed

Lindisfarne
Bamburgh

GALLOWAY

Brunanburh?

ENGLISH NORTHUMBRIA

Tyne

Carlisle

Hexham

CUMBRIA

Eden

Tees

Brunanburh?

DANISH NORTHUMBRIA

Man

Ribble

Ouse

York

IRISH SEA

Aire

Humber

NORTH
SEA

Manchester

Mersey

Trent

Lincoln

The Wash

Runcorn

Elmham

Anglesey

GWYNEDD

Eddisbury

Chester

Derby

Nottingham

EAST
ANGLIA

Dee

Watling

Shrewsbury

Lichfield

Brunanburh?

Nen

Dunwich

WALES

POWYS

Tettenhall

Tamworth

Leicester

Stamford

Bridgnorth

Severn

Warwick

Bedford

Ouse

GUTHRUM'S
KINGDOM

ENGLISH

Hereford

Wye

Towcester

DANISH MERCIA

Leighton
Buzzard

Lea

Hertford

MERCIA

Gloucester

Oxford

Malden

Brecon

Cirencester

London

Usk

Bristol

Chippenham

Kingston

Watchet

Wedmore

Avon

WESSEX

Rochester

Canterbury

Dover

Glastonbury

Exe

Parret

Winchester

Pevensey

Tamar

Exeter

Dorchester

Avon

Chichester

CORNWALL

Wight

ENGLISH CHANNEL

Map 5

SUDREYS

Edinburgh
Clyde
LOTHIAN
Carham
Tweed

SCOTLAND

BERNICIA
Chester-le-Street

Holy Island
Bamburgh

ENGLAND
ON THE EVE OF THE
NORMAN
CONQUEST

Scale 1 : 6,000,000
English Miles
0   100

CUMBRIA

NORTHUMBRIA (MORCAR)

Eden

WESTMORLAND

Tyne
Jarrow
Durham
Tees

Man

Ribble

Derwent
Stamford
Bridge
Ouse
York
Fulford
Tadcaster
Ricall

IRISH SEA

NORTH
SEA

Humber

Manchester
Mersey

Aire
Don

Gains-
borough

Anglesey

NORTH WALES

Chester
Dee

MERCIA

Lincoln

Derby
Nottingham

The Wash

EAST
ANGLIA

Norwich
Thetford

Stafford
Shrewsbury

(EDWIN)
Trent
Leicester
Stamford

Nen
Ely
Huntingdon

Teifi

Coventry
Warwick
Worcester
Avon

WASTHEOF
Northampton

Ouse

GYRTH

Ringmere

Leominster
Wye
Hereford
Usk

Bedford
Ipswich

LEOFWINE

Towy

Gloucester

Hertford
Maldon
Waltham
London

F.field
Oxford
Brentford
Thames

Sherston
Wallingford

Thanet

Bristol
Avon

WESSEX
(HAROLD)

Otford

Sandwich
Canterbury
Dover

Watchet

Wedmore
Wells

Penselwood
Avon
Winchester

Battle

Hastings
Pevensey

Glastonbury
Parret

Tamar
Exe
Exeter

Southampton
Bosham

Wight

ENGLISH CHANNEL

Admiral Lord Viscount Horatio Nelson
(1758–1805)

HORATIO NELSON was born at the rectory of the village of Burnham Thorpe, in Norfolk.

He entered the Royal Navy at the age of twelve, in 1770, joining the *Raisonnable* as a midshipman. Despite famously beginning every voyage with seasickness, he would spend thirty of the next thirty-five years at sea.

After the *Raisonnable*, he served as midshipman on the *Triumph* and the *Seahorse*, travelling to the Caribbean and the Arctic. His next voyage was to India, where he picked up a bout of malaria and had to be sent home. It would leave him with recurrent partial paralysis for the rest of his life. Despite this setback to his health, he passed for Lieutenant on 9 April 1777, two years after the American War of Independence had begun.

In September 1778, Nelson was made first lieutenant of the *Bristol* and in the same year, France allied with American rebels against Britain. With Britain at war, Nelson was appointed commander of the sloop *Badger* in December and made captain at the astonishingly young age of twenty, in June 1779.

He served in the American war before returning to the Caribbean to enforce sanctions on the new American states. He interpreted the law rigidly, which earned him the dislike of both traders and local governors. However, attempts to have Nelson removed came to nothing after he petitioned the Admiralty and George III directly in defence of his actions. On the Island of Nevis, he met and married Frances (Fanny) Nisbet.

This first stage of Nelson's life could easily have set the pattern for the rest. His relationship with the Admiralty had suffered during his time in the Caribbean – and even the King was unhappy at Nelson's association with his disreputable son, Prince William Henry. For five years, Nelson was 'beached' – on half pay and unable to find himself a command. If war with revolutionary France had not come in 1792, he may well have remained in that state for the rest of his career.

In January 1793, he was appointed in command of the *Agamemnon* and sent out to the Mediterranean fleet under Lord Hood and then Admiral Hotham. At first, Nelson was not pleased to be given a 64-gun ship-of-the-line as he believed his seniority entitled him to command a 74. However, he was very impressed at the *Agamemnon*'s agile handling – in part the result of a complete refit and a new copper bottom.

The *Agamemnon* was one of fourteen ships sent to intercept a French convoy early in 1795. When the two fleets came within sight of each other, the French decided to withdraw, but two of them collided in the excitement. The *Ca Ira* came off worse from the impact and visibly lost speed.

Nelson saw his chance and attacked the 84-gun ship, giving her a whole broadside from close range, with each gun double shotted. He continued to pound the French ship for two hours, sweeping back and forth across her stern. At that point, Admiral Hotham signalled for Nelson to disengage, rather than lose him to French ships returning to save their stricken colleague. The incident went a long way to associate the name of Nelson with quick thinking and excellent seamanship.

Nelson was given the task of securing Corsica as a base for the Royal Navy. This too was a successful endeavour, though he was blinded in the right eye by a stone splinter from a parapet struck by an enemy shell. Despite this injury, he returned to duty the following day.

The Battle of Cape St Vincent (1797) involved fifteen British ships of the line defeating twenty-seven Spanish ships of similar power. As more and more Spanish vessels appeared on the horizon, Admiral Jervis told Captain Calder to stop counting them out loud, saying, 'Enough, sir, no more of that, the die is cast and if there are fifty sail I will go through them.'

The fleets met off the coast of Portugal as the Spanish ships were making a run for Cadiz. With a straight thrust, Admiral Jervis split the Spanish line, then ordered his ships to tack in succession (turn into the wind) to prevent the gap being closed. Nelson was last but two in the line and saw that the manoeuvre could not be completed fast enough to prevent the Spanish escaping. He made a decision to disobey orders and turn his ship, HMS *Captain*, into the gap. In doing so, he took fire from seven Spanish ships, including the largest in the world, the 130-gun *Santissima Trinidad*. Despite heavy damage, losing the wheel and part of his masts, he led a boarding party onto the *San Nicolas* and then immediately across her to the *San Josef*, entangled and damaged on the opposite side. Nelson's cry was 'Westminster Abbey or glorious victory!' and in this way, he captured two Spanish ships of the line. He took the surrender of the Spanish captains and remained on board, cheered by every British ship that passed. His extraordinary part in the battle was later humorously referred to as 'Nelson's patent bridge for boarding enemy vessels'.

Nelson had distinguished himself again, this time as commodore, with captains under him. Despite his seniority, he had taken a huge risk in 'interpreting' orders received from Admiral Jervis. If he had failed, he could well have been court-martialled, but the Spanish fleet was smashed: outsailed, outgunned, outfought. Jervis was generous in his praise.

Nelson's great friend Captain Cuthbert Collingwood was there, as was Thomas Hardy, not yet a captain, in the ship *Minerve*. HMS *Victory* was also present as the flagship of the Admiral. Nelson was knighted as a result of this success and promoted to rear-admiral.

In the same year, his right arm was shattered during a failed attempt to capture Spanish treasure ships in the Canary Islands. It was amputated without anaesthetic. The following year, in 1798, Nelson took his ship across the Mediterranean in pursuit of the French fleet that had landed Napoleon in Egypt. The Battle of the Nile is one of Nelson's most impressive and crucial actions.

The Battle of the Nile

Napoleon had taken control of Alexandria on 2 July 1798. He revered its founder, Alexander the Great, and it must have been a moment of special glory for him to be in that ancient place. His army pushed on to take Cairo by 24 July. Nelson was in Syracuse on the east coast of Sicily when he heard the news of the French fleet's whereabouts in Aboukir Bay off the western mouth of the Nile. He put to sea immediately and on 1 August, a British lookout sighted the French at anchor. The French fleet had landed guns to defend their anchorage and felt themselves secure. What was to follow would deny Napoleon his chance of an eastern empire and cripple him at sea. In a very real sense, the future of the world pivoted on one man at that moment. It is possible there would not have been a British Empire to resist the Nazi machine 150 years later if Nelson had lost in Egypt.

The French fleet consisted of four frigates and thirteen ships of the line, including Napoleon's own 120-gun flagship, the *Orient*. Under Admiral Brueys, they were anchored close to shore and were ready to fight at anchor, gaining the advantage of a steady firing platform. They had even dismounted cannon from the land side to fire out to sea.

In contrast, Nelson had thirteen ships of the line. He attacked as darkness fell, his ships cutting *between* the French fleet and the shore. The French were thrown into confusion. Their guns and crews were all on the wrong side for the action and Nelson's captains hammered the enemy unmercifully. Within twenty minutes, the first three French ships had been silenced and the first five surrendered by eight o'clock.

During the battle, Nelson was struck by flying iron, tearing free a flap of skin that blinded his one good eye for a time. Seeing him stunned and bleeding copiously, his officers led him below, believing he was dying. He too considered the possibility and prepared letters to be sent to his wife. He refused treatment ahead of his men, and by the time he was finally stitched, news came that the *Orient* was on fire. Nelson insisted on being helped up on deck once more.

The *Orient*'s magazine exploded around ten o'clock that evening, an explosion that could be heard thirteen miles away in Alexandria. The French Admiral Brueys was amongst the dead. Nelson sent his only undamaged boat to pick up survivors, though the battle would not finish until the afternoon of the following day.

Not a single British ship was lost and only 218 killed. The French losses are estimated at around 1,700, with 3,000 more taken as prisoners. Nelson was made a baron and became an English hero. The French fought on to the very end, but of the seventeen ships that had faced the British in the beginning, only four survived, withdrawn by Admiral Villeneuve, a man who had a part yet to play in Nelson's life.

By 1801, Lord Nelson sailed with the fleet to Copenhagen as second in command to Admiral Sir Hyde Parker. The fleet had been sent to Denmark to break the armed neutrality of the Baltic states. Nelson entered the action on board HMS *Elephant*, with Thomas Foley as Captain and Captain Thomas Hardy present as a volunteer. The British ships engaged the Danish fleet and both sides took terrible losses. Famously, Parker sent Nelson the signal to disengage. When it was brought to his attention, Nelson put his telescope to his blind eye and claimed he could not see it. From this, the expression 'turning a blind eye' entered the language.

Another interesting presence is that of Captain William Bligh at the battle, in command of the 50-gun *Glatton*. Following his acquittal at court martial over the mutiny on the *Bounty*, Bligh had resumed active service.

The Danes fought with great courage against the veteran British fleet, but eventually succumbed and accepted Nelson's offer of a truce to spare them further losses. An armistice was quickly arranged and signed. Nelson was made a viscount for the part he had played. His old commanding officer, John Jervis, now Earl St Vincent, was among many who complimented Parker and Nelson in the Houses of Parliament. It was Jervis who said of the chances of a French invasion, 'I do not say they cannot come. I only say they cannot come by sea.'

Nelson was one of the most famous men in England at this point. When he walked to his ship before Trafalgar, people knelt in the street. Others held up their children to catch a glimpse. The bulk of French ships were blockaded in Cadiz in the south-west of Spain and Brest, the most westerly point of France, with the prowling British fleet beating up and down the Atlantic off the coasts, waiting for them. The chance to end the sea threat once and for all would come in 1805, off the coast of Spain.

Trafalgar

At Trafalgar, Nelson was in command of the fleet, with Collingwood as second and the Earl of Northesk third. The battle was fought on 21 October 1805, ever after known as Trafalgar Day. Nelson commanded twenty-seven ships of the line against thirty-three of the French equivalent. However, his gun crews could fire at twice the rate of the French and the British shooting was more accurate. Courage, gunnery and seamanship would prove decisive, as they had throughout the war.

In August 1805, Napoleon had written to his admirals: 'Come into the Channel. Bring our united fleet and England is ours... all will be over and six centuries of shame and insult will be avenged.' He had 90,000 men along the coast of France, but did not have the ships to take them across the English Channel. In desperation, he ordered Villeneuve out from Cadiz to engage the enemy.

Admiral Villeneuve came out on 20 October, watched by British frigate captains who signalled their movements in relays out to the main British force. Nelson wanted Villeneuve's ships and at first merely maintained a parallel

course southwards. Before the attack, Nelson arranged his fleet into two divisions. He led the first himself from the *Victory*, with Thomas Hardy as captain. Collingwood led the second division from the *Royal Sovereign*. Instead of sliding along the French line of ships, Nelson had decided to cut straight through it, as had proved so successful at Cape St Vincent. The French and Spanish fleet numbered thirty-three ships of the line, with 2,652 guns and 25,200 men. The British fleet had twenty-seven ships of the line, 2,178 guns and 17,076 men. The names of the British ships read like a litany of mythical and historical references: *Victory, Royal Sovereign, Britannia, Temeraire, Prince, Tonnant, Belleisle, Revenge, Mars, Neptune, Spartiate, Defiance, Conqueror, Defence, Colossus, Leviathan, Achille, Bellerophon, Minotaur, Orion, Swiftsure, Polyphemus, Africa, Agamemnon, Dreadnought, Ajax* and *Thunderer*.

Before the fleets joined, Nelson made his will, asking that his mistress Emma Hamilton be well treated and that his daughter Horatia use only the name Nelson, so that his surname would be remembered. He was a devout man, as might be expected from the son of a Church of England rector. His diary records the prayer he wrote that morning, recorded for posterity.

> May the Great God, whom I worship, grant to my country and for the benefit of Europe in general a great and glorious victory, and may no misconduct in anyone tarnish it, and may humanity after victory be the predominant feature in the British Fleet. For myself individually, I commit my life to Him who has made me and may His blessing light upon my endeavours for serving my country faithfully. To Him I resign myself and the just cause which is entrusted me to defend. Amen, amen, amen.

As mentioned in the Naval Flag Codes chapter, Nelson intended to send the signal 'Nelson confides that every man will do his duty.' He accepted 'England' as a change and then 'expects', as it was in the code book as a single flag, and so would be quicker. The final signal was 'England expects that every man will do his duty', which caused his friend Captain Collingwood to say 'What *is* Nelson signalling about? We all know what we have to do.'

The first shot of the battle was fired at the *Royal Sovereign*, who raked her attacker, a Spanish three-decker named the *Santa Anna*. The British squadrons bore the French guns without being able to reply as they approached the wide enemy line, but at last they were in amongst them and the air screamed with shot. The *Victory* was attacked by five ships, but fought her way through with the *Temeraire* in support. Nelson and Hardy didn't move from the quarterdeck, though Hardy's shoe buckle was dented by a splinter. The air was filled with smoke to such a degree that they were practically blind. Nelson certainly did not see the sniper on the French ship *Redoutable* aiming at his distinctive uniform. Nelson was hit and Hardy held him as he collapsed.

Nelson was carried below, pausing only to order the tiller ropes of the *Victory* adjusted. He was bleeding internally and had a musket bullet lodged in his spine. He told the doctor that he had felt it break his back and knew he was dying. The chaplain came to him and Nelson reminded him he had left a will and that his daughter and mistress, Emma Hamilton, were to be looked after. It was a world removed from the chaos topside, with French ships being hammered and striking their colours to the British fleet. Nelson asked for his old friend Hardy to come down to him. Hardy was in the thick of commanding the *Victory* and could not leave command for another hour. When he did arrive, he was shocked to see Nelson's condition. Nelson asked Hardy to send his personal effects to Emma Hamilton.

Despite having lost more than a dozen ships of the line, a French attack on the *Victory* was under way and Hardy was called back on deck.

The surgeon confirmed to Nelson that there was nothing he could do.

When Hardy returned an hour later, the battle was won. Nelson's captains and crews had carried the day. Nelson asked Hardy again and again to look after Lady Hamilton after his death. Then he said the famous words, 'Kiss me, Hardy', and Hardy kissed him on the cheek. Nelson murmured, 'Now I am satisfied. Thank God I have done my duty'. Hardy stooped and kissed him again on the forehead and Nelson called out, 'Who is that?' 'It is Hardy,' the captain replied. 'God bless you, Hardy.' Death did not come with great swiftness for Nelson and he continued to speak to those around him, mentioning again and again that Emma Hamilton and his daughter should be looked after.

It is an interesting point that having Hardy kiss him goodbye was never questioned until rather prim Victorians suggested he might have said 'kismet'. It is true that the words were almost unintelligible and that Nelson was only partly coherent from his wound. However, he was a man who inspired fanatical loyalty and love from his band of brothers. Hardy had been with him almost from the beginning and would have seen nothing wrong in kissing the great man farewell as he went where they could not follow at last.

His tomb is exactly under the centre point of St Paul's dome in London. The wooden coffin inside was made from the timbers of Napoleon's flagship, the *Orient*. Nelson actually had it with him on the Victory and kept it propped behind his desk.

To preserve his body, it was soaked in brandy and the coffin encased in lead. It lies in the crypt alongside Cuthbert Collingwood and other captains who fought on that day. Both men have monuments above ground and they share the crypt with another famous name from British history – Arthur Wellesley, Duke of Wellington.

BUILDING A WORKBENCH

—✱—

BEFORE WE COULD MAKE a number of the things in this book, it was obvious we needed a workbench. Even the simplest task in a workshop becomes difficult without a solid vice and a flat surface.

We kept this as simple as possible. Pine is easiest to cut, but it also breaks, dents and crushes, which is why classic workbenches are made out of beech – a very hard wood.

Complete beginners should start with pine, as mistakes are a *lot* cheaper. Planning is crucial – every table is different. Ours fitted the wall of the workshop and is higher than almost any workbench you'll ever see. Both of us are tall and prefer to work at a higher level. Draw the plan and have an idea of how much wood you will need.

The suppliers cut the wood square to save time and we spent two days cutting mortice and tenon joints before assembling it.

RULE: Measure twice and cut once. Carpentry is 80% care and common sense, 20% skill, or even artistry. You do not have to be highly skilled to make furniture, as long as you *never* lose your temper, plan carefully and practise, practise, practise. The reason a professional is better than an amateur is because the professional cuts joints every day.

MORTICE AND TENON JOINTS

A mortice is a trench cut into wood. The tenon is the piece that fits into the trench.

NOTE: Using sharp tools is not to be undertaken lightly. A chisel will remove a finger as easily as a piece of wood. Don't try this unless you have an adult willing to show you the basics. There are hundreds of fiddly little things (like how to hold a chisel) that we couldn't fit in here.

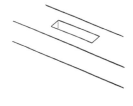

We started by making two rectangular frames to go at each end of the table workbench. This is a very simple design, but mortice and tenon joints are strong on the corners.

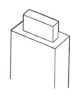

Make sure that the top of your tenon is not too close to the top of the upright. When it comes to cutting the mortice, you do not want to break through.

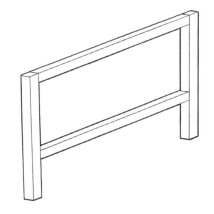

For simple 'through' joints, the tenon length is the same as the width of the upright. To create the tenon, you have to make four saw cuts (accurately!) down to a marked line that is equal to the depth of the upright. In the picture, only the middle rectangle will remain. After the four cuts, you saw away the waste pieces and use a chisel to trim any splinters or roughness.

When you have your tenons cut, number them in pencil. Use the tenons as the template for the mortice trenches, also numbered. We also pencilled a cross on the top side so we wouldn't lose track. Obviously, they should all be identical, but it's odd how often they aren't. Mark the mortices with extreme care, taking note of the exact position. The first upright will be relatively easy, but the second has to be absolutely identical – and that's where the problems creep in.

Next, cut the mortice. Great care is needed here – and some skill with the chisel. Take care also not to crush the edges as you lever backwards. Ideally, you should use a chisel as wide as the mortice itself – though some prefer to use narrower blades.

Once you have your pair of end pieces, you need bars running lengthways to prevent wobble. We used mortice and tenons again, as the beech joints seemed easily strong enough for our needs.

In the picture, you can see that we put both beams on one side. We wanted to have access for storage underneath, so we left the front open.

The rope arrangement in the picture is called a 'windlass'. It is used when a piece of furniture is too long to be clamped. Most tables will have this problem and it's good to know you can overcome it with nothing more than a double length of rope and a stick to twist it tighter and tighter. The same technique has even been used to pull wooden ships out of the sea. Be sure to protect the wood with cloth, or you'll cut grooves into your uprights.

The top planks can be glued together if they have perfect edges, or simply screwed in place. The simplest possible method is to screw down into the end pieces, but this does leave ugly screw heads visible. We used a corner piece underneath, screwing across into the end piece and also up into the underside of the top. It worked well enough for our purposes.

To finish, we sanded like madmen for the best part of a day, used filler for the gaps we could not explain in the joints, then wiped it all over with linseed oil. The oil soaked in very nicely to seal the wood – just in case we spill paint on it in the future.

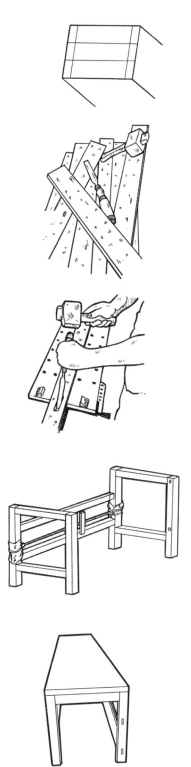

THE STEADY-HAND TIN

THIS IS AN EXTREMELY simple circuit toy that will be instantly recognisable. It is also fun – and portable. You will need a tobacco tin – and they're not easy to find these days. Ask at car-boot sales, or badger the elderly. Try to get more than one, in fact, as they are fantastically useful.

> **You will need**
>
> - A battery – ideally one of the square 9V ones.
> - A torch bulb.
> - Two pieces of bare wire about the length of a ruler.
> - Duct tape.

If you have access to a soldering iron, soldered connections are more reliable, but this can be made without.

1. Attach one wire to the positive terminal of the battery (+). If you do use a soldering iron, make sure the battery is firmly held and don't rush – it isn't easy to place a blob of solder where you want it without it cooling down too fast.

2. Attach the end of the other wire to the end of the bulb, as in the picture. We soldered it.

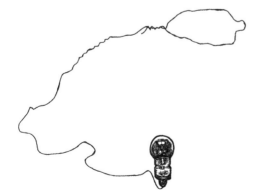

Using small strips of tape, you could hold it steady, but try not to cover the barrel of the bulb – you'll need it for the last connection. Make a loop out of the other end, as shown.

3. Attach the barrel of the bulb to the other terminal. Note that the bulb should go sideways rather than be pointing up, or the tin might not close properly. This a good point to try the circuit. With the bulb in contact with the anode (–), the bulb should light when the wires touch. If it doesn't, check every connection – and make sure the bulb works.

You now have a circuit that will light a bulb when two wires touch. Install it in the tin with more tape.

To use, bend one wire into an assault course of curves and use the loop to go from one end to the other without touching. Here is where you need the steady hand. The whole thing can be carried in a pocket.

There is a slight chance the wires will form a circuit through the metal of the tin, so it's not a bad idea to line it with the tape. At the time of writing, ours has lasted more than a year without breaking or the battery wearing out – despite regular use.

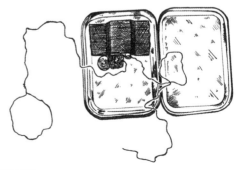

FIVE PEN AND PAPER GAMES

1. HANGMAN

This is the classic word game for two or more players. Think of a word and mark out the number of letters in dashes – – – – – – –. The other player guesses letters one at a time. If they guess correctly, write the letter. If they get one wrong, draw a line of the hanged man and write the letter on the page. Incorrect guesses of the whole word also cost a line.

There are twelve chances to get the word right. If the hanged man is completely finished, they lose. Take it in turns and try some really hard words, like 'paella', or 'phlegm'.

2. HOUSES

This one is silly, but enjoyably frustrating. It looks very easy. Draw six boxes anywhere on the page. Mark three of them with G, E and W – Gas, Water and Electricity. Number the others 1, 2 and 3. The object of this puzzle is to provide vital services to the three numbered houses. You do this by drawing a pipe line from one to the other. Lines are not allowed to cross and they may not go through a house or a service station.

In the example, you can see one of the houses has Gas and Water but no Electricity. Try moving the squares around but remember you are not allowed to cross any lines. This puzzle looks possible, but it actually isn't. No matter where you put the boxes you cannot connect all three services without crossing a line. It is perfect to give to someone who thinks they are

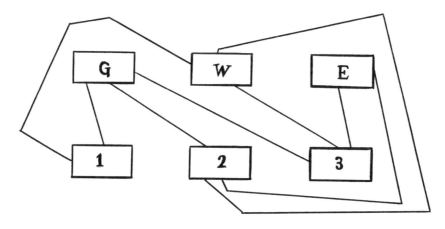

really clever (like an elder brother). It will completely fox them. Pretend you know the answer, refuse to tell them and watch them struggle. (There is a cheating way to complete the puzzle. You take the last pipe line out to the edge of the paper, run it back on the other side and then punch a hole through to the house. This does not impress onlookers.)

3. SQUARES

This is a very simple game for two players that can be fiendishly difficult to win. Draw a grid of dots on a piece of paper, say nine by nine or ten by ten. Each player can draw a line between two dots as his or her turn. The aim is to close a box, making a square. If you can do this, you get another go.

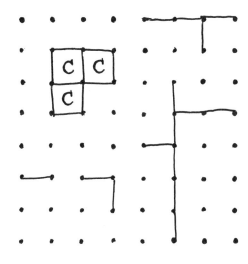

The game tends to follow a pattern of easy steps as most of the lines are filled, then sudden chains of boxes made, one after the other, until the grid is complete. It may be a good idea to sacrifice a small line of boxes so that a larger one is yours. Mark the boxes clearly so they can be counted – either with different colours or a symbol. The player with most boxes at the end wins.

4. BATTLESHIPS.

This is a classic. Two grids are drawn, with x and y axes numbered 1–10 and A–J. Larger grids will make the game last longer. Draw ships on your grid – an aircraft carrier of five squares, a battleship of four, two destroyers of three, a submarine of two and another cruiser of two. Any reasonable combination is possible as long as both players agree.

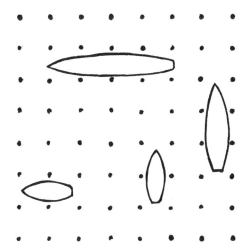

Once these have been drawn in private, each player then calls out shots in turn, using the grid references – A4, C8 and so on. The aim is to sink your opponent's ships before yours are sunk.

An interesting alternative is to replace the ships with words chosen by each player – of two letters, three letters and so on. The aim is still to find and 'sink' the words, but with a score of five points for every word – or *ten* points if the word can be guessed before the last letter is hit. The winner then is the one with the most points at the end.

Another one that looks easy, but is in fact fiendish. Begin by drawing a grid – school exercise books always make these things easier, which may be why an awful lot of these games are played at school.

Three by three is not enough of a challenge, but will do for the explanation. Five by five is much better.

The player using *O* fills in two corners, while the opponent puts an *X* in the other two. Decide who moves first by flipping a coin.

Each player can only place a symbol on adjacent squares to the ones he already has. You can't 'move' diagonally.

Any of the opponent's adjacent symbols are changed into yours by the move – including diagonals. In diagram number 2 it would make sense for *O* to put one in the middle-right square.

You'll need an eraser! The *X* in the corner will be erased and turned into an *O*.

Of course, now *X* can respond. If they put their *X* in the middle of the top row, it will win two more *X* squares.

…and so on. In fact, *O* must win this one.

The game ends when one player has nothing left, or when the grid is filled. This is just a taster. With larger grids, the game can be fascinating and complex.

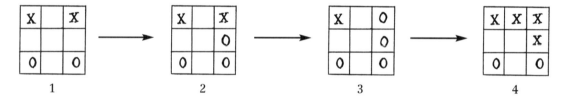

THE GOLDEN AGE OF PIRACY

THERE HAVE BEEN PIRATES for as long as ships have sailed out of sight of land and law. The period known as 'the golden age' of piracy began in the seventeenth century and continued into the early eighteenth. The discovery of the new world and vast wealth there for the taking caused an explosion of privateers – some, like Francis Drake, with the complete authority and knowledge of Queen Elizabeth I.

The word 'buccaneer' comes from European sailors who caught wild pigs on the islands of Haiti and Tortuga in the Caribbean and smoked the meat on racks to preserve it. The French '*boucaner*' means to dry meat in this fashion. The men referred to themselves as the 'Brethren of the Coast' and it is from their number that the most famous names came, like Calico Jack Rackham and Blackbeard. Perhaps the most astonishing thing about the golden age is the fact that many pirates were given pardons, sometimes in exchange for military aid or a cut of the loot. The Welsh privateer Henry Morgan was not only pardoned, but knighted by Charles II, made acting Governor of Jamaica, a vice-admiral, Commandant of the Port Royal Regiment, a Judge of the Admiralty Court and a Justice of the Peace!

Although the skull and crossbones, or 'Jolly Roger', is by far the most famous pirate flag, there were different versions and many other flags that would send fear into the hearts of merchant sailors and their captains. Here is a selection of the most famous, as well as the men who sailed under them.

Walter Kennedy

Bart Roberts

Henry Every

Edward England

Richard Worley

Christopher Moody

Stede Bonnet

Edward Low

Bart Roberts (2nd Flag)

Jack Rackam

Blackbeard (Edward Teach)

Emanuel Wynne

Thomas Tew

Christopher Condent

A SIMPLE ELECTROMAGNET

AN ELECTROMAGNET is just a copper coil with a current running through it. The classic use is the junkyard crane, lifting cars into the crusher. Ours lifted two iron screws.

You will need a few feet of copper wire and something iron to wrap it around – a piece of metal coat hanger or a nail. You will also need a battery and preferably one of the plastic battery holders you can see in the picture. Model shops sell them for very little. It is possible to attach batteries to a circuit using no more than duct tape and elastic bands, but it's fiddly and the connections are unreliable.

1. Insulate the iron nail with tape. It still works without, but the battery terminals heat up and can burn.

2. Wrap the copper wire round the nail, leaving a few inches of the first end free to attach to the battery later. The more turns of wire, the stronger the magnet, so use the longest length you can find. The one in the picture has more than one layer of wire, up then down the rod. Each layer should be insulated from the next with electrician's tape.

3. Make a switch if you like – it's less fiddly than poking wires through the battery terminals, even when you have a holder. We used a couple of black screws – one attached to positive (+), one to negative (–). It is crucial to complete the circuit, or this won't work.

Now use the iron tip to pick up paperclips! In theory, with enough wire, or stronger batteries, the magnet could become quite powerful – a car battery would work very nicely – and then you have applications like dangling the magnet into dark spaces to retrieve screws and iron tools.

SECRET INKS

ANYTHING ORGANIC (animal-based) that is clear or almost clear can be used as a heat-activated secret ink. Put simply, being organic means it contains carbon and carbon things will burn. Milk, lemon juice, egg white and, yes, urine will work as a secret ink. In the picture, we used milk.

In our first attempt we wrote a sentence down the side of a letter. Unless you were looking for it, it wasn't easy to see. The letter on top helped to disguise it. We let this dry and then applied a flame directly to the hidden words. Try to avoid setting fire to the paper or your clothing. The letters appeared as if by magic.

You can read the words 'the army lands at midnight'. Though it sounds very dramatic, this is a clumsy sort of message. Far better to have your spy waiting for a time, then put 'mid' somewhere on the piece of paper. That would be much harder to find.

The trouble with this sort of thing is that the cover letter must look real, but not so real that your spy doesn't look for the secret message. As with the section on codes, some things work better with a little planning. Invent a sister – and then they will know that every letter that mentions the sister by name contains secret words.

Secret inks allow you to send confidential information by post. If it's not expected, it's not at all likely to be spotted.

SAMPLING SHAKESPEARE

No writer of any age has come close to rivalling the creative genius of William Shakespeare. He was born in 1564, on 23 April – St George's Day, in Stratford-upon-Avon. Anyone alive should know *Macbeth*, *Romeo and Juliet*, *A Midsummer Night's Dream*, *King Lear*, *Othello* and *Hamlet*, or have seen them in a theatre.

Here are a few of the better-known quotations. Shakespeare has added countless commonly used phrases and words to English – so common in fact, that we often hardly recognise them as Shakespearean. He really did write 'I have not slept one wink' before anyone else, as well as 'I will wear my heart upon my sleeve' and hundreds more.

1.

What's in a name? that which we call a rose
by any other word would smell as sweet.

Romeo and Juliet, Act 2, Scene 2

2.

This royal throne of kings, this sceptered isle,
This earth of majesty, this seat of Mars,
This other Eden, demi-paradise,
This fortress built by Nature for herself
Against infection and the hand of war,
This happy breed of men, this little world,
This precious stone set in the silver sea,
Which serves it in the office of a wall,
Or as a moat defensive to a house,
Against the envy of less happier lands,
This blessed plot, this earth, this realm, this England.

Richard II, Act 2, Scene 1

3.

If music be the food of love, play on.

Twelfth Night, Act 1, Scene 1

4.

But screw your courage to the sticking-place,
And we'll not fail.

Macbeth, Act 1, Scene 7

5.

Out, out brief candle!
Life's but a walking shadow, a poor player

That struts and frets his hour upon the stage,
And then is heard no more; it is a tale
Told by an idiot, full of sound and fury,
Signifying nothing.

Macbeth, Act 5, Scene 5

6.

Cry 'Havoc!' and let slip the dogs of war.

Julius Caesar, Act 3, Scene 1

7.

Once more unto the breach, dear friends, once more;
Or close the wall up with our English dead!

Henry V, Act 3, Scene 1

8.

Neither a borrower, nor a lender be;
For loan oft loses both itself and friend.

Hamlet, Act 1, Scene 3

9.

All the world's a stage,
And all the men and women merely players.

As You Like It, Act 2, Scene 7

10.

Uneasy lies the head that wears a crown.

Henry IV, Part 2, Act 3, Scene 1

11.

The lady doth protest too much, methinks.

Hamlet, Act 3, Scene 2

12.

To be, or not to be: that is the question:
Whether 'tis nobler in the mind to suffer
The slings and arrows of outrageous fortune,
Or to take arms against a sea of troubles,
And by opposing end them?

Hamlet, Act 3, Scene 1

13.

Let me have men about me that are fat;
Sleek-headed men and such as sleep o'nights.
Yond Cassius has a lean and hungry look;
He thinks too much: such men are dangerous.

Julius Caesar, Act 1, Scene 2

SAMPLING SHAKESPEARE

14.
We are such stuff
As dreams are made on, and our little life
Is rounded with a sleep.
(Usually rendered as '...dreams are made of')

The Tempest, Act 4, Scene 1

✤

15.

Why, then the world's mine oyster,
Which I with sword will open.

The Merry Wives of Windsor, Act 2, Scene 2

✤

16.

I am a man
More sinn'd against than sinning.

King Lear, Act 3, Scene 2

✤

17.

There's a divinity that shapes our ends,
Rough-hew them how we will.

Hamlet, Act 5, Scene 2

✤

18.

There are more things in heaven and earth, Horatio,
Than are dreamt of in your philosophy.

Hamlet, Act 1, Scene 5

✤

19.

Something is rotten in the state of Denmark.

Hamlet, Act 1, Scene 4

✤

20.

Double, double toil and trouble;
Fire burn and cauldron bubble.

Macbeth, Act 4, Scene 1

✤

21.

Is this a dagger which I see before me,
The handle toward my hand?

Macbeth, Act 2, Scene 1

✤

22.

Yet do I fear thy nature;
It is too full o' the milk of human kindness.

Macbeth, Act 1, Scene 5

❋

23.

Why, man, he doth bestride the narrow world
Like a Colossus.

Julius Caesar, Act 1 Scene 2

❋

24.

Et tu, Brute!

Julius Caesar, Act 3, Scene 1

❋

25.

This was the most unkindest cut of all.

Julius Caesar, Act 3, Scene 2

❋

26.

Good-night, good-night! parting is such sweet sorrow.

Romeo and Juliet, Act 2, Scene 2

❋

27.

A plague o' both your houses!

Romeo and Juliet, Act 3, Scene 1

❋

28.

Now is the winter of our discontent.

Richard III, Act 1, Scene 1

❋

29.

We few, we happy few, we band of brothers.

Henry V, Act 4, Scene 3

❋

30.

I thought upon one pair of English legs
Did march three Frenchmen.

Henry V, Act 3, Scene 6

EXTRAORDINARY STORIES –
PART THREE

Touching the Void

In May 1985, two young English climbers set off to conquer the unclimbed west face of Siula Grande – a 21,000-foot (6,400 m) peak in the Andes. There are no mountain rescue services in such a remote region, but Joe Simpson (25) and Simon Yates (21) were experienced, confident and very fit. Their story is an extraordinary one. Apart from being made into a book and a film, it has inspired intense debate among that small group of expert climbers with experience enough to judge what happened.

The two men tackled the face in one fast push, roped together and taking everything they needed with them. They carried ice axes and wore boots with spikes (crampons), using ice screws and ropes for the ascent.

They climbed solidly that first day until darkness fell and they dug a snow cave and slept. All the second day, they climbed sheet ice, reaching 20,000 feet when high winds and a blizzard hit them on an exposed vertical slope. At that point, they were climbing flutes of powder snow, the most treacherous of surfaces and incredibly dangerous. It took five to six hours to climb just 200 feet in the dark before they found a safe place for a second snow cave.

The third morning began with a clear blue sky. By 2 p.m., they reached the north ridge at last – the first men ever to climb that face of Siula Grande. Both men felt exhausted after some of the hardest climbing of their lives, but they decided to follow the ridge towards the peak.

They reached it, but with the weather uncertain, they couldn't stay for long. Only half an hour into the descent, clouds came in and they were lost in a whiteout on the ridge, completely blind. On one side was a drop of thousands of feet and the ridge itself was made of overhanging cornices of snow that could break off under their weight. Yates saw the ridge through a break in the clouds and climbed back up to it. The cornice broke under his weight and he fell, saved by the rope attached to Simpson. He shouted up that he had found the ridge. In such conditions, progress was very slow. By the time darkness came, they were still at 20,000 feet.

The fourth day began with good weather once more. The two men came to a cut in the ridge and Simpson started to climb down a face of sheer ice. He hammered in one of his ice axes and didn't like the sound it made. As he pulled one out to get a better contact, the other gave way without warning and he fell.

He hit hard, his shinbone going through his knee and into the upper leg. As Yates climbed down, he tried to stand on it, appalled at the pain and grating of the bones. The two men looked at each other in desperation. Simpson expected his friend to leave him. There was no other choice – a broken leg so far from civilisation meant that he was dead. Instead, Yates stayed and they discussed a plan to lower Simpson on two ropes, knotted together. Yates would dig himself a seat in the snow and lower Simpson the first 150 feet. The knot wouldn't pass through the lowering device, so Simpson would dig in until Yates had retied it and could lower away once more.

The laborious process began, with Simpson face down. His broken leg jarred constantly, but it had to be fast as neither their endurance nor the light would last for long. Yates's snow seats crumbled quickly in the time it took to lower his friend. As the hours passed, a full storm hit the mountain with wind chill of −80 degrees. Darkness came upon them and both men were exhausted. They had no gas to make tea or get warm. They continued on in the dark, one rope at a time.

Simpson felt the powder snow change to hard ice and called out to stop. His voice wasn't heard and he slipped over the edge of an overhang, dangling below it. He couldn't reach a surface and, crucially, was unable to take his weight off the rope. Above him in the dark, Yates waited alone and freezing, with the wind roaring around him.

At first, Simpson attempted to climb back up the rope using a 'prussic loop', a knot that locks solid once pressure is applied. He needed two and managed to fix the first with frozen hands. The second one escaped his numb fingers and he watched it fall with his last hopes. He waited then to drag Yates to his death.

Yates waited and waited as his seat began to crumble under the unrelenting weight. All he could do was hang on until he began to slide down. He remembered he had a penknife and made a decision in an instant, using it to cut the rope. The rope snaked away and below the overhang, Simpson fell into darkness, losing consciousness. Yates dug himself a snow cave out of the storm and waited for daylight.

Simpson awoke in pitch blackness on a narrow slope, sliding. He had fallen more than a hundred feet into a crevasse, ending up on an ice ledge next to another drop into infinite darkness. He screwed in an ice screw anchor very quickly.

His helmet torch revealed the rope going up to a small hole eighty feet above. He thought Yates was on the end of it, dead. Simpson thought the rope would come tight on Yates' body. He pulled it to him and it fell. When he saw the end, he knew it had been cut and guessed what had happened. He was pleased

Yates was alive, but realised his own chances of survival had dropped to almost nothing.

In the dark, he turned off the torch to save the batteries. Alone, he despaired.

Yates continued to climb down the next day, feeling desperately guilty about cutting the rope. He lowered himself past the overhang and the crevasse, convinced that Simpson was dead. He went on numbly, following tracks back to the base camp that he had made with Simpson only days before.

When no one answered his shouts, Simpson tried to climb out of his crevasse, but eighty feet of sheer ice was impossible with only one working leg. He didn't believe anyone would ever find him. His only course seemed to be to sit and wait to die – or to lower himself into the crevasse to see if there was another way out in the darkness below. He took this terrifying decision, but didn't put a knot on the end of the rope. He decided that if he reached the end and there was nothing beneath him, he would rather fall than be stuck and slowly freeze.

Joe lowered himself eighty feet and found he was in an hourglass-shaped crevasse. He reached the pinch point and found a crust of snow there that had a chance of taking his weight. He heard cracking and movement beneath him, but there was light nearby, at the top of a slope he thought he could climb, bad leg or not. This was the way out.

Though every jarring step brought him close to fainting, he made it onto the mountainside to see a blue sky and bright sunshine. He lay there and laughed with relief at his deliverance.

After the initial exhilaration, he looked further down and realised that he still had miles of glacier to cross as well as a treacherous maze of crevasses. He thought at first that he couldn't

do it, but there was no point in simply sitting and waiting. He could see Yates' tracks and knew that they would lead him through the crevasse field.

He made progress sitting down, with his legs flat on the snow and pushing himself along backwards. Snow and high winds came again, and he kept going as darkness fell, terrified at losing sight of Simon's tracks.

The tracks had gone by the morning of the sixth day, but Simpson struggled on, reaching at last the jumbled boulders that meant the end of the glacier. He wrapped his sleeping mat around the broken leg, using his ice axes to try and support himself over the broken ground. He fell at almost every step and each fall was like breaking the leg again. Somehow, he kept going. He ate snow for water, but there was never enough to quench a brutal thirst. He could hear streams running under the rocks, but maddeningly he could not find them. He pushed himself on and on until he collapsed and lay looking at the sky as it grew dark once more.

As Day 7 dawned, he could barely move at first. He believed he was going to die, but kept crawling. He found a trickle of water and drank litres of it, feeling it make him stronger. Despite this, he was becoming delirious.

Simpson reached the lake by the camp by four in the afternoon of the seventh day. He knew the camp was in a valley at the far end, but he had no idea if Yates would be there. He tried to make faster progress, plagued by the thought that he would get there too late.

Clouds came down as the day progressed and by the time he looked into the valley, it was white with mist. He lay there for a long time, delirious and hallucinating. Eventually, he moved on as night fell and it began to snow once more.

He dragged himself through the latrine area of the camp and the sharp smell acted like smelling salts, bringing him back. He began to call for Yates and when no one came at first, he believed he had been left behind.

Yet Simon Yates had stayed and he woke as he heard his name called. When he heard his name again, he went out and began to search. He found his friend a couple of hundred yards from the camp and dragged him back to the tent. Yates could not believe it. He had cut the rope and seen the drop and the crevasse. He *knew* Simpson could not have survived.

As Joe Simpson became conscious, he sought to ease his friend's guilt. His first words were, 'Don't worry, I would have done the same.'

Adapted from *Touching the Void* by Joe Simpson, published by Jonathan Cape

GRINDING AN ITALIC NIB

ALTHOUGH THE PEN we used is an expensive model, this should absolutely not be tried with a valued pen. There is a reasonable chance of destroying the nib completely and the nib is usually the most expensive part to replace. The rest, after all, is just a tube.

The first thing to know is that *almost all* italic nibs are hand-ground. In theory, there is no reason why you should not be able to grind a nib to suit you, with a little common sense and care.

Before you begin, it is a good idea to get hold of an italic nib and try writing with it. The writing style is quite different and they tend to be 'scratchier'. It is extremely satisfying knowing you have ground your own nib – and the handwriting is attractive.

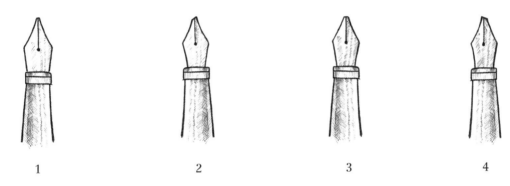

1   2   3   4

Picture 1 shows a standard nib. Picture 2 would be best suited to a left-handed writer. Picture 3 is suitable for both and 4 is best suited for right-handers. It's difficult to change from one to the other if you are not happy with the result – which is why you should try a shop-bought italic nib first.

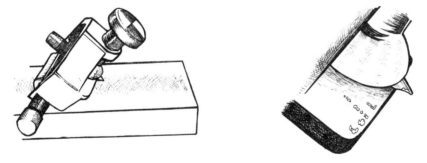

We used a sharpening gig – a useful little gadget that helps to hold chisels at the required angle. It can be done completely by hand, but no matter how you choose to do it, stop often, dip the nib in ink and try it out. Do not be discouraged by scratching at this stage. A fine sharpening stone will take longer, but as delicate as this is, it is probably a good idea.

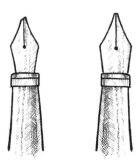

You should arrive somewhere near the nib on the left – if you are left-handed. It was identical to the nib on the right before grinding. Attempts at writing with the new angle were initially discouraging. Very fine sandpaper (or wet and dry paper) was needed to smooth away roughness and dust from the grindstone. It is a matter of personal preference how far you smooth the corners, but I found it helped the easy flow of ink.

All the King's horses and all the King's men

All the King's horses and all the King's men

NOTE: This is not italic or copperplate lettering. Those alphabets have to be learned, though they are based on the wide and narrow strokes of an italic nib.

NAVIGATION

THE FIRST THING TO understand is that a compass points north because it is magnetic and the earth has a magnetic field caused by the rotation of a liquid metal core. The magnetic north pole happens to correspond reasonably well with the true pole – but they are not the same. Magnetic south is off Antarctica and can be sailed over. Magnetic north is near the Canada/Alaska border. They are both very deep within the core of the planet and move over time.

If you are interested, a compass will actually jam on the magnetic poles as it tries to point either 'up' or 'down' – ninety degrees to the surface. A gyroscopic compass is invaluable in such circumstances – that is, a gyro that has been set to point north and then holds its position regardless of changes in direction. Pilots find gyroscopic compasses invaluable. The International Space Station (ISS) has thirteen of them.

Admiralty charts plot the lines of 'magnetic variation' across the globe, showing whether the variation from true north is to the east or west and increasing or decreasing. As you can imagine, this is crucial for navigation. A compass in New York will be approximately 14° W off true north. If you were plotting a course north, you would have to subtract 14 degrees from your compass direction. If the difference was 14° E, 14 degrees would have to be added.

The compass is the universal means of finding your position anywhere on the surface of the planet. The earth rotates east, so in *both* hemispheres, the sun rises in the east and sets in the west. It is true, however, that water swirls the other way down plugholes and toilets in the southern hemisphere.

The figure below shows the thirty-two points of the compass. In the northern hemisphere when the sun is at its highest point in the sky, it will be due south. In the southern hemisphere this noonday point will be due north.

KEY: Read the word 'by' for the symbol –, so N–NW is north *by* north west.

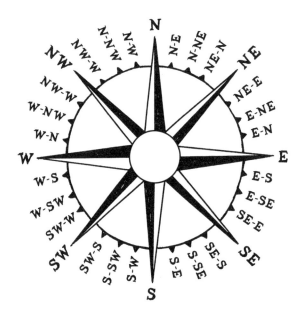

The hemisphere can be indicated by the movement of the shadow cast by the sun: clockwise in the north and anticlockwise in the south. This shadow can also be a guide to direction.

SHADOW STICK

Place a three-foot stick upright on flat ground and mark where the tip of the shadow falls – point 'a'.

Wait fifteen minutes and mark where the tip of the new shadow falls – point 'b'.

Now draw a line from 'a' to 'b' and you have east–west, 'a' being west. Dissect this line at right angles and you have north–south with 'a' on your right and 'b' on your left, you are facing south. This works in both hemispheres – feel free to heat your brains up trying to explain why.

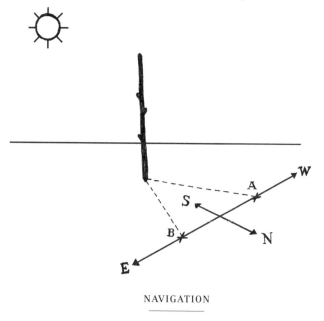

A watch with two hands can tell the direction. It must have the correct local time (excluding daylight saving: this is when you put the clocks back and forward – 'spring forward and fall back' – so in summer you should *subtract* an hour and in autumn *add* one to use this technique). The nearer to the Equator you are, the less accurate this is.

In the northern hemisphere, hold the watch horizontally. If it's summer, wind it back an hour; if it's winter, wind it on an hour. Point the hour hand at the sun. Bisect the angle between hour hand and 12 to give you a north–south line. In the southern hemisphere point 12 at the sun, and the mid point between 12 and the hour hand will give a north–south line.

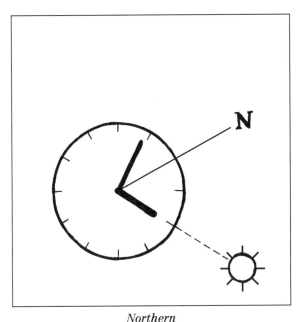

Northern

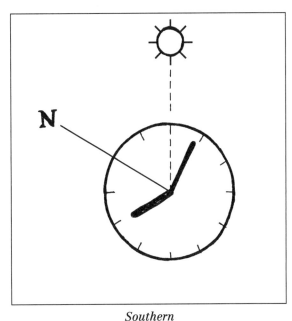

Southern

NEEDLE COMPASS

Get a piece of ferrous (meaning iron) wire – a sewing needle is ideal – and stroke it in one direction repeatedly against silk. This will magnetise it. Suspend the needle on a length of thread and it will point north.

Stroking the wire with a magnet in one direction will work better than silk. This aligns the atoms in the needle. Heating the needle also works, though not as reliably. Try it and see.

If you have no thread then you can also float the magnetised needle on a piece of tissue paper or bark on the surface of water and it will turn to indicate north.

An old-style razor blade can also be used as a compass needle. Rub it against the palm of your hand (carefully!) to magnetise it, then suspend it to get the north–south line.

Use as many methods as you can to get your bearings, then mark out your compass, check all your readings against the sun and keep your needle magnetised.

To find north in the night sky you need to find Polaris, the Pole Star. This is discussed in the Astronomy chapter. There are other indicators in the night sky which can be used. The rising of the moon can give a rough east–west reference. If the moon rises before the sun has set, the illuminated side will be on the west. If it rises after midnight, the illuminated side will be on the east.

Stars themselves can also be used to indicate direction. If you cannot find Polaris or the Southern Cross, get two sticks, one shorter than the other. Stick them in the earth and sight along them as shown to any star except the Pole Star. From the star's apparent movement, you can work out the direction you are facing!

If the star you are lined up on appears to be rising, you are facing east. If it appears to be

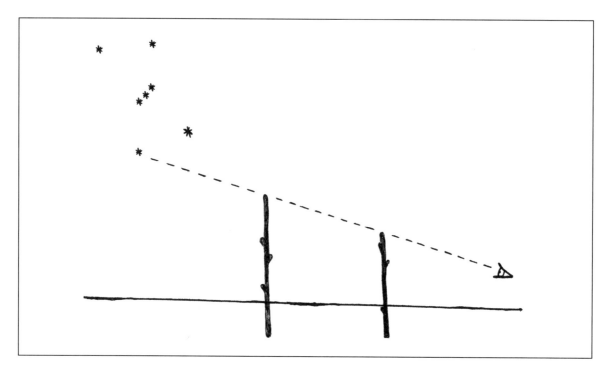

setting (or falling), you are facing west. If the star seems to move right then you are facing south and if it moves left, you are facing north. These are only approximate directions and will be reversed in the southern hemisphere.

Being able to find your bearings at any time of day and night is a pretty impressive thing to know, but try not to show off your knowledge. Keep it safe for a time when you may really need it. As the Scouts say, 'Be prepared'.

NAVAL FLAG CODES

I N 1800, *Telegraphic Signals, or Marine Vocabulary* was published by Sir Home Popham, a Royal Navy captain. Before this point, there were crude systems available, so that messages such as 'Enemy in Sight' could be passed along the ships of the line. Sir Home Popham's system was extremely simple to use.

Just ten flags could be used to represent all the letters of the alphabet. The first ten were shown by one flag. Each letter after could be shown by two flags read from the top down – 1 and 3 to make the thirteenth letter, for example. An extra flag was needed for nought to make numbers like 10 and 20. For added efficiency, Popham made the number 9 flag represent both 'I' and 'J' – a letter only rarely used.

A 'substitution' flag was used for numbers like 11 and 22, as only one of each type was available.

Finally 'preparation' and 'finishing' flags were needed to signal the beginning and end of a message.

Spelling every word of a long message would have been dangerously time-consuming, especially in a complex sea battle. Popham came up with code combinations. 'Expects' was No. 269, for example. If a word was not in the codebook, such as the name of a small port, it could of course be spelled out. With telescopes, it was possible for admirals to contact their captains over vast distances – a crucial part of large-scale battles at sea. At night, the system was recreated in lights, though in a simpler form.

The most famous message of all is the one sent by Admiral Horatio Nelson at the Battle of Trafalgar in 1805, just off the south-west coast of Spain. On the morning of 20 October, he invited his friend Vice Admiral Collingwood and other captains to have dinner with him on *Victory*. Amongst those invited was John Cooke of the *Bellerophon*. As the ship left her place in the line to approach Nelson's ship, *Bellerophon*'s first lieutenant saw signal '370' flying from *Mars,* the next ship in the line. Number 370 is 'Enemy Coming out of Port'. Before *Bellerophon* could relay the message, *Victory* acknowledged, having seen the signal. Nelson cancelled the dinner and called for 'General Chase – south-east.'

With the enemy ships in sight, Nelson decided to send this message to his captains: 'Nelson confides that every man will do his duty.' One of his officers suggested changing 'Nelson' to 'England' and Nelson agreed the change, crossing to Lieutenant Pasco who would send the flag combinations. He told Pasco it must be quick, as he wanted to send his old favourite 'Engage the enemy more closely'. Pasco suggested that 'confides' be changed to 'expects'. 'Expects' was in the signals book, but 'confides' would have had to be spelled out. Nelson replied, 'That will do, Pasco; make it directly.'

(Note that the 'Y' of 'duty' is 24 and not 25 because of the double use of 'I'/'J'. Also, in the eighteenth century, the alphabet put 'U' after 'V' and not before it, as we do today. That is why the 'U' of 'duty' is number 21.)

On seeing this signal, cheers could be heard throughout the fleet. When his famous 'Engage the enemy more closely' went up next, the cheers were heard again.

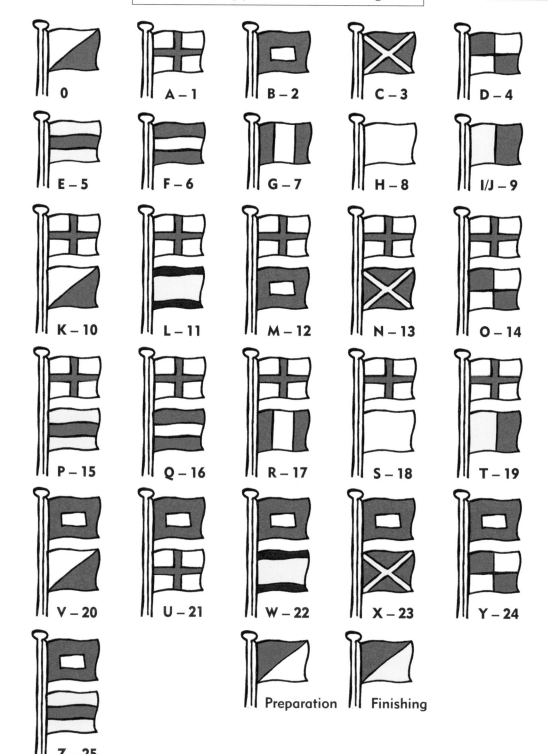

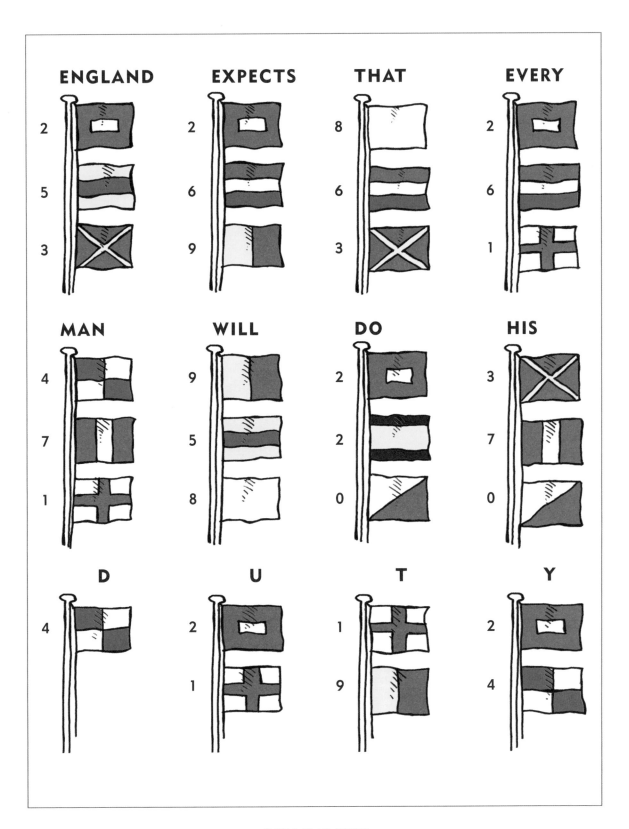

THE PATRON SAINTS OF BRITAIN

THE UNITED KINGDOM is made up of four main countries: England, Scotland, Wales and Northern Ireland. The Union Flag was first created in 1606. It is a combination of the cross of St Andrew for Scotland, the cross of St George for England and the cross of St Patrick for Ireland. Wales was joined with England in 1536 as a principality rather than a separate kingdom and is therefore also represented by the cross of St George.

1. ST GEORGE – 23 APRIL

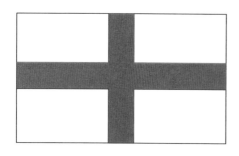

The story of the patron saint of England slaying a monstrous dragon is known by all schoolchildren, but whether he existed at all and how he became the English patron saint is still a bit of a mystery. One light-hearted story suggests that St George made a huge fortune selling bacon to the Roman Army and that's why the English, 'a nation of shop-keepers', adopted him as a saint.

The man who was canonised as St George was a Roman soldier who served in England. One of the few solid facts around this enigmatic man is that he was killed in AD 303, during the persecution of Christians by the Emperor Diocletian. The Archbishop of Genoa compiled a collection of the lives of the saints and tells us that after St George had slain the dragon, he gave up his knightly wealth and preached about Jesus Christ until he saw Diocletian's cruelty. He scolded the emperor and was tortured and beheaded for speaking out.

Edward the Confessor was the patron saint of England until the Plantagenets adopted St George in 1348. The Order of the Garter was created by Edward III. He and his son (also Edward, known as the Black Prince) were the first members of what is one of the world's oldest surviving orders of chivalry. A gold collar is part of the insignia, carrying a representation of George and the dragon known as 'the Great George'. When not wearing the Great George, Knights of the Garter are required to wear 'the lesser George', a small image of the saint.

The annual Order of the Garter service takes place in St George's Chapel at Windsor, built by Edward III in the same year as the founding of the order. A heart, supposedly St George's, rests there as a holy relic. Interestingly, there were foreign knights in the order almost from the beginning. Edward III and his son had conquered areas of France, eventually capturing the King of France and holding him in London. As a result, Edward was Lord of Gascony, for example, and could accept the allegiance of French nobles. The tradition of 'stranger knights' has continued for centuries, with foreign kings and princes joining the order. That said, the German Kaiser had his membership cancelled when the First World War broke out.

St George's Day is celebrated on 23 April, when his red and white flag is flown from every

Anglican church in England. He is also the patron saint of Portugal and Malta and even has his own country named after him, Georgia.

2. St David – 1 March

The life of David of Wales has its own elements of mystery. The primary source for information on his life comes from an eleventh-century Latin manuscript. David was not actually adopted as patron of Wales until the 1800s – another reason why he is not represented in the Union Flag.

He lived in the sixth century AD and is said to have been a son of the King of Cardiganshire in west Wales. He was deeply devout and must have been a man of great eloquence and charisma. He was a priest, a monk and eventually a bishop. He established churches and monasteries, went on pilgrimage to Jerusalem and, against his will, was made an archbishop after impressing other churchmen with his piety and the miracles that followed in his wake. More than once, spring water is said to have come from stone at his touch and he is credited with raising one young boy from the dead. When the crowd complained that they could not see him, the ground is reported to have risen under him until he was visible to all.

David settled in south-west Wales, founding a very strict religious community there. The monks were not allowed to use animals for labour, to give just one example, so that they had to plough the fields with their own strength alone. He himself drank only water and ate bread and herbs. He is said to have been tall and strong and the diet obviously suited him. He reached a very old age – some say over a hundred – and died in AD 589. In his last sermon, he urged parishioners to 'do the little things' – the small examples of kindness and decency that are so important in our lives. He was canonised (made a saint) in 1120. St David's Day of 1 March is a popular event in Wales and across Britain, marked by the wearing of daffodils, or leeks, Welsh national emblems.

3. St Patrick – 17 March

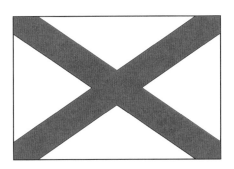

St Patrick was born around AD 385–7. The exact location is unknown, though he is generally supposed to have been Anglo-Roman. His parents were Romans living in Britain in the final days of empire.

When he was still very young, he was captured by sea raiders and taken to Ireland as a slave. He escaped while in his early twenties, making his way to the coast and finding sailors who returned him to Britain. There, he studied to become a priest and was later made a bishop. He returned to Ireland as one of the first Christian missionaries and began a life of extraordinary energy and leadership. His first convert was a chieftain named Dichu who intended to kill the stranger on his shores. However, Dichu found he could not raise his arm in anger against Patrick and accepted the new faith he brought with him.

Like David in Wales, Patrick created monasteries and convents all over Ireland, making his base in Armagh in the north. He preached and taught constantly, building churches and converting whole areas. It was no easy task. Ireland was pagan and bloody when Patrick came. He struggled against ancient sun worship and dark statues of fertility gods like Crom-Cruach, whose followers sacrificed themselves and their children in his honour. Patrick cast down its statue and cursed it, an act of both faith and personal bravery. In far lighter vein, he is said to have banished all the snakes from Ireland. The proof of his effectiveness is the fact that there are no snakes in Ireland.

Miracles followed Patrick and he lit a fire of faith in Ireland that burns today. Perhaps the most famous example of his teaching is in the three-leafed clover known as a shamrock. Patrick used it to show how a trinity – father, son and holy spirit – could also be one, just as the three leaves were one shamrock. It has been Ireland's national symbol ever since. After years of living in poverty, travelling and enduring much suffering he died in AD 461, on 17 March. His life is celebrated on that day around the world wherever there are Irish gathered together.

4. St Andrew – 30 November

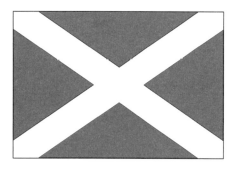

The Order of the Thistle is a form of knighthood restricted to the King or Queen and sixteen others. It was established by James II in 1687. It is also known as The Order of St Andrew.

Andrew has the distinction of being by far the oldest of our patron saints. He was the first of the original apostles, a fisherman in Galilee and brother to St Peter, the first Pope. Andrew is the apostle who introduced a boy with five loaves and two fishes to Jesus. Very little is known about his life after his involvement with Jesus, though he is said to have taken the new faith into Asia Minor (modern-day Turkey) and Greece. He was eventually crucified by the Romans for spreading the Christian faith.

His path to becoming Scotland's saint began when his bones were moved from a simple tomb three hundred years after his death. The Roman emperor Constantine was a fervent Christian convert. He wanted the relics of one of the original apostles of Christ moved to his new eastern capital, Constantinople – now called Istanbul.

Andrew became the patron saint of Byzantium, the eastern Roman empire. There are a couple of tales as to how his bones found their way north. One is that a Greek monk had a dream where an angel told him to take them to the ends of the earth. He removed some of the bones and was shipwrecked off Scotland trying to fulfil his mission. They may also have been brought back by Acca, the bishop of Hexham, in the eighth century. A church was built to house them and in the twelfth century St Andrew's Cathedral was erected on the site. Sadly, the original Scottish bones have been lost, though Pope Paul VI sent relics of the saint to Scotland in 1969. They are displayed in St Mary's Roman Catholic Cathedral in Edinburgh.

The Constantinople bones were taken to Amalfi. They remain today in the beautiful cathedral of St Andrew there, just a minute's walk from the sea.

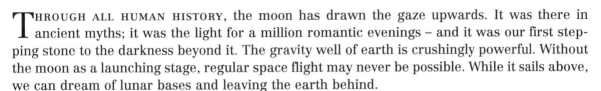

THE MOON

T<small>HROUGH ALL HUMAN HISTORY</small>, the moon has drawn the gaze upwards. It was there in ancient myths; it was the light for a million romantic evenings – and it was our first stepping stone to the darkness beyond it. The gravity well of earth is crushingly powerful. Without the moon as a launching stage, regular space flight may never be possible. While it sails above, we can dream of lunar bases and leaving the earth behind.

The first landing on the moon was on 20 July 1969, one date *everyone* should know. It is the only object in space that we have visited, after all. The *Apollo 11* spacecraft reached the moon and fired braking rockets to take up orbit around it. Neil Armstrong and Edward 'Buzz' Aldrin descended to the surface in a landing module named 'Eagle'. Michael Collins remained in the command module. After announcing to the watching earth that 'the Eagle has landed', Armstrong stepped out onto the surface of the moon.

There have been many momentous events in our history, from Caesar crossing the Rubicon to the first use of an atomic bomb, but having a human being set foot on another, stranger soil may be the most extraordinary.

Armstrong's first words were, 'This is one small step for man, one giant leap for mankind.' Famously, he had intended to say 'a man'. Without the 'a', he seemed to repeat himself.

The two men spent twenty-one hours on the surface and brought back forty-six pounds of moon rock. The moon has no atmosphere – and therefore no protection from meteorites. Its surface has been battered and melted by these strikes over billions of years, resulting in a soil called a 'regolith' – made of dust, rock and tiny beads of glass that are slippery underfoot.

The *Apollo 11* landing was the first of six successful landing missions during the twentieth century. In sequence, they are: *Apollo 11*, *12*, *14*, *15*, *16* and *17*, ending in December 1972. *Apollo 13* suffered technical problems and had to return to earth without landing on the moon. There will be others. An unmanned probe named *Lunar Prospector* found ice in 1998 at both moon poles – one of the most important requirements of a future colony!

THE PHASES OF THE MOON – AS SEEN FROM EARTH

The phases of the moon are such a part of our world that they should be common knowledge.

1. This is a new moon. The moon is between the earth and the sun and shows no light. This position creates the strong vernal tides on earth.
2. A waxing (growing) crescent. This use of the word 'waxing' is now almost completely restricted to describing the phases of the moon. As the moon moves on its cycle, we see the sunlight reflecting on its surface. The crescent will grow as it moves around the earth.
3. First quarter moon. Quarter of the way around the earth, one clear half of the moon is visible.

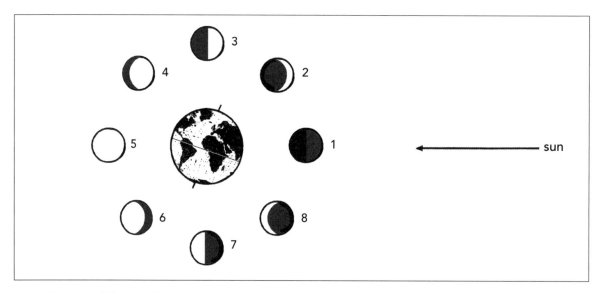

4. Waxing gibbous. The word 'gibbous' is another one that tends to be used only in descriptions of the moon. It means convex, or bending outwards. This is a good time to take pictures of the moon. Surprisingly sharp images can be made by the simple action of putting a camera up against the lens of a telescope on a tripod.

5. Full moon – also a time of strong tides, as both the sun and moon pull at the earth's oceans.

6. Waning moon – beginning the path back to the new moon.

7. Last quarter, with a perfect half of the moon again visible.

8. Waning crescent.

Moon Facts

1. Distance from earth: because of an elliptical orbit, this varies, but on average is 240,000 miles (386,000 km).

2. Gravity: about 1/6 of earth.

3. Day length: 27.3 earth days.

4. Time to orbit earth in relation to a fixed star (sidereal month): 27.3 earth days.

5. Time in relation to the sun (new moon to new moon/synodic month): 29.5 days.

6. Because it takes 27.3 days to orbit earth *and* turn on its own axis, we always see the same face. (See Questions About the World – Part Two.) However, there is no dark side in the sense of lacking light. Like earth, there is a night and day side, but both receive light during the cycle. The 'dark side' of the moon just doesn't exist!

7. The moon has no atmosphere, which means no wind, so Neil Armstrong's original footprint will still be there exactly as it was in 1969 – unless Buzz Aldrin or one of the others scuffed it over.

8. Daytime temperatures can reach up to 273 °F (134 °C). That is almost three times as hot as the Sahara Desert on earth. Night-time temperatures can be as low as –243 ° F (–152 °C). Needless to say, human beings cannot survive such an extreme range without a great deal of protection.

9. The American flag planted by the *Apollo 11* astronauts had to be made out of metal. Without an atmosphere, a cloth flag would have hung straight down.

10. The moon is silent. Without air or some other medium, sound waves cannot travel.

11. We owe many of the beautifully named parts of the moon to Galileo. It was he who thought he saw oceans on the moon in 1609, giving us Mare Tranquillitas (Sea of Tranquillity), Mare Nectaris (Sea of Nectar), Mare Imbrium (Sea of Showers), Mare Serenitatis (Sea of Serenity) and many more. Sadly, they are dry depressions and not the great oceans of his imagination.

SOME KEY FEATURES

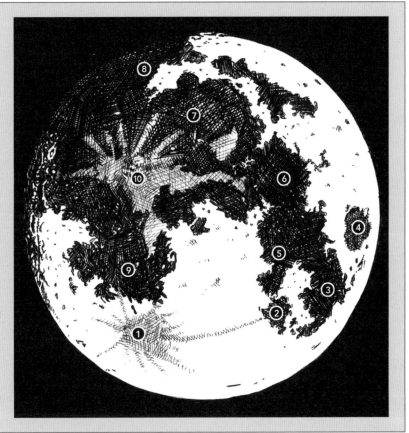

1. Tycho Crater.

2. Mare Nectaris (Sea of Nectar).

3. Mare Fecunditatis (Sea of Fertility).

4. Mare Crisium (Sea of Crises).

5. Landing point of *Apollo 11*, on south-west edge of Mare Tranquillitatis (Sea of Tranquillity).

6. Mare Serenitatis (Sea of Serenity).

7. Mare Imbrium (Sea of Showers).

8. Mare Frigoris (Sea of Cold).

9. Mare Nubium (Sea of Clouds).

10. Copernicus Crater.

Every month, at full moon, the earth goes between the sun and the moon. However, the exact line-up required for a lunar eclipse is not so common. Usually, the moon's tilted orbit takes it out of alignment. At most, there are only two or three full eclipses of the moon each year. You might expect to see around forty in a lifetime.

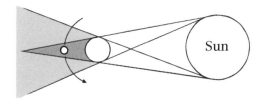

If you were standing on the moon at the time of a lunar eclipse, you would see the earth slowly blotting out the sun. In a lunar eclipse, the earth's shadow falls across the moon, though red sunlight scattered from the earth's atmosphere sometimes means a red moon can still be seen. Given the relative sizes, the earth's cone of shadow completely covers the moon and the eclipse can be seen from anywhere on the earth's surface.

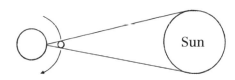

A solar eclipse is a far rarer event. In these, the earth is the smaller partner and the full eclipse can only be seen along a narrow track, never more than about 200 miles wide. Obviously, these can only take place at the time of a new moon, when the shadow of the moon falls onto earth.

There are two kinds of solar eclipse, 'annular' and 'total'. Annular eclipses are about twice as common and far less impressive. They occur when the moon is too far from earth to block the sun completely. The sky will not darken as completely and a bright ring will still be visible around the moon. Annular means 'ring-shaped'.

A total solar eclipse is well worth travelling to see. It is one of the marvels of the natural world. First, a tiny bite appears in the ring of the sun, which deepens until the sun becomes a crescent and the day darkens towards an eerie twilight. The corona of the sun can then be seen around the black disc. The temperature drops and birds often return to trees to roost. Then the light begins to reappear and the world as we know it returns.

SKIMMING STONES

THIS IS QUITE A TRICKY skill, but it is possible to bounce a stone on water five or six times without too much trouble. Barnes Wallis used the same principle when designing the bouncing bomb for raids on the Ruhr Valley in Germany. You will need several things in your favour to skim like the Dambusters.

First of all you need to pick your stone, as flat as possible without being too thin. It needs some weight to carry, but if it weighs much more than an apple, you won't get the range. Most beaches will have a variety of stones to choose from but if you find the perfect 'skimmer' in the park, hang on to it.

Skimming on the sea is harder because of the waves. If you try it on a lake, watch out for swimmers, who object to having stones thrown at them.

The skill is in the grip and the angle. Curl your forefinger around the stone, resting it on your middle finger. Secure it with your thumb.

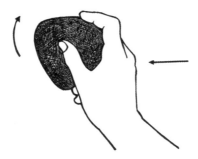

The action of throwing the stone is all important – too steep and the stone will just plonk into the water. Bend your knees to keep the angle of descent around 25° and try to get the flat side to hit the water when you release, to help it bounce on the surface.

The power you use to throw the stone can be increased once you get the hang of the technique.

More than one bounce and you are 'skimming', though you will have a way to go to beat the current world record of *thirty eight*.

PINHOLE PROJECTOR

You will need

- Long cardboard tube.
- Sheet of card or A4 paper.
- White tissue paper.
- Adhesive tape.

THE SUN IS A BRIGHT shining star that gives life to our planet. It is also very dangerous to look at directly and can damage your eyes. How then do we study the eclipses and transit of planets across its surface? With a pinhole projector, one of the best tools to view solar events as they take place.

As the name implies, a pinhole projector projects an image (upside down) of the sun so you can watch an eclipse without actually looking at it.

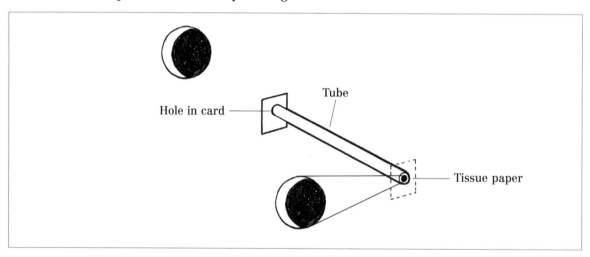

Hole in card

Tube

Tissue paper

To build the projector, use glue or adhesive tape to attach the sheet of card at one end of the tube, as shown in the diagram. Make a small hole in the card over the tube. Attach a thin sheet of tissue paper to the other end with glue.

To make it work, simply lift the card end towards the sun and an image will be projected onto the tissue paper 'screen' at the other end. Remember, only look at the projected image.

You can also build a projector with a magnified image, which is far more impressive and can be focused. You will need a telescope or binoculars and two pieces of white card.

First cut a hole in one of the pieces of card so that it fits over the end of your telescope or one side of your binoculars to shield the image from unwanted light. Now aim the telescope (or binoculars) at the sun and hold the other piece of white card a couple of feet from the eye-piece. An image of the sun should appear, which you can sharpen by changing the focus or moving the card. Never, *ever* look through a telescope while focusing or aiming it at the sun.

With a similar contraption, we saw the transit of Venus cross the sun in 2004. These transits usually come in pairs and the next is due on 6 June 2012. Partial eclipses are not particularly rare, though whether you can see one depends on where you are in the world. Here is a list of the more impressive total solar eclipses coming up in the next few years. Each date is followed by the latitude and longitude that will give the best view. For Britain (with a longitude of zero at Greenwich), the one in 2015 will be the easiest to see – especially from the western side of Scotland.

1. 01/08/2008	Latitude: 65.6N	Longitude: 72.3E
2. 22/07/2009	Latitude: 24.2N	Longitude: 144.1E
3. 11/07/2010	Latitude: 19.8S	Longitude: 121.9W
4. 13/11/2012	Latitude: 39.9S	Longitude: 161.3W
5. 20/03/2015	Latitude: 64.4N	Longitude: 6.6W
6. 09/03/2016	Latitude: 10.1N	Longitude: 148.8E
7. 21/08/2017	Latitude: 37.0N	Longitude: 87.6W
8. 02/07/2019	Latitude: 17.4S	Longitude: 109.0W
9. 14/12/2020	Latitude: 40.3S	Longitude: 67.9W

In 2038, there will be seven solar and lunar eclipses. A total lunar eclipse is a strange and wonderful sight, as light is scattered by the earth's atmosphere to turn the moon a dark red, as if it were made of copper.

Set up your pinhole projector and enjoy the sights.

CHARTING THE UNIVERSE

THE ANCIENT GREEKS were the first recorded people to try and explain why natural events took place without reference to supernatural causes. Astronomy started to become a science and began its long journey from superstition to enlightened understanding. They were beginning to uncover the 'rules' of the universe but these often conflicted with the prevailing beliefs and the conflict between faith and science continues even today.

Thales was a Greek philosopher and explorer who lived in the 6th century BC. He travelled to Egypt to study geometry. On his return, he demonstrated a high level of mathematical skill, even predicting the eclipse of 585 BC. His legacy is the belief that natural events could have natural causes. It is true that he thought the world was flat and floated on water – but, on the other hand, he realised earthquakes could be explained as more than a bad-tempered Poseidon.

Aristotle (384–322 BC) was one of the most influential of all Greek philosophers. He was a student of Plato, and became the teacher of Alexander the Great in Macedonia. He constructed three experimental proofs to show that the earth was round. He was the first to classify plants and animals. He thought that the earth was at the centre of the universe and that all the planets and stars were fixed in the heavens in a sphere around the earth. He believed earthquakes were caused by winds trapped beneath the earth.

Aristarchus flourished in the century after Aristotle and made a model to show that the sun was at the centre of things and not the earth. His theories were more scientific but history only briefly records his heliocentric ideas. However, no less a figure than Copernicus (see below) gives him credit in *De revolutionibus orbium coelestium*, writing, 'Philolaus believed in the mobility of the earth, and some even say that Aristarchus of Samos was of that opinion.'

Ptolemy of Alexandria was another gifted Greek astronomer. In AD 150, he published an encyclopedia (the *Almagest*) of ancient science with details and workings of the movements of the planets, showing an intricate mathematical system of circles within circles that buttressed his arguments for an earth-centred universe surrounded by unchanging spheres. This 'Ptolemaic system' was to rule the world of astronomy for 1,500 years.

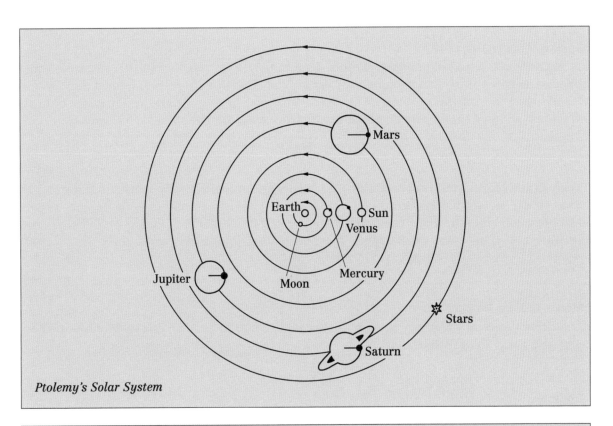

Ptolemy's Solar System

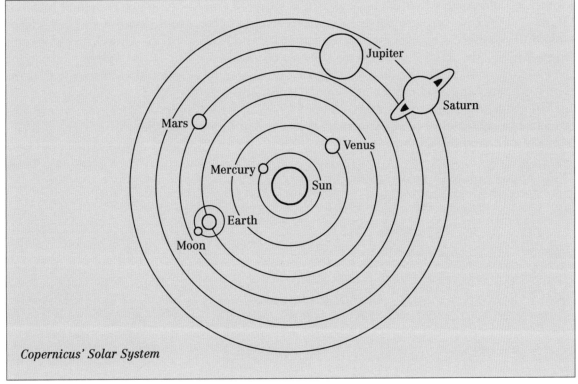

Copernicus' Solar System

Nicolaus Copernicus (1473–1543) was a Polish astronomer. Just before his death, he published his masterwork, *De revolutionibus orbium coelestium* – 'On the Revolution of the Celestial Spheres', which was to change humanity's view of the cosmos. Copernicus claimed that the sun was at the centre of the universe. This met with great hostility from the Christian Church, which had adopted the Ptolemaic geocentric (earth-centred) system.

Tycho Brahe (1546–1601) was a Danish astronomer who in 1572 saw a brilliant new star in Cassiopeia. This was a supernova – the explosion of a dying star, and in 1604 another supernova blazed forth in the sky. These events shattered a cornerstone of Ptolemaic thinking: that the outermost sphere was unchanging. The heavens had joined the renaissance.

Johannes Kepler (1571–1630) was Tycho Brahe's assistant and with his combined notes produced three laws of planetary motion. This enabled him to predict the positions of planets more effectively than Ptolemy.

Galileo Galilei (1564–1642) was an Italian scientist, who in 1609 took a telescope – then a new invention – and pointed it at the night sky. He discovered that the giant planet Jupiter had four moons clearly revolving around it in simple orbits, a miniature version of the Copernicus system. He published his discoveries, and in 1616 was warned by the Church to change his views. In 1632 he published *Dialogue Concerning the Two Great World Systems*, ridiculing the Ptolemaic system. He was forced to recant and abandon his beliefs that the sun was at the centre of things and lived out his days under house arrest.

The Catholic Church later absolved Galileo from any wrongdoing. In 1989, a spacecraft was launched to study Jupiter and its moons; it was called *Galileo* and those moons are still collectively known as the Galilean moons.

These names should be known to all.

DOG TRICKS

TEACHING A DOG simple tricks helps the bond between you. Dogs enjoy pleasing their owners and a well-trained dog is a happy dog! The only difficulty is in making the dog understand what you want. Commands should be given in a firm, low voice. Don't expect them to understand perfectly the first time. Be prepared to come back to the same commands again and again, leaving a few days between. Most dogs are perfectly willing to jump through hoops (literally) for their owners.

1. 'Speak.'
This comes under the group of tricks from observed behaviour. If a dog does something and a command word is uttered and a treat given every time, they will quickly associate the treat and the pat with the command word. Say 'Speak!' when they bark and in a short time, they will bark on command. Saying 'Are you sleepy?' when they yawn works in exactly the same way.

2. 'Sit.'
Everyone is familiar with this one. It is important that a dog should know to pause at every kerb rather than rush across. Sitting helps to mark the importance of roads. Repetition is the key here – even bright dogs like collies can take two years to become well trained. Do not expect overnight results with any of these. Press the dog's hindquarters down firmly, whilst saying 'Sit'. Then give a treat – a fragment of biscuit, for example. It doesn't have to be much. A pat on the head will probably do, but you'll find training easier with some sort of small reward to hand out.

3. 'Down.'
Always follows 'Sit'. Point firmly at the floor in front of the dog's head. As with teaching them to 'speak', you might try this when they are on their stomachs naturally. Otherwise, you can try placing them in the 'down' position manually, then express delight and give them a treat. They should remain upright, like a sphinx.

4. 'Die for the Queen.'
Usually follows 'Down'. 'Dying' involves lying completely flat on their side. You may have to press your hand gently against the dog's head to indicate what you want it to do. Dogs love this and though they lie still, their tails wag madly. Keep your voice very low and touch the tail, saying slowly, 'Dead dogs don't wag...' Hold it for two or three seconds, then get them up and give them a pat and a treat.

5. 'Paw.'
This is one you have to demonstrate. Simply lift the dog's paw in your hand and shake hands gently before giving them a treat. Follow with the command 'Other paw' for them to swap over. It won't be long before they offer paws on command. I had a terrier who took for ever to get this, but he managed it in the end.

6. 'Over.'
This is used when you want the dog to run – to cross a road swiftly is the most common use. Train the dog by holding their collar and raising your tone in excitement, holding them back. When all is clear, say 'Over!' loudly and let them run. They will probably not cross neatly the first few dozen times, so don't train them near cars.

7. 'Heel.'
Crucial when walking a dog on the lead. It is tiring and annoying to have a dog pull as it walks along. Curb the habit early with a sharp jerk of the lead and a very firm tone as you say the command word. Puppies are excitable and curious. They often take a long time to learn this. Be careful not to hurt them and do not worry about looking a fool. Anyone who has

ever had a puppy has walked along a road saying 'Heel' over and over and over again without any clear effect. To state the obvious, the dog does not understand why you are calling out parts of your feet. You are setting up a link in their minds between the word and the action of being jerked back. It will probably take a good year for this to work, depending on how young the puppies are when you get them. Be patient. It's good practice for controlling your temper when you have children later on. Seriously. Like a lot of things in life, early work bears fruit when it really matters.

8. 'Stay.'

This is another important one to teach early. Most dog owners have been surprised by a situation where the dog is far away and suddenly there's a car coming towards you. If you can tell the dog to 'Stay' and have it remain still, a serious accident can be avoided. This is taught with the aid of a pocketful of treats and many afternoons. You have the dog sit and say 'Stay!' in your deep command voice. You hold up your hand at the same time, showing the dog a flat palm. You take a step back. If the dog follows you, return it to the same spot and begin again. Begin with three steps and then give it a treat and a pat, making a big fuss of the dog. When they can remain still for three steps, try six, then a dozen and so on. You should be able to build up to quite long distances in only a short time. Dogs do like to be able to see you, however. If you turn a corner, almost all dogs will immediately move forward to find you again.

9. 'Gently.'

This is usually said with the second syllable elongated. A dog must be taught not to snap at food, though their instincts tell them to grab things before another dog gets it. You must never tease a dog with food – they will learn to snap at it and someone will be hurt. Always present food firmly on a flat palm. If they lunge at it, say the word 'Gently!' in a firm, low voice. They will hear the tone and hesitate.

10. Begging.

I'm not really sure if this is a trick or not. Small dogs do this almost automatically. If you hold a biscuit slightly out of reach of a terrier, he'll probably sit back on his haunches rather than leap for it. Collies are almost all hopeless at begging and fall over when they try. If you do want to try teaching it, the same requirement of treats, patience and common sense applies. Have the dog sit and hold the treat just out of reach. If you have taught them the command word 'Gently...!' it could be used to stop them snapping at your fingers. Let them have the first treat just by stretching, then move the next a little higher so their front paws have to leave the ground. Repeat over months.

11 'Drop!'

This is a very important command. Puppies in particular are very playful and as soon as you touch something they are holding, they will pull back and enjoy the game as you desperately try to save your shoes from destruction. It's best to take them by the collar to prevent them tugging too hard and say 'Drop!' in a loud, fierce voice. Repetition, as with all of these, is crucial.

12. 'Over! Over!'

Different families will have different command words, of course. This one is probably not that common. Our dogs are always taught to jump at hearing this. You may be out walking and need them to jump a low fence, for example, or jump up onto a table to be brushed. Begin with a higher surface and simply pat it firmly, saying 'Over! Over!' to them in an excited voice. If this doesn't work, do not pull them up by the collar. They could be frightened of being off the ground and that won't help. If you can, lift them to the higher level and then make a huge fuss of them, giving a treat. Repeat pats and lifts until they are comfortable with the higher position.

This is quite fun to see. Like cats, dogs can really jump, but they aren't taught to do it on command very often.

13.

Police dogs are taught to evacuate their bowels and bladder on command. It's done by using the command word – make your own one up – at the time when the dog is going to the toilet, and then the usual routine of making a fuss and giving a treat. In all honesty, this is only useful when, say, a dog will spend most of the day inside an airport and must not pee on luggage. For pets, it isn't worth it.

14. Jumping through your arms.

Not all dogs can do this – the terrier absolutely refused point-blank. The command 'Over! Over!' is useful as the dog knows it is for jumping. Begin by making a circle on the floor with your arms and having the dog called through for a treat. You need two people for this. After a few successful repetitions, raise your hands from the floor, so the dog has to step up a little to pass through. They're probably far too excited by then, so try it again the next day. Raise your hands higher and higher, then stand upright, holding your arms out in the largest circle you can make. Dogs the size of collies can do this, though some will thump you in the body or hit your hands as they go through. They improve with practice and it is a great trick to impress other dog owners.

15. Finally, attack commands.

There is no secret to having an attack word for a dog. Be aware, however, that unless it was absolutely justified, the dog is likely to be destroyed. Children accompanied by dogs are *much* less likely to be troubled by strangers, regardless of the breed of dog. Dogs are known to be aggressive and territorial, especially with strangers – men in particular. They do not need to be taught higher levels of aggression.

The opposite of this is what to do if you come into contact with an aggressive dog. First of all, it is a risk to put your hand out to pat any strange dog. If you must take the chance, let the dog smell your hands first, coming in slowly and low down so as not to startle them. If they show their teeth, move away. Mankind is the only animal on the planet who shows his teeth to smile. The rest of them are saying 'Go away or I will attack.' The same applies for growling. It is never playful. Never growl back. That is what another dog would do and the aggression will increase dramatically. Most dogs have the courtesy to warn you. Take the warning and back away.

If the dog does attack, remain on your feet and protect your face. Don't scream. Break eye contact if you can, as dogs see a direct gaze as aggressive. Dogs are almost never interested in serious damage. They simply want to remove you from the area. Do not run, however. Walk slowly away. Big dogs like Alsatians will hit you hard in the chest or back to try to knock you down. On the ground is not a good place to be in a full attack.

If you do end up on the ground, curl up to protect your face and neck. Again, they will do a lot more barking than actual biting in almost every case. Remain as still as you can and don't call for help or scream. The noise may excite them.

A well-trained dog will not be aggressive with other dogs or people, or at least they'll bring the poodle back when you call them. They will guard your home, force you to remain active to walk them, play with you whenever you have the slightest interest and adore you with complete trust in all weathers, on all days.

WRAPPING A PARCEL IN
BROWN PAPER AND STRING

NOT A VERY 'DANGEROUS' ACTIVITY, it's true, but it is extremely satisfying to know how to do this. There are two main ways: one without sticky tape of any kind and a more ornate one that needs the ends held with tape. I think they both have a place when sending a present or something thoughtful to someone else – just to give them the old-fashioned pleasure of tearing it open. It is true that you could simply cocoon a parcel in tape, but there is a certain elegance in doing it without.

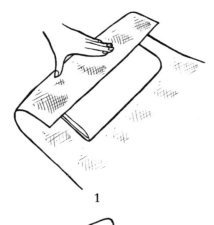

1

2

You will need brown paper and string, available from most post offices and all stationers.

Place the item to be posted on the sheet and cut a piece to fit it. Leave as much as half the height again and three times the width. Be generous rather than mean with the paper. If it really is too much, you can cut some off later, but you can never put it back on.

If you were using sticky tape, you'd use less paper, fold one sheet under the other and then tape the edge. Here, we are going to fold the edge down over itself in strips. This will create a 'spine' of paper that is very useful for rigidity and finishing it off. It also looks quite good, if you are careful with the folds.

Take a little time getting the ends right. Fold in a middle piece on each side, so that you end up with a duck's bill in brown paper, as in the picture. This is not the classic 'folding triangles in on themselves' technique. It is better.

Fold that duck's bill over itself into a neat point on both ends. You don't need to tape it, just leave it loose. The folded spine will prove very useful to hold it all together while you tie the string.

3

4

5

6

WRAPPING A PARCEL IN BROWN PAPER AND STRING

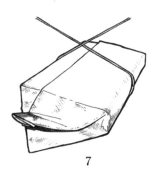

7

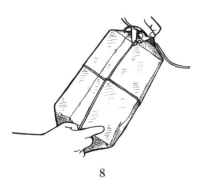

8

Now for the string. Cut a good long bit – three or four feet (90–120 cm). Once again, you can always shorten it. Begin on the side where the final knot or bow will go. Take the string around to the other side and then cross the two pieces as shown above, changing directions at ninety degrees. Take the two lines round the other ends of the parcel and back to the middle of where you started, for tying. It is helpful to have someone put their finger on the knot to stop it slipping.

One useful tip is to tie an extra knot before tying the final bow, linking the two lines together on top. This makes it more secure and is a good habit to get into.

The spine of folded paper is underneath. The parcel is neatly wrapped. Well done.

The only drawback to this method is that the crossed strings go right through where you would usually put the address. It is possible to tie the string so that it doesn't, but we found this way needed a bit of tape to hold those ends down.

Instead of starting in the middle of the parcel, start at one end, running the middle point of a long piece of string underneath. For this method, there is nothing more annoying than running out of string halfway through, so we suggest five feet (150 cm).

Wrap the string around, but this time cross at the three-quarter mark rather than at halfway. Run the strings around the other side and do it again and again, crossing at the corners until you can finally tie it off. As you'll see from the picture, the ends are not held by the string, but this is robust – and it leaves a space for the address.

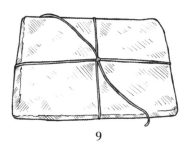

9

10

11

WRAPPING A PARCEL IN BROWN PAPER AND STRING

STAR MAPS: WHAT YOU SEE
WHEN YOU LOOK UP...

Facing south in the **northern hemisphere**, turn the book so the current month of the year is at the bottom. This will be accurate at around 11 in the evening.

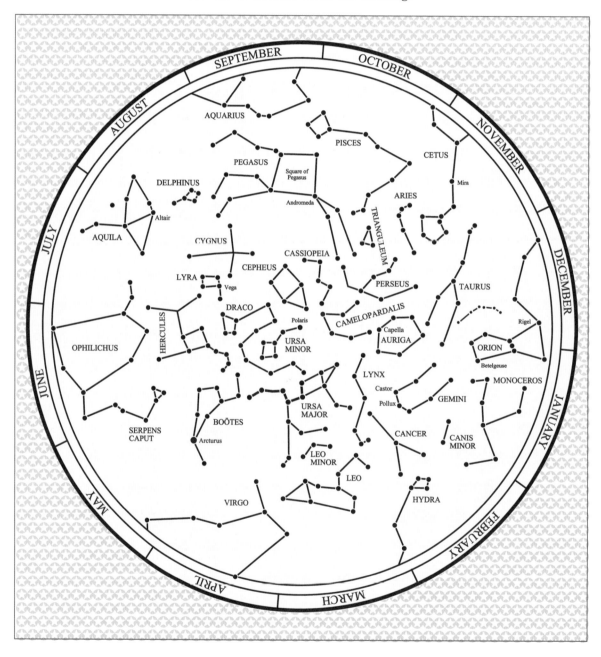

Facing north in the **southern hemisphere**, turn the page again to put the correct month at the bottom and these are the constellations visible on a good clear night at 11 p.m.

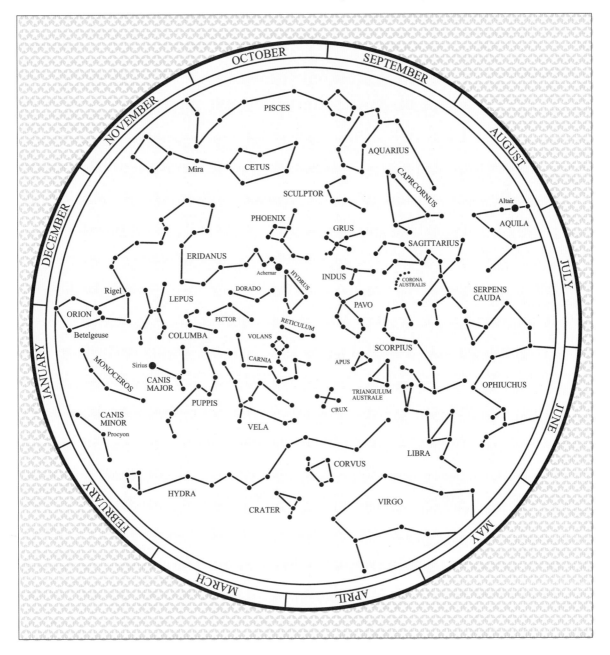

STAR MAPS: WHAT YOU SEE WHEN YOU LOOK UP

MAKING A PERISCOPE

You will need

- Saw, hammer, glue, small tacks.
- Two mirrors – 2 x 2 in (5 x 5 cm).
- Plywood – three-ply or five-ply. Cut two pieces of 18 x 2 in (45 x 5 cm), two pieces of 16 x 2 in (40 x 5 cm), two end pieces of 2 x 2 in (5 x 5 cm).
- Duct tape.

THIS IS A QUICK and easy one. It took just over an hour to put together once we had everything to hand. It does, however, involve work with a saw, hammering and glue, so if you are unsure, ask for help.

First get yourself two small square mirrors. Any glass shop will cut a couple of bits for you. Ours cost a pound each, which is a high price, considering what they are. You may well do better. For the actual periscope tube, we used plywood we had lying around. Ours was five-ply, which is more robust than you actually need. Three-ply would be better and is also easier to cut.

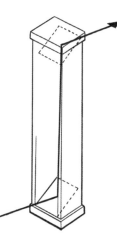

A periscope works by reflecting from one mirror to another and finally to the eye. Its simple effect is the ability to look higher than your head. It can be used to peer over fences or check enemy positions without exposing yourself to sniper fire. The classic use is in submarines.

We used small tacks to create the box, leaving a space (at the top of one side and the bottom of the other) for the mirrors. We kept ours simple and fairly rough, though obviously your periscope can be smoothed, painted or even joined and glued properly if you wanted one that would survive a generation or two. As a woodwork project in mahogany with brass corners, it would be very impressive.

The only difficulty was in securing the mirrors. By far the best way is to glue tiny wood strips in place on the inner surfaces, like runners. The mirrors slide between the strips and lock neatly into place against the end pieces. We used heavy insulation tape, however, and that seemed to do the job almost as well.

Having relied on the tape, it seemed sensible to cut one of the sixteen-inch sides down to fourteen inches, so that the top mirror could actually rest on its edge. Obviously, if it sat in neat little wooden runners, it would be perfectly all right to leave the piece at sixteen inches, a neater look.

The angle of the mirrors should be 45° for the right reflection. This isn't easy to judge, however, and the easiest way is just to position the first mirror until you can see the other end of the periscope tube in it. Once that is secured, position the second by hand, marking lines so you can find the correct position easily. Then either tape it or glue the wooden runners.

In theory, you could build quite a long periscope. We found eighteen inches was about right for our mirrors, but you could use larger pieces and experiment with a longer box.

FIVE POEMS EVERY BOY SHOULD KNOW

YES, A BOY SHOULD BE able to climb trees, grow crystals and tie a decent bowline knot. However, a boy will grow into a man and no man should be completely ignorant of these poems. They are the ones that spoke to us when we were young. Find a big tree and climb it. Read one of these poems aloud to yourself, high in the branches. All the authors are long dead, but they may still speak to you.

IF -
BY RUDYARD KIPLING (1865–1936)

If you can keep your head when all about you
  Are losing theirs and blaming it on you,
If you can trust yourself when all men doubt you,
  But make allowance for their doubting too;
If you can wait and not be tired by waiting,
  Or being lied about, don't deal in lies,
Or being hated, don't give way to hating,
  And yet don't look too good, nor talk too wise:

If you can dream – and not make dreams your master;
  If you can think – and not make thoughts your aim;
If you can meet with Triumph and Disaster
  And treat those two impostors just the same;
If you can bear to hear the truth you've spoken
  Twisted by knaves to make a trap for fools,
Or watch the things you gave your life to, broken,
  And stoop and build 'em up with worn-out tools:

FIVE POEMS EVERY BOY SHOULD KNOW

If you can make one heap of all your winnings
And risk it on one turn of pitch-and-toss,
And lose, and start again at your beginnings
And never breathe a word about your loss;
If you can force your heart and nerve and sinew
To serve your turn long after they are gone,
And so hold on when there is nothing in you
Except the Will which says to them: 'Hold on!'

If you can talk with crowds and keep your virtue,
Or walk with Kings – nor lose the common touch,
If neither foes nor loving friends can hurt you,
If all men count with you, but none too much;
If you can fill the unforgiving minute
With sixty seconds' worth of distance run,
Yours is the Earth and everything that's in it,
And – which is more – you'll be a Man, my son!

We recommend *Puck of Pook's Hill* as an example of Kipling's prose. Tragically, his only son John was killed in the First World War, in 1915.

Ozymandias

BY PERCY BYSSHE SHELLEY (1792–1822)

I met a traveller from an antique land
Who said: Two vast and trunkless legs of stone
Stand in the desert … Near them, on the sand,
Half sunk, a shattered visage lies, whose frown,
And wrinkled lip, and sneer of cold command,
Tell that its sculptor well those passions read
Which yet survive, stamped on these lifeless things,
The hand that mocked them, and the heart that fed:
And on the pedestal these words appear:
'My name is Ozymandias, king of kings:
Look upon my works, ye Mighty, and despair!'
Nothing beside remains. Round the decay
Of that colossal wreck, boundless and bare
The lone and level sands stretch far away.

This poem was written as a commentary on human arrogance. It is based on a broken statue near Luxor, Egypt. The actual inscription (translated) reads 'King of Kings am I, Osymandias. If anyone would know how great I am and where I lie, let him surpass one of my works.'

INVICTUS
BY WILLIAM ERNEST HENLEY (1849–1903)

Out of the night that covers me,
Black as the pit from pole to pole,
I thank whatever gods may be
For my unconquerable soul.

In the fell clutch of circumstance
I have not winced nor cried aloud.
Under the bludgeonings of chance
My head is bloody, but unbowed.

Beyond this place of wrath and tears
Looms but the Horror of the shade,
And yet the menace of the years
Finds, and shall find, me unafraid.

It matters not how strait the gate,
How charged with punishments the scroll,
I am the master of my fate:
I am the captain of my soul.

'Invictus' is Latin for 'unconquerable'. As a child, Henley suffered the amputation of a foot. He was ill for much of his life and wrote this during a two-year spell in an infirmary. He was a great friend of Robert Louis Stevenson and the character of Long John Silver may even be based on him.

VITAE LAMPADA
SIR HENRY NEWBOLT (1862–1938)

There's a breathless hush in the Close tonight –
Ten to make and the match to win –
A bumping pitch and a blinding light,
An hour to play and the last man in.
And it's not for the sake of a ribboned coat,
Or the selfish hope of a season's fame,
But his Captain's hand on his shoulder smote –
'Play up! play up! and play the game!'

The sand of the desert is sodden red, –
Red with the wreck of a square that broke; –
The Gatling's jammed and the Colonel dead,
And the regiment blind with dust and smoke.
The river of death has brimmed his banks,

And England's far, and Honour a name,
But the voice of a schoolboy rallies the ranks:
'Play up! play up! and play the game!'

This is the word that year by year,
While in her place the School is set,
Every one of her sons must hear,
And none that hears it dare forget.
This they all with a joyful mind
Bear through life like a torch in flame,
And falling fling to the host behind –
'Play up! play up! and play the game!'

Though the poem makes reference to a British square of soldiers being broken in the Sudan, the poem is actually about the importance of passing on values to the generations after us. In the poem, the young soldier remembers his old Captain's words to rally his men. 'Vitaē Lampada' came out in 1898. It means 'the torch of life'.

SEA-FEVER
BY JOHN MASEFIELD (1878–1967)

I must down to the seas again, to the lonely sea and the sky,
And all I ask is a tall ship and a star to steer her by,
And the wheel's kick and the wind's song and the white sails shaking,
And a grey mist on the sea's face and a grey dawn breaking.

I must down to the seas again, for the call of the running tide
Is a wild call and a clear call that may not be denied;
And all I ask is a windy day with the white clouds flying,
And the flung spray and the blown spume, and the sea-gulls crying.

I must down to the seas again, to the vagrant gypsy life,
To the gull's way and the whale's way where the wind's like a whetted knife;
And all I ask is a merry yarn from a laughing fellow-rover,
And quiet sleep and a sweet dream when the long trick's over.

Masefield, who later became Poet Laureate, wrote 'Sea-Fever' when he was only twenty-two. It contains some fantastic examples of onomatopoeia – words that sound like their meaning. You can hear the wind in 'wind like a whetted knife', for example.

There are hundreds more poems that have stayed with us as we grow older. That is the magic perhaps, that a single line can bring comfort in grief, or express the joy of a birth. These are not small things.

COIN TRICKS

COIN TRICKS ARE EASY to do and very effective. Here we will show you some simple sleight-of-hand 'vanishes'.

Any coin will do, the bigger the better, though I would suggest nothing smaller than an English 2p coin or an American quarter.

Most tricks are over quite quickly but a little 'patter'(spoken introduction) is still required. The speed of the trick is not important. It's all about the smoothness of movement and that takes practice. Misdirection and the final flourish will make you seem like a seasoned magician. When performing, let your hands move smoothly and confidently.

One of the oldest coin sleights is called 'the French Drop', a simple, effective 'vanish'. The reappearance is also important and we will suggest some examples such as taking it from behind a spectator's ear, but with a little ingenuity and practice you will come up with some ideas of your own to keep the spectators captivated.

THE FRENCH DROP

If you are right-handed, hold the coin by the edge in your left hand between your first two fingers and your thumb, make sure the hand is turned palm up and the fingers are curled in.

With the right hand palm down, go to grab the coin, with the thumb of the right hand going underneath the coin and the fingers above it. Close the right hand into a fist to take the coin.

At this point, release the coin, letting it fall into the cupped fingers of the left hand. The right hand now moves forward, supposedly holding the coin. The left hand drops to your side with the real coin.

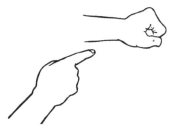

This sleight is quite elegant and needs to be performed smoothly and naturally. A good way to practise is to alternate between the French Drop and actually taking the coin, so when you perform the sleight you precisely duplicate the action of taking the coin.

Check occasionally in the mirror to see if it looks natural. Do not try to hide the coin in your left hand, just let the hand drop to your side. You could point at the right hand with a left finger, to misdirect the attention of the spectators. Always keep your eyes on the right hand, and then drop the left hand to your side.

Everyone watching will think the coin is in the right hand, so hold it out straight, focus on it and open the hand finger by finger. It will have vanished! Now reach towards a spectator with your cupped left hand and produce the coin from behind their ear! They can't see the approach round the back, so this is fairly easy.

THE EASY VANISH

The Easy Vanish is simple to perform yet very deceptive. Hold both hands palms up with a coin on the second and third fingertips of the right hand. Hold the coin in place with the right thumb.

Now turn that hand over and slap the coin into the palm of the left hand. Close the fingers of the left hand over the fingers of the right; withdraw the right hand, but hang onto the coin, using your thumb. Drop your right hand down by your side and reveal an empty left hand!

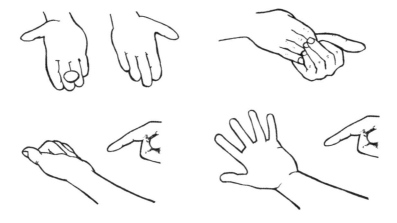

THE BASIC VANISH

Hold both hands out, palms up, with a coin in the centre of the right hand. The right hand approaches the left hand from below so the palm of the right hand touches the fingertips of the left hand.

The legitimate move is to drop the coin into the left hand as the right hand passes over it, closing the fingers of the left hand over the coin and dropping the right hand to one side.

Now to create the sleight, place the coin in the centre of your right hand and close the fingers and thumb slightly, gripping the coin with your palm. This is called 'palming'. As you pass over the left hand with the back of the right hand to the audience, you can retain the coin in your right hand. This will take some practice. Getting the coin in the right position for the palm needs confidence and a little patter to bounce it around until it's right.

As before, practise the sleight and check in the mirror so it looks natural.

Outlined above are three easy vanishes, but as I said at the beginning, it is the reappearance that is important. One great reappearance that can be used for any of the vanishes is called 'cough up'. It involves a little patter and a flourish.

At the beginning of the sleight, let the people watching know that you have a hole in the top of your head. Lean forward and let them look. Ask them if they can see it. They should say no and when they do, look a little confused and state that you can prove it. Smoothly perform one of the vanishes above, let's say the French Drop, but do not reveal the empty right hand. Instead, slap the top of your head with it. Then move your left hand to your mouth and cough, letting the coin drop. Catch it with your right. This really does look as if you have passed a coin through your head! Remember, it's smoothness that counts and if people ask you to do it again always decline. Don't give your tricks away too easily.

LIGHT

WHAT IS LIGHT? Without the human sense of sight, the word 'light' would have no meaning. Light enters our eyes and we 'see' things. Seeing things is a mental sensation and light is the physical cause of this. The mental effect that light causes is still one of the mysteries of the mind but we do understand a great deal about light on the physical side.

The thing we see might have its own light source – like a light bulb, or light might be reflected off it from somewhere else – like the sun. We see most things by this reflected or borrowed light.

The origin of any light source will begin with the vibration of atoms. A light bulb, for example, uses electricity to heat a filament to the point where it gives out energy in the form of white light. That light travels at about 186,000 miles per second (300,000 km/s) in empty space. It travels in waves or a steady flow of waves, like ripples on a pond. The waves have a very short wavelength (this is measured from the crest of one wavelength to another): 1/40,000 inch (0.00006350 cm) to 1/80,000 inch (0.00003175 cm), depending on the colour.

When light shines on a non-luminous body (like a table), it stimulates the atoms to varying degrees. Some atoms absorb all the light that falls upon them, while other atoms absorb some of the light but allow the rest to be reflected. The light finally reaches the eye, producing on the retina an image of the object viewed. Thus we 'see' and recognise the different parts of an object.

Light waves of various wavelengths create the sensation of colour when they fall on the eye.

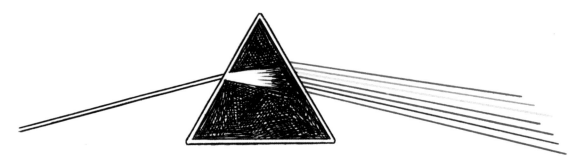

These waves can be identified by passing light through a prism, a coloured strip called 'the spectrum' being produced, red at one end and passing through orange, yellow, green, blue and indigo to violet at the other end. 'Richard Of York Gave Battle In Vain' is a good way to remember the colours of the spectrum.

By mixing colours, using coloured glass and a white background, any colour whatever can be produced, including some that are not present in the spectrum, like brown. The eye cannot tell the composition of the light that produces any given colour; for example, the colour yellow is a simple colour, but may be produced by mixing red and green in the correct proportions. Whiteness is caused by a mixture of all the simple colours. The classic way to see this is to colour a card disc with the shades of the rainbow and punch a pencil through the middle. When spun quickly, the colours will blur into whiteness.

When we look at a raindrop, we call it transparent, and think that the light goes straight through. Actually some of it is reflected from the inner surfaces. The light is bent or 'refracted' as it enters the raindrop and again when it leaves.

Raindrops act in the same way as rough prisms of glass or ice and cause rainbows. The drops of water split up the sunlight into the colours of the rainbow by 'refracting' each of the different colours of light to a different degree.

You will always find that your shadow points directly to the middle of the rainbow. You might also hear of a 'crock of gold' where the rainbow ends. Unfortunately, a rainbow has no end. As you move your position so the rainbow will move with you. Curiously no two people will ever see exactly the same rainbow. They generally appear when the sun is fairly low in the early morning and afternoon. The lower the sun, the higher the bow.

Colour is an affair of the mind, whilst light is purely physical, but you cannot have one without the other.

LATIN PHRASES EVERY
BOY SHOULD KNOW

There are hundreds of thousands of Latin roots in English. If that wasn't enough, some Latin words have become so common they are often believed to *be* English! 'Agenda' (things to be done), 'alter ego' (other self), 'exit' (he/she leaves), 'verbatim' (word for word) and 'video' (I see) fall into that group. There is satisfaction in understanding your own language – and that includes its origins.

Latin phrases crop up in conversation as well as the law courts. It is still the gold standard of education, but be warned – showing off is not a suitable reason for learning this list.

The precision of Latin can be a pleasure, but the main reason for this chapter is cultural. The three pillars of British culture are the King James Bible, the complete works of Shakespeare – and Latin. If you know English, you should know a little Latin. What follows can only ever be a small sample of the whole.

Learn one a day, perhaps. After each phrase, you'll find a home-made phonetic pronunciation guide. Stressed syllables are in capitals (SCIssors, DINosaur.) For some, you'll find an example of it being used.

1. **Ad hoc** (ad-hok). Literally 'to this'. Improvised or made up. 'I wrote an ad hoc poem.'
2. **Ad hominem** (ad HOM-in-em). This is a below-the-belt, personal attack, rather than a reasoned response to an argument.
3. **Ad infinitum** (ad in-fin-EYE-tum). To infinity – carried on endlessly. 'And so on and so on, ad infinitum…'
4. **Anno Domini** (AN-no DOM-in-eye). In the year of our Lord. Example: 'This is the year of our lord, 1492 – when Columbus sailed the ocean blue.'
5. **Ante meridiem** (AN-tay Mer-ID-ee-em). Before noon – 4 a.m., for instance.
6. **Aqua vitae** (AK-wa VIT-eye). Water of life. Most often used to refer to whisky or brandy.
7. **Audio** (ORD-i-o). I hear. Romans would probably have pronounced this like Audi cars.
8. **Bona fides** (BONE-uh FIDE-eez). Bona Fides are credentials establishing good faith or honesty. Technically it is nominative singular, though it is usually heard with a plural verb these days, because it ends in 's'.
9. **Carpe diem** (CAR-pay DEE-em). Seize the day, or use your time.
10. **Cave canem** (CAV-ay CAN-em). Beware of the dog. Found preserved in a mosaic floor in Pompeii, to name one place.
11. **Circa** (SUR-ca). Around – approximately. Julius Caesar was born circa 100 BC.
12. **Cogito ergo sum** (COG-it-o ER-go sum). 'I think, therefore I am' – a famous conclusion form René Descartes, the French philosopher. He considered the statement to be the only defensible proof of existence. All else could be fantasy.
13. **Curriculum vitae** (cur-IC-you-lum VEET-eye). The course of life – or school and work history. Usually abbreviated to CV.
14. **Deus ex machina** (DAY-us ex MAK-in-a). Literally, a god out of a machine, as when Greek playwrights would have Zeus lowered on wires to solve story problems. It has come to

mean poor storytelling, where some outside force makes it all end well.

15. **Dulce et decorum est pro patria mori** (DOOL-chay et de-COR-um est pro pat-ri-ya MORE-ee). 'It is sweet and fitting to die for your country.' A line from Horace. Later used ironically by Wilfred Owen in a World War I poem.

16. **Ergo** (UR-go). Therefore.

17. **Exempli gratia** (ex-EM-pli GRAR-ti-ya). For (the sake of) example – usually abbreviated to 'e.g.'

18. **Fiat lux!** (FEE-at lux). Let there be light.

19. **Habeas corpus** (HABE-e-as CORP-us). Literally 'You must have the body'. This has come to mean that a person cannot be held without trial – the 'body' must be brought before a court.

20. **Iacta alea est** (YACT-a Ali-ya est). The die is cast. Julius Caesar said this on the Rubicon river, when he was deciding to cross it. He meant 'It's done. The decision is made.'

21. **In camera** (in CAM-e-ra). In secret – not in the open. 'The meeting was held in camera.'

22. **In flagrante delicto** (in flag-RANT-ay de-LICT-o). In 'flaming crime' – caught red-handed, or in the act.

23. **Ipso facto** (IP-so FACT-o). By the fact itself. 'I have barred my house to you. Ipso facto, you are not coming in.'

24. **Magna cum laude** (MAG-na coom LOUD-ay). With great praise and honour. 'He graduated magna cum laude.'

25. **Modus operandi** (MODE-us op-er-AND-ee). Method of operation – a person's professional style of habits.

26. **Non compos mentis** (non COM-pos MEN-tis). Not of sound mind. Cracked.

27. **Non sequitur** (non SEK-wit-er). Does not follow – a broken argument. 'He never takes a bath. He must prefer cats to dogs.'

28. **Nota bene** (NO-ta BEN-ay). Note well. Usually abbreviated to 'n.b.'. Note that 'Id est' is also very common and means 'that is'. 'Id est' is usually abbreviated to 'i.e'.

29. **Paterfamilias** (PAT-er-fam-IL-i-as). Father of the family – paternal figure.

30. **Persona non Grata** (Per-SONE-a non GRART-a). An unwelcome person.

31. **Post meridiem** (POST me-RID-ee-em). After noon – usually abbreviated to 'p.m.'.

32. **Post mortem** (post MOR-tem). After death. Usually taken to mean investigative surgery to determine cause of death.

33. **Postscriptum** (post-SCRIP-tum). Literally 'thing having been written afterwards'– usually abbreviated to 'p.s.'.

34. **Quis custodiet ipsos custodes?** (kwis cus-TOAD-ee-yet IP-soss cus-TOAD-ez). Who guards the guards?

35. **Quod erat demonstrandum** (kwod e-rat dem-on-STRAN-dum). Which was to be demonstrated. Usually written as QED at the end of arguments.

36. **Quo vadis?** (kwo VAD-is). Where are you going?

37. **Requiescat in pace** (rek-wi-ES-cat in par-kay). 'May he or she rest in peace' – usually abbreviated to RIP.

38. **Semper fidelis** (SEMP-er fid-EL-is). Always faithful. The motto of the United States Marines Corps. The motto of the Royal Air Force is 'Per ardua ad astra' – through difficulties to the stars. The Royal Marines motto is 'Per mare per terram' – by sea, by land.

39. **Senatus Populusque Romanus** (sen-AH-tus pop-yool-US-kway rome-ARN-us). The senate

and the people of Rome. Imperial legions carried SPQR on their banners. Oddly enough, it is still to be found on drain hole covers in modern Rome.

40. **Status quo** (state us kwo). 'The state in which things are.' The existing state of affairs. Example: 'It is crucial to maintain the status quo.'

41. **Stet** (stet). Let it stand. Leave it alone. Often used in manuscripts, to indicate that no editing change is necessary.

42. **Sub rosa** (sub ROSE a). Under the rose – secret. From the custom of placing a rose over a doorframe to indicate what was said inside was not to be repeated.

43. **Tabula rasa** (TAB yool a RAR sa). Literally a 'scraped tablet'. Blank slate. A state of innocence.

44. **Terra firma** (TER a FIRM a). Solid ground.

45. **Terra incognita** (TER a in cog NIT a). Land unknown. Used on old maps to show the bits as yet unexplored.

46. **Vade retro satana!** (VAR day RET ro sa TARN a). Get behind me, Satan. This is an order to crush desires or temptations to sin.

47. **Veni, vidi, vici** (WAYN ee WEED ee WEEK ee). I came, I saw, I conquered. Said by Julius Caesar after a rebellion in Greece that he defeated in one afternoon.

48. **Versus** (VER sus). Against – usually abbreviated to 'v' or 'vs.'

49. **Veto** (VEE tow). I forbid. Another one so commonly used as to appear English.

50. **Vox populi** (vox POP yool ee). Voice of the people. Often abbreviated to a 'Vox Pop' – a short interview on the street.

AND THE NUMBERS...

There are only seven kinds of Roman numerals. These are: I, V, X, L, C, D and M. (1, 5, 10, 50, 100, 500 and 1000.) From just those seven, all other numbers can be made. The only difficulty comes in recognising that some numbers, like four and nine, are made by IV and IX – one less than five, one less than ten. This pattern is used all through Roman numerals, so nine hundred and ninety nine will be IM. That's it. Spend ten minutes on this page and then go and read any gravestone you wish.

I II III IV V VI VII VIII IX X **(1–10)**

XI XII XIII XIV XV XVI XVII XVIII XIX XX **(11–20)**

XXX **(30)** XL **(40)** L **(50)** LX **(60)** LXX **(70)** LXXX **(80)** XC **(90)** C **(100)**

The year 1924, for example, would be represented as MDCCCCXXIV.

HOW TO PLAY POKER

EVERY BOY should know how to play this game – but be warned. Luck has very little to do with it. High rollers in Las Vegas stay clear of poker because playing against experts is a humiliating way of giving money to strangers. In many cases, the roulette wheel is more attractive to those people – at least when they are thrown out wearing nothing more than their underpants, they have only themselves to blame.

There are dozens of variations of poker, so we're going to cover only two popular games: Five-Card Draw and Texas Hold-'Em. It is worth mentioning at this point that poker is a game that must be played for money. There is no *risk* in throwing all your matchsticks into the pot – and therefore no chance to bluff. It *is* possible to limit the bets to a level where it doesn't mean you have to sell the dog, but you can still feel as if you've won something.

FIVE-CARD DRAW

The aim is to beat the other players and that can be done by sudden changes in betting, bluffing or simply having a better hand. The very first thing to learn is the value of hands. Here they are, in order:

The best hand possible is the **royal flush** – all cards in sequence, from ace to 10, and of the same suit. The odds against being dealt this hand are 650,000/1. It would be a lifetime event to see one of these in the first five cards. Below that is a **straight flush** – again, all the cards in sequence and of the same suit, but lower down the line: 4, 5, 6, 7, 8 in spades, for example. Even that has odds of 72,000/1.

Four of a kind. Odds against being dealt it: 4,000/1.

Full house. Three of a kind and a pair. Into the realms of possibility, perhaps, at 700/1.

Flush. All cards of the same suit but of mixed ranks. Odds: 500/1.

Straight. All five cards in sequence, but of different suits. 2, 3, 4, 5, 6 for example, or the high one seen in the picture. Odds: 250/1.

Three of a kind. Three cards of the same rank. Odds: 50/1.

Two pairs. Odds: 20/1.

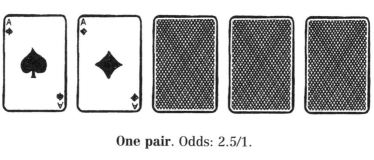

One pair. Odds: 2.5/1.

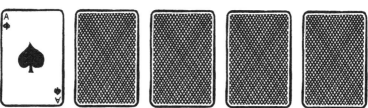

High card or **no pair.** Odds: 2/1.

Memorise these rankings and what they mean. You really can't check them while playing.

Four players is the classic home game number, but five or even six can be accommodated.

Begin by placing an agreed amount in the pot. This is to prevent weak hands being automatically folded. If one player does nothing but hold on, he may scoop the pot – and that should be worth something.

A dealer is nominated to start. Whoever is dealer will go clockwise round the table. It is common practice for the dealer to shuffle the cards, then slap the shuffled pack onto the table for the person on his right to cut.

When the dealer is ready, he deals five cards face down to each player. These are examined without showing them to anyone.

A round of betting follows. Betting also goes in a clockwise direction, so the person to the left of the dealer puts an amount of money into the pot. For the sake of the example, we'll say the bet is ten pence.

Going round the circle, each player now has three choices.

1. They can pay ten pence to stay in, saying 'I'll see that ten'. The word 'call' is also used.
2. They can raise the bet, saying 'I'll see that ten and raise you another ten.'
3. They can fold their cards, saying 'Fold,' and drop out of the hand.

The person opening the betting has a further choice of saying 'Check,' meaning 'No bet.' It could be a bluff, or it could be a weak hand. Other players can also say 'Check' in response, but if someone puts money in, everyone has to match it or fold.

If the ten-pence bets go around the table, the betting round ends. It cannot be raised by the first better.

If someone *does* raise it, saying 'I'll see that ten pence and raise you another ten,' they are showing their confidence in their hand. To stay in now, everyone else will have to match the combined bet of twenty pence.

When the round of betting is over, the dealer offers the person to his left the chance to exchange up to three cards. If the player already has an excellent hand, he might refuse the offer. Most players will exchange, though, keeping the pair of sevens they were dealt and hoping to be given another one.

If you are thinking that mathematics is your weakness, you really should not be considering playing poker for money. Give it to charity instead – it will be better used than ending up as someone else's pocket money.

A FEW USEFUL IMPROVEMENT ODDS

• Three of a kind, change two cards: odds on four of a kind or full house –	9/1
• Three of a kind, change one card: odds on four of a kind or full house –	12/1
• One pair, change three cards: odds to improve to two pairs –	6/1
• One pair, change three cards: odds to improve to three of a kind –	9/1
• One pair, change three cards: odds to improve to a full house –	98/1

There are dozens more – and the good players know them all.

Another calculation that comes in is whether winning a particular pot is worth the bet.

$$\frac{\text{size of pot x 'probability of winning'}}{\text{potential loss}} = \text{investment odds}$$

If the answer comes to more than one, it's probably a good bet to make – but note the fact that 'probability of winning' is expressed as a fraction and could be guesswork.

$$(50 \text{ pence x } 0.4) / 10 \text{ pence} = 2.0 = \text{good bet}$$

The final aspect of poker is the ability to read other people – not just their expressions, though this is the game that created the phrase 'poker face' – someone who hides their emotions. Patterns of betting can also be read. Perhaps when you sit with Jim you notice that whenever he has a good hand, he puts in a very big bet at the first opportunity. You might avoid hands where he does this, but there is always a chance he is deliberately setting up a pattern on good hands, to then do it on a bad hand and watch everyone else fold... that's bluffing.

In essence, that's about it for draw poker, except for invaluable experience. The chances of good hands are increased by 'wild' cards. If you get these in a hand, you can call them anything you like, which throws the odds right out of the window. Suddenly, unheard-of hands become possible, like five aces.

This is the type of poker used at the world championships. First, the two players to the dealer's left put up 'the small blind' and the 'blind' – usually half the minimum bet and the minimum bet. This becomes more significant as the game goes on and bet limits increase.

Two cards are dealt face down to each player. These are the 'hole cards'.

A round of betting takes place, exactly as described above, with raises, folds etc. It is customary to say 'Call' when matching the current bet without a raise.

When betting comes to an end, the dealer deals the 'Flop' – three more cards, this time face up where everyone can see them.

After the Flop, another round of betting takes place, beginning with the player to the left of the dealer. He has the choice to bet, fold or check, as with Five-Card Draw. If he checks and the next person bets, he will have to match it – but will now have a better idea of the sort of hands held. As a result, checking can be tactically useful.

The dealer plays another card face up – the 'Turn', beginning another round of betting from the left. When that ends, the final card is dealt – the 'River'.

Now there are five cards face up on the table and two face down in each player's hand. Although seven cards are available, the aim is to make the best five-card hand.

Bluff plays a large part in this version of poker – and the betting tends to be much higher than five-card draw, as players hang on to see if later cards help their hand.

The final round of betting starts with the player to the dealer's left, as before.

SOME OF THE ODDS FOR TEXAS HOLD-'EM

1. HOLE CARD ODDS

• Any pair –	16/1
• Ace, king of different suits –	110/1
• At least one ace –	5.7/1
• Two cards of same suit –	3.25/1

2. IMPROVING ON THE FLOP

You hold	Flop gives you	Odds against
A pair	Three of a kind	10/1
Any two	Two pairs	48.5/1
Two same suit	Flush	118/1

3. IMPROVING ON THE TURN

From	To	Odds against
Four cards of a flush	Flush	4.2/1
Three of a kind	Four of a kind	46/1
Two pairs	Full house	10.8/1
One pair	Three of a kind	22.5/1

4. IMPROVING ON THE RIVER

From	To	Odds against
Four cards of a flush	Flush	4.1/1
Three of a kind	Four of a kind	45/1
Two pairs	Full house	10.5/1
One pair	Three of a kind	22/1
Nothing	A pair	6.7/1

The last piece of advice is 'Never try and fill an inside straight.' If you were playing draw, say, and have 4, 5, 6, 8 and a king, you might be tempted to exchange that king in the hope of a seven – to make 4, 5, 6, 7, 8, a high hand. There are forty-seven cards you have not seen and only four of them are sevens. 47/4 is almost 12/1. Making a straight at either end is twice as likely, however.

It really is important to realise that poker is a difficult game. The golden rule is 'If you can't spot the sucker at the table – it's you.'

Douglas Bader

'Rules are for the obedience of fools and the guidance of wise men'

– Douglas Bader

DOUGLAS ROBERT BADER was born on 10 February 1910 in London. His father Frederick was a civil engineer and when Douglas was just a few months old, he and his wife Jesse went out to work in India. They considered the climate too harsh for a baby and Douglas did not join them until he was two. The Bader family came back to England in 1913, though with the outbreak of World War I, Frederick Bader went with the army to France.

Douglas never saw his father again. He died there after complications with a shrapnel wound.

His mother Jesse remarried, but Douglas spent a great deal of time with his aunt Hazel Bader and her husband, Flight Lieutenant Cyril Burge, who was adjutant to the RAF college at Cranwell. Through that relationship, Bader discovered a love of planes and flying that would last him the rest of his life. He had been a superb sportsman at St Edward's school in Oxford and after becoming a cadet at Cranwell in 1928, he represented the college at boxing, cricket, hockey and rugby. His academic studies were not as impressive and he came second for the sword of honour at graduation. One of the students said, 'To us, Bader was a sort of god who played every conceivable game and was the best player in every team'. He was commissioned as an RAF officer in 1930.

He was an extremely gifted pilot and gained a place in his squadron aerobatics team, winning the pairs title at the Hendon pageant of 1931. He was absolutely without fear and pushed his bi-plane a little too far on 14 December that year. He was showing off to friends with low rolls barely above the ground. One wingtip touched and the plane crashed, doing terrible damage to his legs. Dr Leonard Joyce had to amputate his right leg above the knee, his left below.

The twenty-one-year-old Bader was not expected to survive, but he had a fierce will to live and a furious temper. He began the slow painful path to recovery and was transferred to the RAF hospital at Uxbridge. He met the great love of his life, Thelma Edwards, there and married her in 1935.

Bader was given metal artificial legs and had to learn to use them, as well as grow callouses on his stumps. The right leg was particularly tricky as the metal knee joint required great balance and perseverance. He was told he should use the sticks to help his progress as he would never walk without them. Bader replied, 'On the contrary, I will never bloody walk with them.' He never did, relying instead on his reflexes, coordination and sheer will. His life had altered for ever. Later, Bader recorded the event in his flying log with these words:

'X-country Reading. Crashed slow rolling near ground. Bad show.'

After being discharged from the RAF, Bader went to work for the Asiatic Petroleum Company. As he couldn't fly, he drove a specially adapted sports car like a maniac along country lanes, but there was more to come in the life of this extraordinary man. When the Second World War broke out in 1939, Douglas immediately attempted to re-enlist. He was refused at first, being told that there was nothing in the King's regulations allowing a man in his condition to fly. He retorted that there was nothing in the King's regulations to say a man in his condition couldn't fly!

He had the support of his fellow officers, especially those who had known him from before the accident. Britain needed pilots and Bader was taken back into the RAF and made flight commander of 222 Squadron, flying and making his first kill as they covered the retreat at Dunkirk. He was promoted after that action to command the Canadian 242 Squadron. They had lost half their number in casualties and were severely demoralised. With his metal legs, they assumed at first that he would lead them from behind a desk, but instead, he demonstrated aerobatics to them for an hour, flying a Hurricane fighter. Douglas Bader was the right man to restore their morale through his peculiar brand of stubbornness and charismatic leadership. From the beginning, he trained them in his own style of fighting, ignoring the Fighter Command official tactics. In fact, his ideas would prove their usefulness and became effective tactics for the RAF in resisting the German bombers and fighter escorts.

Under Bader, 242 Squadron first fought in the Battle of Britain on 30 August 1940 against the German fighter waves, taking down twelve German planes in a single hour. They would go on to fly three or four sorties a day for as long as their Hurricanes would stand up to the punishment.

Bader himself was responsible for 22½ air-to-air victories – the half after he and a friend shot up a German plane together and both agreed to claim half the kill. The total made him the fifth highest ace in the RAF. The importance of this cannot be overestimated. Without air superiority, Britain could not have defended her cities or airfields in WWII. German bombers would have had a free hand as they had over in Europe. Bader was awarded the Distinguished Flying Cross (DFC) and the Distinguished Service Order (DSO) for gallantry and leadership at the Battle of Britain.

In the lull after the battle, Bader continued to take his squadron out to attack German E-boats and the occasional lone Dornier bomber. He was a key player in the revision of RAF and US Air Force tactics, commanding the Tangmere wing of three squadrons as they prowled over the Channel looking for the enemy. When returning from successful missions, Bader was in the habit of opening his cockpit canopy and lighting a pipe with the control stick held between his metal knee and his good knee. When other pilots saw him do this, they kept a good distance in case he blew the plane up with petrol fumes.

In 1941, he was involved in a mid-air collision over France with a German Me 109 whilst dog-fighting. The tail of Bader's plane was torn off and he was began plummeting towards the ground. He got the canopy off and climbed out into the wind to parachute clear. His right leg caught and he found himself nailed to the fuse-lage by the slipstream, heaving and tugging at the metal leg before it took him down with the plane. At last, the belt holding the leg to him snapped and the leg went off through his trousers, allowing him to break free of the plane and parachute to safety.

In German captivity, he asked if a message could be sent to England for his spare right leg to be sent over. It is an astonishing thing, but the Germans agreed to this and the RAF dropped it in a crate during a normal bombing run. The leg was slightly damaged in the land-ing, but the Germans repaired it and took it to Bader in the hospital where he was being held. He put in on and while no one was paying attention, walked casually out of the hospital, in an attempt to escape. They caught him, but he maintained this spirit of cheerful defiance in various POW camps, inspiring respect from those around him. All British prisoners under-stood that escape attempts meant that more guards would be used who might otherwise be killing allied forces. Even failed attempts had value. Eventually, the Germans sent Bader to the famous Colditz Castle, which was meant to be escape-proof.

More than three hundred attempts were made over five years and thirty-one people did in fact get completely clear. The inmates built a complete glider, walked out dressed as German soldiers and generally forced the Germans to use vast resources and manpower to keep them in. Airey Neave was the first Briton to escape the castle. He later went on to become an MP and was killed in an IRA car bomb in 1979.

Bader attempted escape so many times that the Germans took his legs away. A great outcry was raised over this and the Germans were shamed into returning them. Bader promptly escaped again and had to be brought back. He was still there when the Americans liberated Colditz in 1945 and he returned to England, where he was promoted to group captain. With the war over, he couldn't see a future for him-self in a peacetime RAF and instead joined Shell Oil's aviation department, a job that came with its own plane.

Bader raised money and campaigned for disabled people, flying all over the world visit-ing veterans' hospitals. He inspired others by his example and his willpower.

One day in 1955, he went back to speak at his old school in Oxford. A fifteen-year-old pupil saw Group Captain Bader coming through the gates with his instantly recognisable gait. Bader was carrying cases and it was a hot day, so the boy ran across and offered to help with the bags. Bader's response was to tell him to 'bugger off!' in a very angry tone. The head-master came to see the boy later. He said that he had done the right thing in offering, but 'Group Captain Bader will not be helped. He regards carrying his own cases on a blazing hot day as a challenge.'

The book and film 'Reach for the Sky' tell the man's story better than we have here. Bader was always a prickly, difficult person-ality, but his courage and stubbornness were legendary. He died in 1982, but his story is still an inspiration.

MARBLES

THE ROMANS played marbles. They were made from stone, clay or marble (aha!), though marble marbles were the most accurate. These days, glass and china marbles are still available in most toy shops. Do not be deceived: the version of marbles called Ring Taw can be frustrating and demanding – but it is the best. All you need is a flat surface, a bit of chalk, a bag of marbles – and a competitive streak.

We thought about trying to make a couple of marbles, but the temperatures involved would have meant you reading something called *The Suicidal Book for Boys*. Molten glass has different-coloured glass injected into it before being cut into cylinders and dropped into a rolling tray where the marble rolls itself to perfection.

Marble Names

Any marble you use to take a shot is called a **Shooter**, or a **Taw**. For the rest, there are as many names as kinds of marble. Some of the better-known examples are: Ordinaries, Oilies/ Petrols, Chinas and Dobbers.

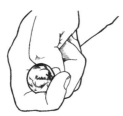

Fulking

Fulking is the name of the classic schoolboy technique for shooting.

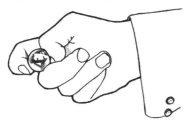

The professionals, however, (and they do exist) use '**knuckling down**'. Greater accuracy is possible with that steering finger, though we liked the one we remembered from school. With fulking, there's a danger of letting it fall out and roll across the circles, which can be embarrassing. This can also lose you the game.

The Three Games You Need to Know
Ring Taw

1. Draw two circles in chalk, as you see below. The small one is twelve inches across, or a ruler's length (30 cm). The larger one is six feet (1.83 m) across. Remember that the distance from your elbow to your wrist is roughly a foot (unless you are tiny, obviously). Otherwise, find someone who is six feet tall and ask them to mark out the circle using the distance between their outstretched arms, which will also be six feet.

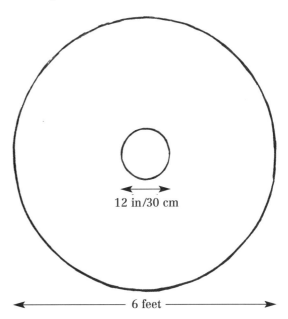

12 in/30 cm

6 feet

2. Choose which marbles will be risked from each bag – equal numbers from each player. This is a skill game – it doesn't matter which

ones you lose or win, just how many. Put them in the inner circle. We found tactical placing of one at a time worked well, taking it in turns.

3. The Taw can never be lost. It can be a personal favourite, a rare one, metal, marble, china, glass or even wood. Practise with your Taw and never allow it to be a stake in the game.

4. Decide who is going first.

5. First shot. The aim is to shoot the Taw from any point on the outer ring at the ones in the centre. Any marbles knocked out of the inner circle are pocketed by the shooter, who then takes a second go, unless the Taw has vanished inexplicably. If you *can* find it, shoot from where it lies.

6. If you miss, or fail to knock one out of the inner circle, play passes to the next player. If your Taw stops in the outer circle, it stays where it is for Rule 7. If it stops in the *inner* circle, it must be bought out with a replacement marble from the offending player.

7. When a Taw is stuck in the outer circle, it becomes a target. The next player can choose to go for the centre or the Taw. If he hits the Taw, he has to be given a marble by the owner. He may not strike it twice. If *his* Taw gets stuck, play moves on again.

8. The game continues until the inner circle is clear.

Bounce About

This game is a throwing rather than shooting game – the marbles are in the air during the shot. Bigger marbles are better for this game.

1. The first player throws his marble forward about five feet.

2. The second player does the same, trying to hit the first marble. (Other players can hit either and so on. This can be played by quite a few.)

3 All shots are underhand and from where the Shooter lands.

4 If a marble is hit, the owner either loses it or pays a marble forfeit from the bag. It's better to pay the forfeit so as not to lose your Taw.

That's it. All the tactics come from the play.

Hundreds

This is a surprisingly addictive accuracy game for two players.

1. Draw a small chalk circle – diameter twelve inches (30cm).

2. Both players shoot a marble at the circle from an agreed distance.

3. Both in or both out gets nothing.

4. One in the circle earns ten points and another go.

5. First to a hundred wins.

Fouls

1. In Ring Taw, the shooter's knuckle must touch the outer circle. Lifting is a foul.

2. 'Fudging' is pushing the hand forward – and a foul. The marble must be shot with the thumb alone.

3. After the game has begun, no contact with marbles in the inner circle is allowed, except by the Taw.

The world championship is played every year in Tinsley Green, West Sussex, England. In essence, it is Ring Taw, with forty-nine marbles in the inner ring, worth a point each. The winner is the first to knock out twenty-five with the Taw.

Playing marbles is not about how many marbles you can buy, it's about the ones you win and lose – it's about skill and your Taw.

A BRIEF HISTORY OF ARTILLERY

The ability to strike an enemy from far away has always appealed to soldiers and generals alike. Bows have been found from as early as 7400 BC, preserved in a bog at Holmegaard, Denmark. They may go back as far as 20,000 BC. Though such weapons were powerful and accurate, there has always been a search for more destruction and greater range. A city cannot be battered into submission by archers, after all.

The Meare Heath yew bow from Somerset, England – dated to c. 2500 BC.

Archimedes is one of the most famous early inventors of artillery weapons. In the defence of Syracuse in 214 to 212 BC, he used Bronze bronze mirrors to focus the sun and burn enemy ships.

The truth of this story was doubted for a long time. In the early 1970s, a Greek scientist, Dr Ioannis Sakkas, employed sixty Greek sailors in an experiment to see whether it was possible. All the men carried large oblong mirrors and used them to focus the sun onto a wooden ship one hundred and sixty feet away. The ship caught fire almost immediately.

Archimedes was an extraordinary thinker, the Leonardo da Vinci of an earlier age. He invented a number of other artillery weapons to sink Roman galleys, or hammer them from the city walls. He was not alone, however. The Greeks developed knowledge of pulleys, water pumps, cranes, even a small steam engine. It was a period of extraordinary scientific advancement – all of which was useful in creating weapons of long long-distance destruction.

Early weapons were based on the spring power of a bow arm, pulled back by muscle or by a ratchet, as in this picture. Understanding pulleys in particular means that a man can repeat an easy action over and over to move large forces very slowly. In other words, heavy weapons can be wound back with the use of a few simple principles.

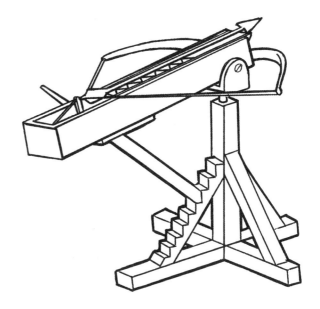

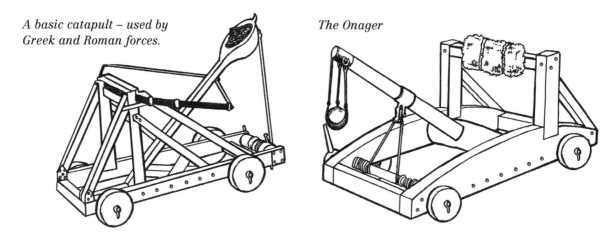

A basic catapult – used by Greek and Roman forces.

The Onager

'Torsion' is the force gained by twisting. The Romans improved on Greek inventions, perfecting the use of ropes of woven horsehair and sinew as their 'spring'. The heavy Roman **'Onager'** was capable of sending a 100 lb (45 kg) rock up to 400 yards (365 m). An 'Onager' is Latin for a wild ass or donkey – with a fearsome kick. It is similar in principle to the catapult, with a sling-like cup and a single torsion bar.

The **Ballista** was a Roman bolt or stone shooter. It used two torsion springs and had a range of up to 450 yards (411 m). The Romans also perfected a *repeating* ballista, invented by Dionysios of Alexandria. By simply winding a handle, the ratchet came back, an arrow dropped into place and was fired as soon as the winch reached its maximum point. This was the first machine gun – long before gunpowder.

Every Roman legion carried heavy onagers and thirty **Scorpion** bows – a smaller form of the weapon that could be carried on a single cart. Roman success in war depended on much more than discipline and a good gladius!

The last type of this sort of engine is a **Trebuchet**, powered by counter-weights. This form of artillery was able to launch heavier weights than any other kind. However, the enormous counterweight needed meant that they were practically immobile once set up and worked well

The Ballista

The Trebuchet

only when battering city walls. They were in use throughout medieval times until the invention of cannon. Pulleys and ratchets were used to pull down the arm and load it. When released, the arm snapped forward and the second section whipped over at high speed.

Later, gunpowder and iron-foundry techniques combined to create smooth-bore cannons. Compared with early engines of war, these had a much longer range and were faster to load. Although China had gunpowder in the eleventh century, it was European countries that really exploited its use as a propellant in the thirteenth century. Roger Bacon, the English Archimedes, wrote down a formula for gunpowder in code in the thirteenth century. The combination of sulphur, charcoal and potassium nitrate, or saltpetre, would change the western world.

The picture above is of 'Mons Meg', a Flanders cannon cast before 1489 and currently kept in Edinburgh castle. It fired a stone ball of 330 lb (150 kg) more than one and a half miles (2.4 km).

For the next six hundred years, cannons would remain essentially the same – smooth-bore muzzle loaders, lit by a taper or a flint-lock. Iron balls would be used instead of stone as they were easier to mass-produce and make uniform. Cast-iron barrels took the place of softer wrought iron. Cannons at sea could fire chain, or bar shot to destroy enemy rigging and clear the decks of boarding parties. In the basic principles, though, Nelson's cannons fired in the same way as those from the thirteenth century. As with most long-lasting technologies, if they weren't replaced, they were perfected.

Mortars and **Howitzers** were also perfected during the nineteenth century. A mortar fires at very high angles compared with a cannon, a howitzer between the two. Progress was fast and furious as a single clear advantage could mean the difference between winning a war and being invaded.

Types of Royal Navy Bar and Chain Shot

World War I British field piece, firing sixty-pound explosive shells.

Rifling a barrel involves casting spiralling lines inside that make the ball or shell spin as it leaves, giving gyroscopic stability. Although it had long been in use for hand weapons, the practice was first applied to artillery around 1860. The new breed of artillery would be breech-loading, have reinforced barrels and be able to fire shells with astonishing accuracy.

The heaviest versions of these shell-firing weapons could be miles behind the lines, firing huge shells in a parabola (arc) at the enemy positions.

The twenty-first century – British Challenger 2 tank.

No chapter on artillery could be complete without a mention of **tanks**. From WWI onwards, these awesome machines have changed the face of warfare by allowing powerful artillery to be extremely mobile and well armoured.

In modern times artillery can take the form of inter-continental missiles, striking from hundreds or even thousands of miles away and with a greater force than anything else in this chapter. In a sense, artillery has reached its ultimate stage, where cities can be flattened without a single soldier entering the combat zone.

Shells can now be armoured in 'depleted uranium' – uranium with most of the radioactive isotopes removed. This is a heavy metal and hard enough to be ferociously efficient as an armour-piercing round. Though it is actually less radioactive than naturally occurring uranium, it is chemically toxic and should not be ingested. Dust and fragments from DU shells remain dangerous for a very long time.

We have come a long way from bow-based spring weapons. Until the invention of the machine gun, it was still possible to march into cannon fire and expect at least some of your army to reach the enemy. World War I changed that, the obsolete tactic going the way of the cavalry charge. It is difficult to predict the course of the future, with such immensely powerful weapons now available. Wars nowadays tend to be fought on a small scale, with major players being very careful to limit the destruction. In theory, Britain could have dropped nuclear weapons on Argentina during the Falklands War, or America on Iraq in the first or second Gulf War. Neither country took that step. Let us hope it does not happen in our lifetimes.

THE ORIGIN OF WORDS

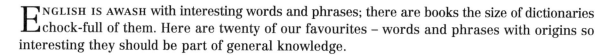

ENGLISH IS AWASH with interesting words and phrases; there are books the size of dictionaries chock-full of them. Here are twenty of our favourites – words and phrases with origins so interesting they should be part of general knowledge.

1. **Boycott**. Captain Charles Cunningham Boycott was a rent-collecting agent for an English landlord in Ireland in the nineteenth century. He was considered particularly harsh and locals refused to have anything to do with him. His name became a word meaning 'to ostracise'. It is used as a verb – 'to boycott', and as a noun – 'the boycott went well.'

2. **Halloween**. 'Hallow' is an old pronunciation of 'Holy', still sometimes found in the alternative version, 'All Hallows Eve'. The '-een' part is a common contraction of the word 'evening'. 'Halloween' means 'Holy evening' – also known as 'All Saints Eve'.

3. **Hooligan**. Almost certainly derived from the surname of an Irish family, 'Houlihan', whose name became synonymous with bad behaviour in the late nineteenth century.

4. **Quisling** (pronounced 'kwizling'). Norwegian Major Vidkun Quisling was a Norwegian politician who supported the Nazis in WWII. His name became synonymous with 'traitor'. He was shot for treason.

5. **Thug**. One of many Hindi words adopted into English (like 'pyjamas' and 'bungalow'). The 'Thugs' were a sect of robbers and murderers in India.

6. **Gerrymander** (pronounced 'jerry-manda'). A word derived from the surname of Elbridge Gerry, a US politician who in 1812 rearranged electoral districts to gain advantage for the Republican party. The new district was jokingly said to be shaped like a salamander and was depicted as such in a political cartoon that coined the term 'Gerry-mander.' His name has come to describe schemes to win elections dishonestly. His name began with a hard 'g', strangely enough, but the sound is soft on the word.

7. **Assassin**. The Arabic word 'hashshashin', meaning 'hashish eaters', was the name given to a violent Syrian sect in the Middle Ages. To create a murderous frenzy, they took hashish (cannabis) amidst chanting and dancing. The English word 'assassin' ultimately derives from this.

8. **Whisky**. From the Gaelic 'uisge beatha' (Ishka Ba-ha) –, meaning 'water of life'. Other languages use very similar phrases – 'aquavit' for strong spirit in Scandinavia, 'eau-de-vie' for brandy in France, 'aqua vitae' in Latin. Vodka is Russian for 'little water'.

9. **Tawdry**. Meaning cheap and flashy. This word comes from the phrase 'Saint Audrey's lace'. St Audrey was a seventh century princess of East Anglia, who took religious orders. As a girl, she had been very fond of necklaces and when she succumbed to a throat disease, she felt it was punishment for her vanity. 'St Audrey's lace' or 'Tawdry lace' was tainted, or flawed, and came to mean flashy and poor quality.

10. **Cor blimey/Gorblimey**. Still heard around Britain, though mainly in London, sometimes contracted just to 'blimey'. This is a corruption of an old oath – 'God blind me.' In a similar way, 'Bloody' is thought to be a corruption of 'By our Lady' and one that has fallen out of use, 'Gadzooks!' is a form of 'God's hooks', making reference to the nails used in the crucifixion of Jesus. The Australian 'Strewth!' similarly, is a contraction of 'God's *Truth*.' Even oaths can have interesting histories.

11. **Exchequer**. In Norman England, money-counting tables were often covered in a chequered cloth. The practice was common enough for the table to become known as an 'eschequier', meaning 'chessboard', and the word transferred to English as 'exchequer', a word for the Treasury.

12. **Auspicious/augury**. In English, the words have to do with telling the future. 'It seemed an auspicious moment to apply for his job, when Jenkins fell down the well.' Both have their roots in the Roman practice of using the flight of birds to tell the future. An expert in this field was known as an 'auspex', derived from a combination of 'avis', meaning 'bird', and 'specere', 'to look'. These charlatans were literally 'lookers at birds', and the word survives two thousand years on.

13. **Chivalry**. The moral code of knights, who tended to ride horses. The name is derived from the French word for horse, 'cheval', which in turn comes from the Latin 'caballus'. 'Cavalier', meaning off-hand or 'too casual' (a cavalier attitude), also comes from the same root.

14. **Chortle**. A word invented by Lewis Carroll (writer of *Alice in Wonderland*) as a combination of 'chuckle' and 'snort'. This type of combination is known as a 'portmanteau' word. He also invented the word 'portmanteau' to describe words of this type, like 'brunch', which is a combination of 'breakfast' and 'lunch'. Clever man.

15. **Conspire/Expire/Respire**. All these words have their origin in the Latin, 'spirare', to breathe. Conspirators breathe their plots together. A man who 'expires' has the breath go out of him. Respiration is breath.

16. **Denim**. This is one of many products linked to its place of origin. The hard-wearing cloth was created in Nîmes, a southern French industrial town. It was known first as 'serge de Nîmes' and then as 'de Nîmes'.

17. **Laconic**. The region inhabited by the Spartans of ancient Greece was named Laconia. Philip of Macedonia (the father of Alexander the Great) sent this warning to the famous warriors of the city, to frighten them into obedience: 'If I enter Laconia with my army, I shall raze Sparta to the ground.' The Spartans replied with a single word : 'If.' 'Laconic' means terse, or to the point, in recognition of the Spartan style. The word 'Spartan', meaning bare and without ornamentation, also comes from that warrior culture.

18. **Shambles**. Although it is now used to mean a chaotic scene, this word originally meant a slaughterhouse. In fact, reference to the fact that shambles were relocated after the great fire of London in 1666 can be found on Christopher Wren's Monument, (next to Monument tube station in London). The word origin goes even further back to Old English for a table, 'scamul', which is connected with the Latin for 'bench', 'scamnum'. Rows of these would form a meat market.

19. **Mob**. This word is simply a contraction of the Latin phrase, 'mobile vulgus' (MOB-e-lay, VULG-ous). 'Mobile' means fickle and 'Vulgus' means crowd.

20. **Quick**. In Old English, 'cwic' meant 'alive', a meaning we still see in 'quicksilver', another name for mercury, as the liquid metal seems almost to be a living silver. You may also have heard the phrase, 'the quick and the dead', meaning 'the living and the dead', or 'cut to the quick', meaning 'cut to the living flesh'. 'Quick-tempered' also retains some sense of the original sense, though the modern meaning is mainly to do with speed alone.

THE SOLAR SYSTEM
(A QUICK REFERENCE GUIDE)

THE SUN. THE CENTRE OF THE SYSTEM

- 93 million miles from Earth (149 million km).

- The Sun alone makes up 98% of all the mass of the solar system. If it was empty, it would take 1.3 million Earths to fill it. The temperature on the surface is a mere 6,000 °C/ (11,000 °F), while the internal temperature is 15 million °C (27 million °F).

- Age: Best current guess is 4.6 billion years. We expect it to survive for another 5 billion years before becoming a red giant, then a white dwarf, before finally burning out. Do not worry about this – the Earth and everything else in the solar system will be destroyed during the red giant stage.

MERCURY

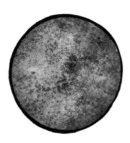

- Mercury is the closest planet to the Sun, at only 36 million miles (57 million km). Second smallest in the system. The surface is cratered in a similar way to Earth's moon. There *is* a thin atmosphere, containing sodium and potassium from the crust of the planet. Most of Mercury seems to be an iron core.

- Temperature: Hot. 430 °C (810 °F) by day, –180 °C (–290 °F) by night.

- Rotation around Sun (Mercury's year): 87.97 days. This is the fastest in the solar system and as a result, Mercury was named after the Roman messenger to the gods, who had wings on his feet.

- Moons: None.

VENUS

- The second planet from the Sun, at an average 67 million miles (108 million km). Venus has been called the morning or evening star, also Hesperus and Lucifer. Venus is the brightest object in Earth's sky apart from the Sun and our moon.

- Venus can be seen crossing the Sun in 2012. If you miss that one, you'll have to wait until 2117, which is quite a long time. Remember that pinhole or reverse projection from a telescope is a good idea when looking at the Sun – **never** look at it directly, especially with a telescope. The Sun would be the last thing you ever see.

- Rotation around Sun (Venus year): 224.7 days.

- Moons: None.

- Atmosphere: Complete cloud cover resulting from 97% carbon dioxide, the rest nitrogen. Hostile to life as we know it. Surface pressure 96 times that of Earth, so before you could even begin to choke, you'd be squashed flat. The average surface temperature is 482 °C (900 °F). Uncomfortable, to say the least.

- Venus was named after the Roman goddess of love because lonely men sitting in observatories can be quite susceptible to shiny, pretty things in the sky. Its movement across the heavens has nothing to do with actual love, however.

EARTH

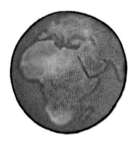

- The third planet from the Sun, at 93 million miles (149 million km).

- Like baby bear's porridge, Earth is neither too hot nor too cold. It is *just right*. Its atmosphere is made of nitrogen, oxygen, 0.03% carbon dioxide and trace gases, such as argon.

- Earth is the fifth largest planet in the system. It has a magnetic field and a liquid nickel-iron core.

- Rotation around the Sun (Earth year): 365.25 days.

- It has an elliptical orbit that means the Sun–Earth distance varies from 91 to 95 million miles at different times. The Earth rotates on the same plane as nearly all of the other planets in the system (except for Pluto), as if they are imbedded in the surface of an invisible plate. Very neat. We call it home.

- Moons: One, which rotates around the Earth in 27.3 days. With an astonishing lack of imagination, we call it 'The Moon'. (This is a bit like the London *Times* calling itself *The Times* because it was first, while all other *Times* newspapers include a city – the *Boston Times*, the *New York Times* and so on.)

MARS

- Fourth planet from the Sun, at an average of 141 million miles (226 million km).

- Gravity: One third that of Earth's.

- No significant magnetic field, which suggests the core is now solid, though it may have been liquid in the past.

- Rotation around Sun: 686.98 days.

- Average temperature: –55 °C (–67 °F).

- Mars has ice caps at both north and south poles, made up of water ice and frozen carbon dioxide. It has an atmosphere of 95% carbon dioxide, 3 % nitrogen and 2% argon and trace gases. Like Earth, it is tilted on its polar axis and experiences seasons, which can involve ferocious dust storms. Despite various probes and landings, we have yet to set foot on the red planet.

- Moons: Two, named Phobos (Fear) and Deimos (Panic). Mars was named after the Roman god of war. The Greek version of Mars was the god, Ares, who had two sons. The moons are named after them.

JUPITER

- The fifth planet from the Sun, at an average: 484 million miles (778 million km).

- Jupiter is by far the largest planet in the solar system and the fourth brightest thing in our sky, after the Sun, the Moon and Venus. It takes twelve years to orbit the Sun. It is sometimes called the amateur's planet, because it can be found easily with a basic telescope, or even binoculars.

- We haven't been to Jupiter and we probably never will – so our knowledge is based on observation and the occasional orbiter and probe. Science means we are not blind, however. For example, an effect of gravity is that it causes a passing object to accelerate, which is why you will occasionally see film sequences of spaceships using a 'sling-shot around the Sun' effect. The increase in speed can be measured and compared to other figures we already know. Piece by piece, we build up a picture of a planet – even one where the pressure and gravity is so crushing that we are unlikely ever to ever get a probe down to the surface.

- Jupiter's mass can be predicted from its effect on its moons – 318 times that of Earth. However, if Jupiter were hollow, more than a thousand Earths could fit inside, which means it must be composed of much lighter gaseous elements. This was confirmed by the *Galileo* probe in 1995, which dropped into the outer reaches of the atmosphere and found them composed of helium, hydrogen, ammonia and methane. In many ways, Jupiter is a failed sun – 80 times too small to ignite.

- Beneath the gas layers, pressure increases to more than 3 million Earth atmospheres. At that level, even hydrogen has properties of a metal and Jupiter has a solid core that must be one of the most hostile places imaginable. Winds there will range up to 400 mph and at those pressures, the chemistry of the universe that we think we understand will be completely alien. At temperatures of between –121 and –163 °C (–186 to –261 °F), ammonia will fall as white snow.

- Moons: Around 61, with a faint ring of debris. There are hundreds, perhaps thousands, of rocks orbiting Jupiter. Whether they are referred to as moons or not is a matter of opinion. Galileo discovered the four largest in 1610. They are: Io, Europa, Ganymede and Callisto. Given their size, they deserve a special mention. They are named after lovers of the chief god of the Greeks, Zeus, whom the Romans called Jupiter.

  1. **Io**. The closest to Jupiter, pronounced 'eye-oh'. It has a diameter of 1,942 miles, (3,125 km) a little less than the Earth's moon. It is intensely volcanic and its closeness to Jupiter's magnetic field generates three million electrical amps that flow into Jupiter's ionosphere. It orbits Jupiter in 1.77 days, at a distance of 220,000 miles (354,000 km).

2. **Europa**. The smoothest object in the solar system. It takes 3.55 days to orbit Jupiter. Its surface is ice, but a weak magnetic field of its own may indicate that there is liquid salt water below the surface. It has a diameter of just over 1,961 miles (3,155 km). Europa orbits Jupiter at a mean distance of 420,000 miles (670,000 km).

3. **Ganymede**. The largest moon of Jupiter and the largest moon in the solar system, with a diameter of 3,400 miles (5,471 km). It orbits Jupiter at a mean distance of 664,000 miles (1,068,000 km), taking 7.15 Earth days. Ganymede is larger than Mercury.

4. **Callisto**. The last of the Galilean moons. It has a diameter of 3,000 miles (4,828 km) and orbits at 1,170,000 miles (1,880,000 km) from Jupiter. It is similar in size to Mercury and orbits in 16.7 Earth days.

SATURN

- The sixth planet out from the Sun, at 856 million miles (1,377 billion km).

- Like Jupiter, it is a gas planet, with atmospheric pressure condensing hydrogen into liquid and even metal towards the core. Still, we think the overall density would be low enough for Saturn to float on water. It takes 29.5 years to orbit the Sun.

- The atmosphere is composed of 88% hydrogen, 11% helium and traces of methane, ammonia and other gases. Wind speeds on the surface are more than 1000 mph (1,600 kph).

- The rings stretch out more than 84,000 miles (135,000 km) from Saturn's centre. They were first seen by Galileo in 1610, though he described them as handles, as he saw them end on. The Dutch astronomer, Christiaan Huygens was the first to recognise them as rings, separate from the planetary surface.

- Temperature: –130 °C (–202 °F) to –191 °C (–312 °F). (Very cold!)

- Moons: Quite a large number if you count very small pieces of rock, but there are fifteen reasonably sized moons, ranging from Titan, the largest (second only to Ganymede in the solar system and even possessing a thin atmosphere), down to Pan, which is about 12.5 miles (20 km) across. The NASA probe, *'Huygens'* landed on Titan in 2005.

- Saturn is the Roman name for the Greek god, Cronus, who was father to Zeus.

URANUS

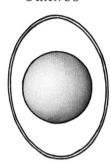

- The seventh planet from the Sun, at an average distance of 1.78 *billion* miles. (2.86 billion km).

- It has 11 rings and more than 20 confirmed moons, though as with Saturn and Jupiter, there are probably many more we haven't spotted yet. It is 67 times bigger than Earth, but has a mass only 14.5 times that of Earth, qualifying it for gas giant status, though on a smaller scale to Saturn and Jupiter.

- The space probe *Voyager 2* reached Uranus in 1986, our only source of knowledge at the time of writing, apart from Earth observation.

- Rotation around Sun: 84 Earth years, though it spins on its own axis even faster than Earth – 17.25 hours.

- Uranus has an atmosphere of 83% hydrogen, 15% helium and 2% methane. The planet core is nothing more than rock and ice. It has a huge tilt on its polar axis, so that one pole then the other points at the Sun. This means each pole receives sunlight for 42 Earth years. Average temperature: –197 °C (–323 °F) to –220 °C (–364 °F).

- Moons: 27. All named after Shakespeare characters, with names like: Cordelia (closest), Ophelia, Bianca, Puck, Rosalind, Desdemona, and so on.

- In mythology, Uranus was the father of Saturn, grandfather to Zeus/Jupiter.

NEPTUNE

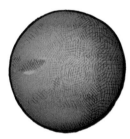

- The eighth planet from the Sun at 2.8 billion miles (4.5 billion km).

- Neptune is the fourth largest in the system. It has four rings and eleven known moons. It is the last of the gas giant or Jovian planets – seventy-two times Earth's volume, seventeen times its mass.

- It is believed to be composed of ice around a rock core, under an atmosphere of hydrogen, helium and methane.

- Every 248 years, Pluto's erratic orbit brings it inside the 'shell' of Neptune's orbit, making it the furthest planet from the Sun for a twenty-year period. The last time this happened was from 1979 to 1999, when Pluto moved back out. Neptune is the last of those planets that orbit on the same flat plane as Earth.

- The existence of Neptune was predicted before it was seen, like Halley's comet. The orbital track of Uranus seemed to be affected by the gravity of a large mass. The path and location of that mass were mathematically plotted, then searched for – and Neptune was found. It was first observed in 1846.

- The only vehicle from Earth to reach Neptune was *Voyager 2*, in 1989.

- Rotation around the Sun: 164.79 Earth years. It has an axial tilt of 29.6° compared to Earth's 23.5°, suggesting it has a similar movement of seasons, though to be honest, it's so cold, you'd hardly notice, or care.

PLUTO

- The ninth planet from the Sun at 3.65 billion miles (5.87 billion km).

- Pluto is what happens when a stray lump is slowly drawn into a neat solar system. However, Pluto is grown up enough to have a moon and has a tiny effect on the orbits of Neptune and Uranus. It is so small and distant that, even knowing it was there, it still took the telescopes of the world twenty-five years to find it for the first time in 1930. It took until 1978 for anyone to spot the single moon, Charon.

- We haven't managed to get a probe out that far, but the Hubble telescope has mapped 85% of Pluto's surface. It has polar caps and seems to be a ball of rock and dirty ice. It does have a thin atmosphere of nitrogen, carbon dioxide and methane.

- Being a dark and miserable place, Pluto was named after the Roman god of the Underworld (Hades to the Greeks). Charon was the boatman who ferried the souls across the River Styx.

- In 2004, Dr Mike Brown of the California Institute of Technology announced the discovery of a tenth planet – one about three-quarters the size of Pluto, more than 84 billion miles (134 billion km) away from the Sun. Sedna is reddish coloured, has no moon and its classification as a planet is somewhat dubious. There are, after all, more than a few scientists who think that Pluto should be declassified, never mind this tiny lump of ice. At least Pluto has a moon.

And Finally, Comets, Asteroids and other debris...

- The Sun is such a massive object that its gravity affects a vast volume of space, trapping objects such as **Halley's Comet**. These tend to be dirty balls of ice, sometimes just a few miles across. Halley's was large enough to have an effect on the orbital paths of the system and Edmund Halley's achievement is that he predicted this mathematically without seeing the comet. In fact, he never saw it. It wasn't until sixteen years after his death, in 1758, that sky watchers on Earth saw the comet once more. It is visible from Earth every 75–9 years and has been recorded since 240 BC. The next appearance is in 2061. It is extremely unlikely that the authors of this book will see it, but there is a chance you will...

- The **inner asteroid belt** lies between the orbits of Mars and Jupiter. It is composed of hundreds of thousands of rocks varying in size from grains to large ones hundreds of miles across. It may be debris from a planet-sized collision, or just the building blocks of the system, left over after everything started cooling.

- **Meteors** reach the system as it travels in space on the end of the milky way galaxy. They are usually made of stone silica, more rarely iron or nickel or a mixture of all three. They can make a bright trail as they reach the Earth's atmosphere and hit friction. If they don't burn up, they can hit the planet below with more force than an atomic bomb – but that almost never happens. (See Dinosaurs.) The best time to look for them is the 9–16 August and the 12–16 December. Meteors in the summer shower are known as the Perseids, as they appear in the constellation of Perseus. At its height, one a minute can be seen. Meteors in the winter meteor shower are known as the Geminids, as they appear in Gemini, near Orion. Both showers should be visible even from urban locations. They won't last for ever – the Geminids only came into existence in 1862.

- That's it. The rest is space and cosmic radiation.

THE TEN COMMANDMENTS

WHAT COMPILERS of modern versions of the Bible sometimes fail to appreciate is that the language of the King James Version has a grandeur, even a power, that their versions simply lack. It is no hardship to 'walk through a dark valley'. On the other hand, 'the valley of the shadow of death' is a different matter. Frankly, the rhythm and poetry are part of the effect and not to be lightly cast aside. We can find no better example of this than the Ten Commandments themselves. Book of Exodus, Chapter 20, Verses 1–17:

And God spake all these words, saying, I am the Lord thy God, which have brought thee out of the land of Egypt, out of the house of bondage.

1. Thou shalt have no other gods before me.

2. Thou shalt not make unto thee any graven image, or any likeness of any thing that is in heaven above, or that is in the earth beneath, or that is in the water under the earth: thou shalt not bow down thyself to them, nor serve them: for I the Lord thy God am a jealous God, visiting the iniquity of the fathers upon the children unto the third and fourth generation of them that hate me; and shewing mercy unto thousands of them that love me, and keep my commandments.

3. Thou shalt not take the name of the Lord thy God in vain; for the Lord will not hold him guiltless that taketh his name in vain.

4. Remember the sabbath day, to keep it holy. Six days shalt thou labour, and do all thy work: but the seventh day is the sabbath of the Lord thy God: in it thou shalt not do any work, thou, nor thy son, nor thy daughter, thy manservant, nor thy maidservant, nor thy cattle, nor thy stranger that is within thy gates: for in six days the Lord made heaven and earth, the sea, and all that in them is, and rested the seventh day: wherefore the Lord blessed the sabbath day, and hallowed it.

5. Honour thy father and thy mother: that thy days may be long upon the land which the Lord thy God giveth thee.

6. Thou shalt not kill.

7. Thou shalt not commit adultery.

8. Thou shalt not steal.

9. Thou shalt not bear false witness against thy neighbour.

10. Thou shalt not covet thy neighbour's house, thou shalt not covet thy neighbour's wife, nor his manservant, nor his maidservant, nor his ox, nor his ass, nor any thing that is thy neighbour's.

Verses 18 and 19:
And all the people saw the thunderings, and the lightnings, and the noise of the trumpet, and the mountain smoking: and when the people saw it, they removed, and stood afar off. And they said unto Moses, Speak thou with us, and we will hear: but let not God speak with us, lest we die.

COMMON BRITISH TREES

IN ABOUT 4000 BC the whole of Britain was covered by woodland. The natural environment in temperate regions does favour trees, but human activity does not. Most of Britain has been cleared of its ancient woodland by the migration of people using fire and axe. Millennia later, Britain rose as the pre-eminent sea power on the back of English oak.

To our ancestors, forests were an essential part of the rural economy, providing timber for houses, animals to trap, charcoal for fuel, wild mushrooms and herbs. A system evolved called 'coppicing', where an area of undergrowth and small trees was grown for periodic cutting, managed like any other crop.

There are still hundreds of different varieties of trees all over the country, too many to list here. However, it is a good idea to know the common trees of towns and countryside and how to identify them. It is as important to understand the earth around you as it is the heavens above. It might even come in useful when it comes to making things from wood.

The identification of trees can seem a formidable task. Overhearing a botanist wandering around murmuring '*Sequoiadendron giganteum*', may be a little scary. There is nothing wrong with recognising varieties by a process of categorisation and elimination, however. Here are a few of the most common – the ones we think *everyone* should know.

THE ENGLISH OAK (*QUERCUS ROBUR*)

The most important forest tree in north-west Europe, varying in size from 70 to 130 ft (21–40 m). Oak forms extensive woods and is fantastically long-lived, often surviving for centuries. Beech is more common in the south of England and ash and pine in the north. However, in the English midlands, oak reigns supreme.

- **Bark:** Grey, with fine cracks and ridges. The twigs bear rounded but pointed buds.
- **Leaves:** Clear and separate lobes.
- **Fruit:** The familiar acorn, on long stalks in clusters. Groups of seedlings can often be seen because squirrels bury them to ensure a winter food supply.

The Common Lime (*Tilia x europaea*)

A magnificent tree, tall and elegant, (75 ft/23 m), a well-established hybrid of the small- and large-leafed limes which form woods on the limestone slopes around Bristol and south Yorkshire. Traditionally planted in avenues. Lime flowers when dried can make a wonderful tea that is helpful in aiding sleep.

- **Bark:** Grey or grey-brown, long ridges and cracks and lumps.
- **Leaves:** Heart shaped, narrowing to a point, dark green, with tufts of white hair underneath. The twigs themselves are hairless.
- **Fruit:** rounded Rounded and faintly ribbed when ripe; fall in clusters.

Hawthorn (*Crataegus monogyna*)

One of the most familiar sights in lowland Europe as well as Britain. A dense thorny shrub, but which can also grow as a small tree (40 ft/ 12 m). Common on all soils as a hedge plant.

One of the old names for the Hawthorn hawthorn blossoms is 'May', which led to the ancient advice: 'Ne'er cast a clout til May is out' – don't remove a vest until spring comes. It's still good advice.

- **Bark**: Light brown and flaky.
- **Leaves**: Variable but lobed.
- **Fruit**: Distinctive small, deep red, round haws (fruit).
- **Flowers**: Appear in early June in white clusters, turning pink as they mature.

Silver Birch (*Betula pendula*)

Silver birch is a common tree of dry and sandy soils. Fast-growing, they rarely last longer than 100 years. At maturity, they can reach 100 ft (30.5 m). Distinguished by stiff branches and dropping twigs. Spring sap can be tapped into bottles and tastes like clear, sugary water. However, if the hole is left unplugged or too much is taken, the tree will die.

- **Bark:** Pinkish brown in young trees, turning white with black patches.
- **Leaves:** Oval with a long pointed tip, serrated around the edges.
- **Fruit:** Catkins (small twig). Shed lots of papery winged seeds in autumn, yellowy in colour.

Beech (*Fagus sylvatica*)

An impressive tree, which can grow up to 140 ft (42.5 m), with an enormous spreading crown. Dominant in chalky soils. Beeches survive for centuries, growing immense, twisting trunks. The wood is extremely hard and used in school carpentry benches.

- **Bark:** The trunk is smooth and grey, branching out horizontally.
- **Leaves:** Oval and pointy with clear veins at the edges. Spring – yellowy, summer – dark green, autumn – a rich brown. Twigs are brown with narrow pointed buds.
- **Fruit:** A hard glossy brown nut in a hairy shell. The inner nut can be eaten and tastes delicious.

Horse Chestnut (*Aesculus hippocastanum*)

A very familiar suburban tree, but not a native of Britain. Introduced from south-east Europe in the seventeenth century. Shakespeare never played conkers! The name comes from the resemblance to the edible chestnut. Can grow up to 80 ft (24 m).

- **Bark:** Orangey-brown.
- **Leaves:** Green oval, with an unmistakable spread.
- **Fruit:** Dark, sticky buds, beginning to open in April, forming green, spiny fruit cases towards the end of summer. These fall in September, the shells splitting to reveal brown nuts known as conkers.

Sycamore (*Acer pseudoplatanus*)

By far the most common maple in Britain. A beautifully domed tree that can grow up to 120 ft (36.5 m). In Britain, it is the most common tree in upland areas.

- **Bark**: Smooth and grey, becomes cracked and rough. Twigs are short and have fat green buds.
- **Leaves**: Large and green with five pointed lobes.
- **Fruit**: Form in pairs and spiral when in flight.

ASH (*FRAXINUS EXCELSIOR*)

The trunk is often long and straight. In northern England it is the main hedgerow tree, the only British tree that is of the olive family. Usually 70–80 ft (21–24.5 m), but can grow up to 140 ft (42.5 m).

- **Bark**: Smooth and grey, long cracks with age. The twigs are sticky, and have big black buds.
- **Leaves**: Pinnate (meaning 'pairs either side of stem'). Green, small and pointy.
- **Fruit**: In October, it sheds seeds that resemble a long, narrow, brown wing.

Robert the Bruce (1274–1329)

AFTER A LONG and successful reign, King Alexander III of Scotland died in 1286 after falling from his horse. He left no surviving children and only one four-year-old granddaughter, Margaret, the daughter of the Norwegian king. Rather than see the realm splinter into factions, the Scottish lords proclaimed her queen, despite her youth. The King of England, Edward I, intended to marry her to his son, himself a baby at this stage. Sadly, Margaret died at the age of eight before even making it back to Scotland.

There were then *thirteen* claimants to the Scottish throne. Edward I of England was asked to adjudicate between them and he came north with an army to do so. In the end he chose John Balliol, who had a direct line back to King David I of Scotland (1124–1153). Robert the Bruce was the next strongest contender for the throne. He had a near identical claim back to David I, but he seems to have been an extraordinarily charismatic leader and practical politician, which Balliol was not. Balliol had English estates and Edward assumed he would not resist the annexation of Scotland after his coronation. However, Balliol did just that. He refused to give judicial or feudal authority to Edward, or to acknowledge his superiority in any form. Edward's attempt to gain Scotland by stealth and subtlety had come to nothing.

To put this period in historical context, it should be remembered that the great eras of expansion were still centuries away. The Elizabethan period was from 1558–1603. England and Scotland would not have a joint throne until James I and the beginning of the seventeenth century. England in the fourteenth century was feudal and bleak. Though cathedrals and universities soared in her cities, every aspect of life was ruled by the land-owning class and the Church of Rome. At the secular head was Edward I, King of England, a hard

Robert the Bruce

man intent on unifying his realm. He had already conquered Wales, naming his son as Prince. (There is an old story that when the Welsh were unhappy at the thought of an English prince to rule them, Edward said he would give them a prince who spoke no word of English. They cheered this, but then he held up his baby son to them . . .)

Robert the Bruce saw the reigns of two very different English kings. The first was Edward I, a man who has on his tomb the words 'Hic Est Edwardus Primus Scottorum Malleus' – Here lies King Edward, the Hammer of the Scots. In his younger years, Edward travelled as far as Jerusalem and Tunisia on the Crusades. After returning home, he conquered Wales, borrowing money from English Jews to do it. His solution to the mounting interest on his debts was to have 300 heads of Jewish families executed and the rest exiled in 1290.

When Edward turned his gaze on Scotland, hard years came to that country. When Balliol resisted Edward's authority, he knew war would follow and prepared an army to invade the north of England. Edward had also expected his support against the age-old enemy, France, but Balliol actually made a pact with France against him.

In a cold rage, Edward drove north with his professional soldiers, smashing all resistance with extraordinary savagery. At Berwick, his army butchered many thousands of men, women and children, killing for two days. The Scots destroyed crops and livestock, starving his men while they launched attacks into Northumberland. The north bled in thousands of skirmishes and murders. Edward captured the 'Stone of Destiny' from Scone, on which all Scottish monarchs had been crowned, taking it back to Westminster. It was placed in 'King Edward's Chair' (named after Edward the Confessor) in Westminster Abbey. All British monarchs since that time are crowned whilst sitting on that chair, including Elizabeth II in 1953. The actual stone was given back to the Scottish people in 1996, though it will be returned for future coronations, as the thrones are linked in a 'united kingdom'.

Balliol was forced to abdicate at Kincardine Castle, only five months after he had gone to war with Edward. He spent three years in the Tower of London before he was allowed to go to estates in France. Edward chose Berwick as the place where he would receive a formal oath of homage from 2,000 Scottish nobles that year. Robert the Bruce was one of those who swore fealty in 1296.

The Scots rebelled again and years of conflict followed – a turbulent period for Scotland that produced, amongst others, William Wallace, a romantic rebel against the English king. His life inspired Walter Scott to write *'Exploits and Death of William Wallace, the Hero of Scotland'* and he was also the inspiration for the film *Braveheart* in 1995. Wallace and Robert the Bruce did not always see eye to eye. Robert the Bruce was a better diplomat and Wallace supported John Balliol's right to be king of Scotland, saying his abdication was achieved under duress. Wallace achieved some extraordinary victories against the English armies, even when heavily outnumbered, as at the Battle of Stirling Bridge in 1297. For that action, Wallace was knighted by Robert the Bruce and named 'Guardian of the kingdom of Scotland and leader of its armies'.

However, in 1298, Wallace saw his army broken at the Battle of Falkirk. Wallace resigned as Guardian and the post was then shared between Robert the Bruce and John Comyn, another of the original thirteen with a claim to the throne. Wallace escaped and spent time in France while Robert the Bruce made peace with Edward in 1302, staying at court in Carlisle. All the leading Scots were forced to swear fealty to Edward again in 1304 – except for Wallace. He remained at large for another year, a popular hero wherever rebels met. He was finally caught in 1305 and was hanged, drawn, quartered and beheaded at Smithfield Market in London along with his brother, their heads placed on London Bridge. It must have seemed like the end of Scottish independence, but Edward was growing old and sick and his son would never be the man to rule the hard lands of the north. Edward II lacked charisma and personal authority. He would be one of the worst kings England ever had.

Robert the Bruce met with John Comyn to put the case for one of them becoming king of Scotland and breaking faith with Edward I. Though Comyn agreed at first, he announced the treachery in letters to King Edward. Warned by a friend, Robert was forced to ride from Carlisle to Scotland before he could be caught and executed. He arranged a meeting with John Comyn in the sanctuary of a Scottish church and he and his men killed Comyn there, in revenge for the betrayal. Robert the Bruce was later excommunicated for this act by Pope Clement V.

He was crowned King of Scotland by his own mistress in 1306 at Scone – though not with the famous stone under his feet. His reign did not start well, with a string of defeats against the English forces in Scotland. Three of his brothers were killed by Edward, his wife was taken prisoner and he was forced into hiding. The legend is well known that when he was on the run and forced to take shelter in a cave, he saw a spider trying to complete a web and failing, over and over. As Robert the Bruce watched, it tried again and succeeded. The example gave him hope.

In 1307, Robert the Bruce began a new rebellion and Edward I took an army north to crush him. Edward was old and exhausted and as he reached the borders of England and Scotland, he was taken ill at a place called Burgh-by-Sands, where he could actually see Scotland across the Solway Firth. He told his son not to entomb him in Westminster, but instead to boil the flesh off his bones and then carry the bones in every future battle until the Scots were destroyed. His son failed in this, as he failed his father in almost every way. He faced problems of rebellious lords in England and returned there, leaving Robert the Bruce alone to consolidate his position.

In 1308, the tides of war changed for Robert the Bruce. He fought the Comyns first to establish his claim and then had the French king recognise his right to rule Scotland, which was a great aid to his cause. Considering that Edward II had married the French king's daughter Isabella, it was an astonishing feat of diplomacy. In fairness, the marriage could not have been a happy one. One of Edward II's first orders as King was to bring his lover, Piers Gaveston, back from France, where his father had banished him.

Robert the Bruce was also aided by Sir James Douglas, known as 'The Black Douglas'. Under his command, the Scottish clan forces drove out the English garrisons Edward I had left and invaded the north of England twice in 1311, laying the land waste.

Edward II had no choice but to respond. He took a large army north against the forces under Bruce. An absolutely crucial battle followed – Bannockburn, still seen today as one of the classic dates in Scottish history. The Scottish forces were badly outnumbered and facing professional soldiers well armed with crossbow, longbow, sword, axe, pike and horse. The lie of the land played a part, as the English found themselves hemmed in by marsh ground and bog, negating their numerical superiority. The battle itself took place over two days, with the most serious clash on 24 June 1314. The English cavalry charge was ineffective on that ground and was beaten back. The Scottish advance rolled over the English archers and the victory was complete when Edward II fled the field, his nerve deserting him.

Robert the Bruce would go on to many other victories over the next decade. The Irish lords even offered him the throne of Ireland. Robert sent his brother Edward, who was crowned High King of Ireland in 1316.

In England, Edward II managed to sire two boys and two girls with Isabella, despite his inclinations. He lacked the ruthlessness and tactical skill of his father, and Robert the Bruce was laying waste to cities and towns and sacking monasteries as far south as York. Edward II lost power to a committee of his own lords, lost his throne to his wife and eldest son and, after being held prisoner and tortured, was eventually put to death in 1327 by being impaled on a length of red-hot iron, considered at the time to be a suitable comment on his lifestyle and failures.

It would be Edward II's son, Edward III, who would sign a peace treaty in 1328 that recognised Scotland as an independent nation and Robert the Bruce as King. It was the crowning moment of Robert's life and he died the following year in 1329.

As he signed the treaty, Edward III was only sixteen and under his mother's legal power. When he reached his majority, he repudiated the treaty. English kings continued to call themselves rulers of Scotland, but Scotland did remain independent until 1603, when James VI of Scotland became James I of England and joined the thrones. Unlike his hopeless father, Edward III ruled successfully and wisely for no less than fifty years.

Robert the Bruce's final instruction was that his heart be taken to the Holy Land. It has since been returned and is buried in Melrose Abbey in Roxburghshire in the east of Scotland.

HUNTING AND COOKING A RABBIT

UNDER UK LAW, it is illegal to use an airgun under the age of fourteen. From fourteen to seventeen, an air rifle may be given as a gift and used legally, though it is still illegal to buy one before seventeen. It is also worth considering the lesser-known fact that if an air rifle is used in the commission of a crime of *any* kind, it is considered to be 'a firearm' – with serious penalties applied.

The legal limit for an air rifle sold without a firearm certificate is twelve foot-pounds of pressure. There are two main types: those you cock by pulling the barrel back on itself and those that work from compressed air held in a canister under the barrel. The type that cocks is cheaper and doesn't need recharging every 100 shots. It should last practically for ever. Target shooting can be a highly enjoyable pursuit, but a powerful air rifle can also be used to hunt game – rabbits, pheasants and pigeons.

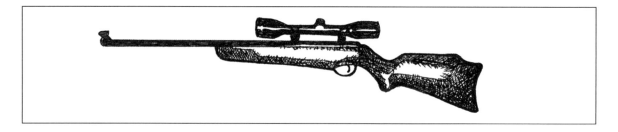

To do so is not a game, nor is it a sport. We believe the experience is valuable as it gives an insight into the origin of those neat meat packages you see in supermarkets. The aim, however, should be to get lunch – if you kill something, you have to eat it.

It is possible to hunt rabbits with a bow and arrow, but the movement involved in pulling the string back tends to spook them and we cannot recommend this unless you are capable of holding a drawn bow motionless for ten or twenty minutes. Believe us when we say it is extremely hard to hunt rabbits with a bow. You tend to lose the arrows as well.

Before you go anywhere near a live shoot, spend time with a target set up at twenty or thirty yards. You can make a simple bull's-eye by drawing round two cups in circles on a bit of paper. Bring drawing pins with you to fix it to a tree.

A yard is a normal walking pace, so it's easy to set up the range. You need to be certain that when you have something in your cross-hairs, the pellet will hit where you point it. The method here is to find a steady aiming spot, a tree stump, for example, and fire five shots at the bull, taking note of where they hit. If you are steady, they should be close together. If all of your shots at bull are hitting low and to the left, say, you'll need to adjust your sights to fire up and right. Practise until you can hit the bull regularly. You should not stint when buying the pellets – you want ones that are checked for quality and heavier than usual. Don't bother with the pointed-head pellets. Weight is far more important. It does cut the range a little, but is more likely to result in a clean kill.

Finding the Rabbit

Get out into the countryside, for a start. It is not illegal to fire an air rifle within the confines of your own garden, unless the pellets pass outside the boundary, in which case you are likely to have an armed police team turn up. Be sensible – look for rabbits where there are fields. Note that it is also illegal to walk around with an uncovered weapon, but if the weapon is in a carrying sleeve, you can walk on public land with one. That said, the law can change and may have by the time you read this. Check with your local police station before taking an air rifle on a public highway.

Rabbits never move far from their warrens. If you have ever seen one in a field, their burrow will be very, very close by. The best thing to do will be to note where they are seen over a period of time, to have an idea of where to find them. It is possible to come upon them on a ramble, but it's a little hit and miss.

This is one place where exercising a little common sense wouldn't hurt. Go and ask the owner of the land if you can shoot rabbits. If it's a field, or a farm, there's a very good chance they will say yes. Rabbits breed like maniacs and are not much loved by farmers. You may even be given directions to the best spots. However, shooting a pheasant will provoke a very angry reaction. These birds are a cultivated crop whose value lies in the shooting fees paid for them. Poachers are not appreciated and illegal poaching carries heavy penalties.

Once in the area, find the warren. You might see rabbits in the distance, but as you come closer, they will all vanish. After you locate the complex of burrows, you should get between 60 and 90 feet (18–28 m) away (20-30 yards) – the effective range. Much further and you are likely to miss a kill. Much closer and they will remain nervous in your presence.

Have a pellet ready in the rifle, settle down flat on your stomach and wait. You will appreciate a warm coat and possibly even a thermos of tea at this point. Your arrival will have startled the rabbit population and you'll have to wait ten minutes or so for them to return.

Don't have a rush of blood to the head and fire at the first rabbit you see. There will be a number of chances, but some will be too far, or the rabbit might be too young. When you are ready, take the shot, aiming at the head behind the eye if you can. There is a great satisfaction in pulling off a difficult shot over distance. If you are with someone else, never point the gun at them, even if you believe it to be unloaded. An accident at that point could last a lifetime.

In the event that you merely wound the rabbit, you should reload, approach and fire point point-blank at the spot behind the eye. Try to avoid causing unnecessary suffering. If you have missed, either move to another position, or read a book for half an hour. It will take that long for the rabbits to come out again.

Rabbits bleed, so have a plastic bag ready for transport. All you have to do now is skin it and eat it.

Skinning the Rabbit

This is not a difficult process, though it is a little daunting the first time. If you have a heavy-bladed cleaver, simply chop off the four paws. If you are stuck with only a penknife, break the forearm bones with a quick jerk, then cut the skin around the break in a ring. Remove the head in the same way. A serrated edge will cut through the bones, but a standard kitchen knife is likely to be damaged if used as a chopper.

Cut a line down the middle of the chest, from head to anus. This can be fiddly if you're on your own, and a serrated edge is very useful. Be careful not to cut into the abdominal cavity – if you do, the stomach and intestines will spoil the meat.

With fingers, you can now pull back the skin to the hip and shoulders, yanking the fur off the legs like sleeves. When the legs are free, take hold of the fur at the neck and pull downwards. The pelt will come off in one piece, leaving you with the carcass. The belly is quite obvious and bulges with intestines.

Holding the carcass upside down, take a pinch of loose skin near the rear legs and cut a line across it. As you turn the rabbit the right way up, most of the intestines will slide right out immediately and anything that doesn't can be scooped out with ease.

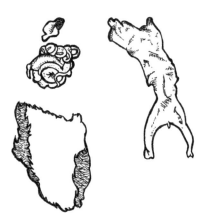

There is a partition between the stomach area and the upper chest that can be broken with a little pressure. Behind it, you will find the heart, lungs and a few other bits and bobs. Pull it all out. The heart, liver and kidneys in particular can be very tasty, but the intestines and stomach should be left well alone.

It is worth taking a moment to have a look at the various inner organs. Male rabbits will have testicles that should also be cut away. This is not for the squeamish, but that is the point of the chapter. If you buy a pork chop, we think you should realise what has gone into providing that meat for you. In a sense, killing for food is a link with ancestors going back to the caves.

PREPARING A MEAL

This isn't the place for a formal recipe, but it is worth covering the next stage. You could spit-roast the rabbit, but it is easier and more common to joint it – that is, remove the legs by cutting through the joints. Fillets can also be taken from pads of flesh near the spine. You can take a fair amount of meat off a single rabbit – enough, with vegetables, to feed two men and provide hot broth against a winter chill.

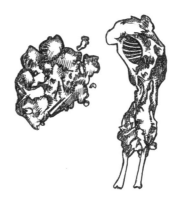

Place the meat in a pot with water and bring it to the boil, adding courgettes, a little garlic, carrots, leeks and celery until the pot is half full. Let it simmer for half an hour to forty-five minutes. Wild game is often pretty chewy because the muscles are used much more often than tame animals'. Nevertheless, rabbit cooked in this way is delicious and the broth is very good indeed.

THE GAME OF CHESS

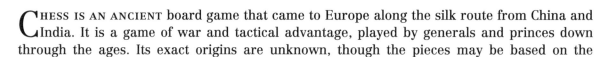

CHESS IS AN ANCIENT board game that came to Europe along the silk route from China and India. It is a game of war and tactical advantage, played by generals and princes down through the ages. Its exact origins are unknown, though the pieces may be based on the ancient formations of Indian armies.

It is a game for two people, played on a board of sixty-four alternately black and white squares. As with most of the best games, it is easy to play badly and hard to play well.

THE PIECES

Both sides have sixteen pieces: 8 pawns, 2 knights, 2 bishops, 2 castles, (also known as rooks), 1 queen and 1 king.

The object of the game is to capture (checkmate) the opponent's king. White has the first move and then both players take it in turns until one triumphs.

SETTING UP THE BOARD

There should be a white square in the right-hand corner when placing the board. The pieces are arranged in two lines, facing each other. The pawns protect the rear line, which is arranged in the following sequence: 1. Rook; 2. Knight; 3. Bishop; 4. Queen; 5. King; 6. Bishop; 7. Knight; 8 Rook.

The queen always goes on her own colour – the black queen on the black square in the middle. The white queen will go on the corresponding white square.

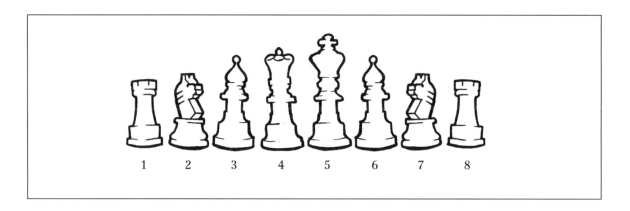

1   2   3   4   5   6   7   8

Each type of piece moves in a different way.

1. **Pawns** are the infantry and move forward, one square at a time – except on the first move, where they are allowed to lurch two squares forward in a fit of martial enthusiasm. They capture diagonally, to the left or right. They are the least valuable pieces, but the only ones that can be promoted. (Value: 1 point.)

Knight

Bishop

2. The **Knights** are the cavalry: mobile and difficult to stop. They move in an 'L' shape of 'two squares and one' in any direction. In the diagram, all the black pawns around the knight can be attacked. Crucially, the knight is the only piece that can jump over others in their path. Even if a rook blocked the way to one of the pawns above, the knight could still take the pawn. (Value: 3 points.)

3. **Bishops** are the elephants. They move along the diagonals, though they are limited to white or black squares only. They work well together, covering both colour squares. They also do well in distance attacks, like machine guns or searchlights. (Value: 3 points.)

Rook/Castle

4. **Castles** (Rooks). These are the chariot forces. They control the straight lines on the board and are particularly useful in the endgame and for castling. (Value 5 points.)

5. The **Queen**. This is the most powerful piece on the board and can move in any direction, without limit. (Value: 8 points.)

6. The **King** is the most important piece on the board. It can only move one square at a time, but in any direction. It can move two squares whilst castling. It cannot move into check. (Value: Game.)

Queen

King

Having the first move is an advantage and most games tend to be won by white. Classically, black plays defensively, countering white's aggressive moves and taking advantage of mistakes.

Capturing. One player removes an enemy piece from the board by landing on the same square. With the exception of a king, any piece can take any other. A king is restricted by the fact that it cannot move into check, so a king can never take another king. Pawns can only capture diagonally, moving forward.

Check/Checkmate. If a piece threatens the king, so that in theory it could take the king, it is called 'check'. The king *must* either move out of check, block the check, or the attacking piece must be taken. If none of these are possible, the king has been caught – a checkmate, which is a corruption of the Arabic for 'The king is dead'.

Castling. After the knight and bishop have moved, the king can shift two squares either left or right, with the rook taking the inside square.

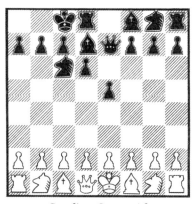

Castling Kingside   *Castling Queenside*

En Passant. This is an unusual form of pawn capture that is now common practice. When a pawn has moved down the board, it looks possible to avoid it by moving the opposing pawn two squares up. 'En passant' allows pawn capture as if only one square had been moved.

In theory, the game can be split into thirds – the opening, the middle game and the endgame.

OPENING

The idea here is to get out all your main pieces, known as 'developing', before castling your king to safety. The centre of the board (the four central squares) is important to control. For example, a knight in the centre has up to eight possible moves. In a corner, he may only have two.

Some openings have names and long histories, such as 'The King's Indian Defence' and 'The Sicilian'. There are many books on openings, but you should find one you like and stick to it, playing it often to understand it better. As an example, we'll show the moves of the King's Indian.

Remember, pawns cannot go backwards, so move them carefully as you develop. Link them into pawn chains, one protecting the next. Try and avoid leaving a piece 'en prise', or undefended.

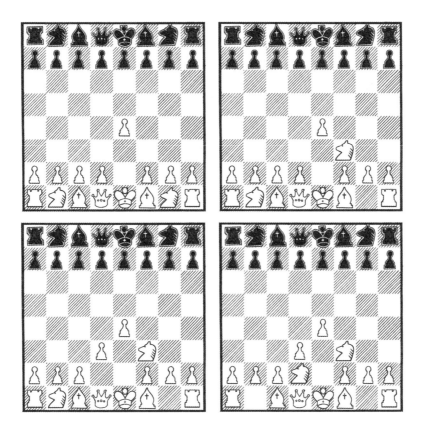

THE MIDDLE GAME

Your pieces should be developed and your king safe. This is where you start to attack.

Advance your pieces to positions that help control the board and capture the enemy units. Even at this stage, you should be looking for opportunities to capture the enemy king, but don't overextend your pieces. If you want to move to a square with one piece, make sure it is protected by another.

A 'pin' is a piece held in place by the danger of losing a more important piece behind it. Pins work particularly well against the enemy king. Your opponent is unable to move his blocking pieces as he *cannot* move into check.

A 'fork' is when a piece threatens two pieces at the same time. The knight is particularly good at this and can be deadly when putting the king in check and at the same time threatening a valuable piece.

A 'skewer' is the opposite of a pin, when a valuable piece is forced to move, thereby exposing a lesser piece to capture. A rook that threatens a queen may not get the queen, but may take the bishop behind her when she moves.

Remember to keep your king protected in your 'castle', stay level on points and try to get ahead. Even a pawn advantage will show itself in the endgame.

THE ENDGAME

It is possible to win in the middle game, while the board is still full of pieces, but most wins occur in the endgame. The board will be stripped of the main pieces and pawns. Strangely, the safest position for the king is now the centre of the board, where its power can be used to attack and shepherd pawns towards promotion.

Promotion. If a pawn reaches the back rank of the opposing side, it can be exchanged for a queen, rook, bishop or knight. (You can have two queens! Just turn a rook upside down to represent the second one.) In the endgame, the threat of promotion can have a serious effect on tactics.

The endgame will involve combinations of pieces, as bishops and rooks, for example, attempt to limit the enemy king's movement, check him and then bring about a checkmate. Rooks are particularly strong in the endgame and should not be sacrificed early.

The aim is obviously to checkmate your opponent's king. This is the hardest part of the game and the last thing the novice learns to do *well*.

This is one of the only games where you get to match your brain directly against someone else. It's a level playing field – except for experience, preparation and intelligence. Do not underestimate preparation. Many a clever boy has been beaten by a better chess player.

It is played all over the world, from magnetic sets on trains to ornate bone carved sets in Indonesia. It's a language we all know and every boy should be able to play chess.

TANNING A SKIN

MAKING LEATHER from skins must be one of the oldest human skills. That said, it isn't at all easy to get right and it's worth knowing that small skins (like those of rabbits) can be air-dried after the fat has been cut away. The result will have the stiffness of a bit of cardboard, but there is a very good chance it will feel no better *after* the tanning process. Larger skins have to be tanned, or they simply rot.

First of all, cut away any obvious pouches of flesh on the inner side of the skin. The best way to do this is to stretch the skin onto a board, held in place with tacks at the edges. Use a sharp knife and a lot of care to remove the marbled pink fat without puncturing the skin beneath it. Stone-Age peoples used flints and bones to scrape hides. They also chewed them to make them soft. You might want to try this, though we thought it was going a little too far.

You don't have to get every tiny scrap of fat, but be as thorough as you can. A rabbit skin can be left in a cool room for about ten days and it will dry. Covering it in a heavy layer of salt speeds the process and also helps to prevent any smell of rotting meat. You may want to change the salt after two or three days if it becomes damp or obviously contaminated. When the skin has dried it will be quite rigid. At this point, you could trim off the rough edges with a pair of scissors.

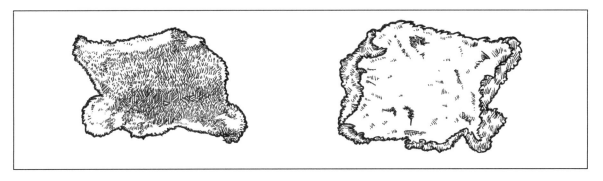

Tanning is the chemical process that makes skin into leather – a waterproof, hard-wearing and extremely versatile material. Almost all the leather we use is from cows, as it is produced as a natural by-product of eating beef. Various chemicals are useful in the process, including traditional ones from boiled brains or excrement. However, we used aluminium potassium sulphate. As well as growing crystals, alum solution can tan skin.

Once the skin is completely dry, it can be dipped in warm water with a little soap to cut the grease. There is a membrane inside all animal skins that must be removed before tanning. One way is to rub the skin back and forth on an edged object, like a wooden board or a large stone. We found wire wool useful, as well as the back of a kitchen knife. It took a long time. It smelled. Peeling off sticky wads of fatty membrane was not an enjoyable experience. Still, no one said it would be easy.

When the skin was about as clean as we could make it, we trimmed one or two of the rougher edges and prepared a solution of 1 lb (453 g) alum, 4 oz (124 g) washing soda (calcium carbonate) and 8 pts (4.55 l) of water. It fizzes as you mix it up, but don't worry.

A rabbit skin should be left in the solution for two days, though larger skins can take up to five. Be careful how you dispose of the liquid, as it's a pretty potent weedkiller and will destroy grass.

When you take it out, it will be sopping wet and the skin side will have gone white. You now need to oil it thoroughly and leave it overnight. Ideally, you would use an animal oil, but those aren't easy to get hold of. We chose linseed oil, which is usually used for cricket bats and church pews. It smells quite pleasant, as well. We placed a plastic bag over it to seal in the oil and left it for another two days.

The next stage is to let the oiled skin dry, fur side out, but only until it is damp. This stage is crucial to create a soft final skin. Whilst damp, you must 'work' it. This means gently stretching it and running it back and forth over a smooth wooden edge, like the back of a chair or a broomstick held in a vice.

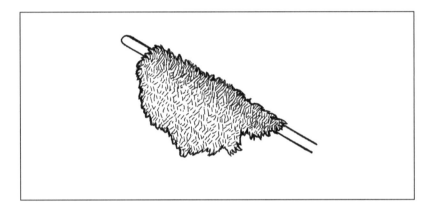

How soft the final version is will depend on how well it was tanned, how much flesh still adhered to the skin membrane and how conscientiously you work it. If it does dry out, and is too stiff, it is all right to dampen it again and repeat the process. It will get softer, but it could take a few sessions.

Finally, a quick dip in unleaded petrol is worth doing, just to clean it and cut through excess oiliness. It will make the skin smell of petrol, obviously, but this fades in a day or two. You really should get an adult to help with this.

Once you have allowed it to dry completely, imperfections can be removed with a sanding block. The skin will resemble waxed baking paper, but it should be strong *and flexible* – and it shouldn't smell like a dead animal. Calfskin has been used as paper and rabbit skin could also be written on, though it would serve better as an outer sleeve for a small book, a drawstring pouch or, with a few more, perhaps a pair of gloves.

THE BRITISH EMPIRE (1497–1997):
'The empire on which the sun never sets'

INDES   AUSTRALIE   CANADA   AFRIQUE   BORNÉO   GUYANE   HAOUSSAS   NIGER

Fıve centuries of energy, triumph and disaster, heroism and invention are too full to be explored here in the detail they deserve. What follows is a summary of the rise and fall of the largest empire the world has ever known. The influence of language, custom, law and tradition continues, but the British Empire came to an end on 30 June 1997, when Hong Kong passed back into Chinese ownership. It is astonishing to think that almost exactly 100 years before, on 20 June 1897, Queen Victoria celebrated her Diamond Jubilee of sixty years ruling 375 million subjects. The idea that the Empire would vanish only a century later would have been laughed at, though Rudyard Kipling saw that the world turns on, regardless of human achievement. His poem 'Recessional'

was read to Victoria. These four lines are particularly poignant.

> *Far-called, our navies melt away –*
> *On dune and headland sinks the fire –*
> *Lo, all our pomp of yesterday*
> *Is one with Nineveh, and Tyre!*

It has struck some that if an empire had to be broken against an enemy, Nazi Germany was a worthy cause. All the countries in the Empire sent men back for that conflict. They came from America, India, Canada, Nepal, New Zealand, Australia, South Africa – everywhere, in fact, where the people could claim a bond with Britain – to give their lives against a dark and terrible enemy. Perhaps that was the purpose of the British Empire – to be there at that time, when the future could have gone another way. As a legacy, perhaps that will do.

On 20 May 1497, John Cabot set sail from Bristol with a royal warrant to claim land for Henry VII. This was the first document of what would one day become the Empire. He made landfall in Newfoundland, on the north-eastern edge of Canada. His son Sebastian established the Company of Merchant Adventurers in London and secured a trade treaty with Ivan the Terrible in Russia. English trade interests were beginning to grow, and by the time of Elizabeth I they would come into conflict with the ambitions of Spain. There were several reasons for the rivalry. The Spanish royals had sponsored Christopher Columbus, they were Catholic where Elizabeth was Protestant, and most importantly of all, the two growing trade fleets competed against each other. English pirates would capture Spanish ships laden with gold, silver and slaves from their colonies in South America. In turn, English crews would be arrested and tortured whenever the opportunity presented itself. It was a brutal period, with fortunes for the taking, which helped to establish the English as a naval nation. Elizabeth I even leased ships to privateers in exchange for a tithe of the profits. It was simple: it rewarded daring and it brought vast wealth to Britain. As Sir Walter Raleigh said,

> Whosoever commands the sea commands the trade; whosoever commands the trade of the world commands the riches of the world and consequently the world itself.

Sir Francis Drake had first sailed with the privateer John Hawkins, a scourge of merchant shipping. In his turn, Drake became the most notorious of privateer captains, taking great pleasure in attacks on Spanish vessels. He saw the 'Papist' Catholic Spanish as enemies to a Protestant England and was happy to ambush their ships and even a mule-train carrying silver from Peru to Panama. He became a popular hero in England and was a dashing favourite of the Queen. He was the second man

Sir Francis Drake

to circumnavigate the globe (after Magellan) – though he missed finding the legendary southern continent (Australia) – and reached California, naming it New Albion. He brought his queen £160,000 profit from just one voyage – in a day when a man could live comfortably on £20 a year. He was knighted on the quarterdeck of his ship, the *Golden Hind*.

When he heard the Spanish were preparing a great armada in Cadiz, Drake took fifty ships out to attack them with fire-ships before they could sail out of the harbour. His fleet did so much damage that the Spanish took a year to rebuild. Drake said that he had 'merely singed the King of Spain's beard', but Elizabeth would not agree to further attacks.

In 1588, the Spanish Armada sailed into the English Channel. Many of the Spanish ships were lost to strong winds and high seas, leading King Philip to comment later that 'God is an Englishman.' In addition to natural forces, the Spanish fleet was beaten by faster gunnery, nimbler ships and better captains, ending the likelihood that the future would be Spanish-led.

*

This was to be the hallmark of the early British Empire. Trade would drive its expansion, then war, almost always with European nations seeking their own wealth. Over the next four centuries, Britain would go to war with almost every European country. Perhaps because of Europe being a cauldron of conflict for the previous three thousand years, the nations of the continent were superior to the rest of the world in terms of arms, tactics, ships, technology and materials such as steel. Holland, France, Spain, Germany and Britain all exploded outwards, using their advantages to win territories and profit. One by one, all of the others were beaten home again. The French were finally stopped at Waterloo and the Germans in 1945. The Empire would eventually become the Commonwealth, in a peaceful transition, as the world headed towards the third millennium.

✳

When James VI of Scotland combined the thrones to become King of England, Scotland and Ireland in 1603, the new century would provide fresh challenges for the nascent Empire.

In 1613, the East India Trading Company established its first settlement at Surat in India. Their aim was to grow spices in competition with Dutch traders. Exploration and adventure led the way, with men such as Captain John Smith, who named New England, and Sir George Somers, who discovered the Bahamas when he was blown off course.

King James was a Presbyterian (of the Church of Scotland) and Puritans in England were deeply unhappy with his rule. In 1620, a disaffected group of them set sail from Southampton in two ships – the *Speedwell* and the *Mayflower*. The *Speedwell* was unseaworthy and they both turned back to Plymouth. The *Mayflower* then went out alone, carrying Puritans, crew and colonists recruited by the Virginia Trading Company. They made landfall first in Cape Cod, but could find no decent shelter in the depths of a hostile winter. The second landing was at Plymouth in Massachusetts, named so previously by Captain John Smith.

Many more would follow and over time Maine, New Hampshire and Connecticut were settled. The new world was opening up and by 1630, Boston and ten other settlements were established. By 1643, New Haven, Plymouth, Connecticut and Massachusetts formed a confederation as the United Colonies of New England.

In England, Charles I had taken the throne and actually lost it in the English Civil War with Oliver Cromwell. The American colonies began to taste their own freedom from the mother country. In 1688 William of Orange was asked by the English parliament to take the throne from James II, who was once again insisting England should become Catholic. William had a claim to the throne through being a grandson of Charles I and he landed with an honour guard, after James II had gone into exile in France. The Crown's grip on the American colonies became oppressive during his reign.

In 1707, the kingdoms of England and Scotland were legally and politically joined by the Act of Union, an important part of British history. Gibraltar (at the southern tip of Spain) became a British port in perpetuity by the Treaty of Utrecht in 1713. Minorca was also turned over to Britain but, more importantly, France was forced to drop her claim to vast territories in Canada. However, it would take military action to enforce British sovereignty over Canada. Even while a new capital was being built in 1748, French attacks on British settlements continued. Eventually, the French colonists were given the choice of swearing allegiance to the British Crown or being deported. Most chose to be deported.

In America, the struggle between France and Britain continued. A French expedition took control of the Ohio Valley and a messenger named George Washington was sent to tell them to withdraw. His small unit was made to surrender by the French. A much larger army that included 1,200 regular soldiers from Britain would be almost annihilated by a combined French and Iroquois Indian force. The rebellion spread, though this particular force was eventually routed and driven back. In 1756, the Seven Years War with France began and in America, Canada and India, as well as closer to home, French and British forces fought bitter battles.

✳

Robert Clive of India might have remained an East India Company clerk if not for the war. Famously he had tried to commit suicide twice, failing both times with a jamming gun. He was made an ensign in the Company army and became almost the archetype of that strange breed Britain could produce – men with an absolute disregard for personal safety and an unshakeable belief in the rightness of their cause. The Mahrattas of India called Clive 'Sabat Jung' – 'Daring in War'.

Calcutta was begun as a settlement by the British East India Company. The Company officials fortified their base in Calcutta against local insurrection. The Nabob of Bengal decided this was an act of defiance and sent a great host against the fort, overwhelming it. The 146 company employees surrendered on the condition that their lives be spared. They were held without water in a stifling room twenty-four feet by eighteen. In the morning, only twenty-three had survived what became known as 'the black hole of Calcutta'.

It could all have been lost in 1756. The French were growing in strength in India, while the East India Company had lost Calcutta and Madras. British colonies in America seemed vulnerable to French attack. In addition, Britain lost Minorca and Spain entered the war on the side of France in 1762.

In England, the Prime Minister, William Pitt (Pitt the Elder), came up with the idea of funding the Prussian army to wage war against the French-led alliance of Austria, Russia, Saxony, Sweden and Spain, allowing Britain to concentrate her troops in far-flung places such as India and Canada. He was particularly lucky in having Frederick the Great as his ally, as the man was a tactical genius. The Seven Years War can be considered the first world war, given the scale of it. It is still the most successful war ever fought by Britain as it brought India and Canada into the fold and practically began an empire overnight. Pitt did not lack confidence: 'I know that I can save this country and no one else can,' he said.

Clive recaptured Calcutta in 1757 and after extraordinary subterfuge and negotiation, fought the Battle of Plassey against a French and Indian army of 50,000 with fifty-three guns. Clive had 1,100 British troops, 2,100 natives and ten guns. The French gunners continued fighting right to the end, but Clive's force routed the enemy and secured Bengal for British rule. It has been said that Plassey was the turning point, but in fact there were hundreds of times and places where the British Empire could have failed. Only when we look back with an Olympian perspective does it seem inevitable. For those involved in its creation, every year survived was a gift and only luck, fortitude, bravery and cunning could hold it for the year after that.

Robert Clive

'The Death of Wolfe' by Benjamin West.

In Canada, Pitt was fortunate to have another gifted soldier – James Wolfe. The fleet took an expeditionary force of 9,000 British regulars and 500 colonials from Halifax to take Louisburg and then Quebec from the French. In 1758, Wolfe led the attack on Louisburg carrying only a cane. The guns of the great fort were taken and turned on French ships in harbour. The first step had been taken to pushing the French out of Canada. However, the fighting was ferocious as fort after fort was captured throughout 1759.

Wolfe was made major general and took command for the assault on Quebec, an almost impregnable fortress above the St Lawrence river. (James Cook was the surveyor of the river, the man who later went on to claim Australia and map New Zealand.) The night before, Wolfe gave a locket to John Jervis, a naval captain, to be sent to his fiancée if he died. As an admiral, Jervis would later play a crucial role in Nelson's career and lived until 1823.

Wolfe's army fought the French on 13 September 1759 on the Plains of Abraham in front of the city. Both commanders were mortally wounded. Wolfe died during the battle and the French commander later that night. Quebec surrendered and the British garrisoned the city.

There were other battles, but on 8 September 1760, the French surrendered their interest in Canada. They had lost fleets to British ships and Britain was free from the threat of invasion. Bells rang in London to celebrate a year of victories.

The American War of Independence could also have been the beginning of the end. In a very real sense, this was a civil war between British forces who wanted to remain loyal to Britain and others who wanted to forge their own identity as a separate country rather than one ruled from abroad. The causes are complex, though part of the reason for the war was the level of taxes imposed by Britain on such products as sugar and, most famously, tea. 'No taxation without representation' was the cry raised against King George III. The cry, needless to say, was ignored and further taxes were imposed on glass, lead, paper and just about anything else the British government could think of. Riots followed in America and bloodshed was inevitable. A change of government in Britain meant that all taxes were repealed except for the one on tea, but it was too late and in 1773 in Boston 342 boxes of tea worth £10,000 were tipped into the harbour – known ever after as 'the Boston tea party'.

Britain had reduced the size of the army after the Seven Years War. Clive had at last managed to shoot himself, Wolfe was dead and Pitt was too elderly and frail to help the situation. George III suffered from porphyria, a disease that rendered him completely insane for temporary periods. From 1773 to 1783, Britain needed a great negotiator, a visionary, or possibly a Wellington or a Nelson. For once, there wasn't one and the war was a shambles. Interestingly, the French played a crucial part, still smarting from their defeat in the Seven Years War. Apart from providing supplies, France formed a league of 'armed neutrality' with Spain, Russia, Prussia, Holland and Sweden to protect American shipping from the Royal Navy. A French fleet brought 5,000 men and 106 heavy guns from Toulon to support their General Lafayette in America. After landing the army, the French fleet attacked British ships waiting for a retreating British force under Cornwallis. With his back to the sea, Cornwallis was forced to surrender at Yorktown. Famously, his military band played 'The world turned upside down'. In September 1783, Britain recognised the independence of the thirteen American states. George Washington became the first president six years later on 30 April 1789 – the year of the French Revolution. Napoleon Bonaparte had arrived on the world scene.

Canada remained a British possession, though limited autonomy was given soon after the American war and perhaps because of it. India was thriving to the point where the British government wanted more influence, and Pitt the Younger passed a law that gave the government oversight control of the East India Company in 1784. India had become the jewel in the Crown, though the Company was a force in the country for another hundred years. Trade continued to grow, though Britain abolished slavery in 1807 and then used the navy to enforce the abolition on the shipping of all other countries.

Napoleon was eventually beaten by an alliance led by Wellington on land, and Nelson's Royal Navy at sea. The Treaty of Vienna in 1815 effectively ended the threat of France to British interests. Parts of north Africa and a number of small islands remain under French control to this day, but the possibility of the world speaking French had passed. Even time would be measured through Greenwich rather than Paris, though the one place in the world that does not recognise Greenwich Mean Time is the part of France directly south of Greenwich. Perhaps unsurprisingly, they keep continental time – one hour ahead.

✳

As the Victorian era began in 1837, the Empire continued to expand. Dutch Boers had established settlements in south Africa by the beginning of the nineteenth century and Britain developed its own outposts in that rich land, though the Boer Wars didn't come till later. Hong Kong was gained by treaty with China in 1839 after trade wars over opium, tea and silver. In 1840, Britain claimed New Zealand and fought the warrior Maoris over the land for the next thirty years. In 1848, Britain made Canada largely self-governing and when that was successful, used the same formula in Australia and New Zealand. This was the seed

Queen Victoria

of the Commonwealth. In 1867, Britain united all the Canadian provinces into one dominion – one country. Afghanistan was occupied and then lost. India had railways, schools and hospitals built across it as part of a complex infrastructure. The Punjab was annexed after wars with the Sikhs, who earned the respect of the British with their courage and tenacity. Tea was introduced as a crop in India and Ceylon (Sri Lanka) by the British, intent on breaking the Chinese tea monopoly.

The Indian Mutiny of 1857 occurred when Sepoy soldiers rebelled against the imposition of British culture. For example, female infanticide had been outlawed and 'suttee', the practice of burning a live widow with her dead husband, was also banned. Attempts to emancipate women did not go down well and the spread of Christianity in India was seen as a threat to Islam and Hinduism.

Famously, the mutiny was set off by a rumour that the British rifle cartridges had been greased with pig and cow fat and were therefore untouchable to Hindus and Muslims. Indian regiments refused the cartridges and mutinied, murdering the white officers and

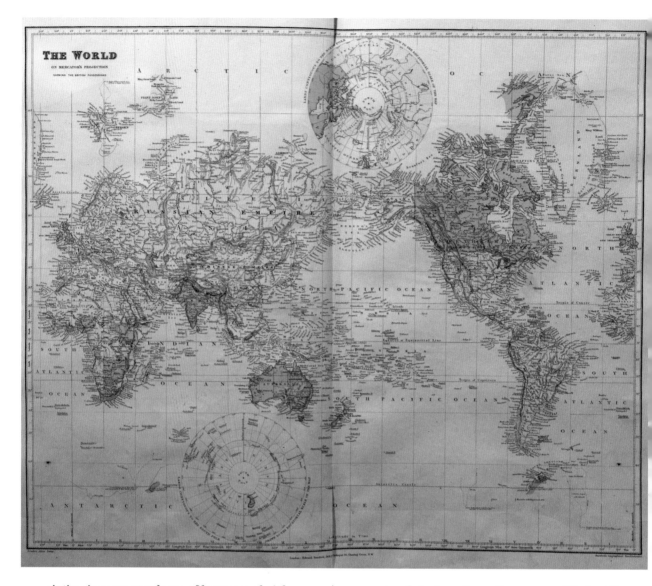

THE WORLD
ON MERCATOR'S PROJECTION
SHOWING THE BRITISH POSSESSIONS

rioting in a great release of horror and violence. British forces were heavily outnumbered by native troops they had trained and were besieged and massacred. The Gurkhas of Nepal and the Sikhs of the Punjab remained loyal. The Siege of Cawnpore was particularly brutal. Safe passage had been promised to a thousand men, women and children. They had barricaded themselves into the small fort for twenty days against an army of ten thousand. When they came out, they were massacred. Five hundred and six children were hacked to pieces and thrown into a well. The British who came too late to relieve them were filled with rage at what they saw. Other atrocities followed, such as the British strapping Sepoys to the mouths of cannons as they were fired. The battles were fierce and brutal, with 182 Victoria Crosses being awarded for courage. Only the First World War would produce more examples of extraordinary heroism (181 were awarded in WWII, 626 in WWI).

Sir Colin Campbell, Sir Hugh Rose and Sir James Outram eventually broke the rebellion and India slipped back into an uneasy peace. The country would not become independent until 1947, after the Second World War.

Victoria's reign ended in 1901, with the Empire still growing. Germany and Austria would be the chief enemy in the new century, though France was always willing to take on new colonies if an opportunity presented itself. South Africa was the first battleground of the century, with Britain clashing with the Dutch over rights to the continent.

Some acquisitions, like the Transvaal in south Africa, were claimed in part to disrupt the power base of other countries before they became a threat. Nonetheless, political decisions had to be carried out by the army and navy, fighting the Dutch Boers.

World War I (1914–18) was fought at sea and on every continent, with Britain leading a block of allies against another block led by Germany. It does not need to be said that millions of lives were lost in the most brutal of conditions. The Germans under Kaiser Wilhelm were beaten after four years of war and the guns in France fell silent at eleven in the morning, on the eleventh day of the eleventh month, 1918. 'Remembrance Day' is still marked every year with memorial services and the sale of poppies.

Former German colonies in Africa became British possessions, such as Cameroon, Togoland and East Africa. In addition, Iraq and Palestine became 'British Mandates', which meant Britain assumed responsibility for them, as well as adding Egypt, Cyprus, Kuwait, the Sudan and a host of other small states. With France on the winning side, Syria and Lebanon became French colonies. In all, nearly two million square miles were added to the Empire and when Britain laid claim to Antarctica in 1919, the Empire was the largest it had ever been.

✳

The Victorian era had produced many who saw the Empire as theirs by divine right. The drive to spread civilisation produced missionaries and reformers like Florence Nightingale and William Wilberforce, who campaigned against slavery. Gentlemen adventurers were the archetypal example of young Christians who were prepared to risk their lives for more than the simple fortunes of Drake and Ralegh's time. The dream had altered to one that brought the light of British rule to those less fortunate, making the world a better place as a result. The British assumed a moral superiority as well as a financial and military one. The result was a spread of culture that altered the world for ever.

Characters like Cecil Rhodes, who ruled what is now known as Zimbabwe, calling it Rhodesia, were from the same mould as Richard Francis Burton, T.E. Lawrence, James Brooke, Kitchener, Napier and a thousand other examples of the breed. Their achievements are astonishing in scale and breathtaking self-confidence. At the same time, Britain produced a stream of reformers and more liberal thinkers who stood against the brutal treatment of native populations and deplored acts of violence. Both types created an Empire capable of merciless ferocity in places like Ireland and India – and a humanitarian philosophy that led to improved health and education for its subjects. As Mahatma Ghandi said in 1915,

> I discovered that the British Empire had certain ideals with which I had fallen in love. One of those ideals is that every subject of the British Empire has the freest scope possible for his energies and efforts and whatever he thinks is due to his conscience... I have said that government is best which governs least, and I have found it possible for me to be governed least under the British Empire. Hence my loyalty to the British Empire.

The idea of a 'Nightwatchman' state, that is one that that does not interfere in every aspect of people's lives, was a peculiarly British idea, quite different from the governments of the continent. It came about because the vast Empire simply could not be governed on the sort of scale that is possible today.

The years between the wars are generally regarded as a golden period by those who lived through them. The *Boy's Own Paper* gives an idea of the attitudes of the day, valuing attributes of manliness, fair play, decency, honour and an ability to play cricket. The idea that the century would see the end of British rule over almost all of it would have been preposterous. Yet, the Second World War was fought to resist the military rise of Germany – carrying with it a quite different and darker philosophy.

As Niall Ferguson said in his book *Empire: How Britain Made the Modern World*:

When the British governed a country – even when they only influenced its government by flexing their military and financial muscles – there were certain distinctive features of their own society that they tended to disseminate. A list of the more important of these would run:

1   The English language
2. English forms of land tenure
3. Scottish and English banking
4. The Common Law
5. Protestantism
6. Team sports
7. The limited or 'Nightwatchman' state
8. Representative assemblies
9. The idea of liberty.

The last of these is perhaps the most important because it remains the most distinctive feature of the Empire, the thing that sets it apart from its continental European rivals. I do not mean to claim that all British Imperialists were liberals: some were very far from it. But what is striking about the history of the Empire is that whenever the British were behaving despotically, there was almost always a liberal critique of that behaviour from within British society.

GROWING SUNFLOWERS

THIS IS SUCH A SIMPLE THING, but it can be fulfilling and if we don't mention it here, a chance could be missed. These plants (*Helianthus*) are called sunflowers because they turn towards the sun and when mature, their large round heads resemble the sun. In French, they are called 'tournesol' and in Italian 'girasole'. You can find sunflower seeds in hamster food or a health-food shop. Growing any plants and flowers can be rewarding, but sunflower seeds are particularly good as sowing to blooming takes only sixty days of a good summer. They grow at an unusually high speed with impressive results.

Plant the seeds in fertile soil in late spring. All you have to do is get hold of some of the black-and-white-striped seeds, put them in a little earth in a plastic cup, add water and wait a few days. They need sunlight, so make sure the cup is on a well-lit window ledge.

The growth shown below is after only one week. The seeds split open and rise on the stalks like hats. Remove the seeds when you can see the leaves.

Eventually, you may have to use thin wooden stakes to support the stems. They will produce one of the largest flowers you can grow anywhere, with a head full of edible seeds. The final height can reach eight feet (2.4 m)!

The second picture is after a month, almost two feet (60 cm) high. They have been repotted, which just means a little extra earth or compost and a good watering. If you have a spot that receives regular sunshine, they will thrive in open ground – but check them for slugs and snails at regular intervals. To sustain this sort of growth speed, they do need water – so don't forget to give them a daily splash.

When the flowers finally fade in late summer, break apart the heads with your thumbs and you will find hundreds of the striped seeds ready to begin again next year. The shells contain a pleasant-tasting inner seed that can be eaten raw. You might also try roasting the shells until they brown, then serving them with salt and butter. They are a good source of potassium and phosphorus, iron and calcium.

QUESTIONS ABOUT THE WORLD – PART THREE

1. **How do ships sail against the wind?**
2. **Where does cork come from?**
3. **What causes the wind?**
4. **What is chalk?**

I. HOW DO SHIPS SAIL AGAINST THE WIND?

When the wind is coming straight at a boat or ship, it would seem impossible to sail into it. It can be done, however, by clever use of the sails and rudder.

Fig. 1 is a plan view of a small boat with the main sail and rudder visible. The wind comes from the direction of the three arrows marked 'a' and would tend to turn the boat in the direction of the arrow 'b'. To counteract this, the rudder is put over as at 'c' and the weight of the water against the rudder pushes the boat in the direction marked 'd'. Between these two forces, like a pip being squeezed, the boat slides ahead in the direction 'e'.

In order to get to a point windward (upwind), the boat must make this manoeuvre first to starboard (right) and then to port (left), as in Fig. 2. The boat sails to starboard, 'a', then after a time, the rudder is put over, 'b', and the sail is set over on the other hand – and the boat heels over and progresses on the port 'tack'. By this changing or 'tacking' from port to starboard and vice versa, the boat can, by a zigzag course, reach a point from which the wind is blowing – and it has sailed against the wind.

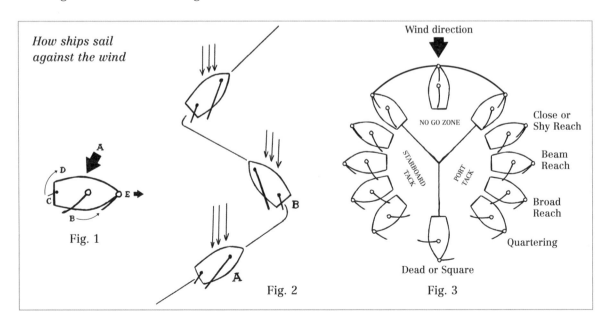

How ships sail against the wind

Fig. 1

Fig. 2

Wind direction

NO GO ZONE

STARBOARD TACK

PORT TACK

Close or Shy Reach

Beam Reach

Broad Reach

Quartering

Dead or Square

Fig. 3

2. Where does cork come from?

When a plant is damaged and its internal tissues are exposed, it is open to fungal and bacterial attack. In a similar way to the human body producing pus, many plant defence mechanisms release a fluid as part of the healing process. From a tissue within the plant, called 'callus', new cells are formed to close the wounded parts. These cells quickly become brown, and assume the nature of true cork.

As man needs cork in rather large quantities, he has found a tree that produces it in large supply, the Cork Oak (*Quercus suber*). The outer bark of this tree largely consists of cork, which can be peeled off in large strips during the summer season. This process injures the tree just enough to encourage it to produce more cork to replace what has been lost. That said, many wine producers are moving over to either plastic corks or screw-top bottles.

3. What causes the wind?

Winds are air currents and their prime cause is temperature differences created by the uneven heating of the Earth's surface and atmosphere by the sun.

Polar regions can be 160 °F colder than equatorial regions. Also relevant is the fact that in the tropics day and night temperatures differ by more than 50 °F. In addition, every mile we rise above sea level wll drop the temperature by an average of 17 degrees.

The Earth's rotation also complicates matters, forming regular winds that were a boon to trade in the days of sailing ships. Currents of cold air from the arctic regions cannot keep pace as it spins and are deflected westward. North winds become north-west winds; the same happens in the southern hemisphere, south winds become south-east winds.

4. What is chalk?

Chalk is a soft kind of limestone (a carbonate of calcium). It occurs in many parts of England and the ranges of hills in the south-east are composed almost entirely of it. It consists of the shells of tiny animals called 'foraminifera' which live in all parts of the ocean. When the foraminifera die, the insoluble shells form a sludgy deposit which hardens under pressure, and we get chalk. It is often found with flint, another stone composed of fossilised organic remains. Despite its relative softness, chalk can be found in huge cliff formations, such as those on the south coast of England at Dover and Lyme Regis.

ROLE-PLAYING GAMES

THIS IS NOT a page telling you *how* to do something – you'll see why as you read. It's a short essay on role-playing games: what they are and how to get started. There are few inventions of the twentieth century that can combine entertainment with imagination so well.

Dungeons and Dragons was put together in 1972. It is still available from online bookshops or gamer stores. To get started you'll need the player's handbook, the dungeon master's handbook, some dice and, eventually, an adventure to play. It isn't that cheap to start, but after the initial outlay, costs are minimal – it's all imagination and the occasional pencil.

In essence, you buy the books, read them and choose a character for yourself. There are basic classes like Fighter, Thief and Magic-user. The character will start out with certain qualities such as dexterity and strength, decided by the roll of a die. With experience, the character grows in power, endurance and knowledge. The game also grows more and more complex. Fighters win more powerful weapons, Wizards gain access to greater spells. When we were children, we progressed from Basic to Advanced to Expert to Immortal levels, before moving on to battling at a national level and building an empire. You never forget the first time you are exiled from a country you raised from nothing.

You do need a few people for this – it is a social game, which is a recommendation. In a very real sense, it is a training ground for the imagination and, in particular, a school for plot and character. It may even be a training ground for tactics. If you want to be a writer, try D&D. For that matter, if you want to be a mathematician, try D&D.

The Dungeon Master (or DM) is the one who runs the game. He will either collect or write adventures – literally set in dungeons or just about anywhere. The characters battle the monsters he chooses and either solve his traps or fall prey to them, suffering horrible deaths. The players will develop characters with extraordinarily detailed histories, equipment and skills.

For us, D&D meant hundreds of hours at school and at home playing with pencils, charts, dice and laughter. If elves don't grab you, there are many other forms of role-playing – from Judge Dredd, to superheroes, to Warhammer, to a hundred more . . . but Dungeons and Dragons is still the original and the best.

UNDERSTANDING GRAMMAR – PART THREE: VERBS AND TENSES

Transitive and Intransitive Verbs

How often will you need to know the difference? Hardly ever, or not at all, but the odd thing is that those who do know these fiddly bits of grammar take *enormous* satisfaction from that knowledge.

Transitive verbs are verbs that must have an object. For example, 'to bury', 'to distract', 'to deny' and many more. You simply cannot write them without an object – 'John denied', 'Susan buried'. John has to deny *something* and Susan has to bury something for it to make sense.

Intransitive verbs are verbs that can be complete without an object: 'to arrive', 'to digress', 'to exist'.

Some verbs can be transitive or intransitive, depending on how they are used in a sentence (just to make things harder): 'The fire burns' (intransitive). 'The fire has burned my finger' (transitive – 'my finger' is the object). 'He has broken the glass' (transitive). 'Glass breaks easily' (intransitive).

Again, though, this is not calculating parabolic orbits – recognising whether a verb is used transitively or intransitively is a matter of care, common sense and memory.

The Tenses

It will come as no surprise to hear that verbs need forms expressing the past, present and future. There are important differences between someone saying 'They have closed the gate' and 'They will close the gate.' The three *principal* forms of verbs, therefore, express these differences. They are known as Present Tense, Past Tense and Future Tense.

The Present Tense
There are five forms for a verb in the Present Tense:

1. Present Simple – *I write.*
2. Present Emphatic – *I do write.*
3. Present Continuous – *I am writing.*
4. Present Perfect Continuous – *I have been writing.*
5. Present Perfect – *I have written.*

The Present Emphatic form, 'I do write', may look a bit odd. It is mostly used in negative statements ('You don't care, do you?') and in questions ('Do you care?') and strong, emphatic statements ('I do care!').

Sometimes, the present can be used to talk about the future – 'I go to London next week' or 'When he arrives, he will hear the news' – but the meaning is clear from context, as it is here: 'Tomorrow, I'm going to the shops.'

The Present Perfect 'I have written' form may also look out of place at first glance. It is used in sentences like the following: '*When I have written this*, I will come and speak to you.' This is clearly an action that is going on in the present, coming from the past.

Similarly, Present Perfect Continuous: '*I have been writing* all my life,' – again, an action which is going on in the general present, if not at that exact moment.

The Past Tense
The Past Tense is usually formed by adding 'd' or 'ed' to the verb (love, *loved*; alter, *altered)*; changing the vowel sound (swim, *swam*; throw, *threw)*; or remaining the same as the present tense (put, *put*; cast, *cast*).

When the verb ends in a single consonant after a short vowel with the stress on the last syllable, the final consonant is doubled before the 'ed' ending (refer, *referred*; fan, *fanned*).

If the letter 'y' ends the word after a consonant, it becomes 'i' before the 'ed' ending (try, *tried*; cry, *cried*).

You'll probably be able to find exceptions to these rules. English has taken so many words from other languages that no rules apply to all of them. However, these work well on most occasions.

There are four standard forms for the past tense:

1. Simple Past – *I wrote.*
2. Past Continuous – *I was writing.*
3. Past Perfect (Pluperfect) – *I had written.*
4. Past Perfect Continuous – *I had been writing.*

There are also a couple of specific constructions, like 'used to', that work in sentences about the past. '*I used to* write about relationships, but now...' Clearly, the writing took place in the past.

Similarly, adding 'going to' is a common construction: 'I was going to call you, but I forgot.' The intention of calling took place in the past.

The Future Tense

First a note on 'shall', a peculiar little word. It is often used interchangeably with 'will'. It survives in commandments as 'Thou shalt not kill.' Its main use is in expressing a future wish. The fairy godmother says 'You *shall* go to the ball!' to Cinderella.

One distinction between 'will' and 'shall' is that 'shall' implies some choice. When I was a boy, I was taught that only God could say 'I will go to the shops' as only he could be certain. The rest of us should say 'I shall go to the shops' because we could be hit by a bus, and not actually make it there. Admittedly, that example rather misses the point that being killed is a little more important than errors of grammar, but it was memorable at least.

The four forms for future time are:

1. Simple Future – *I will write.*
2. Future Continuous – *I will be writing.*
3. Future Perfect – *I will have written*
4. Future Perfect Continuous: *I will have been writing.*

There is also a construction using 'am going to', as in 'I am going to kill you', and various other minor constructions using adverbs of time: 'I am going home *tomorrow*', or adverbial phrases such as 'The bus leaves *in ten minutes.*'

...and that is about it for tenses.

If you've come this far, we know you'll be disappointed if we stop it there. 'What about modal verbs? What about the subjunctive?' you will say to yourself. Prepare to be thrilled at the final two sections. This is the gold standard. Take it slowly.

Modal Auxiliary Verbs

Modal auxiliary verbs are irregular auxiliary verbs – the sort of verbs that give English a reputation for complexity. The language has many auxiliary combinations, mostly using 'to be' and 'to have' in combination with another verb: 'I *am* going', 'I *have been* watching' and so on.

Modal auxiliary verbs are often used to express the speaker's attitude 'You shouldn't do that', or as a conditional tense: 'Don't go any closer. *He could be dangerous.*'

You use them all the time, however, so do not be too worried. Here is a list of them:

will, would, shall, should, may, might, can, could, must, dare, need, ought
won't, wouldn't, shan't, shouldn't, mayn't, mightn't, can't, couldn't, mustn't, daren't, needn't,
* oughtn't*

Note that the use of 'need' as a modal verb, as in 'Need we do this?', is not that common, whereas 'needn't' is used quite regularly: 'He needn't enjoy it, as long as he eats it!'

Modal verbs have no infinitive or '-ing' form – 'to should' or 'maying' do not exist. There is no 's' form of the third person – 'he can' not 'he cans'. They do not stand on their own and are always used in conjunction with other verbs – 'May I go to the cinema?'

The Subjunctive

The **Indicative** mood is the standard factual style of modern English: 'I walked into the park.' The **Subjunctive** mood tends to appear in more formal English, when we wish to express the importance of something. This leads on from the modal verbs, as it too often expresses a wish, an uncertainty or a possibility. It is frequently formed using modal auxiliaries: 'If only they would come!' This is a complex form and scholarly works have been written on the subjunctive alone. With the limitations of space, we can merely dip a toe.

Present Subjunctive

In the present subjunctive, all verbs look like the infinitive but without the 'to' – 'do' not 'to do' – and they don't take an extra 's', even in the third person: 'We demand that *he do* the job properly.'

The verb 'to be' provides the most commonly used examples of the subjunctive form. In the present subjunctive, following the rule in the previous paragraph, 'be' is used: 'Even if that *be* the official view, I must act.' In the simple past subjunctive, we use 'were' throughout. Example: 'If he *were* sorry, he'd have apologised by now.'

Here are some examples of classic subjunctive expressions: 'Be that as it may', 'If I were a rich man,' 'Suffice it to say', 'Come what may', 'God save the Queen', 'If I were the only girl in the world.'

The subjunctive is also used in sentences beginning 'If...', as long as the subject is expressing a wish, an uncertainty or a possibility: 'If I were twenty years younger, I would ask you to dance.'

Lady Nancy Astor once said to Winston Churchill, 'Winston, if I were your wife, I'd put poison in your coffee.' He replied, 'Nancy, If I were your husband, I'd drink it.'

The subjunctive should *not* be used when the 'If...' construction is a simple conditional: '*If you are ill*, the doctor will make you better'. 'If' is used here to indicate that one event is conditional on another. There is no sense of a wish or possibility. 'If my doctor treats you, he will cure you' is another example of a simple indicative conditional. The speaker is expressing a fact conditional on the arrival of the doctor, rather than a speculative possibility.

The subjunctive is also used in certain types of sentence containing 'that':

1. They demanded *that he take* every precaution.
2. It is essential *that they be* brought back for punishment.
3. I must recommend *that this law be* struck from the books.

Past Subjunctive

In the past subjunctive, all verbs take the common form of the simple past tense. 'Have' becomes 'had', 'know' becomes 'knew' and so on. As mentioned above, 'to be' is a little different as it becomes 'were' (and not 'was'), but all the others are regular. Here are some examples:

1. He wept as if *he were being squeezed.*
2. I wish *you were* here!
3. If only *I had worked* in school.

Note that these can be indistinguishable from the standard past perfect 'had worked', as in the table below. The 'If only...' and 'I wish...' beginnings suggest subjunctive.

The following table is almost the end of the grammar section. It covers the subjunctive in all the major tenses, using examples from the verb 'to work' throughout. The important thing to remember is that it might look complicated, but *there is only one form of subjunctive for each verb tense.* If the example is 'I work', then all six persons of the verb use that form.

Mind you, don't expect to 'get it' immediately – this is one of the really tricky forms of English. The answer, however, is not to stop teaching it and watch it wither away as generations come through school with little knowledge of their own language. The answer to difficulty is always to get your hands around its throat and hold on until you have reached an understanding. Luckily, this is happening – especially in America. The subjunctive is on its way back.

Tense	Indicative	Subjunctive
Simple present	*He works*	*He work*
Present continuous	*She is working*	*She be working*
Present perfect	*He has worked*	*He have worked*
Present perfect continuous	*It has been working*	*It have been working*
Simple past	*We worked*	*We worked*
Past continuous	*I was working*	*I were working*
Past perfect	*They had worked*	*They had worked*
Past perfect continuous	*We had been working*	*We had been working*

In addition, here are eight simple sentences in the subjunctive. It is perhaps more common than you realise. Read each one and see how the subjunctive form of the verb is used.

1. He acts as if *he knew* you.
2. I would rather *you had given* a different answer.
3. If only *we had* a home to go to!
4. I wish *I could run* as fast as my older brother.
5. Would that *you were* my friend.
6. I suggest that *he leave.*
7. Thy Kingdom *come,* thy will *be* done.
8. If one green bottle *should* accidentally *fall…*

Now go back to the beginning of Grammar Part One and read it all again.

SEVEN MODERN WONDERS OF THE WORLD

THE SEVEN ANCIENT WONDERS are set in stone, but any modern seven must in some sense be a personal choice. Humanity has created many, *many* wondrous things. A Picasso painting is a wonder, as is a computer, a jewelled Fabergé egg, an aria by Mozart, the motor car, a cloned sheep. The list could be endless.

However, examples such as those don't seem to match the original style and intention of the original ancient wonders. Surely a modern seven should have some echoes in the old ones. Otherwise why have seven, say, and not nine? Our list comes from two rules. 1. It must be man-made, so no waterfalls or mountains. 2. It must take your breath away. Here are seven modern wonders. You cannot look at any of them without this thought: How on *earth* did we build that?

1. THE CHANNEL TUNNEL

An engineering project to bore a tunnel between Folkestone in Kent and Calais in France – a distance of 31 miles (50 km), with an average depth of 150 ft (45 m) under the seabed. France and Britain used huge boring machines, cutting through chalk to meet in the middle for the first time since the last ice age. When they did meet, there was less than ⅔ inch (2 cm) error, an astonishing feat of accuracy.

It took 15,000 workers seven years and cost £10 billion. Part of the structure is a set of huge pistons that can be opened and closed to release the pressure built

up by trains rushing along at 100 mph (160 kph). There is also some 300 miles (482 km) of cold-water piping running in the tunnel to ease the heat caused by air friction.

On the British side, the chalk that was dug out was left at Shakespeare Cliff near Folkestone. As a result, more than 90 acres (360,000 m²) were reclaimed from the sea.

2. The Great Wall of China

At 4,000 miles (6,400 km), it is staggering for its sheer size and the effort required to build it. The Great Wall still stands today, though it is obviously not a modern creation. It was begun more than two thousand years ago during the Qin Dynasty. Qin Shi Huang was not a man of small imagination. When he died, he was buried with more than six thousand life-size terracotta warriors and horses.

The Great Wall was designed to keep Mongol invaders out of China, though it failed to stop Genghis Khan. It has a system of watchtowers and forts to protect inner China. Sadly, some sections have collapsed or been destroyed.

It is a myth that the great wall of China can be seen from the Moon. Many man-made objects can be seen from space at low orbit, like cities, rail lines, even airport runways. From the Moon, however, the Earth looks as if we've never existed.

3. The CN tower in Toronto, Canada

The strange thing is that the CN Tower isn't better known. It is the tallest free-standing man-made structure on earth[1]. To be absolutely fair, its main function is as a television and radio mast and towers just don't catch the imagination in the same way that giant office buildings do. Still, it is 1,815 ft (553.21 m) tall and is a fraction over an inch off perfectly true. It was designed to withstand winds of more than two hundred miles an hour.

4. The Itaipú Dam

This colossal dam stands on the Paraná river on the border of Brazil and Paraguay. To build it, workers removed 50 million tons of earth and stone. The dam itself is as high as a 65-storey building. It used enough concrete for fifteen channel tunnels and enough iron and steel to build 380 Eiffel Towers. By anyone's standards, that is extraordinary.

The hydroelectric power station run by the dam is itself half a mile long. It contains eighteen electric generators, with 160 tons of water a second passing through each one. 72% of Paraguay's total energy consumption comes from this one dam.

[1] There *is* a higher radio mast in America, at 2,063 ft (629 m) tall, but it is supported by guy wires and is a lot less impressive than the CN Tower. Impact matters to get into this list.

One of the reasons the Panama Canal makes it to this list is because it joins two vast oceans and splits two continents. It is 50 miles (80 km) long. Before it was built, a ship travelling from New York to San Francisco would have been forced to go all the way around South America. The canal took almost 8,000 miles (12,800 km) off that journey.

It was originally a French project under Ferdinand de Lesseps. Although he was well respected in France, it took all of his charisma and energy to raise the vast capital needed to begin the enterprise. When work did begin, his men had to contend with parasites, spiders, snakes, torrential downpours and flash floods. Far worse was the threat of disease. Yellow fever, dysentery, typhoid, cholera, smallpox and malaria were all common. In those conditions, up to 20,000 workers died. In 1889, De Lesseps' company went bankrupt and the investors lost their money.

In 1902, the American government agreed to take on the Panama Canal and at the same time supported the independence of Panama from Colombia. The American president, Theodore Roosevelt, told his engineers to 'make the dirt fly'. The Americans rebuilt the site and set to work. By 1910, there were 40,000 workers on the canal and Roosevelt had brought in the army. It was completed in 1914.

The principles are similar to any British canal, but each lock gate of the Panama Canal weighs 750 tons. 14,000 ships go through the canal each year.

6. The Akashi-Kaikyo Bridge in Japan, also known as the Pearl Bridge

The longest suspension bridge in the world. It is miles shorter than the longest actual bridge – the Lake Pontchartrain Causeway is over 23 miles (38 km) long – but there is something particularly awe-inspiring about enormous suspension bridges. This one is 6,532 ft (1,991 m) long. It took ten years to build and cost around £2 billion. It is 2,329 ft (710 m) longer than the Golden Gate Bridge in San Francisco.

After a tunnel, a wall, a tower, a dam, a canal and a bridge, most of the truly impressive human building projects have been covered. The last choice may not be physically enormous, but it represents the next stage and the future to come.

The Space Shuttle may be the most complicated machine ever built. It is the world's first proper spacecraft and though the current shuttles are approaching the end of their useful lives, they were the first step from single-use rockets to the dreams of science fiction. The first one was actually called *Enterprise* after the *Star Trek* ship, though it was only a test plane and never went into space. It is currently in the Smithsonian museum. Five others followed: *Columbia*, *Challenger*, *Discovery*, *Atlantis* and *Endeavour*. *Columbia* first went into space in 1981, beginning a new era of space flight. The programme was temporarily suspended in 1986 when *Challenger* exploded shortly after lift-off, killing the seven-person crew.

On re-entry, shuttle skin temperature goes up to 1650 °C (3000 °F). It is the fastest vehicle mankind has ever designed, travelling at speeds of up to 18,000 mph (29,000 kph).

It is used as an all-purpose craft, capable of launching and repairing satellites and docking with the International Space Station in orbit.

Onwards and Upwards

BOOKS EVERY BOY SHOULD READ

T HE DANGER HERE is that you'll try to read books that are too hard for your age. The choices are from those books we enjoyed, but this is a list that all *men* should have read when they were boys. The first ones are the easiest – though not the best. Every title has been loved by millions. Like a reference to Jack and the Beanstalk, you should know Huckleberry Finn, Sherlock Holmes and all the other characters who make up the world of imagination. The list comes with suggested reading ages – but these are only rough minimums. Reading ability is more important than age.

1. Roald Dahl's books. From five up, these can be read to children. *The Twits* is fantastic. *Charlie and the Chocolate Factory*, *George's Marvellous Medicine*, *The BFG*, and *James and the Giant Peach* are all worth reading. For older readers, his short stories are nothing short of brilliant.

2. The Winnie-the-Pooh books by A.A. Milne. Beautifully written, amusing stories.

3. Willard Price – a series of adventure books, with titles such as *Underwater Adventure*, *Arctic Adventure* and so on. The two main characters, Hal and Roger, are role models for all boys growing up today. Suitable for ages eight and above.

4. All the Famous Five books by Enid Blyton. Also, her Secret Seven series. These are classic adventure and crime stories for those aged eight and above, up to the early teens.

5. *Fungus the Bogeyman* by Raymond Briggs. One of the strangest books in this list, but oddly compelling. For all ages, but probably ten and above.

6. Grimm's Fairy Tales; Hans Christian Andersen; Greek and Roman legends. There are many collections out there, but these stories have survived because they are good.

7. *The Belgariad* by David Eddings. Fantasy series of five books, every one a gem. Eleven and above.

8. *Rogue Male* by Geoffrey Household. An extraordinary story of survival against the odds. Suitable for eleven and over.

9. *The Lion, the Witch and the Wardrobe* by C.S. Lewis. The first of the Narnia series. Superb fantasy stories for confident readers of twelve and above.

10. *Charlotte's Web*, by E.B. White. A powerful story of a pig and a spider! Eight years old and up.

11. *Kim* by Rudyard Kipling – a classic adventure. Also, the *Just So Stories* and *The Jungle Book*. For confident readers, but well worth the time.

12. *The Thirty-Nine Steps* by John Buchan. This is almost the definition of a boy's adventure story, involving spies and wild dashes across the Scottish countryside. Also look for *Mr Standfast* by the same author.

13. The James Bond books by Ian Fleming. For early teen readers and above. These stories are quite dark in places – far grittier than the films.

14. The Harry Potter books by J.K. Rowling. Modern classics.

15. *1066 and All That* by W.C. Sellar and R.J. Yeatman. A funny book of British history, packed with interesting information, though how much it will help with real history is any-one's guess. Early teens and above.

16. Mark Twain – *The Adventures of Tom Sawyer* and *The Adventures of Huckleberry Finn*. For confident readers of twelve and above

17. Isaac Asimov – science fiction. He wrote hundreds of brilliant short stories, available in collections. Confident readers of twelve and above.

18. Terry Pratchett's Discworld books. They are all fantastic, funny and interesting. Start with *Sourcery*. Twelve and above.

19. *Ender's Game* by Orson Scott Card. Fantastic story of a young boy in a military academy. Confident readers of twelve and above.

20. *Midshipman's Hope* by David Feintuch. A space fantasy with a marvellous main character. There are seven in the full series.

21. *The Hitchhiker's Guide to the Galaxy* by Douglas Adams. Funny and clever – the old 'five books to a trilogy' ploy. Twelve and up.

22. David Gemmell's books, such as *Waylander* – the master of heroic fantasy for fourteen and up. Read one and you'll read them all.

23. *Magician* by Raymond E. Feist. One of the best fantasy novels ever written – and a whole series of first-class sequels to follow.

24. *The Lord of the Rings* by J.R.R. Tolkien. The masterwork trilogy. For confident teen readers.

BOOKS EVERY BOY SHOULD READ

25. The Flashman books by George MacDonald Fraser. For confident readers, but a great dip into history and adventure. Fourteen and above.

26. *Animal Farm* and *1984* by George Orwell. Novels to wake the brain. For confident readers of fourteen and over.

27 *Brave New World* by Aldous Huxley. Like Orwell's *1984*, a famous story of a future we should fear.

28. *Lord of the Flies* by William Golding. Superb – but only for accomplished readers of fourteen and above.

29. H.G. Wells's *The Time Machine*, *The Island of Dr Moreau*, *The Invisible Man* – books from one of the best literary minds of the nineteenth century. Fourteen and above.

30. The Sherlock Holmes adventures by Arthur Conan Doyle. The original classic detective mysteries. Loads of short crime stories and longer novels, like *The Hound of the Baskervilles*. Accomplished readers only. Fifteen and above.

31. *Gulliver's Travels* by Jonathan Swift. One that can be read on more than one level. It gave us the lands of Lilliput and Brobdingnag.

32. *Three Men in a Boat* by Jerome K. Jerome. The funniest book ever written, but only for accomplished readers of fourteen or fifteen and above.

33. Stephen King. *The Bachman Books* is a good starting point. His novels are quite adult in subject and can be very frightening. Accomplished readers only – fifteen and above.

IMPERIAL AND METRIC MEASURES

LINEAR MEASURES

1 **mile** = 8 furlongs = 1,760 yards = 5,280 feet = 1.609 kilometres (km)
1 **furlong** = 10 chains = 220 yards = 201 metres (m)
1 **chain** = cricket pitch = 22 yards = 66 feet = 20 metres
1 **yard** (yd) = 3 feet = 0.9144 metres
1 **foot** (ft) = 12 inches = 0.3048 metres
1 **inch** (in) = 25.4 millimetres (mm)

SQUARE MEASURES

1 **square mile** = 640 acres = 259 hectares
1 **acre** = 10 square chains = 4,840 square yards = 0.405 hectares
1 **rood** = ¼ acre = 1,210 square yards = 1,011 square metres
1 **square yard** (sq yd) = 9 square feet = 0.836 square metres
1 **square foot** (sq ft) = 144 square inches = 9.29 square decimetres
1 **square inch** (sq in) = 6.45 square centimetres

CUBIC MEASURES

1 **cubic** yard = 27 cubic feet = 0.765 cubic metres
1 **cubic foot** = 1,728 cubic inches = 0.028 cubic metres
1 **cubic inch** = 16.4 cubic centimetres

CAPACITY MEASURE

1 **bushel** = four pecks = 64 pints = 8 gallons = 36.4 litres
1 **peck** = 2 gallons = 16 pints = 9.1 litres
1 **gallon** (gal) = 4 quarts = 8 pints = 4.55 litres
1 **quart** (qt) = 2 pints = 1.14 litres
1 **pint** (pt) = 20 fluid ounces = 4 gills = 0.57 litres
1 **gill** = 5 fluid ounces = 0.14 litres
1 **fluid** ounce (fl oz) = 1.8 cubic inches = 0.03 litres

WEIGHT

1 **ton** = 20 hundredweight = 2240 pounds = 1.016 metric tonnes

1 **hundredweight** (cwt) = four quarters= 112 pounds = 50.80 kilograms (kg)

1 **quarter** = 2 stones = 28 pounds = 12.70 kilograms

1 **stone** = 14 pounds = 6.35 kilograms

1 **pound** (lb) = 16 ounces = 7000 grains = 0.45 kilograms

1 **ounce** (oz) = 16 drams = 28.35 grams (g)

1 **dram** (dr) = 27.3 grains = 1.772 grams

1 **grain** (gr) = 0.065 grams

MONEY (BEFORE DECIMALISATION IN FEB 1971)

1 **penny** (d) = 4 farthings ('d' from the Roman denarius coin)

1 **shilling** (s) = 12 pence/pennies

1 **crown** = 5 shillings

1 **pound** (£) = 4 crowns = 20 shillings= 240 pennies

1 **guinea** = 21 shillings

INTERESTING NOTE

The reason British currency is called a 'pound' is actually to do with the weight of silver pennies. Alfred the Great set a 'pennyweight' as 24 'grains' in the seventh century. 240 silver pennies, comes to a pound (lb) in weight. That is why the currency is still called 'pound sterling' – 'sterling silver' is silver of very high purity.

British imperial measurements are usually known as US measurements today. The American system is fractionally different to the traditional British measurements – their hundredweight is 100 lb, for example. It is slightly ironic that while the Americans send men and women into space using pounds and inches, Britain has adopted the measurements of the French Revolution. Metric has the benefit of being easy to calculate, with everything based around the number 10. British imperial measurements are based around the number 12 and also the human body: a yard is a man's pace, a foot is the length of a forearm (or a foot), a rough acre is a square of seventy paces by seventy. Having more than one system alive in the world is useful to remind us that they are *artificial* – that the world is man-made.

ILLUSTRATIONS

———— ✦ ————

Illustrations © Richard Horne
(http://homepage.mac.com/richard.horne/)

Acknowledgements:

Sea Fever by John Masefield reproduced by permission of The Society of Authors as the Literary Representative of the Estate of John Masefield.

For the Fallen (September 1914) by Laurence Binyon reproduced by permission of The Society of Authors as the Literary Representative of the Estate of Laurence Binyon.